way? And will Cassie's unshakable faith inspire Jack to make a decision for Christ?

The Protector is the fourth book in **Dee Henderson's** beloved *O'Malley* series. A lifelong Illinois resident and the daughter of a minister, the author is deeply involved in Chicago-area ministries. She's also a fan of basketball's Bulls and baseball's Cubs and Cardinals.

"Dee Henderson had me shivering as her stalker got closer and closer to his victim. The message that we have nothing to fear as long as God is in control was skillfully handled, but I got scared, anyway! I highly recommend this book to anyone who likes suspense."

TERRI BLACKSTOCK, BESTSELLING AUTHOR OF *TRIAL BY FIRE*

"A masterstroke!!... Dee Henderson gives the reader not one but two irresistible heroes."

COMPUSERVE REVIEWS

TRUE DEVOTION

"Dee Henderson has done a splendid job mixing romance with the fast-paced action of a Navy SEAL platoon."

STEVE WATKINS, FORMER NAVY SEAL

"Action, adventure, and romance! *True Devotion* has everything a reader could want!"

ANGELA ELWELL HUNT, BESTSELLING AUTHOR OF *THE IMMORTAL*

"[Dee Henderson] has created a truly stunning tale of love and devotion to God, country, and to those left behind when the missions are done."

COMPUSERVE REVIEWS

"A wonderful story with real and entertaining characters. Ms. Henderson's gift with words makes this book impossible to put down."

WRITER'S CLUB ROMANCE GROUP ON AOL

THE PROTECTOR

BOOK FOUR—THE O'MALLEY SERIES

DEE HENDERSON

Multnomah®Publishers *Sisters, Oregon*

THE PROTECTOR
published by Multnomah Publishers, Inc.

© 2001 by Dee Henderson
International Standard Book Number: 1-57673-846-9

Cover design by Chris Gilbert/Uttley DouPonce DesignWorks
Cover image of firefighter by Index Stock Imagery
Background cover image by Tony Stone Images

Scripture quotations are from: Revised Standard Version Bible (RSV)
© 1946, 1952 by the Division of Christian Education of the National Council
of the Churches of Christ in the United States of America

Multnomah is a trademark of Multnomah Publishers, Inc., and is registered in
the U.S. Patent and Trademark Office.
The colophon is a trademark of Multnomah Publishers, Inc.

Printed in the United States of America

ISBN 0-7394-2143-3

"For God so loved the world that he gave his only Son, that whoever believes in him should not perish but have eternal life. For God sent the Son into the world, not to condemn the world, but that the world might be saved through him."

JOHN 3:16–17

Prologue

The electricity was out. The candle nightlight on the dresser was barely bright enough to scare away the ghosts. Jack watched the dancing shadows flicker on the wall and wished his mom had brought him the torch flashlight his dad used when they went camping. Dim was worse than dark, and the shadows were laughing at him.

If only there were a full moon, not a storm. He could hear the wind picking up. He tugged on the blanket, ready to yank it over his head when the lightning struck. Sometimes lightning could herald action heroes coming to save him and sometimes it was just angry bolts. Tonight the storm was angry.

"Mom?" He didn't shout it. He wasn't supposed to still be awake; he wasn't supposed to be afraid of the dark. But if she would maybe just come check on him...

Thunder cracked.

His dog raced into the room from the hall.

Overjoyed, Jack hurriedly tugged the sheets back up and buried his face against the pillow so he could pretend to be asleep. Mom had let Shep inside the house. The dresser rocked as his dog crashed into it, squeezing around to get into the fort Jack had built earlier that day with blankets over chairs. The candle toppled and disappeared.

Jack squeezed his eyes shut at the sudden blackness. This was not good. This was very bad. He heard his mom talking with his dad, the sounds echoing as they came up the stairs.

The room started to brighten. He opened one eye a little to see if Mom had come to the doorway with her light to check on him. The door stood open, empty. Jack opened both eyes. Fire peeked over the edge of his bed, licking at the G. I. Joe sheets.

Jack watched, wide eyed, fascinated. The flames grew like marching soldiers in a spreading line.

He reached to move the Matchbox car from the foot of the bed and drew back from the heat. "Mom."

The fire alarm in the hall went off.

The noise deafened the sound of thunder outside.

"Jack!" His mom rushed into the room followed by his dad.

She pulled him from the bed and swallowed him in a hug. She smelled like lilacs. His dad yanked back the rug and the covers, attacked the flames, and stomped them out. *Wow.* They had turned to flames fast; it had been just a flicker moments before. "I'd like Superman sheets to replace mister G. I. Joe," he told his mom, watching his dad save him.

She squeezed him. "Superman sheets," she murmured, her voice choked. "I can do that."

One

The house was a total loss. Firefighter Lieutenant Jack O'Malley shone his bright light on the dripping walls, looking for anything that would provide a source for the smoke he was still chasing. Second floor beams above him groaned as the building settled. Fire had shattered what had once been a beautiful, well-kept home. It was like walking around inside a sarcophagus. The place felt like it was dying.

The kitchen smelled of something nasty, the sharp smell of burnt cleaning supplies making Jack's eyes water. Limp bananas were now hanging over a bowl whose apples looked like cooked mush. Coupons fluttered from the counter to the floor, turning to a sodden mass in the standing water. Pictures on the refrigerator had bled away color in the heat, leaving behind the ghosts of people barely discernible.

The big calendar on the wall beside the phone had been reduced to darkened, curling pages. A family's life, documented in dates and times and appointments, gone. Jack let the light linger on the calendar, the month of November half marked off with Xs, today's date of the fifteenth highlighted by something now illegible in bold red ink. Their vacation dates, he guessed. Thanksgiving was next week and they had chosen to travel early. He was grateful they had not been caught in the inferno.

This was so incredibly senseless. The fire looked like it had been set.

Jack could feel the weariness wash over him again, and behind it, building, the tick in his left eye that showed his growing anger. He'd like to find the man responsible for this and deck him.

A wisp of gray caught his attention as the house breathed. Some smoke was coming through the central air ductwork. Jack touched his radio. "Nate, check the utility room again."

"On it."

Jack walked through what had once been the patio door, stepping out into the night. The massive spotlights from the fire engines in front of the house cast strange shadows onto the backyard through holes in the house where windows had never been intended.

Popcorn.

Jack stopped in his tracks when he spotted the white kernels lying at the edge of the deck protected from booted feet by the waist-high wooden railing. The building anger surged and fury swept through him. Someone had stood and watched the house burn, had come prepared to enjoy the sight. It was a signature he'd seen before.

The white kernels were scattered, dropped as though stragglers from an overflowing fistful. Jack searched the area. A few of the unpopped grains that had been flicked into the flames lay burnt with hulls split in two. Jack had hoped with a passion this particular arsonist was going to stick to his nuisance fires of grass and trash. Instead, he'd just escalated to his first house.

Fire was supposed to be an accident, not a weapon, not something enjoyed. Jack kicked a smoldering chunk of wood ripped from a window frame away from the evidence. His job was turning into that of a cop.

He hated arsonists. Painful experience from his past had taught him how ruthless a fire starter could become. Destruction of property. Innocent victims. Injured firefighters. They had to find this guy before someone got hurt.

He could fight a fire, but fighting a man... Jack felt like his hands were tied and he hated the feeling of being helpless. He was an O'Malley. He wasn't a man to duck trouble. He preferred to go after it.

This was clearly trouble. How was he supposed to go after a man who chose to be a coward and hide behind a match?

Thanksgiving was coming, then Christmas, and he had enough on his plate already with his sister Jennifer fighting cancer to want to add this kind of tangle. The holidays were like waving an invitation to make trouble. He couldn't be two places at once. They had to stop this guy soon. But it was tomorrow's problem.

Around him the firefighters from Company 81 were pulling hose and shouting to be heard over the sound of a power saw. They were aggressively searching for hot spots within the burned-out house and trying to find the source of that smoke still rising like a wavering cobra into the air.

Somewhere in the ruins this fire was still alive. Jack pulled back on his gloves and looked over the ruins of the house with an experienced eye. A decade of fighting fires had taught him well, for it was not a forgiving profession.

Fire was an arrogant beast. If in control, it challenged with ferocious disdain anyone who approached. If forced to retreat, it liked to lie low, patiently waiting, then exact a painful revenge.

They'd find it. Kill it. And another dragon would be slain.

"Cole." Jack got the attention of the fire investigator.

There were few men who could dominate a fire scene just by being present; his friend Cole was one. Six-two, one hundred and eighty pounds, prematurely gray at forty-two, Cole Parker had made captain at thirty-six, a decade before most. He now led the arson group. Jack trusted the man in a way he trusted few outside his family.

"What do you have, Jack?"

With his flashlight, Jack illuminated the popcorn.

Cole, a big man with a big shadow, stilled for a moment, then walked over to the deck.

"He's escalating," Jack said.

Cole bent to pick up a kernel. "We knew he eventually would. Five fires in seven weeks, he's not a patient man."

"He's ringing fires around the new boundaries of the fire district,"

Jack suggested, knowing it was at least a clue to figuring out who the man was they had to stop. The smaller, older fire stations had been closing over the past months, their engines and crews dispersed to expanded hub stations. The reapportioned equipment better reflected the new housing construction and demographics of the area, but nothing could change the reality that more territory in each district meant longer response times. This firebug knew how to take advantage of the change.

Cole just nodded. "A dangerous man playing a dangerous game." He ate one of the popped kernels. "Salt. He's bringing his own refreshments."

"I really didn't need to know that."

His friend rose gracefully to his feet. "I thought this had the sound of one of his. Late at night, edge of the district." He looked over at Jack. "Gold Shift."

The implication that his shift was being targeted hadn't escaped Jack's attention. They worked twenty-four hours on, forty-eight hours off, yet all the fires had been fought by his shift, none by Black or Red Shifts. Jack would not easily admit he'd started to sweat when the tones sounded. It was hard to hold his trademark good humor when someone out there appeared determined to make sure he was going to face flames.

Cole brushed his hands on worn jeans. He'd been paged to the scene from his home. "Tell me about this fire."

"It was in the walls."

First on the scene, Engine 81 had pulled up as smoke began to pour from the attic vents and around the eaves. Jack had pushed his way into the front hallway, shining his light, and had watched the paint bubble from the heat inside the walls. No flames had been visible, but as soon as he had poked his ax into the wall, the dragon had leaped out, roaring. "We had a hard time getting water onto the face of it."

Nate on the nozzle, Bruce pulling hose, they'd lost precious time cutting into the walls. With no moon and the neighbors' homes a distance away, the fire had not been reported until it already had a good hold. Jack had been thinking it ignited because of an electrical short until he saw the intensity of the fire. He illuminated the smoke line and burn pattern with his light as they walked.

"Center of the house?" Cole speculated.

They slogged across the yard now turned into mud by the hours of streaming water. Jack stopped by a dogwood tree. "I think so. There was too much ambient heat to assume it started on the second floor and worked down within the walls, not enough fire scarring on the siding to show an origin point in an outside wall."

Arson for profit didn't fit this guy's pattern—probably a guy—Jack decided. It didn't feel like the work of a young offender either. These fire locations were carefully planned. And it was odd for a fire starter who did it for enjoyment to acquire the taste late in life. "Think he's after the press attention?"

"Bold enough to stand around after the fire starts and flick popcorn into the flames, arrogant enough to set fires frequently. Now escalating in the type of fires he sets. Yes, he wants the attention—ours, the media's, and ultimately the public's."

"We'll have a panic on our hands if we don't stop him before the press connects the fires."

"Not to mention copycats."

Smoke twisted in their direction, the heavy ash particles making Jack cough. "What time is it?"

Cole sent him a sympathetic smile. "Something after 2 A.M."

Two and a half hours. Jack felt like he had run a marathon. The fire turnout coat sat heavy on his shoulders and it stuck and rubbed at his neck as he moved. The last hours had turned his blue uniform shirt and cotton T-shirt under the coat into a sweaty mass. Jack knew he could forget any idea of sleep tonight. It would be dawn before they got the fire mop-up complete.

His left knee was still complaining about the force of the impact earlier when he dropped from the engine to the asphalt street with more speed than care. The initial sight of the house with smoke beginning to pour from the roof vents had made him push faster than safety would dictate.

It might have appeared haphazard to the spectators watching their arrival, but the company had executed a well-coordinated attack on the fire. The crew from Ladder Truck 81 had gone after the roof and ventilated the fire; the men from Engine 81 had surged to lay hose and get water on the face of the fire; and the crew of Rescue Squad 81 had hit the ground reaching for air tanks, ready to go in if people were trapped.

The drills and teamwork had paid off; no time had been lost during the attack. There were benefits to working with the best. And a few drawbacks. First engine on the scene, last engine to leave.

He'd kill for a shower. The smell of smoke and sweat was a stench he didn't mind as long as he was moving and was downwind of himself.

"You did a good job of knocking it down."

He was pleased at the praise for Cole didn't give it lightly. "Thanks."

Jack would prefer to be on the roof or pulling down scorched plaster, even coiling hose, than to be the guy tapped to manage the scene. But the captain of Company 81 had been called to the site of a chemical spill, so the job passed to Jack.

He retrieved two bottles of ice water from the rescue squad and handed one to Cole. As he drank, Jack scanned the few remaining spectators—neighbors hurriedly dressed, a couple kids entranced at the sight of the red engine and ladder truck, local media, a cop blocking the street from thru traffic.

Some firebugs were watchers. They acted just so the firefighters would get called out. They'd stand and watch the battle, their own personal entertainment. No one stood out among those gathered.

Jack turned back to the house and watched guys turn a nozzle back on to deal with a pocket of fire found smoldering in the wall between the garage and the breezeway. "This isn't going to be his last fire."

"Safe wager."

"Any ideas?"

Cole drank deeply, then shook his head. "No ideas, no assumptions, no conclusions. You know how this job is done."

Jack did. It took patience he didn't have. "My men are at risk." His words were quiet because he knew the memory Cole carried, knew how the words would resonate.

Cole reached over and squeezed his shoulder.

Jack didn't know if he ever wanted to make captain, knowing how much the privilege and burden of command had cost his friend. Cole had led Company 65 before moving to head the arson group. He'd moved because an arsonist had made it personal. Jack wanted to ask about Cassie, about Ash, but found himself in this situation hesitant to voice the names.

"Lieutenant?" A firefighter from Truck 81 stepped to the open front door. "You're going to want to see this."

The heat from the floor came through his boots. Jack could hear the fire, a rushing sound, huge, consuming. Every step took him closer to it. The hallway turned and he felt the stairwell post. He started up the stairs. There was someone still in the house. They had to get her out.

The smoke was coming down in rolling waves. Fire brightened the darkness ahead of him, surging through the smoke in licks of vicious flames.

The heat was too intense.

The smoke was too low.

No one in this house could still be alive.

It was a grim realization that firmed with each step and by the sixth step Jack stopped. He wanted to rush through the flames, he desperately wanted to change reality. His sister Rachel would be crushed at the news her friend was dead, and Tabitha's husband— Jack couldn't change what had already happened. He was responsible for his men's lives. Jack put out his arm, stopping Ben, the lieutenant of Black Shift who had taken the place of the rookie on Jack's crew for this attempted evacuation. "There's nothing we can do."

Bruce and Nate in the rear of the group turned at his words to lead the way out. Ben Rohr hesitated. Jack squeezed his shoulder. The lieutenant was the veteran of the group, in his early forties but still had more fires under his belt than Jack had ever seen. He understood how torn the man was to turn back from a victim—there was no choice. Ben headed down the stairs.

The fire roared behind Jack, reaching out to touch the back of his heavy fire coat. It had already claimed a victim. They couldn't afford to give it another. Jack felt the post at the bottom of the steps and turned the corner into the hall as the fire roared down the stairway landing and part of the ceiling buckled.

The sound of sirens screaming outside provided direction. Jack followed the noise toward the door they had entered. Water slapped against the side of the house, hissing as it turned to steam. Men rushed to meet them and clipped shakes of heads passed the painful word. Hard hands slapped their shoulders, counting them. "Last man," Jack shouted. "Drown it." The firefighter on the nozzle nodded and pulled hose into the doorway, then opened it.

Jack pushed off his gear. The night air felt cold after the oppressive heat. They would join the fight to stop the fire, but it would be a grim fight with no good outcome. People, property—they had already lost both. How was he supposed to tell his sister that Tabitha was dead? The thought of doing so was enough to drive the sickness deep.

Neighbors, cops, and spectators had gathered to watch the scene and Jack saw the reaction as word a neighbor had died swept through the crowd.

"We could have made it," Ben said, staring at the flames, absorbed in watching them.

"Going up, but we couldn't have made it back out," Jack murmured, watching the veteran firefighter weighing the odds of which could move faster: firefighter or flames. It would have been a suicide mission.

"Get out of my way!"

Jack turned to see a man surging past police. Gage Collier, the reporter a familiar face to local firefighters and police. This was Gage's home. Gage's wife. Jack stepped forward to meet the man before he reached his crew. There were no words for what he felt. "Gage, I'm sorry. I'm so sorry."

Jack saw the punch coming but did nothing to block it.

"She was pregnant!"

Jack jerked awake, breathing hard. He shoved himself upright to get away from the heavy, haunted sleep. The nightmare always came after a fire now. Two years old, and it was still a living memory. It merged with other memories: the victims he hadn't been able to reach, the screams of people caught in flames, the nursing home—always the inevitable memory of the nursing home fire. Jack loved being a fireman but the costs were building. Did the arsonist know what he was doing? Not only destroying property but the firefighters who battled the fires.

Jack would have called his family, just to hear another voice tonight besides the fading ones in his head, but the one person who could help him the most to talk through the trauma was his sister Rachel. And she already had to live with the fact it was her friend who died.

He got up to pace and forced the memories down again. They'd linger and he would live with them. Tabitha died because they had been late to the fire.

Ben still called that the department's blackest day, for a brush fire on the other side of the district had cost them precious minutes in response time. A new lieutenant and a veteran both haunted by the same memory. It wasn't a bond Jack would have chosen, but it was one that went deep. He didn't know how Ben coped. Jack had better learn because otherwise he would have to think about walking away from the profession he loved. This was slowly killing him.

Two

The fertilizer bags were in his way, and after the fourth trip into the garage, he kicked one of them and succeeded in hurting his foot. The Thanksgiving meal today would be chicken from the local fast-food place, the pie a frozen thing that was put in the oven. It was a far cry from the home-cooked feasts of years past, but since the divorce he'd been making do. It had only been a week since the last fire, but he wanted to go burn something. They were destroying him and his family. He had to get their attention, had to get things changed.

The newspaper had relegated the fire investigation to the seventh page in the city section. A short statement by the investigating officer—the fire is under investigation. A quote from the homeowner about how thankful his family was for the support of friends and family at this holiday time. Soft stuff, routine stuff, no hard news in the article. The community had five fires in seven weeks, an arsonist stalking their fire department, and what did they do? Yawn.

Well someone was going to notice; someone was going to hear, if only Jack. He slammed the trunk of the gray sedan. It wouldn't change what he lived with, what his family lived with, but it was a place to start. By the time he was done he would have all of them paying attention.

He'd have to leave a message this time.

The phone rang right next to his ear. Jack was startled awake. His face was inches from the clock on the nightstand, the digits blinking 5:40 A.M. A week since the arson fire and he was finally enjoying sleep again. He hated getting awakened from the dream of his mom hugging him and smelling like lilacs. He loved that memory, it was one of the clearest from his childhood.

A photo of his parents was in a silver frame behind the clock, crowded by car keys, his beeper, and a tattered wallet. His parents had died in a car crash, way before Jack was ready to let them go. He'd been eleven. Another frame beside the photo sat empty, one of his sister's not so subtle ways of suggesting he get a girlfriend. He'd never gotten the courage to move the empty frame to a drawer.

Jack reluctantly reached over to answer the phone. Thanksgiving Day inevitably meant people choking on turkey sandwiches, grease fires in the kitchen, kids playing together banging heads and chipping teeth. It was going to be a long day and he was in no hurry to start it. "Hello?"

"Jack, I need you," Kate whispered.

He wedged the phone tighter to his ear. What was his sister doing up at this time of day, and why was she whispering? Neither fit her. "What's wrong?"

"You really don't want to die, do you? Come on, put it down. Don't eat it," she crooned.

Jack shoved himself up. His sister was a police hostage negotiator, a good one. She was having two conversations. "Where are you?" Where was the rest of her team? She normally tugged in their oldest brother Marcus when she needed help.

"My apartment roof. No, don't go out on the ledge. Don't." Her voice sounded frustrated and that was rare for Kate. She was known for her apparent boredom during a crisis. "I need an extra pair of hands. Marvel got into the turkey bones and he's going to kill himself eating them. I can't catch him. You've got the magic touch."

He had his shirt half on. That stopped him. "Your cat? You woke me up for a cat?"

"Jack—" The phone clattered against stone and he heard the unmistakable sound of Kate lunging. Her apartment roof was flat, gravel topped, with a large concrete ledge around it, and that noise was gravel scattering. "That does it. He's now in the elm tree clutching the turkey leg and hissing at me."

"Let him be."

"Dave gave me that cat."

Jack closed his eyes. Her fiancé, Dave Richman, had given her the cat. And Kate hadn't had a cat since someone shot her last one through her living room window. Jack looked with regret at his pillow and instead reached for his keys. "I'm coming."

"Thank you."

An O'Malley called, an O'Malley came. They needed a cat rescued, gutters cleaned, his sisters called him. If they had a real crisis, they called one of the others. Jack smiled and reached for his billfold, not entirely minding his role in the family.

They'd celebrated Thanksgiving together two weeks ago, as several of them were working this long weekend. He had a lot to be thankful for today, and family headed the list.

The seven of them were close, a group bound together not by blood, but by choice. They were all orphans. At Trevor House over two decades ago they had chosen to become their own family, and had later legally changed their last names. It was unique but it worked. He'd lost so much when his parents died, had been so lonely. By the time the legal logistics had been sorted out, he'd been twelve, at the foster home, and adoption was unlikely. Trevor House had become his home. The O'Malleys had filled the huge void. They were family, even when the calls came at the most inconvenient times for something only family could understand.

Jack found the street Kate lived on in downtown Chicago blocked off, the street and the sidewalks marked with fluorescent red spray paint and big, new drainage tiles sitting on the small strips of grass. No city crew was present to actually work on the project, but they still left the street blocked off. Jack parked a block away and hiked back to Kate's building, taking the outside fire escape up to the roof. Kate often sat on a lawn chair up here at night to watch the city she risked her life to protect.

She was at the east corner of the roof, half leaning over the ledge. Jack summed up the problem in a glance. "You can negotiate with a man holding a gun but can't negotiate with your own cat."

She looked over her shoulder, relief and frustration both showing on her normally impassive face. "Just help me get to him before he gets a bone splinter stuck in his gut and bleeds to death."

Jack winced at the image. He pulled on gloves and opened the canvas backpack he kept for rescuing critters. Fires often trapped pets and he'd learned early on to be prepared. "What were you doing up before 6 A.M.?"

"Do you have any idea how long a turkey takes to bake?"

"Yes. I gather you didn't."

"I try to avoid the actual meal preparation on holidays so that it's actually a holiday. Dave is coming to dinner. I've got to work today, and I do not have four hours to sit and watch a turkey cook. I put it in about one this morning when I got home from a page, and then got up at a horrible hour to get it out."

Kate would have been smarter just to take turkey out of the freezer from all the leftovers or buy her turkey already baked from the store deli. "You had to take the meat off the bones?"

"I don't exactly have room to put that massive carcass in my refrigerator."

Jack stepped up on the ledge. "Let me guess. Marvel got into the trash."

"He grabbed the turkey bones and bolted."

Marvel sank his teeth into the turkey leg and flattened his ears back, offering a threatening rumble. The old yellow tabby was not a house cat, had never been a house cat, and only Kate would try to domesticate him. Dave had been feeling sorry for Kate when he handed her the stray that liked to wander his property. It was doubtful he'd considered what Kate and an opinionated scrapper would be like together.

The old elm tree was one of the few that hadn't been slaughtered in the attempt to rid Chicago of an Asian beetle infestation. Jack hoped the limb hadn't been hollowed out so it would break under his weight. He took the big step from the ledge onto the tree.

"You're not content to set off Dave's alarm system, get in fights and come home bloody, and eat my sister out of house and home. Now you have to pretend you're a squirrel and trees are your home," he said softly, edging out on the limb toward the cat. The next limb was too far away for the cat to jump to and still hold the turkey bone. The cat was cornered.

"Come here, you big lumbering furball." Jack reached for the tomcat. He got a swipe with a greasy paw for his troubles. The claws caught the back of his wrist just behind the glove protection. The turkey bone fell to the ground.

"Nice, Marvel. Very nice," Jack remarked grimly, gripping him. The deep scratches stung. And it was obvious why the cat had acquired the name. It really was a marvel he was still alive.

Jack tucked the cat inside the backpack, then flipped over and latched the canvas flap to keep him inside. He would have tossed the pack to the roof, but Kate wouldn't appreciate it. He worked his way out of the tree back to the roof.

He offered her the squirming bag. "One mad cat."

Kate took the canvas satchel and wisely kept it closed. She patted Jack's chest. "Come down to the apartment and I'll fix you breakfast," she offered over the cat howls.

"Make it coffee to go. I'm due at work."

"Any leads on your arsonist?"

"Sure. He likes to burn things." He was getting philosophical about it. His job was to put out the fires; Cole's was to find the man setting them. And Jack knew better than to bet against Cole.

Her pager went off. Kate glanced down at it on her belt. "Jack—" He took the cat before she asked. Kate was already dialing. The conversation was short. "Someone just shot up a liquor store over on Princeton."

"Sounds like we're both going to have a long day."

She was already jogging across the roof to the fire escape. "Lock him in the bathroom?"

"Go. It's handled. Be careful."

"Always am. I owe you one."

"Remember that next time we play basketball."

She laughed and disappeared.

Jack whistled over the noise as he carried the cat back to Kate's apartment. Her home showed the evidence of her late night return— her gym bag dropped inside the door, tennis shoes in the hallway, her jacket tossed toward the chair, and mail sliding off the hallway table.

Jack warily let Marvel out in the bathroom and watched the cat settle with a huff on the toilet seat cover that matched the rugs. At least the frills were good for something. Jack tugged the door firmly closed.

Out of habit, he checked to make sure the bedroom windows were closed and locked, checked that the fire alarm was flashing to show good batteries. He walked back to the kitchen to fix himself coffee. He could get some at the fire station, but that was a twenty-minute drive and he'd never last that long. Jack wondered how many car wrecks he would work before his shift ended. Too many. And probably at least two kitchen fires. Holidays were predictable that way.

Pulling a piece of paper from the pad, he wrote Kate a note and put it under a magnet on her refrigerator. She'd need a laugh by the time her day was done. Somehow he didn't think her dinner with Dave was going to happen on time and uninterrupted. He understood the hope though; he had major plans for his own evening if he could keep the workday under control. A plaintive howl came from the bathroom. Jack locked Kate's apartment and headed to work, taking the coffee with him, relieved to leave the cat behind.

———❦———

The Smokehouse Eatery parking lot was crowded tonight. Jack slapped mud off his slacks, splattered from an attempt to stop a dog from darting across a ditch into tollway traffic. He'd rearranged his schedule in order to be here early, even if it meant coming with mud-splattered slacks. He didn't see Cassie's car, but there was always a chance she'd caught a ride with someone.

It was a typical firemen's holiday. They were crowding into Charles and Sandra's restaurant, taking over the Smokehouse Eatery to celebrate Thanksgiving together. The firehouse down the street might have been closed in the department consolidations, but the restaurant had been a tradition for decades and the holiday was just a good excuse to come back.

He worked his way through the crowd, and within moments confirmed Cassie was nowhere in sight. Jack paused to greet their host and was waved with a laugh toward the buffet table. He was grateful; lunch had been a long time ago.

Twenty minutes later he found Cole. "Think Cassie will come?" Jack asked his friend while he watched the door to the restaurant.

Cole picked up a toothpick and stabbed another Swedish meatball from the buffet hot pot to add to his plate. "She won't come."

Jack looked at his friend, hearing the certainty.

"She's tired, Jack."

"She shouldn't be alone on Thanksgiving."

"Her choice. Let her make it. She hasn't been able to make many of them in the last year and a half."

"She won't cook Thanksgiving dinner for one."

"I took her a pumpkin pie," Cole said.

"She was home?"

"I left it at the bookstore. Knowing Cassie, she'll end up there."

Jack fought the disappointment. He had really been hoping to see her here tonight.

Jack kept one eye on the local news, still worrying about Kate in a quiet corner of his attention. The liquor store crisis had ended about noon, but he knew the likelihood that it had just been followed by another page. He kept expecting to see the breaking news banner and a reporter pushing a microphone in Kate's face.

As a substitute for a day with his family, this party was a pretty good replacement. But while the celebration wasn't muted, neither was it complete. They were missing Cassie and Ash.

Tony was here, in his wheelchair from a fall six years before. Chad had come. Ben's nephew was now on temporary disability from smoke damage to his lungs, for fires made no allowance for rookie mistakes. Cassie Ellis and Ash Hamilton needed to be here—to know they still had a place, to know they were still part of the family. And Jack needed to see Cassie, make sure she was doing okay. The guilt from a busy summer and unfulfilled plans didn't sit well.

He turned to reach for a chip he didn't want to cover the emotions that surged back.

He'd been in some tough fires over the years, but nothing that could compare to the event they simply called The Fire. The nursing home had burned, trapping patients and staff alike. Over a dozen firefighters had been hurt by the time it was over. but only two still haunted everyone involved. Cassie and Ash.

The ceiling had come down. Burning plaster and beams, chairs, tables, and filing cabinets from the floor above had trapped them. Cassie had been pinned and burned. Ash hadn't been able to shift the debris to get her free.

For an agonizing eighteen minutes, a battle that had been focused on rescuing patients and staff had been overlaid with the grim reality of a missing team. The frantic calls from Ash had been chilling, and then they had gone silent.

Jack had joined up with Rescue 12 for the search, penetrating into the heart of the fire through pitch-black corridors, thick toxic smoke, trying to find a way around the collapsed section of the hallway. The heat had been so oppressive it broiled what it touched.

They had found them just past the commons area. Cassie, facedown with her right arm twisted, pinned down in agonizing pain. And Ash—buddy breathing with Cassie to get her oxygen as her tanks had chimed and went empty, tears pouring from the man as she tried to die on him.

"Has anybody heard from Ash?"

Cole shook his head. "He disappeared after Cassie's final surgery and doesn't want to be found. He left no forwarding address."

"It's been three months."

"He'll be back," Cole replied. "Knowing Ash, he's out on his bike traveling the country, blowing the cobwebs out of his brain. He won't do anything crazy."

Jack had been there. He still occasionally disappeared on his two days off to ride as far as his bike would take him. But three months was a little steep.

"I thought Rachel was coming with you tonight?" Cole asked casually.

Jack narrowed his eyes as he watched his friend reach over to stab a turkey rollup. He'd never been able to figure out if there was something there or not. "She decided to track down Gage," Jack replied, not bothering to hide his opinion of that. Rachel was going to get herself hurt in that relationship, but there was no reasoning with her.

He watched for a reaction, but Cole merely glanced over at him. "Does Gage still hate your guts?"

"What do you think?"

"I think you're a lot like Ash. Feeling guilt you figure you deserve to carry."

Jack acknowledged the hit with a slight raise of his punch glass but countered with the truth. "He really does hate my guts."

"His wife is dead. He's sued the furnace repair company out of business. Money's not going to solve the hurt. Hating you is one way to cope."

"We pulled back from the fire. We were late."

"Tabitha was dead long before you got your air tanks on," Cole countered softly. "Long before the fire alarm came in. Someday he'll accept the autopsy report."

"Kind of hard to read past the word *pregnant.*"

"And you scold me for feeling guilty that Cassie got hurt on my watch." Cole pointed to an empty table. "Sit. We'll talk about our popcorn man and leave the past where it belongs for both of us. In the past."

The bookstore was closed for the holiday allowing Cassie a chance to work uninterrupted on shelving books and updating her inventory. She had begun to play Christmas music a month early. While the rest of the world enjoyed Thanksgiving Day, Cassie set her heart on Christmas and hummed along with "Silent Night."

Christmas was going to be her turning point. There was a new beginning waiting for her—to what she hadn't figured out, but it would at least be a new beginning. She was out of the hospital and was never going back. She was thankful just to have the chance to move on. Last year, no one had been willing to give her odds she'd be through the surgeries within a year.

She missed Rescue Squad 65. Oh, how she missed it. The rescues. The close-quarter recoveries. Cutting people out of car wrecks. Being first to go into the smoke while firefighters from the engine crews worked to get water on the flames. The job was gone for good. She had no illusions that she would ever recover sufficiently to go back on active duty.

Cole wanted her to come work for him. It was a sincere offer but she couldn't generate any enthusiasm for it. Being on the sidelines when rescue squads rolled out would cut into her heart. It was better to move on. But life was boring without Rescue Squad 65.

She hated being bored.

Like a coward, she hid from her friends in order to spend Thanksgiving as she chose to: alone, working. She needed the quiet peace of music, books to shelve, and paperwork to do. She needed the time to think.

Lord, You kept me alive for something, and all I'm doing at the moment is spinning my wheels, waiting…for what, I don't know. What do You have

*in mind for the future? I know You love me too much to ask me to endure that
last year of agony without already having a plan to turn into Your glory.*

The questions she'd been putting off until the end of the year were
before her now and decisions had to be made. The vinyl records were
thirty years old without a scratch on them, the music excellent. The
books from the Sandoval estate auction were genuine gems. The paperwork…she planned to ignore it a while longer. Cassie shifted books to
fit a copy of *Tom Swift in the Caves of Ice,* copyright 1911, onto the second shelf of the glass-enclosed bookcase. The store was hers, pur-
chased two months ago.

*I don't mind selling books, but is this it? For all its challenge, it's a pale
comparison to what I had.*

She'd been selling rare books on-line as her part-time hobby for
years. But she never intended it to become more than a hobby that
earned her pocket change. She loved books, but not enough to make
them her life. For now, this was a compromise, a place to store her
growing collection of books and keep herself busy while she figured
out what she wanted to do with the rest of her life.

Thirty, single, burned. The dream of winning a beauty pageant
someday could be scrapped.

Her sense of humor was vicious when she was in a bad mood.

Her right hand cramped as she reached down to pick up another
book. Cassie closed her hand into a fist, watching the scars on her forearm flex. Fire did strange things to skin.

She was thankful to be alive. She wanted no pity for the rest. Part
of it was her independent streak that meant accepting the risks that
went with the job. She'd had the misfortune of becoming one of the sta-
tistics. Complaining that it had been her and not Ash was anathema.
She had pulled nine people from that nursing home and been on her
way back for the tenth when the ceiling had come down. She didn't
regret the decision she had made.

When she wore long sleeves, the evidence of the surgeries of the last
year and a half disappeared. If her glasses were strong prescriptions, they
at least allowed her to read. It was a vast improvement over the days of

wondering if she would have use of her arm or if her sight would survive.

She was recovering. Friends wanted her to be recovered. It was a fine line that took some maneuvering to manage. She could not yet stop the crushing fatigue that hit when she was around a crowd of caring people. Spending Thanksgiving alone had been the right decision, a necessary one. But not everyone had been fooled.

Cassie was fairly certain Cole had left the pumpkin pie. Only a handful of people had a key to the store. The gift had been left on her desk in a white box with a blue bow on top. It was something her former captain would do.

She should call him. Cole wouldn't mind getting a call at home and it would do her good to make it, to talk with a friend who understood the fine tension that underscored the holidays.

She didn't call.

She wasn't the only one who needed to move on with life. Cole did too.

And Ash. Cassie forced herself to pick up the next book. Her partner had stayed through the surgeries, kept her sane through the pain, only to disappear once she was released. To walk away and give her no clue where he was going...She knew Ash. He'd taken what happened personally. And she didn't need either one of them carrying that guilt.

She needed to see Ash for Christmas. After she hugged him, she was going to slug him for worrying her this way. *Please, Jesus.* She let the two words carry the prayer. The emotions were too deep for more words. She really needed to see Ash.

She'd been a fair-weather Christian before the last eighteen months. But in the recent black days, she'd touched bottom, and God was still there. Still bigger than the problems. She hit Him with her anger, her pain, and He'd taken it in and not reflected it back. Cassie was clinging to that peace she had found. Life was tough, but God was tougher.

Another record dropped on the turntable and "Do You Hear What I Hear?" began to play. She'd never taken the time to really celebrate Christmas before. She let the busyness of the season push aside the deeper meaning. Before this year she wasn't even sure she understood what Christmas was really about.

It wasn't just about a baby in a manger, although that was what the world tried to limit it to. It was a day that had begun the final confrontation between good and evil.

Jesus had won. And in the last year Cassie had met Him. Not the soft Jesus that a commercialized Christmas conveyed, but a Jesus so comfortable and secure in His authority He'd come to confront Satan on his own turf.

Jesus had chosen to lay aside the trappings of power that were His right and come humble and approachable, a servant. Man saw it as weakness; Jesus did it from strength. He had arrived with nothing to prove but His Father's love.

It would be nice to spend this Christmas with a deeper appreciation for the celebration.

What she was going to do that day was still an open question. She didn't want to spend Christmas alone, but she didn't want to get involved in the fire department activities either. She had no family in the area—her parents had died years before, and she'd talked her brother into accepting a job offer in Florida last year. She could get absorbed in events at church, but they would demand energy she really didn't have.

There was no good solution, just a lot of options with different drawbacks.

She reached for another book.

What she really wanted to do was spend Christmas with a couple good friends. Ash led that list. And if she had to spend Christmas without him, she was going to give his gift to Goodwill.

"Gage, where have you disappeared to now?" Rachel O'Malley muttered the question to herself when leaning on the doorbell to his town house failed to get a response. Shifting the sack she carried, she pulled out her keys, flipped through the ring to the one marked with a gold crescent, and used it to let herself into Gage's home.

She was invading his space, but she'd done worse in the past. He'd finally given her a key after he found her sitting on the front stoop at 1 A.M., having waited patiently there since 8 P.M. for him to get home. He was shocked sober enough to bawl her out for being careless with her safety. The scowl and the anger had set her back on her heels, but still…it had been nice to see that he cared.

After that, when he'd gone out drinking and knew she was in town, he wore his beeper and carried a phone. He wasn't a man who wanted others to worry; he just wanted to passively kill himself.

Rachel did not like to worry about friends and Gage had her worried. If he couldn't handle Thanksgiving, there was no way he would be able to handle Christmas. She knew what it was like to grieve; Tabitha had been her best friend. And since losing his wife in the way he had, there was a big hole to grieve, but still, Gage was alive. Someday he had to start remembering that.

He was a good man. An award-winning reporter with the *Chicago Tribune,* he fought his battles with the power of his words. And while burying himself in work was a decent short-term answer, it was a lousy long-term one.

He'd fired the housekeeper again. Rachel knew it as soon as she walked into the kitchen and saw the dullness of the linoleum and the stacked, washed dishes in the draining rack. Gage was too neat a man to leave unwashed dishes around. But he wouldn't see the rest of the small details that made a house a comfortable home; he'd only feel them as they accumulated.

She opened the refrigerator to store the Cool Whip to go with the cherry pie she'd brought over. Gage had a sweet tooth.

The milk was sour. She didn't have to smell it to tell; she only had to pick up the plastic gallon to see it. It was the little things that made the grief intense: buying milk by the pint instead of the gallon, cooking for one. Her heart hurt to see the signs of continuing grief.

She was half in love with Gage herself, had resigned herself to living with that fact. Friendships under the stress of the last two years either fractured or melded people together, and Rachel felt like her heart had been soldered together with his. She was going to get him through this if it killed her. She owed it to Tabitha. She'd wrestle with her own emotions later when it was time to move on.

She took off the cap and poured the milk down the sink.

Getting Gage through this second year of holidays was going to be more difficult than she thought. She picked up his phone, saw there were six messages blinking on his answering machine, and since she knew five of them were hers, got further annoyed. The least he could do was listen to her worry about him.

She was surprised when she caught her sister at home. She had expected to leave a message on the answering machine. "Kate, could you rescue my gray-and-white suitcase and shove it in a closet?" She had been planning to head back to Washington, D.C., and already had tickets for an early morning flight out of O'Hare. As Kate had offered to give her a ride to the airport, Rachel planned to spend the night at her sister's place and had already moved her luggage to Kate's trunk.

It was best to put those plans on hold.

On call with the Red Cross and the Emergency Services Disaster Agency to handle trauma situations involving children, Rachel traveled so much she kept apartments in both Chicago and Washington. Staying longer in Chicago would create headaches as she was serving on the presidential commission on school violence next year. The preparation work was just ramping up, but she would figure out a way to work around it.

"That bad," Kate commented.

"If he didn't love so deeply, he couldn't grieve so deeply. But he's drowning in it."

"Drinking?"

Rachel checked Gage's trash and didn't see any liquor bottles. "Doesn't look like it." He'd promised her and he was a man of his word. "But he could use a friend. I'll stick around for the holidays."

"It will be good to have you around. If I'm out when you swing by, help yourself to dinner. I'm buried in turkey; Dave and I barely made a dent in it. There's no need to try and get to the grocery store tonight to replace perishables."

"I appreciate it."

"Give Gage a hug for me? I like him."

At least someone in her family did. Gage's lingering animosity toward Jack had polarized her family. "I'll do that."

Rachel hung up the phone, then looked around the kitchen trying to decide what to do. She had prepped herself to have Gage answer the door, to smile and keep her emotions to herself. She even searched out the *TV Guide* in case he didn't want to talk. For him, she'd tolerate a football game.

Gage called her sticky, sometimes as a compliment, sometimes with a touch of irritation in his voice. She stuck no matter how hard he tried to shake her off.

He thought it was because her overactive sense of doing good wouldn't let her leave him alone. She didn't tell him he was essentially a nonpaying patient. He'd be ticked and she really didn't want to explain the notes she kept out of habit. How did she explain she was just worried enough to want to stay close without sounding paranoid?

She needed Gage. She was thirty-five, and the last few years had drained her more than she would admit even to family. The old stuff she had buried from her childhood was back disrupting her dreams. Her sister Jennifer's cancer had pushed the subject of mortality back center stage, and she just wanted a chance to stop moving for a while and catch her breath. With Gage, there was a reason to stop. As much as she helped him, he helped her. He listened.

She picked up his jacket from the chair at the kitchen table, caught the faint smell of his aftershave, and rubbed her hand on the fabric as she walked to the closet to hang it up.

Where was he?

A check of the garage showed his car was missing. Knowing Gage, the odds were good he had stayed local. Rachel found her keys and locked his house. Shoving her hands in her pockets, she set out searching.

Three

C assie? Open up. I know you're in there. I can see the lights are on."
Jack tried to keep the frustration out of his voice. She was going to
ignore his thumping on the door. The blinds on the front window
had been lowered and the door had stained-glass panels preventing a
look inside, but the lights were on and her car was still here. So much for
wondering what she'd think about unexpected company.

The street was deserted. The chill in the November evening made
Jack wish he'd thought to wear more than a windbreaker. Her bookstore was in the old section of Lincoln Hills' downtown, nestled
between a candy store and a bike shop. The businesses were part of one
old brick building sharing a common roof and parking lot. He'd leave,
but he was beginning to worry and he hated that feeling.

Jack heard a sudden scramble inside to throw locks. The front door
opened so fast he saw Cassie wince as the corner of the door caught her
left foot. She wasn't wearing shoes. "Sorry, I didn't hear you." He heard
the loudness of the Christmas music playing and felt stupid. Deaf, why
hadn't he remembered the obvious? She was now partially deaf.

And she was still gorgeous. Her hair had grown back. She'd always
looked a bit like a pixie, but now her face was framed by curling brown
hair. The suppressed pain had disappeared from those dark chocolate
eyes.

She had gone with the oval frames for glasses that had a thin band of gold at the top, and they drew more attention to her spectacular eyes. Thankfully the fire had just brushed her face and those burns had long ago disappeared under the skill of a surgeon's knife. Overall, it was a great face. He leaned against the doorpost, enjoying it.

"Jack. You were looking for me?" Cassie asked, her words breaking into his thoughts.

"I missed you." He saw her blink and realized what he'd said. "At the party. We missed you at the party." She grinned as he dug himself out of the quicksand of words he hadn't meant to say. "Sandra insisted you needed a care package."

"That's for me?" She looked at the sack he held. "All of that?"

He felt like laughing at her stunned expression. "I caught a look at some of what she was packing. I sure hope you haven't had dinner yet. It started with ribs and went on from there."

"Smokehouse Eatery ribs. I've dreamed of them. Come in, please." She reached out and caught his jacket sleeve, tugging him inside.

She stepped out of the way, then closed the door behind him.

The bookstore had been transformed since the last time he visited. Not that he often entered bookstores, but hers was worth a visit. It showed her touches. Whimsical. Rare books. Rare toys. The bold red fire engine sitting on the corner of her worktable had to be from the 1950s.

Cassie stopped at the counter and leaned over to nudge down the music volume. No radio or CDs for Cassie; she had a stack of vinyl records on a turntable. "White Christmas" ended and "Jingle Bells" began. It set a festive mood.

Jack made a place for the sack on the table that dominated the center of the room. It was custom built to be her come-and-linger table where she put out coffee and cookies for her customers. He slid his jacket over the back of a chair.

It was obvious she'd been sorting and shelving books. Several books with colorful jackets were spread out in a semicircle on the floor beside the glass-enclosed shelves. Curious, he studied the two turned his direction: *Wings for Victory,* with its World War II vintage B-52 and parachuting soldier, and *Gene Autry and the Redwood Pirates,* the horse and its rider racing up a trail. Popular children's books from another decade.

"I think you'd like *Uncle Wiggily in the Country.*" Cassie pointed to the book nearest him on the floor. "It's got pictures in it."

He shot her a smile. "That book looks older than I am."

"1940. The jacket is in good condition, and the color-plate pictures are excellent."

"What's it worth?"

"Ninety."

"That's highway robbery."

Her laughter was a delight to hear. "If I wanted to hold it a while and sell it as part of a set, I could get in the low three figures."

Cassie rolled down her long sleeves and looked down to catch the buttons at the cuffs. "Was Cole at the party?"

Jack wanted to tell her not to roll them down for his sake. But he didn't know how she felt about the scars, if they made her self-conscious or embarrassed. If he said nothing, did he make it worse than if he acknowledged them? They looked a great deal better than the day the doctors first removed the gauze to air the burns.

"Cole was there, most of the firefighters, a good percentage of the dispatchers. The place was packed."

She glanced back up and smiled. "I'm glad. Charles and Sandra have been getting squeezed lately with the station closing right after the movie theater. They not only lost the business of firefighters stopping by the restaurant before and after their shifts, but Charles lost the extra income he earned working paid on call with the station."

"He seems to be weathering the transition. And Sandra is happy to have him off the fire runs."

A new record dropped and "Santa Claus Is Coming to Town" began to play.

Their conversation had already veered through its normal course of subjects and she looked to be searching for a new topic. They were casual friends, the kind you could be comfortable around, the kind with whom you could share a laugh and a smile when paths crossed. There was respect, trust, humor…and not much that was personal beyond work.

His plans to change that hadn't worked out as he hoped. Cassie had been in and out of the hospital with the surgeries, and he'd walked into a summer of crises in his family that had absorbed his time and attention.

He hadn't wanted Cassie catching grief because of him. So he flirted a bit when he saw her at a fire scene or a fireman's gathering, made a beeline to sit beside her when they ended up at the same certification training, but otherwise let the relationship drift as casual friends. He should have never let the distance between where they lived, the schedule clashes, what other guys in the small community of firefighters would say keep him from asking her out.

He was paying for it now. He wanted her feeling comfortable to talk about her plans, to stretch beyond that and talk about the holidays, family, what it was like to have dreams about a fire…but he didn't know how to begin. Stalling, Jack reached over and picked up one of the cars on the table destined for her rare toys shelf. "They don't make cars like this anymore."

The Model-T was heavy, made of metal, its black paint still shiny. The tires were thick rubber, the steering wheel an aged white plastic. He turned it over and found stamped on the bottom the signature Hubbley Toys of Lancaster, Pennsylvania.

"Raise the hood and check out the engine."

He did and smiled with pleasure. It was accurate down to the grillwork. "Now *these* are collectibles."

"I think so."

She liked old cars. It was a small thing, but he hadn't known it.

"Have you eaten yet?" Cassie asked.

Jack looked up from the car he held. Cassie pushed away from the counter and disappeared through the side door to the storage room. She came back with plates and napkins. "Say you haven't even if you have. I hate to eat alone."

"Cassie, I never turn down barbecue spareribs."

She moved books from the table to a blue plastic tote, clearing a space for them. "Just stack the pink pages and drop them back into the in-basket on the desk. They're on-line customer wish lists. I'll get back to them later."

"Business is good?"

"It's in the black. At the prices these books command, I only need to sell a few a month to cover the overhead."

When he'd visited her at the hospital he often found her on-line doing deals or researching the value of books she had found, using the hobby as a distraction against the ever present pain. She hadn't been much for TV beyond CNN and old Westerns.

Dealing with the burns, the surgeries, the painful recovery—day after day she had kept moving forward. He'd sat on the weight bench opposite her in the hospital rehab and told her jokes as she struggled to lift a three-pound barbell through twenty-rep exercises. He learned a lot about her ability never to quit. This business was yet another way to move forward. He was proud of her.

The papers moved to safety, Jack started unloading the sack.

She looked tired. As Cassie quietly fixed her plate with a sample of the items Sandra had sent, he could see now what Cole had referred to. There were lines around her eyes and the good mood and lightness in her voice couldn't hide the fact she was relieved to sit down.

He waited while she silently prayed. He knew she was a Christian. It hadn't taken more than a couple visits to the hospital to see her faith was more than words with her. Her Bible on the bedside table, a few of the books she read were on prayer, and the radio had been tuned to a Christian station. Cole believed too, and Jack had at times interrupted some very serious conversations between the two of them.

He found the subject of religion a difficult one. In the last few months four in his family had chosen to believe, and it was no longer a subject he could avoid. Jack didn't understand it. Jesus seemed to be the serious myth that people believed in at Christmas, Santa Claus the childish one. It was the season for children to think someone really did come down the chimney with gifts and for the adults to set aside reason and believe there was a God who had become a man.

Cassie lifted her head, ending her silent prayer, and reached for a napkin.

"You're looking forward to Christmas."

Cassie flashed him a grin as she nudged the box of Christmas decorations on the floor with her foot. "How could you tell?"

He had always loved the color and excitement of the Christmas season, the stocking stuffers, and the excuse to give gifts. It was harder this year with Jennifer sick, harder to retain the smile when there was a chance this would be her last Christmas.

Cassie's gaze sharpened as she must've caught something in his expression. He didn't want to talk about his sister's cancer, didn't have words to keep the emotions he felt in perspective. He spoke before she could. "You need a Christmas tree."

She looked at him a moment, then nodded, accepting the redirect. "I'm going to put a big one in the window and decorate it to the point it wants to topple under all the lights and ornaments. I've got a set of handmade glitter ones that are messy but look beautiful."

Jack seized on that comment. There weren't many obvious ways to put himself back into her world and he would take any opening he could find. She would need help with the Christmas tree.

"Has anyone heard from Ash?"

He wished he could give her a positive answer. He wanted to shake the guy for worrying her this way. Jack knew how close partners got. He had watched Ash and Cassie tease each other mercilessly during speed drills and hose hauls, but let someone else suggest their team wasn't the best and the two of them would turn as one to reply. He envied them both. "No one has heard from him."

Cassie pushed aside her disquiet and picked up the first sparerib on her plate. "Knowing Ash, he'll be back when he's ready and when I least expect it."

Jack didn't think Cassie and Ash had been more than good friends, but he knew they were very close. When your life depended on the person at your side, the trust went deep. And it went both ways between Ash and Cassie. Jack didn't understand why Ash had left without a word.

Cassie closed her eyes as she tasted the first sparerib. "Oh, these are good."

Jack turned his attention to his. "It's the sauce."

"And the smoke and the time and Charles's magic touch." She finished the first one and licked sauce off her fingers.

Jack reached over and wiped a spot from her chin. "Messy."

She laughed. "You can try and clean me up later. Somehow I don't think I'll have to worry about leftovers."

"You didn't have dinner."

She glanced at the box on her desk. "Pumpkin pie."

"Good priorities."

"Absolutely."

"I'll stop asking questions so you can eat dinner now."

The laughter reached her eyes as she picked up another sparerib. "Appr'ciate it."

Jack relaxed. Cassie hadn't changed, not all that much. Her eyes still reflected her thoughts; her emotions still came easily to the surface. "I miss having you at the fire scenes."

She studied him over her dinner. "I miss being there."

The first time he met her he'd been working with Company 81, Cassie for Company 65.

He was facing a grease fire in a restaurant, all his guys committed, with fire leaping to the business next door. Company 65 arrived and he yelled at her as he did any other guy, tagging her number from the back of her helmet, no idea who she was, sending her and Ash into the smoke next door to confirm the building was clear.

When she dumped water over his head to cool him down before cleanup started, he'd taken a mouthful of it as he realized C. Ellis was a woman. She'd laughed so hard at his expression she started to hiccup, then went back to hauling out smoldering bench padding to the street. Jack shook his head like a wet dog and followed her back to work.

"I can image the mop-ups are a bit more boring now," she teased.

"No one to talk literature with," he agreed, smiling.

Cassie put everything she had physically and then some into whatever job she was doing. His biggest caution had always been that she save some of that energy for the end of the fire.

He'd heard that when she returned to her fire station she'd crawl away, crash with a book, and ignore the world to get her energy back. He enjoyed teasing her about that at a scene while they were doing cleanup.

She'd always been one to laugh at his jokes and his gag gifts. She was quieter now, more reflective, and the experience she lived through was there just below the surface. But she was coming back with the same steel that had driven her to excel at her job. He was grateful. She'd had her life upended, but she found the strength to deal with it.

He wasn't sure how he'd handle it if he were put in a similar situation. He wanted to be a firefighter ever since he'd seen the fire in his bedroom as a young boy. His parents had encouraged the dream with trips to the local fire department and to the firefighter museum. The car crash that had killed his parents— It had been the fire department first on the scene to try and save them and Jack had never forgotten that. He'd gotten into the fire academy as soon as he could qualify. Being a fireman wasn't a job as much as it was an identity.

"Do you have plans yet for Christmas?" Cassie asked.

"Working. We'll probably have the O'Malley gathering the weekend before."

"I've heard about those O'Malley bashes."

They were legendary for the fun, family, and food. "If it's one thing the O'Malleys know how to do well, it's have fun."

"I envy you the big family."

He'd love to talk her into coming with him. He looked at her, started to ask, then bit his tongue. If Cassie said no to the invitation, he wanted enough time to convince her to change her mind, and the clock above the door was taking away his options for having such a discussion. It was 8:10. Jack didn't want to leave but knew he'd have to if he was going to get to the fire station on time.

Cassie saw the direction of his glance and wiped her fingers on a napkin. "You're working tonight?"

"I told Greg I'd cover part of his shift so he could get away early in the morning. His family is having a weekend reunion."

"Nice of you."

"I wish now I hadn't said yes."

She chuckled and pushed the frosted pastry his way. "Take dessert with you."

"Can I come back sometime?"

She leaned back in her chair and left his question hanging a beat too long for his comfort. When she answered, her smile reached her eyes. "Come over and I'll put you to work. Next time I'll bring the food."

Of all the reasons he liked Cassie, that undertone of laughter in her voice was near the top of the list. He pulled on his jacket and dug out his keys, then picked up the pastry and took a bite. There was raspberry inside. "Deal."

She was a vision walking in the door of the Smokehouse Eatery. Cole nearly choked on his soda. Where had Rachel gotten a cashmere sweater to match her eyes? Her black jacket hung open, her hands pushed into the pockets. She was wearing jeans and a sweater the color of emeralds.

Rachel was the classic beauty in the O'Malley family with an innate sense of how to dress well to make an impression. She was making one. Tall, slender, she walked like a model with her graceful stride. Cole was aware of men shifting their gaze as she crossed their line of sight. Rachel skirted around people coming his direction where he sat on a stool at the counter. He straightened, hoping…

"Cole, have you seen Gage?"

The vision spoke and he scowled. "Gage wouldn't risk coming here. He might cross paths with your brother."

She winced. "They have got to call a truce."

"Not up to you."

She shot him an annoyed look and turned to scan the room, her shoulder length brown hair swinging across her jacket collar. "Where is Jack? I thought he was coming to this gathering."

"He left an hour ago. I could make an educated guess where he went."

Rachel smiled. "So could I."

She picked up a matchbook from the basket beside the cash register out of habit and slid it into her pocket. He knew it had nothing to do with the fact she smoked—because she didn't—and everything to do with the fact she often worked disaster situations where the electricity was out. She gave new meaning to the adage: Be prepared.

"Sit. Stay a minute. You just walked in." She looked like she was getting ready to head out again.

"I'm looking for Gage."

"He won't be any more lost in five minutes than he is now."

She hesitated, then slid onto the stool next to him. She had a politeness that wouldn't let her refuse the request. She slipped off her jacket. He told himself not to stare. She was beautiful and it was a pleasure to look at her. Her sweater had three-quarter length sleeves, and it set off the fact she still had a tan acquired from her recent work in Texas and Florida. A silver bracelet holding an emerald stone bracketed her left wrist.

Cole turned on his stool and caught the attention of the lady on the other side of the counter. "Sandra, do you have any more of that hot apple cider? Rachel could use some."

"I'm not that cold," Rachel muttered, pushing the hands she had been rubbing into the pockets of her snug jeans.

"Honey, your nose is red, not to mention your ears."

Now her face was red. He watched that blush and was surprised when she didn't say anything as a comeback. He'd always been able to count on her for one. As a silent apology he slid over the basket of deep-fried mushrooms he'd been working on. "Eat. And tell me about Jennifer."

Her straight posture wilted on the stool. She picked up one of the mushrooms and bit into it, her gaze turning inward as she became absorbed in her own thoughts. "Cole, it's going to be a miserable Christmas."

He rested his forearms against the counter and crowded her space and she didn't even notice. "Why?"

Four

I wondered how far you would walk before you came back here. You should have paged." Caught off guard, Rachel looked up. Gage was sitting on the front stoop of his town house, his gray sedan parked behind her car at the curb rather than in his drive. It was after nine o'clock and Rachel had given up any hope of locating him, having checked all his normal haunts.

"I tried. Your pager batteries must be dead."

He pulled the pager from his belt clip to check. "Sorry. I didn't realize."

Rachel sat beside him on the steps, relief releasing the tension that had built up as she walked back from the restaurant.

Gage picked up her right hand and retrieved the watch she was holding. He fixed the loose link, put the watch back around her wrist, and refastened the clasp. "I was driving. Not drinking and driving. Just driving."

She nodded, appreciating the news.

"I'm sorry you were worried."

She shrugged her shoulder. "I like to worry."

He chuckled and, rather than get up, rested his elbows back on the step behind him and stretched out his legs. "You look good, Rachel."

His mood had lightened since the last time she had seen him. She searched his face and met his gaze, found the first glimmer of acceptance there.

"Thanks. You don't," she pointed out kindly. Thirty-eight, six two; dressing well and staying fit had always been priorities. It was a sign of the grief that what he valued most he'd let go of first.

He stroked his chin. "You don't like the pirate version of me?"

"It's still scruffy."

"Holidays are for beards."

"Is that what you call it?" It suited his chiseled features.

He smiled at her. "Why do I hear an echo of Tabitha in this conversation?"

"She would have started with the hair."

"True."

He let her tease him about it, and that alone told her something had fundamentally changed recently. Hope kindled. Tabitha had softened the man's personality, but the last two years had brought back the edge of cynicism that made his smile rare. Seeing the smile come back was a very good sign.

"I went back to work," he commented.

"I heard."

"No—really back to work. I accepted the Weekend Focus news slot."

A hard-hitting news story for the weekend paper, a chance to go in-depth on stories around the city. He'd won his Pulitzer there four years ago, and the prestige and pressure of that job were some things she remembered. "I'm pleased for you."

"I'm terrified."

He said it so bluntly and with a smile dancing around his mouth that she had to smile. "Welcome back to the living."

"Jeffrey wore me down. My junior partner wants to earn a Pulitzer too."

"He's young, ambitious. Sound familiar?"

"I was never young."

She laughed.

"The piece is ours to research, investigate, and write. I find it somewhat annoying to wear a tie when I go into the office now, but I'll be working from home most of the time."

"Are you ready for that?"

"I'm going to find out. So what were you looking so grim about as you paced back to your car?"

"Cole."

"Not a what, but a who." He got to his feet and offered her a hand up. "You like him; you just don't want to admit it."

"He watches out for my brother; I'm grateful for that." She would be fair and give Cole that. "He's worried about these fires."

"What fires?" Gage's good mood disappeared. Rachel knew how volatile the subject was for him, but she needed his help.

"The house that burned last week...apparently it matches other fires they've had recently. Would you consider taking a look?"

His expression told her no, but he reached out and rubbed her chin with his thumb and sighed. "For you, yes, I'll take a look. As long as you don't rag on me about the housekeeper."

"I'm that predictable?"

He wrapped his arm around her shoulders and turned her toward his front door. "Only to people who like you. So what did you bring me to eat? I'm starved."

"Cherry pie." She glanced at her watch. "I can't stay long. Kate's expecting me at ten."

"Stay long enough to share a piece. I hate to eat alone."

The medallion from Jack's key chain had fallen off. Cassie rubbed the smooth metal between her thumb and forefinger as she walked through the store turning off lights. The man carried a Bugs Bunny medallion on his key chain. It had brought a laugh when she found it. The man was a charmer. And tonight anyone who fed her was in her good graces.

Cassie stopped in the storeroom to retrieve her jacket. She'd have to dig out a pair of needle nose pliers at home and fix the link that had opened. Maybe she would get Jack a matching Road Runner to go with it. They sold them at the corner store, on a spin rack by the cash register right next to the baseball cards and the lock de-icer.

She hadn't intended to stay this late. It was going to be after eleven before she got home. She would get gas in the car, stop by the twenty-four-hour pharmacy, and then it would be home and bed. It sounded like a lovely plan.

Cassie slipped the medallion into her pocket. It was a bit painful to be looking across the table at a young Robert Redford. Rugged good looks, broad shoulders, blue eyes—he was a guy who attracted attention just by walking into the room, who didn't have scars to mar his looks. It wasn't fair to hold Jack's looks against him. Everything she knew about the man she liked. She hoped Jack O'Malley did stop by again.

The fire department community was a small one, and she had worked with his paramedic brother Stephen on a few occasions before the restaurant fire had put her in a place to meet Jack and get to know him.

Dumping water over Jack that day had been a practical way to say hello. It had been a hot day, an intense fire, and cooling down was critical for everyone at the scene. It had also been a laughter-filled way to make sure he would remember her.

She enjoyed his friendship. He was one of the few who hadn't been stiff when he dropped by the hospital to say hi. He was the one more likely to bring her a tape of the Saturday morning cartoons than a magazine. He had always been good for a joke designed to make her laugh.

She saw behind the humor a serious man making a deliberate choice. He made a point to offer her what others were not—a reminder that life outside the hospital walls was still going on, was still there waiting to be enjoyed when she got out. She deeply appreciated that.

Cassie locked the back door of the store. She planned to build shelves in the storage room. She'd see if Jack wanted to help hold boards and swing a hammer some day when he was off work.

Something was wrong.

Cassie stopped, scanning the area and the shadows, searching for why the impression had formed. It was a sensation not unlike being in a fire when she couldn't see but could feel a check from her subconscious not to move, that danger was near.

Her hand coiled around her keys, slipping them between her fingers, turning them into sharp weapons. It was a safe area and she was accustomed to working at night, but if trouble was around the best defense was a good offense.

And then it registered.

Smoke.

She was smelling smoke.

Her head came up like a hawk. She looked toward the sky and saw a faint haze shimmering. Stars began to disappear.

Five

Sam was snoring.

Jack turned his head and considered throwing a pillow across to the next bunk to shut him up. That's what Sam's wife said worked. The dorm room at the station house slept twelve, the bunks basic and the mattresses thick enough to be better than camping out but not comfortable enough to make it reach the level of even a cheap motel bed.

Stretched out on top of his sleeping bag, Jack wasn't sure why he couldn't sleep. It was 11 P.M. and shutting off to go to sleep had never been a problem before. He shifted his head over to the right side of the pillow. He was on the fourth bunk and if he moved his head to the left, the triangle of light coming in the window from the streetlight would be in his eyes.

The sleeping bag smelled like smoke and this late at night it was irritating him. He'd have to remember to drop it off at the cleaners to run through their heavy duty washers. Since the bunks were used by three different shifts, most guys stuck to bringing sleeping bags rather than mess with sheets.

It was different down the hall in the women's dorm. There were two women paramedics and one woman firefighter on this shift. They took time to add nice touches to their lives like sheets, even though it meant changing bedding every time they came on duty.

Middle of the night and he was thinking about how women liked sheets and guys went for sleeping bags. He tucked his hands behind his head and wondered what his sister Rachel would say about that. Probably that he needed some sleep.

Cassie would need to get the Christmas tree up at the store in the next week if it was to make any impact on her Christmas sales. Maybe they could look for the tree this coming Sunday afternoon. He knew she closed her bookstore on Sundays for religious reasons so she would likely be free.

He could borrow his brother Stephen's pickup truck and take Cassie to either a nursery or one of the Christmas tree farms. It would be a good excuse to get a couple hours of her time. The more Jack thought about it, the more he liked the idea.

He was going to have to come up with the right Christmas gifts to put under that tree. She'd probably suggest prettily wrapped empty boxes and there was no fun in that. Besides, he was a great believer in quantity in addition to quality.

Jack smiled. There had to be somewhere he could find some old, rare comic books.

Dispatch tones broke the silence.

Cassie slammed her car into park, killed the engine, and came close to stripping the key as she pulled it out. The streetlights were too far away to give more than an impression of a house set back on its corner lot surrounded by century old trees.

The house was big, old, sprawling, with a wraparound porch. She already hated the two turrets because she knew they would have limited narrow access ways going up. It was the kind of place her grandmother had owned, which Cassie had loved to explore.

Smoke billowed in the breeze. Embers were beginning to illuminate the smoke like fireflies set free from the bowels of the earth.

The spectators consisted of one man in his eighties hurrying down his porch steps across the street and his wife tying the belt of her thick blue robe and scolding him for not putting on shoes.

"Did you call it in?"

"Yes." He was staring across the street in disbelief. "I just got up to get a drink and *wham*, I smelled smoke. For the longest time I couldn't figure out where it was coming from."

It didn't surprise Cassie; she knew how fast fires could erupt, developing from nothing to this. "Who lives here? Is anyone home?"

"Carla and Peter Wallis, their daughter Tina."

Cassie flinched at the child's name. "How old is Tina?"

"Six. They travel frequently, but as far as I know they were staying home for the holidays."

Flames weren't visible in the windows but they were now showing at the crown line of the roof. The house was on the edge of the fire district. The firefighters were on the way; traffic was light. Did she have three to five minutes to wait for them?

She leaned on her car horn. The smoke might not yet be on the first floor, but if it had already descended throughout the second floor, anyone inside wouldn't be waking up.

She felt sweat soak the back of her shirt under her jacket. She didn't want to go in. She was afraid. It might be rational but she was ashamed of it. "Pets?"

The neighbor shook his head. At least there wouldn't be a crazed dog waiting for her inside. If someone was in there, she would never be able to live with herself if she didn't go in. Just do it. Think about it later.

She found her flashlight under the driver's seat and grabbed the roll of duct tape she used to seal boxes of books bought at the estate auction. Cassie was relieved to have the leather jacket but wished she had something better than tennis shoes and ankle-high socks.

She had done rescues before. With Ash. With an air tank on her back, a turnout suit that could reflect three hundred degrees of heat, and a face mask to at least keep smoke out of her eyes even if visibility was nonexistent. She had none of those tonight. And it was Ash in the equation she missed the most.

"When the firefighters get here, tell them I'm doing a bedroom sweep clockwise. Remember that. Clockwise."

She ran toward the house. With every step she got closer to her private nightmare.

Lord, give me courage.

She didn't fear the danger; she feared her memories and the fact she might freeze. As long as she kept her focus and kept moving, she could deal with the risks. But if she had to face the flames...the nausea had started and she was only smelling the smoke.

Another spectator. She saw the man as she turned up the drive toward the front door. "Stay back, please. I'm with the fire department."

She didn't need well-meaning civilians entering the house to try and help. The man stood just inside the property line watching the fire. In the dark, he was simply an impression—a tall man, wearing a light brown jacket and jeans. He slipped his hands into his pockets and idly turned to glance toward her. She couldn't see who it was, but the way he moved...

Ash.

She stumbled.

How many times had she seen that still, relaxed consideration of a situation before he acted? "Ash?" she whispered the word in disbelief. He lived near here. He was back. "Ash." Her voice increased in confidence and was filled with relief.

The man stepped back and disappeared into the shadows.

What was going on?

A hot ember brushed her cheek.

Cassie's attention jerked back to the house. It couldn't have been Ash. Not to watch a fire. Not to ignore her.

Smoke spewed out where the roof met the siding like a chimney pointed downward. Since she had arrived the fire had already grown in intensity.

She needed Ash to be here, not some spectator who thought he'd stand and watch.

How would she get in?

In the past she and Ash would have hit the front door with a battering ram and dropped it in two blows. She didn't have the strength to try a brute force entry.

She saw the child-sized rocking chair on the porch beside two adult chairs. There was no need to be pretty. She picked up the first large chair, its metal cold and hard to grip as all her strength was now awkwardly in her left arm. She sent the chair crashing through the living room window. Only a small amount of smoke swirled out. If the fire was high and held in the roof, there was still a chance.

She knocked out the glass at the bottom of the frame with the flashlight.

For a decade she had loved doing this. She'd been crazy.

She went over the windowsill.

Edge of the district. Late at night. Jack braced his hand on the dashboard as Nate made the difficult right turn onto Holly Street, needing every inch of the road to handle Engine 81's length. The neighborhood was old, the streets narrow, the sirens and lights were waking people up. Jack willed the engine to close the distance faster. 1437 Cypress. They were heading to the blocks behind where Cassie's store was located.

This had the hallmarks of one of the arsonist's fires. But it was not Gold Shift on duty this time, it was Red Shift. It was chance that Nate and Bruce had been available when this call came in. Rescue 65 had been dispatched to a car accident, and Nate and Bruce had arrived at the station in answer to the callback to replace personnel just as the dispatch tones for this fire sounded.

Jack had to assume it was the arsonist and plan for the worst case. The address made it another house—but was it unoccupied or occupied?

"Bruce."

"I'll be at your heels with the fire pole."

Jack nodded. He didn't want a team entering a house with a ceiling ready to come down on them.

Cassie whimpered at the heat. It invaded her jacket and penetrated her long-sleeved shirt. The healing skin from the last surgery screamed. She found the hallway and the stairs going up. The smoke was deceptive. It remained wisps of white in her beam of light on the first floor, but her light shining up couldn't penetrate the blackness at the top of the landing.

She wanted to retreat. She knew what was waiting at the top of the stairs.

Go or get out?

Cassie grasped the railing and took the stairs two at a time.

The smoke drove her to a crouch. Coughing, struggling to get her bearings, she moved right, feeling her way. Air was still breathable low but it was hot. Her eyes burned with the smoke and visibility was abysmal. She didn't waste her breath trying to call out. She would be grabbing and dragging.

The roar of the fire in the roof was deafening. The owners had probably filled the attic and never thought about what a decade of dry rot would do to boxes put into storage and forgotten. Plaster was beginning to drop. Outlets were smoking. Flames were shooting from nail holes marking where pictures had fallen from the wall.

Her options were limited. Breathable air wasn't going to be available for long.

Thirty seconds. Clockwise search.

She hit the first bedroom with the end of the duct tape already tugged free so that two quick twists wrapped it around the hot doorknob. She let the tape stream out behind her as she dove into the smoke to find the bed.

Find a bed that wasn't made and hope her grasping hands touched an arm or leg, pray she didn't find an empty child's bed. Children in a fire had the deadly habit of crawling into closets or under furniture. There was no way she could do a full-room search without gear.

Her right shin hit wood and the painful gasp cost her precious air as she fell against the bed. The down comforter was stretched taut. She cringed at that realization—this was probably a guest bedroom.

Cassie turned and dove back into the hallway. She dropped to her knees, coughing, getting a breath in the clearer air inches from the carpet. The air was so hot it hurt to breathe.

She scrambled into the thick smoke to reach the next door, ruthlessly denying her fear. The next door turned out to be a bathroom. The third door jammed when she tried to force it open. Had someone tried to get to the door and fallen inside?

Cassie set the flashlight by her left foot. She accepted the blisters she was going to get, wrapped her left hand around the hot metal, and put her weight against the door. Her lungs burned as she strained. She managed to wedge her right hand into the crevice and get desperately needed leverage.

There was fire behind the door. As the door inched open she found herself facing the dragon. The door suddenly opened all the way and the flames slapped at her. Plaster. She'd just shoved aside a chunk of plaster and a beam. Cassie jerked away from the flames back into the hallway. Flames shot across to touch the opposite wall. All breathable air became swallowed in the swirling smoke. There was no time left.

Get out.

There was no way to get past those flames.

Cassie turned…and stumbled on a teddy bear lying in the hall.

Six

Jack tightened the wrist straps on his gloves as Engine 81 pulled in front of the house and slightly past it so Engine 65 could take the hydrant. They would buddy tank the water, Engine 65 feeding it forward so they could place four attack lines and keep the water pressure even.

Ladder Truck 81 moved past, sirens still screaming, pulling to the east side of the house. Rescue 81 took the street side of the engines. The fire was already crowning through the roof. Jack swung from the seat to the ground relieved they had rolled all engines. They would need the men. They were going to need to lay a lot of hose to get water on the fire.

Was the house occupied or empty? Jack scanned the spectators, dozens of them, searching to spot the one or two neighbors who might have that answer. Two cops were present and a reporter had already made it to the scene.

"She went in to search the bedrooms." Jack locked in on the words of the distraught elderly man now with the captain. "She said to tell you she was searching clockwise. She was real insistent about that word."

"Who?"

Jack spotted the car. There weren't two people who drove blue sedans with white trim who had chili cook-off bumper stickers saying: Firefighters Like It Hot stuck on the front bumper.

"Cassie," Jack hollered, adrenaline surging. "Has she come out of the house since she entered?" He tried to keep the desperation out of his voice as he grabbed his air tank. He ducked and dropped it into place on his back. Bruce and Nate shifted from hose to grabbing fire blankets and spare air tanks, priorities immediately changing.

The two from Rescue Squad 81 were already racing for the door.

"No. She's been in there three minutes," the elderly man said.

Faced with the possibility of people inside, Jack knew she would have had no choice but to go in. He needed a word with more punch than *fear* to handle the emotion that absorbed him. Shingles slid from the roof and crashed with an explosion of embers onto the walkway.

"Jack, backup rescue." Frank keyed his radio and grabbed the attention of the lieutenant for Truck 81. "Five are going in. Tear open the roof but don't drown it until we know we won't be bringing it down on them as they search."

"No one's home!" The cop struggling to get into the garage had just gained entry. No vehicle. Whoever lived here was away for the holidays. Jack wanted to swear. Cassie wouldn't have known that. And that meant she would take the time to try and reach each bedroom.

She knew how fire moved and breathed. She would know the dangers. But that was a two-edged sword. She would stay inside until the last possible moment. And the smoke would take her down. After eighteen months sidelined she wouldn't know her own limits. Stress, heat, smoke…she should have been out of the house long ago.

Bruce and Nate were at his side as he sprinted toward the house. He wished Ben had been called back to duty. He wasn't coming out without her, and he could use the man's intensity right now.

The paint was blistering. Jack's breath hissed inside the mask as his light picked up the sight he feared. Penetrate these walls and flames would surround them. Let oxygen get to the base of this fire and it would roar. The building was primed to go.

Jack followed the guys from Rescue 81 up the stairs while Bruce and Nate veered off to search the first floor.

Where was she?

Flames had the ceiling, a deep red glowing monster that rolled like waves through the thick smoke feeding on the paint. The two men from Rescue 81 moved forward together into the smoke to literally sweep the width of the hallway with their bodies. Jack knew the reality. They were hoping to trip over Cassie.

She was down on all fours crawling. The firefighter in him applauded her smarts; the guy who had visited her in the hospital wanted to weep. His bright light caught the odd color of blue. She was grasping a teddy bear in her left hand. No wonder she had kept searching. The guys from Rescue 81 swallowed her in a fire blanket to protect her from falling embers and lifted her toward him.

Jack did his best to avoid the healing skin grafts on her arms as he took her weight. Cassie was convulsing with coughs. There was no way she would be able to walk the stairs without stumbling. He put her over his shoulder and turned to retrace his steps down the stairs, moving with only one thought in mind—getting her out of the house fast.

The instant he cleared the front door he ripped off his mask. He shifted Cassie, shoving back the fire blanket, alarmed at the first clear look at her face. Tears streaming, she was gasping for air, gagging. Seared lungs could kill. "Where's the ambulance?"

"Here."

The boots felt like lead on his feet when he wanted to run.

Cole was there as well as two paramedics from the area hospital. Jack was grateful to see it was Neal and Amy who had been on duty. They were pros at fire scenes. He still wished it were his brother Stephen who had received the call as he carefully set Cassie down.

Jack heard the order to drown the fire and knew it meant his men and the rescue squad were clear. An incredible rush of noise followed as water flowed.

Cassie refused to lie back on the gurney. "Hot," she protested.

As Cole peeled away her jacket, Jack spotted the burn spots in the leather. She was going to need another jacket for Christmas.

Amy slipped on an oxygen mask over the coughs.

Jack stripped off his gloves. He unbuttoned the cuffs of Cassie's shirt and carefully rolled up her sleeves. The healing scars on both arms were an angry red, inflamed by the heat, her right arm much worse than her left. Neal handed over cold packs and Jack rested them against her forearms. She flinched.

"Better," she whispered.

Jack tipped up her chin looking for new burns. Her eyes were streaming and she couldn't open them to more than a squint. He carefully slipped off her glasses, relieved to see they hadn't been cracked. The exhaustion he had seen earlier in the evening was swamping her now. "The house was empty, Cassie. The family is on vacation."

Her relief was palpable.

Neal slipped an ice pack behind her neck to help cool her down. "Cassie, hold on, the eye drops will help." He brushed back her hair and carefully opened her eyes to add the drops. He blotted her streaming eyes with sterile gauze. "Let them water and clear."

A fit of coughing doubled her up.

It hurt to hear.

Jack had to get back to his men but he didn't want to leave her side. He could only imagine how hard it had been to face a fire again.

A firm hand settled on his shoulder. Jack looked up to find his captain beside him, watching Cassie. "Company 26 is half a minute away," Frank said. "We're covered. Stay with her. Anything she needs, let me know. Anything."

Jack nodded, grateful.

Neal nudged his arm and Jack looked over. Neal had uncurled Cassie's fingers to slip off her watch. There were blisters on the fingers of her left hand and palm, some already open and raw. Jack recognized the pattern: She'd grasped a doorknob. His own hand spasmed in sympathy.

"Cassie, we're going to get you to a hospital." He stroked the inside of her right wrist, feeling her erratic pulse. "We'll get someone to look at the blisters."

Her eyes opened, and in an uncoordinated way she lifted her right hand to push aside the oxygen mask. "No. No hospital."

There was fear in her eyes, but the hospital wasn't a choice. She had to see a doctor, not just for her hands but her lungs. He didn't need a fight with her, not over this. "Cole." He appealed to the one person she would listen to.

Amy tried to get her to put the mask back on and Cassie pushed it away. She tried to look around to see Cole. "No. I won't go."

The man was her former captain. The history between the two of them extended back a long way before the nursing home fire, and Jack could almost see the silent conversation going on. Cole finally nodded. "Neal, do what you can here. She's not going."

Incredulous, Jack turned, furious at him for that. A look from Cole silenced his words before he could speak.

Cassie closed her eyes and let Amy slip back on the oxygen.

Jack moved aside to give Neal room to work. "Cole—" He was ready to argue the point.

"I want my glasses," Cassie mumbled.

Jack glanced at them in his hand. They were grimy with smoke residue. If he gave them to her, she'd just accidentally knock them off, possibly break them. "Later, Cassie. You can't see right now anyway."

She patted her shirt pocket. "Here. Only pair."

"I won't lose them."

She opened her eyes enough to squint at him. "Swear?"

If she wasn't protesting a pair of glasses, he would have laughed at the irritation in her question. "I promise not to lose them."

She was reluctant to believe him. Jack reached down and gently squeezed her ankle. He understood why she would cling to something so simple. She'd spent three weeks with her eyes bandaged after the nursing home fire. Without the glasses her vision was very poor. "Promise, kiddo."

"Cassie." Neal got her attention. "I need to clean this hand. It's going to sting."

She just nodded at that. Jack supposed everything was relative. A sting wasn't high on the pain meter compared to the pain she'd been through.

Jack turned his attention to his friend and pitched his voice low. "Cole, she needs to see a doctor."

"Tell me something I don't know."

"Then why—?"

"She'd have to be dying before she would voluntarily step foot back into a hospital."

Jack supposed if he had dealt with over a year of being in and out of hospitals, he might feel the same. "It doesn't change the fact she needs to see a doctor."

"So I'll find one who makes house calls." Cole pointed to the fire. "One of his?"

Jack forced himself to focus on the problem they had to deal with. "Fire in the walls," he confirmed. "Better than even odds we'll find his signature."

"Peter Wallis owns this house." The quiet statement was underscored by the significance of the information.

"Chairman of the fire district board?"

Cole nodded.

Jack could feel the open question of motive for the arsonist finding definition.

"That hurt."

Jack turned at Cassie's words, saw the taut edge of pain around her mouth.

"Almost done," Neal sympathized. He had her hand clean, was dealing with a blister forming between her two small fingers. Jack stepped back to her side and let his hand touch her shoulder.

Cassie pushed away the oxygen mask. "This fire was set?"

"It looks that way." Jack nudged the mask back on, wishing she was a better patient. She ignored him.

"He set it," she murmured.

"What?"

She frowned and shook her head.

"Cassie, did you see something?" Cole pushed. "Anything?"

"By the drive. Watching the fire. Weird the way he was watching the fire," she whispered. "A tall man, brown jacket, jeans." She looked down at her hand. "I didn't really get a good look. He was in the shadows."

Jack shot Cole a look. They had been hoping for someone to see the man, but Cassie— Jack was afraid of what that meant. She had seen him; that meant he had seen her too.

Cole dug his keys out of his pocket. "As soon as they say she can move, take her to the station and get her statement," he said quietly. "I'll bring her car."

Seven

Jack knew Cole used his vehicle as his mobile command center. He hadn't realized that meant there was barely room for people. In the back were empty paint cans to use for evidence collection, metal screens for sifting debris, shovel, rake, crowbar, garbage bags, a large red toolbox, and rolls of plastic sheeting to protect evidence.

Jack nudged down the volume on the radio dispatch calls, keeping his attention on the traffic even as his peripheral vision stayed locked on Cassie beside him. "Leave that oxygen on."

"I'm fine."

"You're still coughing between every other word."

"It's not the first time I ate smoke. It's almost cleared."

He frowned at her. "I can tell."

She raised the mask again.

Cole's jacket swallowed her slim frame. Cassie's system had swung from overheated to chilled as it coped with the crashing adrenaline. Jack was feeling very responsible for her as she'd been entrusted to his care and he wasn't all that happy about it. He wasn't a paramedic.

She should have stayed under Neal's and Amy's watchful eyes for at least another hour. But she'd insisted she was ready to move and trying to stop her was like stepping in front of a steamroller.

"You didn't tell me I shouldn't have gone in."

Jack turned his head long enough to look at her, surprised by the touch of irritation in her voice. He'd cleaned her glasses and her eyes seemed huge behind the lenses. They were still red and watering from the smoke irritation and she was blinking to try to clear them. A fact that just made her look cute. "Because I think you did the right thing." He wondered why she had assumed he would have disagreed with her decision. It might have added about ten years to his life, and until she stopped coughing he was going to be wheezing in sympathy, but it had been the right decision. "You needed to go in."

"I didn't want to."

Jack reached over, avoiding her left hand wrapped in a cold towel and settled for touching the grimy knee of her jeans. "You went in anyway." There was admiration and lingering fear in that. She had been touched by fire once, and she still went in. She'd been touched by it again because they hadn't been in time to help her. "It makes you even more of a hero."

"Heroine."

"You're still lady blue," he corrected.

"Thanks." She sounded pleased…even touched.

"You're one of us. Even if you aren't around nearly as often as we would like."

"The guys crowd me," she said softly. "And it's hard on their families."

Jack hurt to hear that even though he understood it. She was the walking reminder of what families feared would happen. "They don't mean it to be."

"It's just reality. I'm not complaining."

"And it's hard to be around what you once had."

"Yes." She shifted Cole's coat. "I smell like smoke. I don't miss that at all."

As a way to lighten the conversation, she had chosen a great point to make. "We both do." The vehicle now smelled like a campfire gone bad. It was not exactly the way to make a good impression on a lady.

"Did you see where my leather jacket went?"

Jack was grateful she hadn't asked how it had fared. The leather had done its job, deflecting burning embers, but it had been destroyed in the process. "Cole had it. I think he tossed it in your car."

She eased open the cold towel to look at her blisters.

"Don't start playing with the bandage and messing up Neal's work." The cold towel kept the gauze wet and the burns moist, a major factor for how it healed.

"Would you relax? They're just blisters. A day or two and they will be calluses."

"What did they give you for the pain?"

"I've no idea, but whatever was in the shot, it's working."

"Your words are slurring."

"I don't make much sense at this time of night anyway, so it's probably not much of a loss." She lost her voice on another coughing fit.

"I wish you had seen a doctor."

"At this time of night they wouldn't have let me go home."

"That's a big deal?"

"Yes."

It wasn't much of an explanation, but the emotions under the word were deep. Home was critical to her now. He tucked that fact away. Did she dream about the fire, need the comfort of her own bed to help her sleep?

"How are your forearms?"

"They hurt."

She raised her hand, then stopped. "I wish I could rub my eyes."

"There's a clean handkerchief in my shirt pocket if you want it." Jack would have reached for it and given it to her, but his hands were far from clean.

Cassie leaned over and tugged it out with her right hand. "Thanks." She slipped off her glasses and wiped at her eyes.

"Need more eyedrops?"

"When we get to the station." She slipped her glasses back on.

Jack rolled his shoulders and did his best to cover a yawn. It was embarrassing to admit how adrenaline sapped his energy.

"I can't say I miss the middle of the night rollouts."

He heard the amusement under her words. He glanced at the dashboard clock. 12:05 A.M. He could forget sleep again tonight, and it was getting to be a bad pattern. When he was in his twenties it hadn't been so hard to deal with. As he neared thirty-four he now felt every minute of the lost sleep. "At least you got me out of cleanup at the scene."

"Oh, great."

"What?"

She lifted her right knee and braced her foot against the dash. "These were my comfortable tennis shoes." There was a hole in the canvas fabric at the top of her right shoe just above her little toes.

"They look like they were fit for the trash bin before this."

"I like old shoes. New clothes, but old shoes." She tugged at the laces with one finger. "Do you know who has my watch?"

"My pocket," he reassured.

"I feel like I've left bits and pieces of me all over the place. I'm not sure what happened with the leftovers I was taking home. I probably tossed the sack in the backseat of my car when I smelled the smoke and managed to spill the food."

"Cole will deal with it."

"I hope he notices that the car needs gas."

"I'm sure he will notice."

"Is Cole coming back to the office? Or is he going to be at the scene for a while?"

"I'd guess he'll be there until he can get the first look inside and get the security in place to close the scene. Regardless, I'm giving you a lift home. You don't need to be driving with that hand."

"I would appreciate it. I need my hair washed and a change of clothes."

"You look like you walked out of a fire."

"I feel like it. Just don't bump us into someone I know or I'm going to be spending forever explaining."

Jack turned into the Station 81 complex and pulled around to the parking lot behind the building. He parked the SUV beside Cole's personal car. "Stay put. I'll get the door for you."

The cold air swirled in as he opened the driver's door and stepped out. He circled the vehicle and opened the passenger door. Cassie braced her uninjured hand on his shoulder to keep her balance as she stepped down. He leaned in to make it easier. She was hurting, and he wished he had the right to lean in and kiss it better. Her hand tightened on his shoulder. "Don't look like that."

"Like what?"

"Interested," she muttered.

"I am."

"Your timing is awful."

He hadn't placed her as easily embarrassed, but she was now. "I think my timing is just fine," he smiled tenderly, rubbing her chin with his thumb. "But I'll let you think about it a bit." Before she could pull back he turned to lead instead. "Come on, this way."

The light at the back door to the station was on. Jack used his key, then held the heavy steel door open for her. He was here more often than home, and it was a comfortable if spartan place. They walked into a wide spacious corridor, the floor tiled and the walls painted cinder block. The corridor was lined with hooks for coats and jackets. To the right was a spacious kitchen with an extra large refrigerator, stove, two sinks, two microwaves, and a large work area. Whichever firefighter had KP duty for the day was cooking for fifteen to twenty for any particular meal.

To the left was the lounge where guys could hang out while off duty, past it the dorm rooms. The architects had changed the historical layout for this station, and instead put the dorms on the first floor, eliminating the much-loved fire pole. Too many men ended up with shin-splint injuries from repeatedly hitting the concrete floor to make it worth having.

The equipment bays were ahead, a huge part of the building, fifty-two feet long, forty feet deep, with twenty feet high ceilings and fast-rising doors. As large as the bays were, they still felt cramped when two engines, a ladder truck, and two rescue squads were pulled inside at the same time.

He eased the coat from around her shoulders. "Okay?" She just nodded. Nothing could hide the fresh tears. Her arms were really hurting. "I'm so sorry, Cassie."

She sniffed and smiled. "Just get me some Kleenex."

"And I'll go grab more eyedrops and another ice pack."

"Cole's office?"

Jack was surprised to realize she hadn't been here before. "Next door in the district offices. Hang a left when you enter the equipment bay and go through the connecting corridor. His office is on the left past the conference room."

Jack watched her turn that way, her steps slow and measured. The only thing he could do was ease the hurt as best he could and hope she didn't end up with nightmares because of tonight.

The station was quiet, a radio was on somewhere as well as the muted sounds of the TV left on in the lounge. Before he headed to the medical cabinet, Jack paused to nudge the magnet by his name on the status board over to show he was in the offices. He got eyedrops, burn cream, and broke out another ice pack for her hand.

Cassie had turned on lights on her way through the dark office building.

There wasn't room to shove another desk into the packed open office area. There had been an attempt last month to squeeze in a desk for the police liaison by angling it in by the emergency exit, sparking a heated debate over whether the fire department should comply with the letter of the law regarding fire safety or the spirit of the law which was to make sure the exits weren't blocked.

The pragmatic people working on the arson squad suggested if fire crews twenty feet away couldn't deal with the fire, having an exit with clearance of more than eighteen inches was irrelevant. The desk had been put in.

Jack found Cassie in Cole's office. She had settled into his desk chair, slouched to be comfortable. It was cool in this building. Jack wished he had thought to grab a sweatshirt from his locker for her.

"I see he's been decorating," Cassie noted.

Children's hand-drawn pictures of a fireman and engine were

taped in a rather haphazard montage on the wall.

"He's been doing a series of presentations at the local schools." Jack pulled out a chair at the small table, swiveling it around and setting down the supplies he carried. The pictures clashed with the pile of books on the table. Two of them—*Investigating the Fireground* and *Fire Investigation*—Jack recognized as course books that Cole was using in his current academy training class.

"What are the latest numbers? Eleven percent of fires are juvenile arsons?"

"Closer to 15 percent."

"Ouch."

Jack reached over for the Kleenex box and set it in her lap. "Eye-drops."

She reluctantly slid off her glasses. "Don't drown me."

Jack chuckled at the warning. "Can't swim?"

"Not funny."

"Bad pun. Tilt your head back."

She leaned her head back but did so by slouching in the chair and looking up. He smiled at her but had his doubts about her ability to see his expression without her glasses. "Don't trust me?"

"What do you think?" She reluctantly leaned farther back.

He missed with the first drop, then got the next four drops sort of in as her blinking messed up his aim. He didn't have the heart to hold her eyes open anymore. "Done."

She didn't comment, just pulled a tissue from the box...and another one and another.

He wisely didn't say anything either as she dried her eyes and slipped on her glasses. He was relieved to see the redness was beginning to clear. "What can you tolerate to drink? More ice water? Juice?"

"Something with sugar. See if Cole has any of his favorite pineapple-orange left."

Jack opened the small refrigerator Cole kept tucked under the side table. He found two bottles of the juice and opened one of them for her.

Cassie accepted it with a quiet thanks, then used the toe of one tennis shoe against the heel of the other to pry off her shoes. "Does Cole like the arson job?" she asked as she looked around the office, sipping the cold juice.

Jack had the odd feeling that Cassie did not want to talk about the fire yet. He set his juice bottle on the table and laced his fingers across his chest. "He's good at it."

"He would be. He's thorough. How are the latest station consolidations working out?"

She was definitely stalling. "There are challenges with learning the new streets and buildings within the expanded district. The station is busier. We're rolling out on probably 20 percent more calls, and it's putting some strain on the paid oncall guys. We'll probably need to move a couple up to salaried positions and put them into the full-time rotation. On the other hand, it is nice having another engine in the rotation for call outs."

"The Company 65 guys are fitting in?"

"Friendly competition," Jack replied, smiling slightly. The drills over the last months were killing them as one engine crew tried to outdo the other, but it was making them all better firefighters. "They seem to be making the transition just fine."

He wished he could read her body language, her expression, better to understand what was going on. He could sort of figure out what his sisters were thinking, but Cassie was a mystery. "What's wrong?"

"What?"

"You're chattering. This place is making you nervous."

She looked away. He waited.

She checked the turned up cuff on her shirtsleeve. It was an interesting tell. He tipped his head to one side and considered why it might be happening. She hadn't been to Cole's office before. She was stalling, and he couldn't figure out why. Curiosity overtook the concern. "Did you ever read the nursing home report?"

"It was offered. I passed."

"I wondered." She had never wanted to talk about the fire when he stopped by the hospital to visit. With Ash it had been the opposite; the fire was the only thing her partner had wanted to talk about.

The nursing home fire had been an unfortunate fire in how it spread. Two of the automatic fire alarms were not working so the fire took hold and spread before other alarms triggered. Two patients died, six had been critically injured from the smoke, and Cassie paid a permanent price. It had been arson. The man suspected of setting it and three other fires had been killed in a car accident in New Jersey two months ago with an outstanding warrant pending for his arrest.

Cassie shifted in her chair. "What do you need to know for your report?" There was grimness under her words, a reluctance to look at him, a tenseness that extended to her body language. She didn't want to think about the fire tonight. He couldn't blame her, not when he just had to think about that hallway and he saw her trying to crawl out clutching a teddy bear.

"What did you see?"

"Not much."

"Do you want to do this tomorrow?"

"With a crowd around here...no thanks." Jack saw her measure the open floor space with her eyes and shift forward in her chair as she thought about getting up to pace. Then she changed her mind and settled back. "I'm tired, Jack. Really tired. But I know how this guy has been hassling you. This is what, his third fire?"

"Sixth," Jack replied softly. He caught her startled gaze.

"You're serious."

"This makes his second house." Jack found a blank pad of paper. "I need to know everything you saw, from the beginning."

She was distinctly subdued as she answered. "I smelled the smoke when I left the bookstore."

"Who were the spectators at the fire when you arrived?"

Jack didn't hurry as he took her through the evening up to the point when they found her in the house. Part of that pace was not to hit her with a question before she was ready for it. The more serious reason was the fact her answers made it hard for him to breathe.

The fire had a powerful hold before she entered the house. Her description of the bedroom with the door blocked was frightening. A beam could have so easily come down behind her, trapping her in the hallway.

"Tell me again about the man you saw."

"He was standing by the oak tree near the turn in the drive."

Cole had found popcorn near that oak tree. Jack didn't mention that fact. That signature was going to remain a very closely held fact even from someone like Cassie.

"Did you notice anything about him beyond the impression—" Jack checked his notes to get her exact words—"tall, brown jacket with pockets, jeans, black tennis shoes, not teens or early twenties, maybe in his late thirties or early forties?"

"How he stood, watching the fire. It wasn't like he had gone still from surprise or shock. I got the impression he was reflecting on it, like he was watching and thinking."

"Would you recognize him if you saw him?"

She scowled at him. "Maybe. I was hoping you weren't going to ask."

"Would you prefer to try to give a description to a sketch artist?"

"I didn't see him well enough to put it into words. I got an impression."

"You could look at the photos tomorrow." They'd have to work around the delay, but if she wasn't up to it Cole would understand.

"No." She rocked the chair back and forth. "Get the arson photo books and raid a candy bar stash somewhere."

Jack closed the pad of paper, understanding the reluctance, his smile one of sympathy. At this time of night he wouldn't be looking forward to studying the photo books either. "I'll see what I can find."

He left and went to find the keys to unlock the cabinet where the books were kept. He had to raid the receptionist's desk to come up with the bite-sized candy bars. She kept a candy dish on the counter; it was a popular place to stop during the course of the day.

He carried the two thick albums and the bag of candy with him back to Cole's office. "Snickers or Milky Way?"

Cassie opened the first photo album and propped her elbows on the table. "Leave the bag."

Jack did so and tugged a lock of her hair. "Thanks."

"Go away."

With a soft laugh, he left her to it.

Jack placed a phone call as he paced through the quiet firehouse back to the dorm, past ready to change into a clean shirt. "Cole?"

"Hold on a minute, Jack." He heard a muffled conversation between Cole and Bruce. "Okay. What was Cassie able to give you?"

"I've got the notes faxing to the captain's car now. You'd best read them. I flagged page four. This fire sounds different—hotter, faster, probably a different accelerant."

"Hold on, let me get them."

Jack stripped off the smoky shirt and tossed it toward his duffel bag.

"She noticed his shoes," Cole said.

"I wish she noticed his face. She's looking at the books but it sounds iffy."

"Jack—we've got a problem. She saw him."

Jack heard Cole's words, knew the man had just made a leap forward connecting information, and felt totally lost. How did he ask Cole what he was talking about without sounding like a fool? Jack sighed. There were days he felt like he was not playing on the same field. "You lost me."

"She noticed his shoes."

"Okay…" Saying she seemed to have a thing about shoes tonight probably would seal the impression that he was a fool.

"She doesn't notice shoes and not notice a face."

"You know what you're saying—" Jack sat down on the side of the bunk, overwhelmed by the idea.

"Even money she could tell you if the guy had a ring on that hand he pushed in his pocket," Cole replied. "She noticed him. Learn something fast: Cassie does what she thinks is right, not necessarily what is right."

Jack was resigning the title lieutenant and going back to caring about how much water pressure was dialed in so he didn't get knocked flat when they put water on the fire. The people stuff of leadership was never going to make sense. "Cole—"

"I'm here for at least another hour. Where is she?"

"Your office, looking through the arson books."

"She'll give you what she can without crossing her own line."

Jack thrust his hands through his hair. "I think you'd better handle this one."

"I'd just get mad at her. Sit down and tug the information out of her. She's got an acute conscience, so nag and you'll get her to spill it."

"Cole."

"You don't have to like it; you just have to do it. It's one of the joys of being a leader. And Jack—if you make her cry I'm going to be annoyed. So choose your words with care."

Jack rubbed the back of his neck and kicked the metal footlocker. "Let me go talk to her. I'll call you back."

Eight

The moon was full and it was shining in her eyes. Rachel shifted her arm under the pillow and turned her head away from the window. She was thirty-five and she was awake in the middle of the night, morose over the fact she was alone. It was a reflection on the choices she had made in her life.

With a groan she buried her head in the pillow. Every time she saw Gage she told herself she was not going to wish for what she didn't have. And every time she did exactly that.

Next year she was going to scale back the amount of energy she put into others and start putting some attention into her own long-term dreams. She had been denying it for a long time. She wanted kids. She wanted to be married. The psychologist in her was amused at the order of those dreams.

Her childhood home had been loud and rough. She tried so hard to be the peacemaker, to fix the problems and the anger and the bitterness between her parents. She was eleven when it had all unraveled. When her parents divorced, she went with Dad. And then her dad didn't have a place for her so she'd ended up at Trevor House.

She wanted a different future. She wanted a happy home and children. Once and for all she wanted to destroy the painful memories of childhood she still lived with.

And her heart was hung up on Gage.

She deserved the mess she was in.

Come the new year, she would be moving on. Her dissatisfaction had been building for a long time but was now ready to be put into words and acted on. She was going to go after those dreams.

All the choices in her life hadn't been bad. Professionally, she could look in the eyes of a hurting child and empathize, reach through and connect with the fear surrounding a trauma. In doing so she could help a child heal. But in putting her focus on her career, she had put her personal life on hold.

No more. The new year was going to be her turning point.

She lifted her head as she heard the distant sound of a siren and relaxed only when it faded. Being around her brother Jack and her sister Kate had made her very sensitive to the sound of a siren.

The apartment returned to silence.

The phone rang.

Rachel tensed even as she reached for it. At this time of night, a phone call for her meant a crisis somewhere and a child in trouble. She did not want to take the call. She couldn't cope with another one. "This is Rachel."

"What exactly did Cole tell you about the fires?"

She blinked at the question. "Gage?"

"Gage. What exactly did Cole say?"

She scowled. "Do you know what time it is?"

"Late."

"I'm sorry you can't sleep. Call me back when it's not late." He was working. She appreciated his help in learning why Cole was worried about the fires but did not appreciate hearing his voice or the question this time of night. "Good night, Gage."

"There was another fire."

She pulled the phone back to her ear and pushed herself up on one elbow. "What?"

"Jeffrey's at the scene; I've got him on hold on the other line. He says the house is a total loss and that Cole is there. Now I need to know what he told you."

She was getting grilled as a source for a story. "Gage, I don't like you."

"Quit thinking and just talk."

Rachel turned on the light. "Deep background, off the record, and all that other reporter legalistic stuff I have to say to get you not to print what I say in the paper."

"I'm not going to quote you, Rachel LeeAnn."

"You've quoted what your wife said in her sleep claiming she hadn't qualified it."

"You are never going to let me live that one down, are you?"

"Never." She had found his Valentine's Day story adorable, if intrusive.

"I won't show Jeffrey my notes. Talk."

It wasn't easy to remember the exact words of the conversation. "As best I can remember—the fires started about two months ago. Cole didn't say what fires, only that there had been a lot of them. That the house fire last week was an escalation and Jack was being kept busy."

"He used the word *escalation?*"

"Yes. He was worried about Jack getting hurt."

"Jack, by name?"

"I don't remember. I could have inferred the concern since we were talking about Jack." She turned the tables on him to get a couple questions of her own answered. "What has Jeffrey said? Is Jack at the scene?" A tone signaled another call coming in. "Hold on, Gage." She answered the other call. "Hello."

"It's Cole."

Cole. He'd never called her before. His tone was worse than grim. She swallowed hard to get back her voice. "I'm dropping the other call. Hold on, Cole."

"Gage, good-bye." She hung up on him. And fought the panic as she waited for the phone to click and give her back Cole. "Jack—he's hurt? Please tell me he isn't hurt. I just heard there's been another fire."

Jack stopped at the door to Cole's office, hating what he had to do.

Cassie was paging through the second arson book. She had her injured hand elevated, idly rocking it back and forth with the melted ice pack lying limp across her open palm. She had neatly arranged six of the bite-sized candy bars end to end, alternating Snickers and Milky Way.

He didn't remember her loving chocolate. He was almost sure she had been a sugar cookie person. Clearly stress changed priorities. The look on her face...

She spoke without looking up. "Do you realize there are kids in this book young enough to still like *Sesame Street?*"

"There's one boy over at Gibson Elementary who has Cole worried. He's already set two fires. The last one did some serious damage to his bedroom."

"Troubled home?"

"His parents were divorced last year. He's an angry young man."

"Sad."

"Yes."

How did he ask? Straight out? Let her talk and see what she said?

Jack sat on the edge of the table, reached over, and closed the album. He'd always preferred directness. "Cassie, what are you not telling me?" he asked gently.

She just looked at him.

"Cole thinks you're hiding something. Is he right?"

Her expression closed up.

Jack was accustomed to people trusting him. Cassie was doing the opposite. On an emotional level it hurt that she chose to respond that way. What was she hiding? He always found it better to face bad news and deal with it than shift into denial mode and lose valuable time.

Who was she trying to protect? And then he tried to get a breath as he struggled to accept the impossible. Another firefighter? "You won't say or can't say?"

The sadness and conflict in her expression... The silence grew.

She'd been biting her nails. Jack reached for her hand and rubbed his finger across the rough edges, feeling that rough himself.

He didn't want to tug it out of her, didn't want to push until she gave him the truth. "I'll take you home."

His quiet words rocked her. "Home?"

She hadn't been expecting him to back off. But if it were a firefighter starting the fires, it was likely someone Cassie knew. Cole could talk to her tomorrow.

And as cruel as it was to consider, it made sense that it would be a firefighter. The fires had been carefully set to make a point. They had started recently. And tonight it had been the chairman of the fire district targeted.

Those facts suggested a motive. Someone laid off in the consolidations, angry enough to be their firebug, might be using fires at the edge of the district line to prove the closed stations needed reopening. And given the location of the fires...it was probably someone from Cassie's old company. If that was what she suspected, Jack couldn't blame her for wanting to keep quiet.

Cassie wouldn't be able to ignore her suspicion. But what would she do if she didn't tell either him or Cole? If she tried to confront the person herself...the thought was horrifying.

Jack found himself backtracking on the decision he had just made. He needed her to tell one of them. He had to at least keep her from trying to act on her own.

Stalling for time, he pulled over the other chair and picked up her tennis shoes. Her pale blue socks were banded with a dark line of ash. "Would you like me to get you a clean pair of socks?"

It tugged a smile from her as she wiggled her toes. "No, but thanks for asking."

He picked apart the knots in her laces, slipped on her tennis shoes, and then retied them.

"Jack." He looked up. She leaned forward and rested her right hand against his cheek, holding his gaze. "Thanks."

He leaned his cheek into that touch, surprised she would offer it but charmed by it and the smile. *Cassie, you're making me feel like a heel because this isn't over.* "You're welcome."

She moved her hand to his shoulder and used him as leverage to push to her feet. "Cole is going to be annoyed with you."

The decision already made, Jack could afford to be philosophical about it. "What else is new?"

"Tell him to call me."

"I will."

She laughed at his immediate agreement.

He'd take her home. It might be easier to have the discussion outside of this place.

They walked through the district building and back to the bays. The sound of their footsteps echoed in the empty, cavernous room. Jack grabbed his jacket and a spare one for Cassie. It wasn't quite as large as Cole's but it still swallowed her.

"We'll take my car." He tugged out his own keys. "Do you have someone who can work at the store for you tomorrow so you can sleep in?"

"Linda covers for me fifteen hours a week. She was already planning to open up in the morning."

Jack held his car door for her. There was a high-pitched squeak as she started to sit down and they both froze.

"Sorry." Embarrassed, Jack reached over her for the rubber cat toy he'd meant to give Kate that had fallen between the front seats.

He waited until Cassie was settled and had fastened her seat belt before he circled the car and slid in behind the wheel. He turned up the heat to the point he would bake but where Cassie might be comfortable, then turned on the scanner.

"What happened to J. J.?"

The small, white lifelike mouse had been a practical joke from Bruce. It had traversed the district showing up in various people's sleeping bags until finally taking up residence on Jack's dashboard tucked between the radio and the scanner. "Lisa borrowed it last week to surprise Quinn."

"How is your sister?"

Lisa was still getting over her too-close brush with a man who had killed more people than the authorities would probably ever be able to discover. "Falling in love smoothes over a lot of stress."

U.S. Marshal Quinn Diamond was the last person Jack would have expected Lisa to fall in love with, but it had developed into a great match. Quinn would keep Lisa out of trouble, or at least be there to get her out of it.

Silence descended as he drove Cassie home and Jack didn't try to break it. If he was going to get her to change her mind and realize she had no choice but to trust him and tell him, giving Cassie time to think was to his advantage. Silence forced her to rethink options.

He had such a good evening visiting Cassie at her store. To have the day end like this... Jack hated having friends hurt. She was moving the ice pack around in her hand, searching to find a way to rest her hand to lessen the pain. The painkillers the paramedics had given her were wearing off.

Jack did not like where she lived. It was an impersonal apartment complex, an older group of eight brick buildings. She lived in building number three on the second floor in a corner apartment. The building foyer did not have good security, the carpet needed replacement, and the hallways were well lit but dreary. The only redeeming feature was the fact that her balcony overlooked the playground in the complex.

Jack knew she had chosen the apartment because it was three minutes from the station where she had once worked. He wondered if she would consider moving now that she was no longer bound by residency requirements.

He parked four spaces away from the building door. The sounds of nearby tollway traffic were intrusive. He walked around to open the car door for her.

He knelt down when he realized she wasn't even trying to release the seat belt. "Cassie?" He leaned across her and freed the seat belt clip. In the dim glow of the dome light he could see the tension.

"Jack, it wasn't what I saw." His hand tightened on the door frame as the words were whispered. She surprised him by saying what she had been unwilling to say before. "It was what I thought."

Jack rubbed his thumb across the back of her hand, wishing he could soothe the turmoil he heard.

"He slipped his hands into his pockets and turned. The way he moved…" Her eyes filled with an incredible agony. "Jack, I think I saw Ash."

He stopped breathing.

Nine

Jack used Cassie's keys to unlock her apartment door. He found the light switch inside the door. Boxes were stacked in the entryway. She was moving? Cassie passed him, stepping around the boxes and moving into the first room on the left. Jack turned the lock on the door and followed her.

His gaze swept the living room with its green recliner and ottoman, couch and rolltop desk. If she was moving she hadn't begun to pack this room; pictures were still on the walls, a jigsaw puzzle was spread out across a cardboard table. She'd been folding laundry. The basket was beside the coffee table and mismatched socks were lined up in a neat row from light colors to dark.

Jack helped her off with the jacket. "Sit."

He headed toward the kitchen, flipped the lights on with an impatient hand, and tugged open cabinets until he found drinking glasses. Like his sisters she kept medicines beside the spices. He scanned prescription bottles, found the one for pain, and dumped two tablets in his palm.

He wasn't surprised at the extensive bandages and gauze she had stocked but it was sad she needed to use them again. He took out supplies for her hand.

He was under no illusions that anything he said in the next few minutes would help. She thought it was her partner setting the fires.

Few things would cut more than that.

The humor he could normally dredge up to defuse a tense situation wasn't there. And he never needed it more.

She was on that brittle edge of tears. He hated being asked to deal with a woman who was ready to cry. Of all the things he could remember with clarity about his childhood, one of the most vivid was how lousy he was at comforting someone who was crying. He wished liked crazy she hadn't told him. Why couldn't she have waited and told Cole? His friend could deal with this.

She hadn't sat as he instructed. Jack set down what he carried on the mahogany end table next to the lamp, settled his hands on her shoulders, and put her into the recliner. He settled on the ottoman and handed her the glass. "Take the pills. This is going to hurt."

She set aside the ice pack as it had warmed. Jack carefully unwrapped the bandage Neal had put around the blisters. It was damp with more than just water; the blisters were weeping.

He carefully added burn cream and replaced the gauze. This he could do. This was practical and tangible. He did his best to ignore the fact she was occasionally sniffing against the threatening tears. "Tell me why you think it was Ash."

"He lives in that neighborhood."

Jack stopped. He wasn't expecting that. "Where?"

"Quincy Street. He moved there about a month before he disappeared."

"Why?"

"Why did he move?"

Jack nodded.

"Something about storage for a boat. He called it his little rowboat."

"The way he stood, moved, reminded you of Ash. What else?"

"His clothes. Jack, the impression I got was a confident, comfortable, reflective man." She shook her head. "It feels so incredibly disloyal to think this."

"Cassie—it wasn't Ash. He would not have started a fire and let you walk into it. It's impossible."

"But what if he did?" she whispered.

"Then he's become a different man than the one we've known for years."

"I can't get the impression out of my mind. I looked through the arson books for someone who looked like Ash. I'm so ashamed of that. I was wishing I could find someone who looked like him."

"Figuring out who you saw will be Cole's job to solve. Trust him. The description gives him a lot to work with."

"Would you talk to him for me?"

He was going to be talking to Cole all right, pushing his friend hard because this arsonist had just made this very personal. It was one thing to go after him, but when Cassie got hurt— Whoever was setting these fires, whatever his motivation, he had hurt a friend. "I'll talk to him," Jack reassured. It was something else practical he could do for her. He rubbed the tape in place. "This should hold for the night. Soak your hand in the morning."

"I will."

He didn't immediately release her hand. "Cassie—" He paused, trying to find the right words. "I hate to leave you alone tonight. Is there someone I can call for you?"

"Amy is across the hall. Go, Jack. I'll be fine and you've got work to do." She lifted her good hand to touch her hair. "Besides, I need to wash my hair."

"Get some sleep first."

"That would be more logical."

The right answer to that was a smile. "Those pain pills are going to knock you the rest of the way out. Come lock the door after me."

She leveraged herself from the chair and walked with him to the door.

"Are you moving?"

She nudged one of the boxes. "My extra inventory of books that are on their way to the bookstore."

She had eight boxes of books in her hallway. "I'll haul them over to the store for you."

"I'd appreciate that. Call me later with what Cole has found?"

"Around noon," Jack promised. He took out his keys as he stepped across the threshold. "Cassie?"

She paused in closing the door.

"Check the batteries in your smoke alarm tomorrow."

It took a moment, but then her smile reached her eyes. "I will. Good night, Jack."

He headed downstairs.

Where did he go next? The fire cleanup would have Cole's attention for the next few hours as he located and secured the evidence. He needed to talk to Cole. This news was going to go over like a lead balloon.

Jack started his car, thought for a moment, and instead drove to Quincy Street. The first fire had happened a week after Ash disappeared. It was too troubling a fact to ignore. Forget what he had said to Cassie. His gut reaction was intense.

Ash setting fires…it was a reach. But Jack could remember the hallway conversations at the hospital. There had been a lot of anger at the cost cutting being made that Ash felt had been a factor in Cassie's getting hurt. The nursing home annual inspection was delayed because the number of inspectors had been cut back. When the drastic cost cutting resulting in fire department consolidations had come down, Ash had been vocal and horrified at what was happening.

He had been so focused on helping Cassie—Jack couldn't see Ash abruptly turning off that emotion and going on a long and sudden vacation. The department consolidations…what if he felt he had no choice but to act? There had to be a reason he disappeared.

Was Ash back?

Dawn was brightening the sky when Rachel shut her car door and started walking, having been forced to park three blocks away from the fire scene.

Engine 81 and Truck 81 were on the scene to deal with cleanup. There were two police squad cars and three news vans. Spectators watching the firemen work were gathered in clusters on the sidewalk across the street. Four of those spectators had brought out lawn chairs to sit and watch the scene in comfort.

The entire scene was sad.

Cole was here somewhere. Finding him was going to be a challenge. Rachel picked her way across a snake's nest of hose lines. Since she came in an official capacity wearing her Red Cross jacket, she was waved across the police lines.

The firefighters were still cooling off what had once been the garage. The water flowing away from the house had cut rivers in the yard. The mud was thick under the men's boots.

She looked for Jack as he had also left her a message but didn't see his distinctive helmet. Jack had painted a yellow smiley face on the back of his helmet and another on the back on his fire coat. He said it was to make it easier when he had to deal with scared kids at a wreck, but Rachel knew the truth. It was Jack's attitude about life. He didn't waste his time worrying about something he couldn't change.

Cole strode through the front door carrying a power saw. He saw her coming up the drive and nodded. She stopped and let him join her.

"Thanks for coming."

She tried to read his face, but the man didn't give much away. "You said it was important." She had been surprised by the request but was not about to show it. She frequently was asked to make assessments about how victims and witnesses were dealing with a trauma, how law enforcement could best get answers about what had happened. But from what she could see of the scene, they didn't appear to need that kind of help here.

"I need your opinion on something." Cole set down the power saw beside the black plastic sheeting at the curbside. Opening the cab door of Engine 81, he reached in back and retrieved a fire coat.

Rachel spotted Gage's partner Jeffrey in an animated conversation with the fire captain. She hoped Gage wasn't here. Hanging up on him hadn't been wise. It would guarantee several pointed questions when he saw her next.

"Rachel."

She took the coat from Cole.

"This stays confidential."

She was annoyed by the reminder. She was bound by professional ethics as well as moral ones. "I'm not going to tell Gage."

"His yappy terrier of a sidekick has been pestering us."

She had to bite her tongue; the description fit Jeffrey perfectly. "You have never liked reporters."

"That's a given."

She struggled into the coat and looked with distaste at the fire hat he held out.

"Quit thinking fashion, woman. No one around here is going to be taking your picture."

"I'm entitled to a little vanity for how my hair looks this early in the morning." To think she had actually lingered in front of the closet this morning debating over what to wear when she met him.

She understood practicality. Her shirt was heavy khaki and the jeans broken in, the shoes near boots. The accessories were anything but practical. The scarf was expensive, the belt braided, the bracelet wide and bold. Cole didn't even notice and now she was annoyed she'd made the effort. "Is Jack around?"

She was surprised at the look of irritation on his face. "Talking to the man who reported the fire." He changed the subject before she could ask what Jack had done now. "When we get in the house, I want you to step where I step."

"There's not someone dead in there, is there?"

"I wouldn't let you near the scene if we had a victim. No one was home."

"This was an arson?"

"Yes."

No hesitation or qualification. "Show me."

Rather than lead the way to the house, Cole pushed his hands into his pockets, took out a roll of lifesavers, and with his thumb offered her the cherry one at the end. "The other night, did you ever find the lost Gage?"

"Yes."

"I wondered. How's he doing?"

"Ask him yourself," she replied, not feeling in a generous mood to talk about a friend. The two men were polite with each other, there was even grudging respect, but Rachel had no intention of stepping between them. Cole did not like reporters probing into ongoing investigations, and she was under no illusions about Gage. The man could irritate a saint.

"You were late getting home."

She raised one eyebrow.

"I called," Cole said simply.

He didn't elaborate and Rachel wasn't comfortable asking. He had a piercing gaze and his brown eyes were warm as they watched her. But she did feel a need to at least offer something. "I shared a piece of pie with Gage and then swung by to see Kate for an hour. Why are you stalling showing me what you asked me here to see?"

"It's disturbing, Rachel."

"I've walked into a fast-food restaurant where a man sprayed an assault rifle and left eight people dead. Disturbing is relative."

"*This* is disturbing."

"Cole."

"Just be prepared. If I didn't need you to see it, I wouldn't ask. If this means what I suspect it does, you and I are going to need to talk."

This wasn't going to be good. She followed Cole up the drive to the house, skirting around worktables made of plywood braced on sawhorses, past sheets of plastic marked with bright yellow criminal evidence tape.

Inside the house the smell of smoke was overpowering. Her eyes immediately started to water. "It was toxic?"

Cole glanced back at her and gave a sympathetic smile. "Onions. A bag of onions in the kitchen pantry burned."

She separated the smells and realized he was right. She wanted to get away from this as soon as possible. "Please tell me we are going upstairs."

"We are. Stay close."

Heavy plastic had been rolled out down the upstairs hallway.

Rachel was surprised at the amount of structural damage. Normally a fire consumed the contents of rooms, the personal items that made fire such a tragedy for people, but left the house itself only scarred. This fire had gutted walls. There were openings torn in the ceiling to get to the attic.

Rachel looked in the rooms as they walked down the hall, getting a sense of the occupants. The bathroom had a melted mermaid shower curtain. "The family had children?"

"A daughter."

Cole stopped at the third doorway. "The fire started in this room." He clicked on his torch flashlight and gingerly skirted the door, hanging half off its hinges, to enter the room. Rachel followed him.

"What do you make of this?" Cole illuminated the message. He'd wiped down the wall to reveal it. Drywall and plaster had fallen away but the letters were huge and the single word was readable. It glowed in a fluorescent red.

Murderer.

She pulled her emotions back, fighting the swamp of reaction that shallowed her breathing. "This is the master bedroom?"

"Yes."

The huge letters were an assault to her senses. She followed the flow of the spray paint, feeling the sensation the man who held the paint can had also felt. Arm straight, fully extended, even reaching, as he walked along the wall. "He moved the furniture before he wrote this."

"Good observation."

The letters tightened and grew smaller, the paint much heavier at the final Rs. It was adrenaline and excitement at the first part of the word and tightly wound anger at the end. The word was huge, the wall a billboard into the arsonist's mind. "How many fires?" she asked, dreading the answer.

"This is number six. Impressions, Rachel."

"He's justifying his actions. He's not just angry, it's become part of who he is. He's working his nerve up to also kill."

She looked over at Cole when he didn't say anything. The intense control the man was exerting over his darkening anger had her taking a step away. "Cole?"

"Rae, I think Jack is in his sights."

Ten

Cassie woke up sweating and sick to her stomach. It was a sensation and a reaction she had unfortunately felt before. She rolled over and carefully put her weight on her elbows, lifting herself up enough so she could hang her head. It had been months since she had to deal with a morning like this. On the worst mornings she had been sick while in bed, in too much pain to risk moving.

When she thought the nausea was at least checked, Cassie slid herself off the edge of the bed and made it to the bathroom. She had changed the fixtures on the sink to long handles so she could turn on the water without having to grip and turn a knob.

She pushed the cold water on full force and lowered her hand into the basin without bothering to remove the gauze. The agonizing pain sharpened and chilled, then eased.

She drew in a shaky breath.

She didn't have the strength to pick up something with her right hand. Her left hand had swollen overnight to the point it was useless. She looked at the phone on the wall beside the light switch. It had been installed as her safety blanket.

The certain knowledge that Jesus was with her wasn't much comfort as she contemplated the odds that in a few minutes she would be sitting on the tile floor in her nightgown, shivering and whimpering and fighting the why-me pity party.

Lord, I hate being alone.

She didn't want to have to call for help. As horrible as this was, the pain was only about a six on her ten-point pain scale. But when she hadn't felt pain above a level of four in several months, it was agonizing.

She laid her head down on her arm as the water continued to lap over her hand. She would just stay here with her head down for a while. If she didn't try to move for the next hour, it would be just fine.

You asked me to go back into another fire. It's haunting me. Please don't let me be sick. I'll cry. I've cried enough these last couple years.

The doorbell rang.

She raised her head too fast and got caught by the dizziness.

Lord, You have a sense of humor in Your timing.

Arranging something like this was just like God—send her help and be polite enough about it to let the doorbell ring ten minutes after she was out of bed instead of while she was still hiding under the covers.

Cassie forced herself to straighten and reach for the robe on the back of the door, whimpering as she lifted her arm higher than it wanted to rise. If help was here, she couldn't ignore the fact she needed it.

She made her way to the front door and looked through the security view hole.

Rachel O'Malley. Cassie had not even had her on the list of possibilities. She was wearing a Red Cross jacket. There was no sign of Jack.

"Just a minute." Cassie worked to release the locks, then eased open the door. "Hi, Rachel."

"Jack called me."

"He didn't need to do that."

"Jack did."

Cassie blinked, then smiled. "Yes, I suppose he did." Ever the protector, Jack had looked more than a little frustrated last night at the idea he was leaving her home alone. Recruiting his sister fit something he would do.

Rachel nodded to the towel and the wet gauze. "It looks like you could use some help."

"I could and thanks." Cassie had learned long ago to set aside her independent streak that made accepting help difficult. She stepped back to give Rachel room in the crowded hall. "Would you do me a favor and start the coffee while I finish getting dressed? I'm dying for a cup."

"Glad to." Rachel locked the door behind her.

Cassie turned back toward her bedroom, already feeling better just knowing someone was around with two good hands. "You saw Jack?"

"Yes. I just left the site of the house fire," Rachel called as she headed to the kitchen. "Both Cole and Jack were there."

Cassie sorted through her closet for something to wear as she listened to Rachel move around the kitchen. She really liked Jack's sister. They met for the first time at a rescue. A trench had collapsed on some utility workers, and Jack had been one of the men working through the night to get the pinned men free. Rachel had been invaluable that night. She'd arranged for sandwiches and coffee to be brought in for both the crews and reporters. She had spent hours talking with the wives of the guys trapped, listening, reassuring.

Cassie had spent most of that night looking at the smiley face painted on back of Jack's fire coat, serving as his eyes for how the ground was shifting as he worked deep inside the trench being shored up. It had put Cassie in a position to be able to relay comments from one of the trapped men to his wife and back. She'd also served as a relay for a very long conversation between Jack and Rachel over baseball games, recent movies, and Jack's habit of leaving stupid jokes on her answering machine. It had been very clear by the end of that conversation that Jack and Rachel were very good friends. She'd envied them that closeness.

Cassie finally chose sweats and a loose blouse she could button and slowly dressed. She needed an ice pack for her left hand; it throbbed in time with her heartbeat.

She headed to the kitchen and found Rachel crouched down looking through the refrigerator.

"You've got eggs and cheese. Would you like an omelette?"

Cassie nudged a chair at the table out with her foot. "Fix me toast and yourself an omelette. I want company for the breakfast I'll pretend to have."

Rachel cast her a sympathetic glance. "Would crackers help the queasiness?"

"Please. There may be a box in the pantry." Cassie spread out the towel she carried and reached for the burn cream left out from last night. "Did you ever play Kick the Can when you were a kid?"

Rachel opened a tube of crackers and brought them over. "Sure. Why?"

"Ever miss the can and kick concrete by mistake?"

"Oh my, yes. Feels like that?"

"A lot like it. The kind of hurt that just circles and keeps coming back in waves." Cassie studied the blister on the inside of her thumb. "I'm so glad the house was empty."

"Jack rescued the teddy bear you were gripping when they found you. He asked me to see what could be done to get it cleaned up before it was returned to Tina."

"That was nice of him." Cassie nibbled on a cracker. "It struck me as probably a favorite stuffed animal given where I found it. Could you hand me an ice pack?"

Rachel opened the freezer. "Oh, Cassie."

"I know; I've got a few."

"Seven is more than a few." Rachel retrieved one of the ice packs and brought it over, along with the first cup of coffee. "I can see how your hand is doing, what about your arms?"

"Not bad. Stiff." She carefully settled the ice pack into her aching hand. She sipped the coffee as she watched Rachel fix breakfast for them both. She had to give Rachel credit. The odds she was here for more reasons than the one she had given were high, but she was starting with the practicalities. "Feel free to tell me the rest of it. Cole was there. I've got the feeling Jack wasn't the only one who suggested you come by."

Rachel pushed down bread in the toaster. "We need to talk. But we can do it while we eat."

Cassie conceded the inevitable. Cole wanted more information about her suspicions of whom she had seen. Her hope she wouldn't have to think again about the fire last night was unrealistic. At least Cole had sent someone who would ask the questions with some gentleness. "About Ash?"

Rachel looked over, her expression grave. "Jack."

"Did you watch this one burn down too?"

Jack turned to face Gage. The insolent tone and the dig at him—there was no attempt to hide it. Jack wished the man would just take a swing at him.

Gage liked to use words and he was very effective with them. He had eviscerated Jack with the article he had written after the fire that had killed Tabitha. Jack figured he had that one coming, but in his world a fight finished the matter. Gage was never going to let it die.

Jack turned his attention back to the hose he was draining. "What do you want, Collier?" Since he decided on his own to see if there was any sign of Ash, Jack was in the doghouse with Cole. There hadn't been, and Cole was annoyed both at his seeking out of a potential suspect and his delay in conveying what Cassie had said. Jack had accepted the rebuke. What he planned to do if Ash had been there was an interesting question that, looking back, Jack was glad he had not faced.

He was now being kept out of the burned-out house for the more serious cleanup. Jack thought it was childish on Cole's part, but he wasn't in a place to complain. It was a crime scene now. He didn't mind the basic tasks of cleanup—the heavy lifting and constant bending—but the wet gloves made him clumsy as he worked, and with an audience Jack found that annoying.

Gage set his foot on the bumper of the rescue squad. "Lincoln Park, Ash Street, the Assley fire…"

Jack forced himself not to react as Gage started naming off the locations of suspicious fires over the last several weeks. He was braced to
be asked how many more fires there had been. Cole would kill him if
he said anything to a reporter.

"Rachel is worried about you."

Jack rapped his knuckles on the concrete as the wrench he was
using to loosen the hose connector slipped. In one short sentence Gage
could shake him up.

Rachel, worried about him and talking about it to Gage.... This he
did not need. "I'll speak to her."

"I'd appreciate it."

"Getting tired of hearing my name?"

Jack caught a glimmer of a smile as Gage lowered his foot, then
turned to leave. "I only use inside sources when I can't find a direct
one."

Jack silently apologized for his assumption that Gage had been
prying at Rachel to get details about the fires. "Talk to Cole."

"Already have," Gage replied. "He was unusually chatty today too."

Jack narrowed his eyes. Cole had voluntarily spoken with a
reporter? That was not like him at all.

Being somewhat out of the loop went with being in the doghouse,
but not being shut out of something newsworthy. Rachel had been at
the scene. Jack started worrying again about why. He had taken her
answer that she had come looking for him at face value, and he should
have realized a phone call would have answered his page to her.

Rachel had been here. Now Gage showed up. Something was
going on Jack didn't know about.

Gage stopped, then looked back. "By the way, where is Rachel?"

Jack would prefer to keep Cassie's name out of the equation, but
Gage could get an answer with just a page to his sister. "Cassie's."

"Really? Brave lady to go into a house fire after what happened at
the nursing home."

Jack heard the reality of Gage seeking out Cassie, knew it was
inevitable. Other news organizations would have found her by now.

Add going into another fire with her history and it was a good human interest story, something reporters craved around the holidays. "Gage, be kind."

Gage took offense at the veiled threat, but then Jack had intended him too. If Gage stung Cassie in a tough interview, Jack was going to return the favor. Someone had to protect her and he'd just elected himself. Jack set aside what he was doing to stand and face the man.

"Something between the two of you?"

Jack went to the heart of the matter. "She's one of us."

Gage finally nodded. "Fair enough."

"The arsonist wrote the word *murderer.*" Cassie felt cold just saying the word.

Across the kitchen table, Rachel circled her coffee mug around her napkin. "Red spray paint. Sweeping letters. He spent some time in the room before he torched it."

Cassie pushed aside the plate that held her toast and reached for the crackers again. The nausea was back with a vengeance.

"Cole thought it was important for you to know."

Not only that, but that he needed to send Rachel over rather than wait until he could come later—it was an extraordinary step. Whoever she had seen at the fire was that angry.... Cassie forced aside the implications. "You said we needed to talk about Jack."

"Have you ever known Cole to be afraid?"

"No."

"He is now." Rachel's hand shook slightly as she lifted her coffee cup.

The arsonist was clearly dangerous, he was escalating, and Jack had fought the six fires.... Cassie froze. "Jack—he's the common factor to the fires."

"Who did you see, Cassie?"

She wished she could answer that question. The truth was painful. "I honestly don't know."

Eleven

"Cole, I want back in."

Cassie closed his office door, shutting out the startled looks of the inspectors, arson investigators, and firefighters she'd surprised as she came striding through the building. She had rushed the words before she lost her nerve to say them.

Rachel had driven her over to the fire scene, where they had just missed Cole. Cassie had been forced to follow him here to the fire district offices. She had passed Jack in the equipment bay replacing air tanks aboard Engine 81. She had not stopped to answer his questions, leaving that to Rachel. Cassie was on a mission.

Cole was in the process of taking off his fire boots, had rolled out a thick sheet of plastic to keep the ash off his carpet. He'd been up all night, but other than looking a little more grim than she remembered, he didn't show it.

Eight hours ago she had left this office relieved to get out of it, and now she was closing herself back in. She was crazy to be doing this. The tension in her gut was incredible. If she were smart she would turn around and leave. Cassie planted her feet and refused to let herself turn.

Cole looked at her in that inscrutable fashion of his. "Sit."

"I'm serious."

"So am I." He pointed to the chair.

She complied, staying on the edge of the seat. "You didn't need to send a doctor to make a house call."

"Cassie, if I'm hiring you again, I get to do whatever I like. Your hair's wet."

"Rachel helped me wash it." She scowled at him for the distraction. "I want back in. So what do you need done? Name it. I want to help. You think Jack's a target. We've got to do something."

"Slow down."

She got up to pace. "Your office makes me feel like I'm back in the principal's office."

"Spend a lot of time there, did you?"

"Cole—"

He held up his hand. "I didn't say no. How'd you like the pumpkin pie?"

He took her enough by surprise she stopped to smile. "You made it."

"Yes."

"Not bad."

"I miss having you take turns on KP. You still owe me a raspberry cobbler."

"I'll deliver eventually."

"How's the hand?"

Rachel had done a good job with the new bandage. In a week it would still be sore but would have begun to heal. That didn't help today. "It hurts like crazy. Now can we talk?"

"If we have to."

"We have to."

He set aside his boots. "I sent Rachel because I figured you had a right to know."

"I came close to seeing that spray painted word while it was still cooking into the plaster."

"Be glad you didn't. If you want in, you're welcome. I need a spy."

"No."

"Listen."

"No. It's not Ash. I don't care what I thought. It's not him. And it's not someone else from Company 65."

"You're talking to the former chief of Company 65. Now sit, and quit jumping to conclusions. I am not suspecting your partner...yet," Cole growled.

She sat.

"Two grass fires, two trash fires, two empty houses, this last one with a message. Whoever this man is, he's setting the fires with a great deal of thought. He's got an escalation plan he's implementing. And you may be our best chance of catching him."

"I can't give you a description, Cole. All I've got is an impression."

"I understand that. What I need is someone who can roll out with Gold Shift and look for him. We know this guy is a watcher. Anyone who strikes you as a possibility, you let the police on the scene deal with it. What I need to know is if you can handle going back on shift."

The hours would kill her. Twenty-four hours on, forty-eight off would be exhausting. But she'd do it if that was what had to be done. "Somehow." She rubbed her eyes. "*Murderer*. He's blaming the department for someone who died."

"A car accident, a fire, a medical rollout that wasn't able to make a difference. We know two things: He called the chairman of the fire district a murderer and he's ringing fires around the boundaries of this district. That makes the focus of his anger the bureaucracy in this district."

"And specifically Jack?"

"Gold Shift fought the first five fires. This fire Jack went on duty early and the arsonist hit again. I've got to conclude from that pattern that he's targeting Gold Shift, specifically Jack, and take what precautions I can."

Cole yanked open his desk drawer that had warped and stuck. He found a new roll of Lifesavers. "Maybe it's because he's got a problem with Jack. Maybe it's the opposite. Jack is the best lieutenant we have. If you wanted to set fires and yet not hurt anyone, who would you ask to put them out?"

She was startled at the suggestion. "The man with the safest reputation."

"Exactly."

"He's setting fires, yet you think he doesn't want to hurt anyone."

"I don't know. This man puzzles me. The locations and times of the fires, how they are set—this arsonist is being very careful. That would suggest the guy has something driving him, an objective in mind. It just doesn't ring true as a thrill seeker. The pattern to the fires suggests he will escalate until he finally gets whatever it is he's after."

"What does he want?"

"Rachel thinks he has already told us and is incredibly frustrated that no one is listening, so he's setting fires to get attention. Rachel is also sure that he will start hurting people if he has to, which is why we've got to stop him very soon."

"Jack doesn't have enemies."

"He's got a few, but no one who strikes me as a firebug," Cole corrected. "For a man to be setting fires out of frustration and anger, either he feels he has no voice or that his voice is not getting heard."

"The guy I saw was confident, self-assured."

"He thinks we're not going to do what he wants and is trying to force it."

"There will be another fire."

Cole nodded. "And soon. Likely targeting Gold Shift. The problem is, accidents happen. Ask Jack to face so many fires and it's not a matter of if he gets hurt, it's when. Jack likes you, Cassie. Use it. Watch his back."

She would have qualified his assumption about Jack's interest if something more obvious had not just occurred to her. "You're not going to tell him, are you?"

"Tell him what? About the word *murderer*? The fact this guy will probably strike harder next time? Cassie, you know Jack. Think about it."

"He'd quit a job he loves if he thought he might be responsible for someone getting hurt in one of these fires."

"Exactly." Cole rubbed the back of his neck. "In this case, Jack's habit for doing the noble thing is more of a headache than a help. You and I are going to make sure it doesn't come to him even thinking about making that decision. You saw the guy. You'll recognize him. And when you do, point him out to the cop on the scene and let us handle it."

"How do I explain my presence to the guys on Gold Shift?"

"Since the department consolidation, we're required to file an efficiency report every ninety days during the first year. You just became the captain's scribe."

"Paperwork."

"You always did love it."

"Like a case of the flu. I need to see the fire reports."

"The red folder on the table. I already had the secretary print the reports for the suspicious fires. There are some items being kept silent regarding the arson methodology and signature; they've been blacked out in the reports."

Cassie wasn't surprised at that; ongoing investigations were always restricted. "How does he know when Jack is working?"

"He's at least got inside access to information, which is why you and I are going to keep this low key. I'll put you on the administrative payroll rather than add you to the duty payroll. You'll do it?"

That decision had already been made at her kitchen table looking across at a worried Rachel. "When do I start?"

"A week give you enough time to figure out how to juggle your bookstore? Gold Shift will be on duty on Thursday. Consider yourself on rotation. Shift starts at 8 A.M."

She groaned. He smiled. "Be here early."

Twelve

Cassie paused the movie when the phone rang that night and struggled to sit up.

"Would you stay put and let me get it?" Jack protested, getting to his feet. He'd shown up after his shift got over, he said to check on her hand, but Cassie suspected it had a lot more to do with trying to figure out why she rushed over to see Cole earlier in the day.

He arrived with three videos and an offer to buy the pizza. Since she had been reading the fire reports Cole had given her, she was more than ready to set aside the work and accept unexpected company. She hadn't realized what that meant. About the only thing Jack had let her do tonight was hold the TV remote—not that that was minor, but still…"It's my phone."

"And you only know everyone in the state. I can say you are fine as well as you can. And you've talked to enough reporters for the day." Jack put his hand on her forehead and pushed her head back on the pillow as he passed the couch. "Stay."

"I'm not a puppy."

"You act like it for all you listen."

"Get me another piece of pizza while you're up."

"I didn't come over to spoil you."

"Sure you did."

He answered the phone in the kitchen. "Cassie's."

It wasn't fair that someone was starting fires and either out of anger or strategy was choosing Jack to put at risk. It must make him miserable to go to work knowing that the odds of a fire being set during his shift were high.

If Cole was right and the fires would likely escalate to put people in danger— In the passion of the moment she knew how high adrenaline surged. No firefighter wanted to back away when someone was trapped in a fire. Jack would take unreasonably high risks to try and rescue someone. Cole had warned her to stay on the sidelines no matter what fire they faced, and she knew that directive was going to be incredibly hard to follow.

Jack reappeared in the doorway. "Luke's Linda. Want to chat?"

She held out her hand for the phone, amused at Jack's way of placing her caller's identity. Luke was the fire department's volunteer chaplain and his wife Linda worked for her at the bookstore. Jack stretched the cord to its limit and handed it to her. She'd talked at length with Linda earlier in the day about the fire.

"Hi, Linda." She glanced over at her guest disappearing back into the kitchen. "Oh yes, he's enjoying himself. He's bossing me around. But since he brought the movies I'm letting him stay. Did we have many customers at the store today?"

An object, which sounded like her phone book, hit the floor in the kitchen.

She covered the phone. "Drop something?"

"Deliberately," Jack called back.

She laughed at that.

She turned her attention back to Linda. "I'll be at the store tomorrow. I wanted to check and see if you could switch schedules with me for this next month."

Jack reappeared a few minutes later in the doorway with a bowl of ice cream. He should be out on his feet from lack of sleep; instead he'd spent the last two hours sprawled on the living room floor laughing over the movie. He said he caught a nap that afternoon, and having worked the twenty-four-hour shifts for years, she knew he probably had. Still, she was surprised to find him so ready to spend an evening with her on the spur of the moment.

When she had her work schedule shuffled around for the coming month, Cassie said good night to her friend and pressed the off button on the phone. "Hang this back up?"

"Sure." Jack took the phone from her.

She nodded to his ice cream. "I'd like some of that too."

"I thought you would. I fixed you a bowl. Do you want this along with or instead of the pizza?"

"I'll wait on the pizza."

"Back in a sec." Jack returned to the kitchen to hang up the phone. He came back with her ice cream.

With chocolate syrup he drew a smiley face on the ice cream and had given it a cherry for a hat. "Nice." And fitting. Jack liked to make people smile.

"Tastes good too."

He dangled a black plastic spider on a string over her face. The things he had in his pockets… She captured it, tugged, and he let go.

"That one is smaller than the one I just killed under your sink. You need to move."

"Don't you start too. Moving is work. I'm not moving." Winter was coming. It meant she had to kill a few more unwanted guests as the building superintendent tried but could only do so much to keep the problem of pests under control.

"How many people owe you favors?" Jack asked.

"More than I can count."

"So collect. This place doesn't have room for a Christmas tree. You definitely need to move."

"It's a waste of time to drag a dying tree up to a second floor apartment, stuff it in the middle of the room, and never be there to see it. Then haul it out three weeks later and spend a few months picking pine needles out of the carpet. I'll do a Christmas tree at the store. That's plenty."

"You need more Christmas spirit."

"Not of the commercialized kind," Cassie countered. "Besides, you know how many fires are started from dried-out Christmas trees over-loaded with lights."

"Just because you have to do it smart, doesn't mean you shouldn't enjoy it. What do you want in your Christmas stocking?"

She looked over at him. "I don't have one."

"Cassie."

"Why do I get a feeling I'll have a Christmas stocking this year?"

"J. J. needs a new home."

"Don't give me your mouse."

"I heard you had been missed in his travels." Jack stretched out on the floor again. "Where's the remote? Let's restart the movie."

She shifted around on the couch to dig it out from between the cushions. She hadn't told him yet that she was joining Gold Shift on Thursday. She should tell him. She needed to tell him. It would not be good just to show up. But the man brought funny movies and five-cent plastic spiders. She didn't want to talk about serious subjects tonight. Cole could tell him.

She circled around the smile on the ice cream with her spoon. "Jack?" He leaned back on his elbows, then looked over at her. "Why did you come over tonight? Really?"

"Rachel told me to."

"Oh." She wasn't expecting that. Was really confused by it. She paused the movie again. "Why?"

Jack shrugged. "Who knows? Rachel said go see Cassie, and I'm not one to question my sister. I learned a long time ago she's smarter than I am."

He had come over because Rachel had asked him to. She had thought he had come over to see her.

Jack reached back, picked up one of the pillows he was using, and tossed it at her feet even as he laughed. "Don't look so disappointed. I was planning to come over this weekend. Rae just gave me an excuse to come over tonight. If you were busy when I rang the doorbell, I was going to blame her for the fact I was interrupting."

His laughter as much as his statement he'd been planning to come over made her feel better. "Were you?"

"Hide behind her, or come over?"

She wanted to say come over, but she offered the safer answer. "Using her as an excuse."

"Sure." He pulled over another pillow to replace the one he had thrown. "That's why guys have sisters, to get them out of awkward jams. And if you buy more ice cream I'll probably come over again."

"Really?"

"Yep."

Cassie started the movie. And made a mental note to buy more ice cream. She could use a friend who made her laugh.

"Did you see Cassie?"

Jack looked up from the disassembled snowblower engine spread across the garage floor to see Rachel coming up the drive. She was skirting around the trash barrel and blue recycling crate he temporarily moved to the driveway to make room for this necessary but messy task in preparation of winter.

"I did. What are you doing here? Not that I'm not glad to see you, but I thought you were heading back to Washington." And what was she doing wearing sweats? He had rarely seen his sister not dressed to make an impression, and if it wasn't so hard to imagine, he would say someone also needed to hand her a hairbrush.

"Change of plans. I'm staying. How's Cassie doing?"

"Better. She's at the bookstore today."

"Got a copy of today's paper?"

"You came over for a newspaper?"

"I came over to show you something."

Rushed over appeared to be more accurate. "Try the kitchen counter."

Rachel opened the door from the garage into the house and disappeared inside. She reappeared a few minutes later brushing the rubber band down the rolled up newspaper. "You haven't read it."

"Read what?" He wiped the grease off his hands, then accepted the city section of the paper she tugged out for him.

"Second page."

The photo of the burned-out house clued him in.

Arsonist Targets District. Gage's byline.

"Rachel."

She took a seat on the steps going into the house, her dejection apparent. "I'm sorry. I didn't know he was going to do it."

It was a long article, under the Weekend Focus banner. Jack started reading. Gage had four of the six arson fires identified. Lincoln Park, Ash Street, the Assley fire, this latest one targeting Peter Wallis. Gage didn't have the popcorn signature yet, but he had most of the details for how the fires had started within the walls of the two homes. There was an entire sidebar on Cassie, including her picture, a long recap of the nursing home fire, and her role in this last fire.

The more Jack read, the deeper his fury grew. From somewhere Gage had found a copy of the letter his sister Lisa had written to the newspaper editor a month ago expressing her concerns with the dangers inherent with the fire department consolidations and the added risk it was placing on him. A forensic pathologist, his sister had to deal with those who had died in fires and her letter was both poignant and personal.

For Gage to turn Lisa's letter into the basis for an article was distressing. Gage used the arson fires to show Lisa's worries had come true. He had shown the series of fires, shown Jack had fought them all, then gone on to show how Cassie had been forced to risk entering a burning house because the new hub stations put help too far away. "How did he get all this?"

"I think I told him some of it," Rachel whispered. "We need to call Cassie."

Jack heard the *we*. Rae intended to duck behind him. "Forget Cassie; someone needs to warn Cole." He saw her dismay. "Rae, Cole doesn't yell at ladies."

"I told Gage what Cole had said because I was worried about you.

I wanted his help to find the guy responsible for these fires. But I didn't mean for this to happen. For you or Cassie to be pulled into it."

She had meant well; it just hadn't turned out well. Gage was her friend and she trusted him. Jack thought the man was driven first and foremost by the anger and grief he still felt. Gage was going to compromise this investigation if he didn't carefully exercise a reporter's discretion. This was the first article to tell the public about the link. The dominoes had begun to fall and they were going to end up with panic and copycat fires.

Jack got to his feet and settled his hand on Rachel's shoulder. "Come on. Go borrow my comb, clean up. I'll talk to Cole."

"Would you?"

"What are brothers for, if not to hide behind?"

Thirteen

Well, at least her life was no longer boring. Cassie struggled to get her shoes on, finally gave up, and kicked her dress shoes across the room. She got up to retrieve the casual flats she had picked up earlier and set aside. She was going to be late to church if she didn't leave soon, but she refused to look like she was falling apart even if it felt like she was.

The phone rang.

"I'm not home," she muttered as she listened to it ring, rejecting the idea of answering it. If she had to tell one more friend the story or duck one more reporter, she was going to scream. That newspaper article had about sunk her.

If she were smart, she would be late to church on purpose just so she could slip into the back row and not have to answer questions. If not for her friend Linda, the last twenty-four hours would have been unbearable. Linda had juggled her schedule and come over to the bookstore Saturday for a few hours just to answer the phone that had never stopped ringing.

Friends called, worried about her after reading the newspaper article. Reporters were leaping all over her actions angling for details to feed further articles. By tomorrow's newspaper, the hype would be unchecked. She'd lived through it once after the nursing home fire. She did not want to live through it again.

Gage had been fair. He kept the quotes he used in context of what she said when they had spoken. But the last thing she needed was a focused sidebar. What she had done was worth a buried sentence late in the article. And the way he had shaped Lisa's letter— Cassie knew Jack would be furious about that. It was way out of bounds to use a letter Lisa had written to further Gage's own purposes.

It didn't help that Cassie was going back on shift. She was nervous. Cole was counting on her. She was going back to work to find an arsonist.

The person she had seen and the impression that it had been Ash continued to haunt her. Time had only strengthened that impression.

Lord, why am I in this position? Who am I supposed to be helping? Protecting? Jack? Ash? Rather than prayer clarifying the issue or bringing a sense of peace, there was an overriding weight coming down on her shoulders. The realization was growing that her first impression may have been the correct one, that she had seen Ash.

I can rationalize him doing it.

Cassie shoved aside items in the bathroom drawer as she searched for her perfume.

Late at night, edge of the district, set to destroy the structure—the fire reports spooked her. She had seen that signature of fires within the walls once before. She had been a rookie still in training. They were conducting a controlled fire as a training exercise at an abandoned house the county was going to tear down. Cassie had watched Ash set the fire using small flowerpots filled with fertilizer set between the joists in the wall. It had created a hot fire similar to an electrical fire beginning in the walls.

The last thing she wanted to do was tell Cole about the flowerpots Ash used ages ago only to find out she had just implicated her partner. The mere thought had the queasiness she was fighting intensify; she reached for the glass of 7-Up she had been sipping through the morning.

Cole had blacked out sections of the reports. She didn't know what the arsonist used as a mechanism for starting the fires. And if it was pottery between joists? Ash had been setting training fires that way for years. How many other rookies going through the academy had seen that signature? A few hundred?

Loyalty to her friend against a suspicion she couldn't prove—figuring out what she should do was impossible. Cole knew her initial impression was Ash. She wasn't hiding it. But without more information to go on, she didn't want to take it further.

Lord, I can't sit idly by while this suspicion lingers, but what can I do?

With no ideas, only churning turmoil, she forced herself to push it aside and start thinking about practical realities.

Where had she stored her extra uniform shirts? It had been a tear-filled spring afternoon after a bad day in physical therapy when she ripped open her dresser drawers, opened the walk-in closet, and sent the evidence of her profession into a pile on her bed. By the time she finished the purge, not only the clothes of her profession but also the specialized tools of the trade she'd acquired over the years had been tossed out. She had no idea where those boxes were stored.

She'd need to find extra socks, sunglasses, and a book to read after the workday portion of the shift ended. It had been so long since she packed to work a department shift she knew she would forget something. And she realized last night that Cole had snuck one in on her with that efficiency report assignment. She'd need to double-check that she had a good briefcase; efficiency reports influenced pay incentives and it would be more than just the reporters who would like to read over her shoulder.

The owl clock over her dresser sounded the half hour. Cassie pulled open the closet and retrieved her long coat. This was not the mood to be in for leaving to go to church.

Lord, forgive me for not being ready to worship. I'm bringing a lot of baggage with me this morning. Calm me down and give me again Your peace that is bigger than these problems. You've gotten me through a lot more uncertain and stressful moments than this, and I should be remembering this last year and relaxing.

She found her purse on the kitchen floor near the pantry beside a case of soda and a plastic grocery sack with cookies and paper plates she had bought for the youth group. A search of the bottom of her purse yielded her store keys but not her house keys. Cassie yanked out her billfold and checked the torn inner lining that seemed to eat her keys every time. Nothing.

She reached for her spare set of house keys in the catchall drawer. There wasn't time to find the missing set. It was frustrating how often it happened when she was in a hurry. With her blistered left hand she reached to tug close the apartment door, which had shut but not latched, and paid for the mistake. The pain rippled. Her hand had settled to a dull throb this morning, so she didn't always stop to think before she acted.

She headed downstairs. A stack of newspaper sales circulars had been delivered to the building and sat on the bottom step. Yesterday her mailbox had been jammed full with Christmas sales flyers. The annual deluge had begun. She opened the building door and shivered as the cold morning air rushed in. She never enjoyed winter and this one had arrived early. When she stepped outside she found her breath was visible.

Jack was leaning against the passenger door of her car. He was dressed for the weather, wearing a leather jacket over a thick black cord sweater and jeans, cradling a Styrofoam cup. Steam rose from the cup, wavering in the cold air. Cassie was stunned to see him.

There must be news about the fire, news either Jack or Cole thought needed to be delivered in person. Ash. Cassie took a deep breath, all the tension she felt coalescing as she braced for the news Ash had returned and it had been him behind the fires. "This is a surprise." Her steps slowed as she approached him.

"I'm here to take you to church. You don't need to be driving until that hand heals."

Church. Cassie struggled to reorient her thoughts.

Jack had protested her driving herself to the bookstore yesterday and she conceded the point, letting Linda give her a lift. But today she could have driven herself. She was surprised that he had not called ahead, only to realize if he had she'd ignored the call. "Did Rachel ask you to do this too?"

"I have a few original thoughts. You look pretty, Cassie."

The compliment delivered with such a lazy smile had her smiling back. She glanced down at the blue pantsuit she was wearing. She'd been after practical and warm. But it was one of her favorites and it did look pretty. "Thanks."

"You're very welcome." His expression turned serious. "I also want to talk to you about the newspaper article."

"Cole called me last night. He said you had been over to see him after reading it."

"You should have told me last night you were coming back to work."

She pushed her right hand deeper into her coat pocket, hating having Jack frown at her. She was worried he would react this way. If he knew part of the reason she was doing it was to try and protect him— "Cole thinks I can help."

"You're going to go out on calls to look for the man you saw."

"I have to do something."

"Not this," he replied grimly.

He was pushing down his anger. It was fascinating to see and realize it was being felt on her behalf. "I appreciate your concern but—"

"He's dangerous."

She had seen a man who was setting escalating fires, who had written the word *murderer*. "I know."

"I don't want you getting involved."

He wanted to protect her. She was grateful, but it left her between a rock and a hard place. "I'm already involved. To do nothing—that's not an option, Jack."

His frustration was obvious, but he glanced away, checked what he was going to say before he looked back at her, then shook his head. "I know, Cassie. But this option is a lousy one." He pushed away from her car and moved over to his. "It's cold. We'll talk as I drive." He opened the passenger door. "How's the hand?"

"Sore." She wrestled to get the seat belt fastened. The heat had been on in his car. And while it had cooled as he waited for her to arrive, it wasn't as cold as her car would've been. She was thankful for that as she settled in.

"You'll have to give me directions."

She thought he'd been to the church the department volunteer chaplain pastored in the past, but that assumption had apparently been wrong. She gave him directions as she shifted her feet to be under the floor heating vent.

Jack backed out of the parking spot. "What time are you coming in to the station Thursday?"

"Cole said the shift starts at 8 A.M. I plan to be in early so I can store gear."

"When there is a rollout you'll ride with Bruce, Nate, and me in Engine 81. We've got room in the jump seat."

Procedure was to roll an engine with a crew of three, then to go with a fourth man if only one engine was responding. It would be crowded on the back U-shaped bench if she was joining a complement of four guys. "I thought I'd be rolling with the captain."

"With the number of calls we respond to he's often moving from scene to scene. And while your stated purpose is to work with him, it's going to take about one shift before the rest of the guys in the company know what you are really doing."

He was right about that. Secrets never lasted very long among a company.

The last thing she wanted to talk about this morning was what she had seen that night, the state of the investigation, and what the upcoming week was going to be like. She tried to change the subject. "Besides chauffeur, do you have other plans for your day off?"

He glanced over at her. "Let's go get a Christmas tree this afternoon for your bookstore."

She was startled by the suggestion. "A Christmas tree."

"Got a better idea?"

"Laundry. Paying bills. Packing for the shift."

"Come on, Cassie." His voice was touched with laughter. "You'd enjoy decorating a Christmas tree more."

"I bet you believed in going out to play before you did your homework too."

"Absolutely."

She knew she was going to need help with the tree; she couldn't move one by herself. Her plans had been to finish pricing books, decorate the front window, then move around furniture to make room for a tree. She could shift that around. "I might be able to find a couple hours if you would like to help haul a tree for me."

"I'd like to help decorate it too."

She smiled at that request. "Are you a tinsel fanatic?"

"Definitely, it's one of my favorite memories from childhood. Life is full of serious people who grew up too soon. I've never been accused of being one of them."

Jack pulled into the parking lot at the grade school where the church met on Sunday mornings.

"Would you like to come to church with me? You know Pastor Luke and his wife Linda. Cole and Bruce both come too. It's a pretty casual crowd since most of the guys help set up the stage and sound and pack it away in the trailer after services each week."

"Thanks, but no. Being a Christmas and Easter churchgoer isn't my style. I'll be back to pick you up after the services."

She was disappointed by that but understood his reluctance. So many people felt unless they attended church regularly it was hypocritical to go. And while her church tried hard to make visitors feel welcome instead of the center of attention, it did happen.

An opportunity to share what she believed was in front of her, and she didn't know how to make it comfortable for Jack to join her. Hearing the truth about Jesus challenged someone to consider what he believed, and it wasn't always a comfortable experience. She could sympathize, but it was reality of the power inherent in the truth.

She stepped out of the car, then leaned down to look back in. "Jack, yes. I would like to get a Christmas tree this afternoon."

His smile made it worth it. "Good. I'll pick you up here at eleven. Tell Luke and Linda hi for me."

"I'll do that."

Fourteen

J ack, that tree is huge," Cassie said, trying not to sound too critical.

"I know. Isn't it great?"

He was straining to hold the center trunk of the tree. He shook it and the branches that had been mashed by the fence the tree had been leaning against settled back into their original shape.

"It looks like a tree that needs to be on a diet. Stuff that falls inside these thick branches will disappear and never be seen again. The lights won't show unless they are on the branch tips."

"Have some faith. This tree will hold up for a month. Think about how great it will look with ropes of popcorn and layers of silver tinsel."

Cassie had been trailing him around the nursery looking at Christmas trees for the last two hours. He was like a kid in a candy store, choosing one, only to go to the next one and decide it was even better.

"Spin it around. Let me see the full thing." She sipped at the hot apple cider she held. The afternoon was perfect for this—crisp air and sunny blue skies. Leaves crunched under their feet as they walked around the nursery. There were hundreds of Christmas trees to consider, and the discussion around large or small, fat or thin, wide needle or slim had been debated on merits all afternoon.

Jack was a riot to walk around with.

"Admit it, Cassie. This is the one. You'll have the best Christmas tree in Lincoln Hills."

"Do you really think you can get that tree into Stephen's truck?" He had borrowed his brother's pickup for this adventure.

"Absolutely."

"Along with about ten feet of pine roping, that gargantuan wreath, three poinsettias, and the musical door chime?"

His grin grew as she reeled off the list of items he had already talked her into. "I'll even make sure there is room for you."

It was a beautiful tree. She only had one reservation. "I don't know if we can get it in the front door of the store."

"Trust me."

She gave him an easy smile. "Oh, I trust you. I'm just trying to decide if I want to jump off this particular cliff with you. It will take about a mile of popcorn rope to decorate it." She was tempted to agree if only for the challenge of it.

The pressure of this morning had been replaced by a relaxing after-noon. She was enjoying Jack. So many men were like Cole, everything close to the vest. With Jack she didn't have to wonder what he thought. She had seen everything from amusement to occasions of worry and anger. The best thing about him was his laughter was contagious.

Her left hand stiffened as the blisters had tightened. She had a headache from the restless night's sleep. But the day had improved because of Jack's company. And it looked like by the end of this day she was going to have spent most of it with him.

"This one?"

She looked at the tree best described as a monster. "This one."

"Sit," Jack ordered.

"I'm fine."

"Cassie."

She tugged over a stool, loath to admit he was right. She was tired enough the tangles in the strands of Christmas tree lights had already won, and she just didn't want to admit it. Cassie pulled the entire mess onto her lap.

"I'll finish them."

She stubbornly shook her head. "I'll get them," she muttered. If only her stiff fingers would simply work. The string of lights were plugged in so that she could find and replace burned-out bulbs. It was a sea of red, green, blue, and white flashes every three seconds. When she tried to hold the strand of lights with her left hand to unscrew a bulb with her right, her left hand would spasm. Clenching her fingers was the equivalent of grasping a live wire. She was beginning to think there actually was a short in the light strand somewhere.

"Patience."

"Patience isn't the problem. I just need some wire cutters."

Jack chuckled as he moved down from the step stool he was using, squeezed her shoulder briefly, and crossed over to the table to get another box of ornaments. He'd long ago finished stringing the lights at the top of the tree.

The tree took over the entire center of the bookstore.

The poor front doorway still showed its scars from where it had lost the fight. The tree won. It had literally been pushed inside, not that Cassie was allowed to help. Jack had called Stephen. She stood by and watched as the brothers wrestled it inside.

They tried placing it by the front window and found, as Cassie suspected, that there was no way to have the tree there without blocking either the counter or the doorway. The guys ended up taking two chairs into the storage room, sliding the main table closer to the display of children's books, and moving the history book display in order to give the tree enough space.

It had been worth it. The tree was going to be beautiful. After all this effort, that wasn't optional. It was going to be beautiful, or it was going to be firewood.

The bulbs finally replaced, Cassie plugged the strand of lights into the end of the previous one on the tree and began working to place them.

Jack stepped back up on the step stool. "Do you want me to use all the glitter balls at the top?"

She glanced up at Jack. He was working from the top of the tree downward. His smile— She shook her head and glitter rained around her. "Now I know why you wanted to do the top branches."

"You look cute wearing the glitter."

What she probably looked like was a six-year-old who had gotten into the glitter sticks. She had to smile at that image. She leaned back on the stool to check his progress. "They look good up there near the room spotlight. Use all of them there." She blew glitter off the back of her hand. "Besides, then they can shed on the tree rather than the floor."

"You need packages under this tree."

"The tree practically hugs the floor. No one could see packages under it." It had already proven to be an effective black hole.

Currently somewhere under the tree were his kicked-off tennis shoes, what she was fairly sure had been an orange glow-in-the-dark superball seen briefly as it bounced past after falling out of Jack's coat pocket, and a handful of French fries she dropped when she tripped over the extension cord to the train set.

"A Christmas tree needs packages."

"I'm going to wrap the books I'll use as my Christmas giveaways." As she now had a twist tie held between her lips, she was forced to mumble her answer as she fought a blue light that didn't want to stay where she placed it.

"Any comic books?"

She got the strand wedged into place and used the twist tie to secure it, triumphant that she had subdued another wayward light. "Sorry. If you want to enter the drawing you have to like to read." A small black spider appeared again dangling and she batted it away with the back of her hand before picking up another tie. Jack and his toys...this one was smaller than the one he had offered at her apartment. He'd probably bought them in all sizes in one of those plastic eggs available from a gumball dispenser.

"How about a coloring book?"

She reached for more ties and conveniently clipped him on the back of his knees.

"I take it that was a no."

"How did you ever pass the lieutenant's exam if you don't like to study?"

Jack laughed. "I've got a good memory and I'm a great talker."

"I agree with the great talker part."

"Just to satisfy my curiosity, where do you buy all these books?"

"Estate auctions. Garage sales."

"You're a Saturday sales junkie?"

"Don't laugh."

"I'm trying not to. Want company some time?" Jack offered.

"Will you carry the books for me?"

"As long as you don't buy one for me to read."

She shook her head at him as she smiled. "You're impossible."

"True. Cassie?"

"Hmm?"

"Thanks for today. I'm enjoying it."

The spider reappeared and she batted it away again. "I'd enjoy it more if you'd quit dangling your spider every time I turn around."

"What?"

It dropped into her lap.

And rather than lie there, it moved.

She flung out her injured hand and slapped the spider away, sending it sailing across the room. The stool tipped. She would have landed in the tree had Jack not flung out a hand to stop her. Instead of getting a face full of pine needles, she fell backward and came close to hitting the back of her head on the table leg.

"Kill that thing," she ordered.

Jack went after the spider scurrying away and stepped on it with his foot. Cassie winced, wishing she hadn't seen that. Wearing shoes was one thing, socks was another.

"Did you hurt your hand?"

She was shaking it to take out the sting. "I caught it on the strand of lights." Half of the bottom strand of lights she had just struggled to put in place were pulled free.

Jack strode back over. He set the stool upright for her.

She looked at it with disgust. "I think I'll sit on the floor for a while. I need to fix the bottom row of lights."

Jack obligingly sat down on the floor beside her. "Let me see your hand first."

"It's fine."

"Cassie—let me see."

There was an edge of lieutenant in his voice, and the command was hard to ignore. She held out her hand. Two blisters had broken on her thumb. She was ashamed at the mess her hand was in. The blisters lay over older scars that had turned smooth skin into stiff ridges. "I don't need your pity."

He looked up, his gaze holding hers. The seriousness never left his eyes but a smile appeared. He curled her fingers closed. "Battle scars don't bother me." He tugged at her buttoned shirt cuff. "Any of them. I've got a few of my own. In rather embarrassing places."

He was doing it again, putting a line of humor under what was very serious. "Do you?" she asked, intrigued.

"I sat on a broken bottle once."

"Sat?"

"Considering I was twelve at the time, sat is more appropriate than lost my balance and tumbled off a railroad tie to land on my tuckus."

"Sat does sound better."

He released her hand. "I'll help with the lights."

She hesitated, then offered him the twist ties. "I'm sorry I thought that was you dangling the spider."

"My fault for having done it before."

"Promise me you'll never use a lifelike snake."

Jack leaned his shoulder against hers. "Promise."

And because he had been nice enough not to laugh at her overreaction to the spider, she leaned back, using his shoulder as a support, and dumped the now tangled Christmas lights into his lap. "Fix this, please."

Jack warily picked up one end of the mess. "Interesting…"

"No, we are not going out to buy more lights."

"I just thought it. I didn't say it."

"I'm a mind reader."

"Do I get to help with the popcorn strands?"

"Are you any good with a needle?"

"I'll learn."

Cassie looked over at him, skeptical. "Buy yourself a box of Band-Aids. You'll need them."

"O ye of little faith."

"One of us has to be practical."

"What's this?" He reached across her and plucked a coin from behind her ear.

"Jack." She was amused by the simple magic.

He walked the gold coin between his fingers and offered it to her. "Your first Christmas gift."

It was a gold foil-wrapped piece of chocolate. "I didn't get you anything."

She expected him to laugh and make a joke. Instead, he just smiled and picked up the Christmas lights.

He gave gifts. She fingered the piece of chocolate stamped as a coin. "Jack?"

"Hmm?"

"Thanks." The word didn't have enough impact to convey everything she was feeling, but she didn't know what else to say.

"You're cute when you're at a loss for words." He tugged over the box of decorations. "I'll flip you for the right to put the angel on top of the tree."

She sent the piece of chocolate spinning into the air. "Call it."

"Heads."

She caught it carefully. He leaned over to look. "I won."

She turned over the coin. "It's a two-headed coin."

"Well, what do you know—"

Fifteen

C ole had said be early. Cassie was early. According to the clock on her car dash, which was known for its creative timekeeping when the weather was cold—and this Thursday morning certainly qualified—it was just after 6 A.M. She was back on shift work. Wide awake at five o'clock, the choice between killing time at home or going to work had been simple. She'd even rushed through breakfast; the old habit of rolling out of bed, grabbing gear, and heading to the station still was ingrained in her thinking.

Where to park had been a problem. She was missing a department sticker for the car bumper to use the official lot but ran a bigger risk of having her car towed if she parked in the visitors' lot for the duration of the twenty-four-hour shift. She compromised by taking Cole's parking place. There was a good chance he was driving the district vehicle and wouldn't need the assigned parking space anyway. If he did…he could find her.

He would certainly know it was her car. Not only had he driven it from the fire scene for her, but he'd left a Post-it note on the rearview mirror suggesting she might want to rethink listening to Saules Trie at full volume. The local band was making a name for itself, and after months in the hospital she'd unwittingly become a fan because the FM radio station DJ was also a fan.

Cassie unlocked the trunk and shoved a box of books out of the way so she could get hold of her duffel bag. She'd bought it at the army surplus store because the canvas bag could easily be tossed into the wash.

She was starting to get nervous. She tugged the cuffs of her jacket down before picking up the duffel bag. The next twenty-four hours were going to be as tough as the day she had arrived at her first station assignment as a rookie.

She'd tried to brace herself for the reaction her presence would trigger. From the firefighters, she knew there would be an overeager effort to show the burns didn't bother them. From those who had only heard about her, it would be an awkward fascination. Eventually they would work up the courage to ask her to tell them about what had happened.

There would be uncertainty over what to say around the kitchen table. Fire crews joked about what they feared, and the dark jokes about fire were legendary. She'd told a few herself during her years at the table. She knew there would be humor that would miss the mark.

For herself—she was worried about her hearing. It was difficult following conversations when she was in a noisy environment. It was acutely embarrassing to try and have a conversation with someone and have to admit she was only able to make out every other word. Concrete floors, large rooms, a constant level of background noise—the fire station was the definition of a place that would give her problems.

Most of the guys had no idea how poor her hearing had become, especially in her right ear. The first time someone called her name and she didn't hear them— She just hoped she didn't come across as rude if it happened.

She had one goal for this first day back on shift: surviving it.

"Morning, Cassie."

She looked up, startled to see Lieutenant Ben Rohr, the head of Black Shift, appear. "Lieutenant."

His smile was welcoming. "Be glad you came early. There are homemade cinnamon rolls coming out of the oven."

"That sounds wonderful."

He took the two straining garbage bags he carried over to the dumpster. The trash was just one of many housekeeping chores done before the shift change. She wasn't surprised to see him pitching in with the housekeeping. The best lieutenants led by being willing to do every job. She waited for him. Ben had seen the department through years of transitions; she was curious to know what he thought of the arson fires.

"How's the hand?" He offered to take her duffel bag for her.

The swelling had disappeared. The blisters had begun to callus over. It was healing. "Stiff."

"Cole is here somewhere." He held the steel door for her. "Can I get you some coffee?"

"I'd appreciate it."

"We cleared a locker for you. Unpack, get settled in, then come join us for breakfast. I'll introduce you around."

A breakfast conversation would be perfect. Ben was heading off duty with the shift change. "Is everyone already up?" She knew how precious those last hours of sleep were before the eight o'clock shift change. It was rare for a firefighter to get a full night's sleep.

There was no getting around the fact the dorm rooms were near the equipment bays. When those massive doors rose and vehicle lights came on, sleep stopped, at least long enough to notice the time of night. Even at the smaller station where she had worked, at least one or two dispatches a night were a given.

"A car accident shortly after five woke the station."

Cassie hung up her coat on an empty hook in the walkway. A yellow caution sign was out to remind people the hall had been mopped recently.

They passed the kitchen. Two firefighters were debating how crisp to cook the bacon and a small group had taken up station near the coffeepot. The rich smell of baking cinnamon rolls hung in the air. The kitchen was always the center of social life at a fire station, the place to linger and talk. "Thanks, Ben." She accepted her duffel bag and turned toward the women's dorm room.

"Cassie." Cole appeared from the equipment bay. "I saw your car.

Dump your bag and come on through. I've got some gear for you to try on. Ben, grab her some coffee? She takes it sweet, but not as sweet as you."

Cassie wanted to laugh as she obediently set down her duffel bag and hurried to catch up with Cole. He had never been a boss to let time slip by.

"I want to get your gear straightened out and then talk through the plan for today with Frank. I'm heading over to the scene of the last fire after roll call, and I want you to come with me and talk me through the report you gave of that night."

Her idea that she'd get a rather leisurely chance to settle in went out the window; it sounded like she would be racing to keep up with Cole today.

She hesitated when she saw the gear Cole was heading toward. Her fire coat had saved her life even if it hadn't been able to prevent all of the burns. There was a new one waiting for her. Her old helmet was there, the Company 65 markings still present, and by the look of it her old fire pants. She'd handled a road crew accident where hot asphalt was being laid and the black tar had permanently adhered to the left pant leg.

She had known Cole would not let her ride along as a spectator. She would be rolling out to fire scenes and for safety's sake would have to be in gear in order to stay with the captain. She thought she was prepared for it, but the emotions came stronger than she was ready for. Difficult rescues, out of control fires, numerous drills—so many years of her life were captured in that gear.

"I wasn't sure about the fire boots. I had several sizes sent over."

"Nines," she said absently, her attention focusing on what she had just seen. Cole had set out the self-contained breathing apparatus. The nightmare flashed by. She hadn't worn a mask since the fire. She'd come close to suffocating because her air tank had run to empty.

Ash had saved her life by risking his own and buddy breathing with her, hoping that help could reach them before he too heard warning chimes. She didn't know if she could handle facing that sensation of breathing on canister air. Using SCBA gear wasn't as simple as the public often thought.

"You need to be able to use it just in case," Cole said quietly. "You're rolling out to fire calls."

"I know."

Faced with picking up the fire coat with her healing left hand or her weaker right arm, she reached for it with her right hand. Heavy, stiff, the nomex cloth feeling like thick rubber, she pulled it on, reaching out of habit for the clips near the collar. Tossing the collar up, she fastened the top button of the coat and worked her way downward. She worked the cinch of the belt tight. When this coat was broken in she wouldn't have to fight the way it lay. Equipment weight would help the material pull and eventually relax.

"Cuffs. Let me." Cole took care to get the best fit possible, adjusting the cuff straps so that with the gloves they would fit tight. Her arms couldn't handle another brush of heat. "Will this coat work?"

"It's a good fit."

Cassie sat down and pulled over the SCBA gear. The best way to fight the nerves was to fall back on training and safety procedures. Cole had set out a sixty-minute cylinder for her.

"Did you bring your recipe box with you?"

She smiled as she turned the tank to check the gauges. "Still thinking about your raspberry cobbler?" She checked the hydrostatic test date and the fill pressure. Eighty-eight cubic feet of air compressed inside the canister should have pushed the pressure up to four thousand five hundred pounds per square inch.

"I'm going to use my informal seniority to put you on kitchen duty sometime in the next few shifts."

"Thanks for the warning." She checked the overpressure plug. The small metal disc was set to rupture if the compressed air refill went past those limits. "If you've got a preference for dessert, what about dinner?"

Ben brought in the coffee. Immersed in the work, she accepted it with a quiet thanks, took a sip, and set it aside.

"Lasagna with Italian sausage, not that bland stuff Bruce prefers."

"An easy request. I was afraid you were going to say fried chicken."

She tightened the cylinder into the harness. The high pressure hose that let air flow from the cylinder to the regulator where it would be lowered to a breathable pressure was finger tight.

Refusing to let her hand tremble, she reached for the face mask. The entire assembly was designed to keep positive air pressure inside the mask to prevent any smoke from entering. A donning switch would shut off the air to the face mask when it was slipped on. She cleared the exhalation valve on the face mask. With the positive pressure it was necessary to forcibly exhale.

The safety checks were done.

She glanced over at Cole. His expression was inscrutable as always. It gave no indication of whether he felt she was stalling or doing the right level of detail.

Calling herself a bit of a coward, she looked back at the gear and let years of training take over.

She grasped the backplate and cylinder with both hands and lifted it above her head, letting the harness straps fall across her shoulders and past her elbows. The harness and air canister slid onto her back in a smooth motion she had done hundreds of times in the past. Only this time the thirty pounds took her to the limits of what her right arm could manage in a controlled way. She secured the straps, pulling them tight to let the weight settle to her shoulder and back muscles.

Fanning the spider straps of the face mask, she took a deep breath and donned it chin first, then straps at the neck, temple, and chin were tightened. She did those moves quickly as her first breathes were now on SCBA.

Breathe in through the mouth, out through the nose. Inhale fast, exhale slow. She heard the litany in her mind and used it to block the surge of adrenaline. She had never felt claustrophobic before, and it hit fast and hard. She locked her attention on the job at hand as a way to fight it, finishing the safety checks.

When she was confident she had missed nothing, she looked toward Cole, a good suspicion on what was coming.

"Your regulator hose just became disconnected."

She scowled at him and quickly moved to execute the emergency procedures. Cole was merciless with the drills. She had to strain to reach straps and hoses. She braced for the possibility he would want to see the movements with a hood plunging her into darkness. The procedures were difficult enough; doing it in the dark as would be the case in a real emergency— She turned her frustration into a focused effort to keep her breathing steady despite the exertion. Cole was going to run her into the ground and she was too stubborn to let that happen.

"Stand down."

With relief that it was close to over, she forced herself to be methodical in how she removed the gear. She lowered the cylinder to the floor with care.

She was drenched in sweat from the nerves and the hot coat.

"Good job. Have breakfast, then come find me." Cole walked away, leaving her to store gear in the empty locker that now bore her name.

Two words. Good job. It had taken her three months as a rookie firefighter to finally earn them. This time—they had never sounded more beautiful.

"Let's get roll call started."

Cassie leaned against the back wall beside Cole as Frank called the shift to order at 8 A.M. The tension that had built over the morning finally broke. This was familiar turf.

Jack raised an eyebrow at her when she didn't choose to cross the room to join the other firefighters from Engine 81. She smiled back and didn't move. There was no way she was going to get sandbagged into a roll-call introduction. She'd been to way too many of these meetings over the years to fall for that tactic.

Get introduced, and end up being the person called on for the remainder of the meeting to answer questions regarding station business. It was an efficient if brutal way to make the point that day one on the job was no excuse for not being fully prepared.

A review of the rollouts for the last forty-eight hours began. Cassie scanned the thick report. Forty percent had been calls for medical assistance. Eight percent had been false alarms. There had been five car accidents, two with injuries. The only fire had been a kitchen grease fire put out before they arrived. With the upcoming holidays and arrival of winter, those numbers would shift dramatically.

Cassie dreaded the first snow. Winter and fires—the water froze to the ground, to the equipment. The fire scenes became skating rinks. Ladders had to be used with extreme caution. For the firefighters bathed with water mist, frostbite became a serious danger. If there was wind, a fire in the winter could become a life-threatening situation.

"In-house, where are we at? Any vehicle problems? Equipment problems?" Frank queried.

Firefighters around the room called out suspected and confirmed problems with starter cords, pumper valves, hose connectors, vehicle brakes, floodlights. Everything went on the white board with men assigned to each issue. If a problem couldn't be addressed immediately after this meeting, it would go up the chain of command.

Frank turned to the training schedule for the day. It was aggressive. The focus of today's drills was on emergency egress procedures. Cassie was relieved. He was doing everything possible to make sure Gold Shift was prepared for the arson fires. "In the spirit of saving the best news for last: Weight training just became mandatory. I want a minimum of an hour in the gym worked into your daily schedules." The announcement was met with a few good-natured groans.

Roll call ended with an order she had heard many times in the past. "Lieutenants, check your rigs." For every problem known about and assigned to be addressed, there were assumed to be two equipment problems coming. Men were not going to be put at risk because of equipment failure if it could be inspected or tested out.

Cole closed his notebook. "Grab your turnout coat and boots, a notebook, and meet me out back at the SUV. I'll get coffee for us both."

His announcement ended any idea of talking with Jack after roll call. She caught his attention and pointed to Cole, then shrugged. It was a twenty-four-hour shift. There would be a moment they'd both be free before the day was over. Jack nodded, his disappointment clear. She smiled at him for that, glad to know it mattered. Turning, she hustled to grab her gear and get out to the vehicle, determined not to leave Cole waiting on her.

Sixteen

Go away." Cassie didn't even bother to open her eyes. If she had to move short of dispatch declaring a five-alarm fire, she was going to snarl at the cause. The official workday was over, even if the shift wasn't, and she had crashed to try and recover from her first taste of being back on the job.

Cole lifted her left foot out of the bucket of hot water. She sucked in her breath as he firmly rubbed at the muscle cramp along the top of her foot curling her toes back. "It will ease."

"You said the same thing an hour ago."

The day hadn't been heavy work, but she'd been on her feet, constantly up and down, hauling paint cans of evidence, carrying equipment, acting as Cole's gofer. The cramps that had hit late in the day had been unexpected and severe. The weight of the boots and the heat inherent with wearing fire gear had eventually taken its toll. Muscles had cramped. It was embarrassing and painful.

She reluctantly opened her eyes. "Cole, you're a slave driver."

"Guilty. Feels good to be back to work though, right?"

She smiled a little at that. "Ask me in the morning."

They were sitting near the horseshoe pit at the back of the fire station. Sunny skies and moderate temperatures in late November were rare and the firefighters were taking advantage of it. The two grills beside the picnic tables had been fired up. There would be barbecued pork chops for dinner.

"You were a good help today."

"Trying to butter me up?"

"Is it working?"

"Some." She sighed and eased her foot back into the hot water. "How do you do it, your job?" She'd spent the day helping him go through the burned-out house, reconciling reports written by the responding firefighters with the police report, and helping create the critical timeline for how the fire had begun and spread.

Walking the upstairs hallway where the firefighters had found her, it had been obvious how foolish she had been to rush inside the house. That was the inherent problem when someone was thought to be in danger—the first instinct was to help and it overrode any instinct for safety.

The word *murderer* haunted her.

She'd seen Cole looking through a report of everyone who had died in the district since the consolidations began. There was nothing easy about the road he had chosen to go down. And she felt a burden for that, knowing one of the key reasons he had accepted a move to the arson group had been what happened to her.

"Someone has to do it," Cole finally replied.

"Do you think he's going to hit again tonight?"

Cole rolled his shoulder. "Fifty-fifty. Don't take chances, Cassie."

"Do I have permission to walk around the fire scene if we do roll out? This guy is not going to be standing out in the open."

"As long as you remain in sight of a police officer or the captain. I know it's going to be a chaotic scene so that burden will rest with you."

"I'll be careful." She did not want to think about the guy she had returned to work to find. "Is Jack back yet?"

Engine 81 and Rescue 81 had been dispatched to a car accident just over an hour ago as she and Cole were returning to the station. It had been hard on her, seeing the rescue squad roll out with lights and siren and not to be on it.

"Jack's on his way; they've been released from the scene. I heard a report of two injuries, both listed as stable."

"I wanted to be on that rig."

"I know."

"How did you handle the first few times the captain rolled out and it wasn't you?"

Cole smiled. "Badly." From behind them came the sound of the engine returning. Cole got to his feet. "Want me to send Jack out once he gets his gear cleared away?"

"Jack won't need the prompting—he'll follow the smell of food. But you might ask him to grab me a soda on the way."

"Glad to."

"I think I like having you feel guilty."

"Thin ice, Cassie."

She laughed softly as Cole walked away, then reached for the book she'd been reading.

Jack spotted more blood in the seam of his left boot and dunked the steel-tipped boot back into the plastic bucket of soapy water. He switched from scrub brush to toothbrush. It had been a bad wreck: a delivery van swerving through traffic and plowing into the side of a red Toyota.

The lady in the car had stoically insisted she was okay, while her five-year-old son had screamed at the top of his lungs. At the memory of the boy's outrage, Jack gave a rueful smile. Kids weren't afraid to be honest and give their real opinion of a situation. She'd bled, the boy had thrown up, and both had survived. They'd just had to be cut out of what remained of the crumpled car.

Jack couldn't find much sympathy for the driver of the van who had broken his leg. The guy had been doing forty on a downtown street.

The side door into the bay opened. Jack glanced over, hoping to see Cassie. He couldn't believe it was closing in on dinner and the day had passed with no more than a brief chance to say hi to her.

Cole came in. "Good run?" He must be out of Lifesavers, he was eating a piece of red licorice.

"Fine."

"The grill is fired up. Pork chops are coming off soon. Cassie appropriated your chair."

His chair—the metal patio chair he had picked up at an auction was huge and swallowed up whoever sat in it. Jack smiled at the mental picture. He got up to begin storing gear in his locker. "Did she?"

"She looks settled in for the night too. Don't hassle her about the foot cramps. The boots weren't broken in and she's paying for it."

"Cole."

"My error. Her feet are up; she's off them for the night short of us getting a dispatch. And she's sensitive about the entire matter."

Jack got the message. Sympathy wasn't the right response. "Feel guilty enough you want to do paperwork for me?" Jack backtracked with a grin on seeing Cole's expression. "Just checking. I'll take it outside with me."

"Snag her a drink on the way."

"Yes, sir."

Cole headed toward his office, tossing a question over his shoulder. "Is insubordination contagious?"

"I'm going to respectfully not answer that," Jack called back, slamming the locker closed.

"Smart man."

Cassie was lost in a book. Jack slowed as he approached for it was clear she didn't hear him. She had escaped into her favorite pasttime.

A folded newspaper and a spare book were tucked by her side in the big chair. Over the arm of the chair hung a pair of black tube socks. Cassie was soaking her left foot. Muscle cramps were a common problem and he wasn't surprised that a full day wearing fire boots had left her fighting them.

Jack leaned over the chair and dangled the item he carried.

"What?" She caught it, turned to look up at him. "Hi." She glanced at the chain.

"Keys to the station. I meant to get them to you earlier. Sorry about that."

Carrying keys in a pocket when entering a fire scene was a bad move. Most firefighters carried them on a belt clip or a chain that could easily be removed. He'd guessed which she would prefer.

She slid the chain on. "I was rather hoping to get locked out."

He tweaked a curl as he took the seat beside her. "Sorry. You're on call like the rest of us." He offered the soda he carried. "Bruce said you were drinking orange today."

"Thanks."

"You've had an interesting first day."

"An understatement." She cracked open the soda.

"You might want to try and get a nap in after dinner. This guy has been hitting around midnight."

Cassie nodded. "I'll do that." Peter lifted the lid on the grill. "There are some things I really missed about station life and this is one of them."

"Good food?"

She shook her head. "A guy fixing it."

Jack stretched out his legs and crossed his ankles, feeling like the Thursday had been going on forever. It was great to finally have a chance to have her full attention.

"How was this last callout?"

"Routine."

He glanced at her, caught an edge of frustration in her expression, and realized he had made a mistake by not covering the details. It had been routine, but she hadn't been on it.

She changed the subject before he could expand his comments. "I've read the reports of the earlier suspicious fires. It was unclear if there has been any indication of someone watching those fires. Is there reason to think he might be staying around to watch every fire he starts? Or am I going to be rolling out with just a fifty-fifty probability of him being there?"

Jack wasn't surprised that Cole had stricken the popcorn signature from the records. Until an arsonist was apprehended any information that might suggest a way to identify him was restricted so that a news report would not reveal it and the arsonist react by changing his MO. Cole would tell Cassie when she needed to know it. "We think he watches all of them. He's got a couple signatures."

He was still frustrated with the underlying decision that she should roll out with them to try and find the man. It was dangerous. If this conversation continued he'd probably say it again. He changed the subject rather than risk it coming up. "Could you use any help at the bookstore finishing the Christmas decorations? My schedule for the next couple days off is free."

"Sure. I've also been intending to build shelves in the storage room. Would you be interested in swinging a hammer?"

"Will you make me one of those super subs I've heard Cole talk about?"

She reached over and patted his stomach. "I'll make you half of one. You'd never manage a Cole-sized one."

He caught her hand and held it up to study her fingers with interest. "What's this?"

She curled her fingers down into a fist.

"Cassie, have you been working on the popcorn chains without me?" She had Band-Aids on her first fingers and thumb. The needle had to be difficult to handle with her stiff hand.

"Don't go there, Jack."

"You're cute when you're embarrassed." Her hand felt rough as the scars had healed in ridges. She didn't need someone to cry for her, and he tapped down the regret he felt. He soothed his fingers around the back of her fist and set her hand down in her lap. He would have held on to her hand, but Peter was watching. "What kind of shelves do you want built at the store?"

He needed to find a good place to watch this fire that would let him linger without being seen. But where? The fire would be huge, multialarm. And perfect—this destruction would embarrass them.

He didn't need Cassie Ellis getting a better look at him. He'd been keeping periodic checks on her since she'd almost stumbled into him, then had determined after the first week she was no threat to his discovery. She'd seen him, but she didn't know him. He'd even crossed her path, said hello, and there had been no recognition.

He'd get one break in his favor but probably not two. He would go for broke with this fire and push hard. He'd get his point across.

His family wouldn't thank him, but then they didn't have to carry the burden of paying the bills. Thanksgiving had been frustrating, but Christmas...

This time he would make sure the newspapers got the message, even if he had to tip someone off to the signature. There was an arsonist loose, and the fire department wasn't up to the job. There would be changes. One way or another, he would force them.

Seventeen

Cassie, are you sure you want to do this?"

"I'm doing it, Gage. If Ash wants to complain, he'll have to show up to do it." She pushed against the back door of Ash's home and found it had very little play in the door frame, but it did have some. She pulled out a laminated video store rental card, slid it into the crack, and started working it around the frame.

"You could just ask his cousin for another copy of the key you lost."

"She's in California for the month." She worked the card downward while she kept the doorknob turned. "You are not printing in your paper an allegation of what I said that I can prove to you is wrong."

Gage ran a hand through his hair. "I already said I wouldn't print it. Would you stop? A cop is going to come by."

"Then I'll tell him exactly what I'm doing. That it's my partner's home, I lost my key, and I am doing what I feel the circumstances warrant. There was a natural gas leak two houses down yesterday that caused a dispatch, and this house needs to be checked."

She wasn't taking this step lightly, but she was frustrated with the idea she had seen Ash, and that the fact lingered in her mind. If Gage hadn't gone probing like a pit bull, her suspicion would not have become known to the press. "And you will print it if you think you can find supporting evidence; I know you." She owed it to her partner to kill the idea now. It was Friday and Gage was in the process of writing his next article.

"I'm not going to apologize for a factual story. The Weekend Focus article last Saturday was accurate."

"Then consider this insurance to remove the basis for your assumption Ash was somehow involved." She gave up on the card and looked around the porch for something else to use.

Ash's home had a decidedly neglected look. His cousin collected his mail from the post office, where it was being held, and paid his bills. His neighbor kept the grass mowed, but it showed the evidence of its vacancy in the weeds that grew, the lack of any Christmas decorations, and the closed window blinds.

She picked up a brick.

"Hold on. Put it down." Gage headed back to the car. He came back with a thin metal strip. "I can't believe I'm doing this."

"You owe me."

"You're the one who asked me to run a background check on your partner. You're not exactly showing confidence in your stated position. Either you think you saw him or you didn't."

"I'm worried about his continued absence. That is all that is behind my request," she insisted. At this point she would love to hear Ash had received a speeding ticket somewhere. It was coming up on Christmas, and she needed to find him.

Gage took her place and popped the lock in a matter of moments. He opened the back door. "Rachel is going to have my head for this."

"Then don't tell her."

Cassie stepped over the threshold and entered Ash's house. It smelled musty. She had been braced to smell natural gas or more precisely the chemical added to it to create a sharp odor. The house had been closed up for months. Her need to check the house was real. During the early months of winter, natural gas home explosions happened more often than most people realized as the ground grew cold and froze, stressing buried lines.

She walked through to the kitchen. The counters were clear. Her note to Ash from her last visit was still on the kitchen table. She opened the refrigerator and found it cool and empty. Ash's cousin had cleared it out after four weeks. Cassie checked the living room. The only thing that appeared to have changed was the formal clock on the mantel had stopped at 7:04.

"He's really not here. I believe you. Satisfied?"

"No." She headed to Ash's office.

Sitting down at his desk, she turned on his computer.

The password was *backdraft;* the same one he had used at the office. She suggested it to him years before and he had never changed it. She brought up his e-mail. It took twelve minutes for all the pending messages to transfer from the server. She should have changed his discussion groups to nomail as she watched all the nightly digests flow in.

The fact so many messages flowed over suggested he was not going on-line to check his messages. There was a chance if in his travels he'd visited friends, someone might have dropped him a note. There were several individual messages. She recognized names of his friends.

The message with the subject line FIRE caused her pause. It was anonymously sent. She checked the date. It had been sent over eight weeks ago.

She opened it. Flickering flames appeared, and the word CHICKEN emerged from the flames, flashed, then disappeared.

"What was that?"

She closed the message. "A firefighter's joke," she told Gage and resumed her search through the messages.

Had Ash been a target before the first fire had been set?

Where was he?

Nothing else in the e-mail suggested anything. She shut down the machine. "Okay, Gage. We can leave. Now what are you writing about this weekend?"

"I hate to burst your bubble, but a suspicion that a firefighter might be starting fires—read the FBI November 1995 report: 66 fire-fighters set 182 fires in the brief review of cases they looked at. When I can prove who this arsonist is, that will be news. The Weekend Focus

article I'm writing at the moment is a devastating look at the manipu-
lation of gas prices at the start of the winter heating season."

"My bills are going up?"

"I strongly suggest you sit down before you open your next bill."

Eighteen

I f the arsonist was going to strike again, he was taking his time about it. And having learned her lesson, Cassie was wisely keeping her nose out of the investigation. It was Saturday, December 9, her fifth shift, and so far she had rolled out only once. Rather than be a suspicious fire as first reported, it turned out to be a chimney fire caused by the home owners' first use of their fireplace this year.

Cole had heard her rather nervous statement about the e-mail message Ash had received, the word *chicken,* and the fact Gage knew about her suspicion. He'd accepted the news with a growing frown, noted down the date she said the e-mail had been sent, and told her not to worry about it. But he had done it with an implicit suggestion that she stop chasing ideas and let him do his job.

Cole believed she had scared off the arsonist. She had seen him, and since then his behavior appeared to have changed. Cassie was quite willing to go along with that supposition if only because it bought her a few weeks to get back into Cole's good graces. No one seemed to think the arsonist would quit setting fires, but as shift after shift passed, there was a growing sense that his MO might change.

Being back on shift work, it was as if she had never left. The twenty-four hour on and forty-eight hour off pace had a rhythm to it, and she adapted back to it much easier than expected.

Cassie opened the oven to check the raspberry cobbler. As

promised, Cole had arranged for her to have kitchen duty for the day. He was getting his requested meal. She was fixing lasagna, hot breadsticks, Caesar salad, and raspberry cobbler for the eighteen firefighters on duty. She promised to make enough cobbler so there would be leftovers for the next shift.

"Cassie, do you have a minute?" Cole asked.

She glanced over to the doorway. "Of course."

"I know you're off duty…"

She smiled at the hesitation. He was being unusually deferential because he wanted to keep in her good graces as well. Technically she went off the clock at 5 P.M. "Bring the paperwork. I know you've got a finance meeting on the eighteenth."

She found working with Cole fascinating. Getting involved in the efficiency reports and the budget paperwork had radically opened her eyes to the scope of his job. She'd thought she would find watching him wrestle with the numbers boring, but instead it was a very big challenge.

"I'd like to try changing these budget figures."

"Which ones?" She held the spoon she was using over the sink, so the grease wouldn't drip on the stove top, and leaned over to see the report.

Cole held it steady while using his pen to highlight a line. "Paid oncall class I. Let's shift the increase to salary class III. And I want to cut the administrative budget another 3 percent and move it to training."

"Given the increase in grounds and maintenance, I don't know if there's another 3 percent that can be cut from the admin figures. You can barely afford a box of paper clips as it is."

"We'll have the fire station auxiliary sell cookies, sponsor a car wash, have another chili cook-off…something. I can beg and cajole the community for things; I can't do that for people. And we've got to squeeze another paramedic and firefighter in under the budget caps."

She agreed with him on the hires. After watching five shifts Cassie would consider the need acute. The guys were getting run ragged with the dispatch rate. If they got back from this last rollout by seven o'clock she would be surprised. She was doing her best to slow dinner preparations so they wouldn't have to come back to rubbery lasagna from overcooking. "I'll get as creative as I can."

"Figure out how to do it and I'll owe you a big one."

"Let me roll out to the next car accident."

He leaned over and pinched some of the grated cheese for the lasagna. "No."

"Cole, I know the job, and you just said you needed the help. I know I can't do everything at a scene I once could, but you know how valuable an extra pair of hands would be. And it's not like you're not already paying me." It was killing her to have the dispatch tones sound and at times be the only member of Gold Shift left at the station. It wasn't the first time she had asked. She didn't understand why he wouldn't agree. "If you think it's a liability issue, could I request a finding from the personnel board?"

"It's not my decision," Cole said quietly.

"Should I talk to Frank?"

"It's Jack's decision to make."

Jack was the one choosing to leave her behind. She blinked as that registered. She had worked hard to show him she was not only up to speed with the status of the rig and the equipment, but also to prove she was not a liability to him on Engine 81. Finding out he was the one blocking her request...it felt like she'd been betrayed. How could he hurt her this way?

"I support his decision."

"Cole—" She needed to understand. "Why?"

"Talk to Jack."

It was the only answer she was going to get. She slowly nodded. "Okay." Cole wasn't going to explain, but she heard what sounded suspiciously like sympathy in his voice. She looked back to the dinner she was fixing. Sympathy ran close to pity. She didn't need either.

She pushed away the hurt. Her issue was not with Cole; it was with Jack. "Leave the budget on the table and I'll do some work on it tonight, if you don't mind my using your office."

Cole gave a rueful smile. "You're welcome to it."

The man worked too many hours. She had found him already at the station when she arrived at a quarter to seven this morning. Unlike the guys on shift, Cole was in the office five days a week. On top of that, he was on call for suspicious fires around the county and had a full court docket to manage as arson cases moved through the courts.

He pinched more cheese. She wasn't sure if he'd had lunch. "There are extra raspberries in the refrigerator."

"Really? I'll accept. Do we have any ice cream?"

"French vanilla. I bought it this afternoon."

"Bless you." He opened the cupboard to retrieve a bowl.

"Jack." It was seven-thirty that evening, after dinner and kitchen cleanup were complete before Cassie was able to search out Jack to raise the subject she had been wrestling with ever since Cole's comment.

"Over here."

She pushed her hands deeper into her pockets and picked her way carefully across the parking lot, trying to avoid the puddles that were actually disguised potholes. The rain had come down in a steady drizzle for most of the afternoon, then had finally stopped, but the mess remained. Several car accidents today were attributed to the weather.

Jack was in the county garage. The building next to the fire station was used to store some of the more infrequently used equipment, including a flat bottom boat and a scaffolding system for construction sites. The large doors were rolled up and the overhead lights glared. He was stretched out under the belly of what the guys affectionately called the Blue Beast.

The old pumper engine had been retired when the Quint—a combine engine and truck—had been bought three years before. The Blue Beast was kept serviced so it could be used when access to a scene was constrained. The narrow wheel bed of the old engine made it the only pumper that could get to certain locations or at major fires where it became necessary to stage water from either the lake or a retention pond.

She could see Jack's boots and not much else of him. "Can I talk to you for a minute?"

"Sure."

"Face to face."

What sounded like a wrench struck concrete. "Just a minute," he muttered through gritted teeth.

"Rap your knuckles?"

"About broke my thumb."

When he rolled out from under the engine two minutes later, his face was still grim and he was shaking his hand to take out the sting.

Now wasn't a good time. "We can talk later."

He sat up and tossed two wrenches into the toolbox. "Now is fine." His expression lightened. "Did I mention it was a great dinner?"

"Several times." She perched cautiously on the metal bins used to store salt blocks.

"Cole was wrong about the cobbler. It's not good. It's fabulous."

"I'm glad you liked it." She smiled but it faded rather quickly.

He moved to sit on the running board of the pumper, his curious look turning serious, his mood changing to match hers. "What can I do for you?"

"I'd like to ride along when there's a dispatch to a car accident and help out. Cole said I should talk to you about it."

She searched his face for an indication of his thoughts. She didn't know what she expected but it wasn't the remote expression that appeared. "I'm not asking to go back on full duty, just roll out and be there if you need an extra hand."

"I'm afraid the answer is no."

"I'd like to know why."

His gaze was calm and resigned. "It won't change the decision," he said quietly. She heard in his answer the caution that it might be better if she would accept that.

She hesitated. She didn't want to push him into a corner, but she needed to know. "Do you think I'd be a liability because of my weaker arm?" He was ruling her out and yet there had to be something she could offer that would be acceptable. "Could I do care and comfort?" Under current department policies, even Luke as a volunteer chaplain was trained in emergency medical response and could provide that kind of help at the scene of an accident.

He turned his attention to wiping grease from his palm.

"Jack?"

"I'm sorry, Cassie."

The rejection hurt. "I need to know why."

He looked at her with sadness and regret, and he gave it to her straight. "You're partially deaf."

She'd asked; the answer cut. Her hearing had been compromised, especially on her right side, but it was not as bad as his answer suggested.

"I can't have you working near traffic when that very traffic would mean you may not hear a shouted warning. You have a problem hearing me across the equipment bay when a vehicle is running; you struggle to follow a conversation at dinner when several separate conversations are going on. Too many firefighters and cops have been hit or almost hit by traffic when working a crash scene. I can't let you ride along."

It was a calm, quiet explanation, a definite one.

She got to her feet, feeling lost. Being around the fire station, hearing the dispatches, seeing the rollouts, going through the refresher training classes…she had let herself think she was really coming back in a limited but real way. She'd been seeing what she wanted to be the truth but not the actual truth. She'd started to hope.

"Cassie, I meant it when I said I was sorry."

She paused, not turning back because she was afraid the tears threatening might show. She'd been judged and found wanting, not because he wanted to do it, but because it was reality. "You made the right decision. You've got a crew to think of beyond me."

—◦◦◦◦—

The paperwork was a haven. She had retreated to it, closing herself into Cole's office, focusing on the numbers. The concentration required allowed her to set aside the emotional turmoil she felt.

She'd seen Cole as she hung up her jacket after coming back in. He hadn't said anything, just squeezed her shoulder. Cole was right. Jack was right. And they'd been forced to intervene and stop her from following down a path that would be a danger not only to herself, but to the other firefighters.

The numbers blurred.

Lord, it hurts.

She set down her pen and pushed back the report. The black three-ring binder she used to collect past drafts slid off the table, hit the arm of the extra chair, and fell open when it crashed on the floor. She looked at the scattered papers. It looked like she felt, cracked open and tumbled out. Stuffing her dreams back together was impossible.

She wiped at the tears. *I let myself hope, and instead of open doors they just slammed shut. Lord, just get me through this day and out of here. I need some place safe to cry.*

She began gathering together the pages. She wondered if she could slip down to the woman's dorm without being intercepted. She didn't want to talk to Jack because she simply wasn't sure yet what to say. Understanding his decision and being able to accept it were different emotions.

Her reason for being here had not changed.

There was still a man out there starting fires.

She would help find him, and she would get on with her life in whatever way that meant. The bookstore business was taking off. She and Linda were struggling to keep up with filling the incoming orders shipping all across the country. Maybe she would implement the plans she had talked over with Linda—hire one more clerk and go forward with plans to expand the business.

Maybe she'd move. The thought had lingered since Jack's comment.

Maybe she would do it. She didn't enjoy making changes, but since she had been reacting to those forced by circumstances, maybe she would add one by choice.

She struggled to find something that felt encouraging to hold on to.

She sighed. For the next few weeks she was in limbo. Having agreed to help Cole, she could not easily pull back from that decision. She went back to work on the budget, although the confidence that she could help out Cole and make a difference was gone. It had simply become paperwork to struggle through.

The math worked, but the numbers didn't, a reality she had observed in her own business. The budget could support either a paramedic or a firefighter but not both. By 10 P.M. Cassie had figured out there was no way to get creative to make the numbers work. Disappointing both Cole and Jack on the same day…she wished she had never thought to hope about a new future possibly working with the department.

Cole couldn't afford to hire her, not to be doing this kind of work on an on-going basis. She understood now why he had placed her on the administrative staff. It was the only way to pay her and justify, by her seniority, hiring her for a few weeks. Cole didn't have the money to pay her into next year. If this arsonist was still out there after January 1, for financial reasons it would be impractical for this arrangement to continue.

The phone rang shortly after ten. It was Cole's public versus private line. She'd been answering phone calls and handling messages for him for the last week. She hesitated to answer it at this time of night. Someone would have paged Cole if it were urgent. Remembering Cole's growl about the voice-mail system's habit of cutting off long messages with its set cutoff time, she reached for the phone. "Hello?"

"I was trying to reach Cole. Is this his assistant or did I dial the wrong number?" The voice was raspy and deep and at first she thought it was being done intentionally, and then she realized why it was also familiar. She sounded much like that during the early days in the hospital. The man was recovering from an injury to his vocal chords.

"This is Cassie. I'm working for Cole, borrowing his office at the moment. Can I take a message for him?"

"Please. Leave him a note that it's Chad returning his call."

Chad. Her pen slowed as she wrote the note, finally placing him and feeling guilty that she hadn't immediately done so. He'd been hurt in the paint factory fire last year. Ben had been by to see Cole early that day to talk about when his nephew Chad could come back from disability, if there would be an opening in the arson group available.

"I'll get him the message," she promised.

"Ask him also to check for an incoming fax."

She tucked the phone against her shoulder and reached for the phone book. "Do you have the fax number or can I get that for you?"

"I have it. You are working late."

"Paperwork," she replied ruefully.

Dispatch tones sounded and jolted her. "I've got to go; we've got a dispatch. I'll be sure he gets the message." She pushed back the chair, still scrawling the note as she stood. She said good-bye and dropped the phone. She rushed through the district offices back into the bays.

Men were suiting up. More tones sounded as additional units were called up. Around her was a controlled rush. The ladder truck, two engines, a rescue squad—dispatch was acting based on a confirmed structure fire, not a report of smoke.

She slid on the pants, stepped into the boots, and reached for her fire coat. She tried to hurry. The men around her were already swinging up into vehicles. The ladder truck kicked on lights to warn traffic on the street they were about to roll out.

The new fire coat fought her as she tried to secure the buttons; she abandoned trying. She'd do it on the way. She grabbed her helmet and gloves.

Nate had Engine 81 running. She moved around to the passenger side.

Jack was there, standing on the running board, one hand on the dash, leaning down to have a hurried conversation with the communications dispatcher. She met his gaze.

The rescue squad to her right moved out.

Jack extended a hand and offered her a hand up.

She stepped up and slid to the back bench next to Bruce.

Jack slid inside and slammed the door. One final sweeping glance around the cab and he nodded to Nate. Sirens and lights came on. Engine 81 rolled out.

Nineteen

J ack had known the address, but he hoped the dispatcher had been wrong on the street number. As they pulled down the street it was clear there had been no mistake. The fire station closed in the consolidation was burning. Flames showed in the burst windows of the dorm wing and smoke spewed from the back of the building where the ventilation system began. The training tower behind the structure glowed like a spire torch.

"This is adding insult to injury."

Jack agreed with Bruce's shouted observation. Jack was willing to bet this would turn out to be their popcorn arsonist. What wood there was within the concrete structure was limited, and yet it was feeding flames well beyond what the normal load would trigger. The smoke was black to the point of ebony and was rolling down suggesting an incomplete burn. The flames had flickers of blue and green indicative of a fire too hot for simply a wood source.

More than just their company had been dispatched. Company 21 had arrived first, thus would have command and control responsibility. Jack reported in to the scene commander via radio and got their assignment.

"We've got the tower along with Ladder Truck 81," Jack called over to Nate. The tower was in danger of collapse, and by virtue of its height it was spreading embers over the surrounding area. It was going to be a difficult fire to fight as it presented a severe containment problem, but at least they wouldn't have to worry about fighting it from the inside with a roof ready to come down.

Jack looked back at Cassie. Her expression was focused ahead on the scene. He'd hurt her with his decision earlier. It would have been easier to ask Cole to make the decision, but doing so would have abdicated his own responsibility as the lieutenant in charge.

He had to admire how Cassie had accepted and dealt with it. She'd wanted his explanation, and even though she did not agree with it, she had not gone over his head to Frank to try and see if it could be changed.

Nate paused the engine long enough for Bruce to step down and pull the five-inch supply line. Nate then rolled the engine forward to join Truck 81, using the vehicle movement to lay hose behind them.

Jack tightened his gloves and swung down to the ground. The lieutenant of Truck 81 already had the aerial ladder moving. The hose line on that ladder would be able to tackle the height of the fire. Jack picked up the radio and linked up with his fellow lieutenant. The truck crew could manage the structure; it looked like the best place for their resources would be fighting to keep the building from collapsing. "We'll take the east face first," Jack shouted over to Nate, who was bringing down the three-inch hose.

Jack caught Cassie's arm and leaned in close to make sure he was heard. "Stay close to Cole." He was convinced this was one of the arsonist's fires. Cassie was going to be looking for the guy. He did not want her wandering around on her own.

She nodded.

He searched her face, worried about how she was going to proceed. She wanted to be fighting the fire; restricted from that, she would want to do anything she could to find the man responsible. And he was comfortable with her doing neither.

"Trust me."

He squeezed her arm, then released it. He had no choice.

He turned to face the fire. The rain earlier in the day was a saving grace as embers landing on roofs of nearby buildings were quenched in the moisture. This was manageable, but it was going to be a vicious firefight.

Was he here?

Cassie kept her back to the fire as she walked around the scene, for it was a personal assault that a fire station had been torched. It would save so much time if she could just find the man. It would release her from the weight of the obligation she faced. It would end the threat to Jack. Cassie stayed within the circuit of the responding units. The fire lit the area and cast flickering shadows.

The roar of the fire and the rush of water mingled with the sound of the men and women fighting it. The smoke had a sharp smell of varnish within it.

She started when someone grabbed her arm. Cole. She hadn't heard him, his grim expression told her that. "Stay with me."

Subdued, she joined him.

"Have you seen anyone at all you consider suspicious?"

"No."

Cole read his watch in the light from his flashlight. "Thirty minutes since the initial dispatch. If he's still watching he's moved back. I want us to systematically canvass a two-block area."

She'd been thinking about it as she walked, trying to find the place where someone would be able to stand in the shadows and have a line of sight to the scene. "What about the high school football field bleachers? That would be a good place to watch from." It was a block away from the fire, but at night with a hot fire raging…that would be a very good vantage point.

"Good suggestion. We'll start in that direction."

"Cole, did you call me and I didn't hear you?"

He didn't speak until she turned to look at him. "I did. And if you get upset about the fact it happened, I'm going to get upset with you. No one holds being hard of hearing against you. We will accommodate

you, not the other way around. And if that means getting your attention before we ask you something, we'll do it."

"I should have never put you in this place when I said I wanted to
come back. Jack's right. I can't do the job."

"If there was a way Jack and I could remove the obstacles to your
being on active duty, we would make it happen. We just haven't been
able to find it. And I seem to remember I opened this conversation five
months ago asking you to come work for me. I'm not losing years of
valuable training by setting you on a bench if I can convince you to get
back in this game. I can't put you back on active duty, but you are well
qualified to join my investigation team."

"As much as I have enjoyed doing your paperwork, you can't afford
me."

"You haven't seen the budget swap Frank and I would make if you
ever did say yes. It's a serious offer, Cassie. You know the job. I'd be
honored to have you working for me full time."

She knew he meant it, and there was some reassurance in that. "I'll
think about it."

He was sweeping the ground with his light as they walked.

"What are we looking for?"

"Anything out of the ordinary."

They walked away from the fire passing spectators heading toward it.
When they reached the football field they found it deserted.

The mud was thick. Cassie stepped up to the bottom row of the
bleachers to walk on it, shining her torch over the bleachers and under
it while Cole swept the ground with his. If someone had been watching the fire from the bleachers he would have probably sat up high to
get a better view.

Her torch picked up something white trailing down the bleacher
seats and on the ground underneath. At first she thought it was someone's band music sheets that had blown away during a halftime pre-
sentation. "Popcorn." She whispered it as it registered…and the
implications hit her like a tidal wave.

She fell off the bleachers and Cole grabbed her arm.

Why hadn't he told her? Why hadn't Cole told her?

"Sit." He turned her and with a smooth motion put her down on the bottom bleacher seat.

She lowered her head toward her knees as it sunk in what she had found and she shuddered with the memory.

Popcorn had also been left at the scene of the nursing home.

Twenty

W hy didn't you tell me?" Cassie whispered. "Has there been popcorn left at all of these fire scenes?"

"It's a copycat. I swear it, Cassie. A copycat." Cole rubbed her back, worried at the reaction he had frankly not expected. The information had been concealed, not to keep it from her, but because it was part of the restricted information in the files regarding the arson signature, and he had already determined it was unrelated to her.

"The man who started the nursing home fire died in New Jersey in a car accident two months ago. I've got the proof, and I went back to the New Jersey police to confirm it." His gloved hand tightened on her shoulder. "Someone else is copying that popcorn signature. He's mocking the arson group, Cassie. This isn't personal to you."

"It is personal against me, just like the fires have been set against Jack."

"No. It's not personal to you. He's using the popcorn signature as a taunt, just like he's been using locations at the edge of the fire district as a way to mock us. The popcorn is the symbol of the worst fire on record. It's just cruel luck that you were the one who chanced into seeing him."

"Then are you sure this isn't Ash? He was very hot about the nursing home fire. He left. Then these fires started."

For her to formally blame her partner…the popcorn had really shaken her up. Cole forced her chin up so he could see her face. "It is not Ash," he replied emphatically.

"I'm not so sure."

"I am."

"You know something else I don't?"

She asked it with such hope that he wished he could give her something. "I believe what I know in my gut. There is no way Ash would let you enter a building fire again."

"You said this arsonist didn't want someone to get hurt...."

Cole had wrestled with the implications of the word *murderer*, of the possibility Ash had been called a chicken. They were taunting words. It was very much like a schoolyard fight. The more he knew about this man, the less he felt he understood.

"He's hitting empty buildings, but he just obviously escalated again."

"Who is he? Do you have any idea?"

Cole rubbed the back of her cheek with his glove, wishing he didn't have to answer. What he had to say he had been trying to avoid concluding for weeks. "I don't think it's Ash, but I'm now convinced it probably is a firefighter." It felt a bit like a death sentence for the department to say it. If he was correct the public implications would resonate for years.

"Then what's the trigger? What set him off this year?"

"I wish I knew. Come on, Cassie. This was one of his. It's going to be a long night." Cole gave her a hand up.

Twenty-one

"Cassie."

She reluctantly opened her eyes as Jack shook her shoulder. As the only thing she was qualified to do now at the scene was to be a well-informed spectator, she'd been trying to get some sleep. The passenger seat of Cole's vehicle had not been the best choice for where to rest. "You're letting the cold air in," she protested.

"Sorry about that."

She stretched and took the kinks out of her back.

"Cole says it's cooled down sufficiently that we can get our first look inside. He'd like you to come."

She pushed up her glasses and rubbed her eyes. "Okay." She looked around him. "It's dawn?"

"Yes. You did get some sleep even though it doesn't feel that way."

She smiled at him for that stipulation as she slid from the vehicle. Jack had been up all night and he looked fresher than she did. She didn't have the endurance she once had.

The landscape had changed. The engines, trucks, rescue squads, and police cars had dwindled down to one engine and one rescue squad from Company 81, one engine from Company 21. Three police cars blocked the adjoining roads and yellow police tape was being put up to keep out spectators.

It was very clear it was now Cole's domain. The arson group tech-

nicians dominated the scene, the bright red stripes on their fire uni-
forms marking them as Cole's team. He stood in the middle of the
chaos, the calm center in the hurricane of the crisis, directing the setup
of what would be a very large investigation.

Cassie walked across with Jack to join him.

"Somebody get Cassie some coffee."

"I'm okay, Cole."

He looked up from his notepad at her. "Coffee and a bagel. You're
working for me, it's an order."

Cassie blinked as she was barked at, then smiled. Cole had definitely been up all night.

"Is that replacement photographer here yet or do I need to send
out a search party?"

"Here, sir." The man was struggling to get equipment out of his
camera bag.

"Don't rush so much that you drop the camera. Someone get him
a helmet and show him how to button that fire coat properly. Have you
ever worked an arson case?"

"No, sir."

"Gregory!"

"Boss!"

"Your pupil—and make sure you get me your own Polaroids for
reference."

Cole looked at the photographer. "How much film are you carrying?"

"Two spools, five hundred frames."

"Plan to use it all. When is your boss getting here?"

"Within the hour, sir."

"Okay. I'm just going to be looking around. Yours are reference
frames, not evidence; we'll leave those to your boss. When Gregory
says take a picture take three, one normal and the other two one step
overexposed and underexposed. You'll get me what I need that way."
Cole looked around. "Now where's my scribe?"

"Right here," his assistant replied. "Get moving, boss; it's freezing
out here."

Cole paused long enough to wink at her. "I'm trying to, ma'am."

Cassie smiled at the interplay. Cole's assistant was comfortable pushing him back, and it spoke to the relationship that Cole deferred to her.

Cole pulled back on his work gloves. "Let's go see what we've got."

The building was cinder block and concrete. While the fire damage was extensive, it was also limited to what would burn. The roof would need to be replaced, windows, doors. Any equipment left in the building after the consolidation would definitely be ruined, if not from the fire, then from the water used to fight it.

Cole led the way.

Cassie stayed a step behind walking beside Jack. The smell of the fire scene made the coffee taste terrible. Jack rubbed the back of his neck. He'd scorched the back of his hand. That sight made her wince. "I'm sorry I dropped out on you to get some sleep."

"I'd call it smart. Cole is going to be pushing you hard today."

They entered the dark building. Torches clicked on. Water dripped from above and splashed into the puddles below. Their steps sounded hollow across the wet concrete floor.

The word *cowards* was boldly chiseled across the concrete wall of the engine bay.

Twenty-two

I hate this guy."

"Let it go, Cassie."

She shoved open the door to her apartment, Jack a step behind her. "There is not a single firefighter in this district who is a coward."

"He pushed a button with you."

"Don't sound so surprised. I've got a right to get mad at what he implied; quit telling me I don't."

"Since the shoe is normally on the other foot and I'm the one people are talking out of being mad, I find it rather interesting to be on the other side," Jack calmly replied. "Where would you like the gear?"

"In the bedroom. I'll unpack it there."

Jack carried it through. Cole had released them at 2 P.M., long after the shift had formally ended, long before Cole himself called it a day. Jack had given her a lift home, carried her duffel bag inside for her.

Cassie moved into the kitchen to check her messages.

"Is Linda picking you up tomorrow morning? Or do you want me to give you a lift in the morning to get your car?" Jack asked as he came back.

"I think we are doing some Christmas shopping. If for some reason I need a ride, I'll give you a call."

"Fair enough. Get some sleep."

"You too." He had been the one up all night.

Jack gave her a tired smile back. "I'm going to shoot for at least eighteen hours," he admitted.

She saw Jack out and locked the door behind him.

Cassie headed back to the bedroom. It was the middle of the afternoon and she was definitely heading to bed. She closed the blinds. She considered just pushing the duffel bag to the floor but forced herself to spend the five minutes necessary to unpack. She separated the laundry that would need to be done from the clothes she would take with her to the next shift.

She set the bag on the floor.

Jack had left his stuffed mouse J. J. on her pillow. She smiled when she saw it. He had promised it would appear and she'd been waiting for it. She reached to pick up the white mouse...and it moved.

Cassie shrieked and hit the floor as she fell back. The mouse disappeared toward her walk-in closet.

She was moving.

And someone else was packing her closet.

Twenty-three

Rewash this one," Cassie ordered.

Jack quickly stepped back to avoid the splash. It was the third glass Cassie had rejected and dropped back into the hot soapy water in the last twenty minutes. There was nothing wrong with his wash job. He'd been assigned kitchen duty for the day and she had been giving him a hard time since breakfast. Jack scooped up a handful of the soap suds and blew them at her. Cassie laughed and tossed the dishrag she was using into the sink, this time generating a splash that did hit his shirt.

"Next time, please don't volunteer to help."

A towel was lobbed over his shoulder. "Throw it in, Jack."

"No way," Jack called back to Peter. He retrieved the glass, nudged the hot water faucet back on to rinse the glass free of suds. The guys were enjoying having Cassie here and had certainly made her welcome over the last weeks.

Jack glanced over at Cassie and waited until she looked his direction before he spoke. The kitchen was noisy and it was his habit now to notice that factor and wait until he had her attention before speaking to her. "Do you—" His pager went off. Jack set the glass down on the drain rack and glanced at the number.

His sister Jennifer O'Malley; it was her emergency code. Jack paled at the sight of it. He grabbed the towel and dried his hands, then reached for his cell phone. There had been less than a handful of emergency pages from his family over the years.

"Jack—"

He held up his hand and cut off Cassie, punching in numbers with his thumb, having to go off memory for the Houston area code. The large kitchen quieted as the men realized something was wrong, but Jack still headed outside where the transmission would be better. Dusk was falling on the late December day. His wet shirt grew icy in the cold air.

The call was answered on its second ring. "Jennifer, what's wrong?"

"Sorry…make it an emergency."

He could barely hear her. "Easy. Slow down and get your breath."

"I fell." She was crying.

And Jack started panicking half a country away. Fell? Or had her spine collapsed? The cancer around her spine, the radiation treatment— "Where are you? Is help there?"

"I fell."

She was worse than shaken up. Jennifer was a doctor, and he'd never heard this kind of confusion before. Jack took a deep breath and focused on one objective. "Jen, where are you?" She called him looking for help from somewhere half a country away. It petrified him. Cole came outside carrying an extra jacket. Jack pointed at him and urgently whirled his finger in a circle, asking for a communication loop.

Cole tossed him the jacket and immediately turned and yanked back open the door. "Get me two phones. Fast."

Jen had to be either home or at the office. But apparently no one was around.

"Laundry." Jack caught Jennifer's faint whisper.

At her house, in the basement, a concrete floor—she'd fallen, or more likely fallen down the stairs. She lived in Texas but it was still cool at this time of year. The basement would be chilly and not somewhere he wanted her with this kind of growing shock apparent. "Don't try to move, Jennifer. Please. I'm getting Tom." He'd find her husband somehow.

Cole reappeared with phones.

"Rachel," Jack whispered. "Then get Houston, Texas, dispatch."

Cole raised an eyebrow and started dialing. Any other time Jack would have found the realization that Cole knew Rachel's number by heart fascinating; at the moment he was simply relieved.

"Tom's car phone," Jennifer whispered. "Don't remember number. You were a speed dial."

"Really? I appreciate that." Jack was sure her husband Tom was also a speed dial but he had no intention of mentioning it for fear in this confusion Jennifer would hang up and try to call Tom. He hoped her phone battery had been recharged. He needed her to keep talking. "What do you want for Christmas?" he asked, grasping for subjects.

"It's soon."

"I know, Jen. What do you want for a present? You never gave me a list," he coaxed from her.

"Coat."

She was cold. "I can do that. What else? What do you want for your kids?" Her patients were personal to her, and she always thought of them at Christmas.

Cole strode over. "They're patching me to dispatch. I've got Rachel," he passed on quietly. "What do you need first?"

"Find Tom. Jen—" he forced himself to put what he feared into words—"spine injury, shock, concussion. The basement at her house."

Cole absorbed that in one long look. "Okay." Cole shifted phones. "Dispatch? I need an emergency break-in."

And Jack started pacing. He was petrified by the rasp in Jennifer's breathing. "Have you bought Tom's Christmas present yet?"

Twenty-four

J ack, it's Tom. I've got her. Spine pain, but she's got mobility."
There was calm steadiness in Tom's voice. Jennifer's husband Tom
Peterson was also a doctor, and in this enormous upheaval of
Jennifer's cancer he had always played it straight on medical information. "She fell down about four stairs, went through the railing, and
landed in a tangle of Christmas decoration boxes. I'll call you from the
hospital. We're heading there now."

Jack heard the sound of people arriving, and from the volume of
the footsteps on the stairs knew Jennifer had been lying near the steps.
"She hit her head."

"The confusion is from a recent change in medication. Hold on, Jen
wants to talk to you again."

"Jack…he bought me a butterball."

She was talking about a brand of turkey. "Okay, Jen. That's good.
Let Tom take you to the hospital now."

"He's so sweet."

Jack had to smile wondering what Tom was thinking of this. "Go
to the hospital, Jen."

A bark nearly shattered his eardrum. There was a clatter as she
dropped the phone.

What? They didn't have a dog.

Tom was the one who came back on the line. "A puppy, Jack. I was out getting her Christmas present. Jennifer, you can't take the dog with you. Let me have him, honey." The phone got set down, leaving Jack listening to a faint conversation.

"Baby."

"Yes, he's a baby. But he doesn't need to go to the hospital."

"Then I don't want to go."

"I know. Let them fasten the straps, honey."

The phone scratched on concrete. "Jack, I'll call you from the hospital."

"You bought her a dog?"

"Only because it's illegal to import the warm water penguin from Argentina she wanted."

"She's confused."

"A little," Tom conceded. "We're weaning her off this med and back to the prior one. A couple days and I promise she'll be back to normal and embarrassed about this."

"I hear you." Jack knew embarrassed would be an understatement. "I'll call the family and give them a heads-up. What do you want me to say?"

"She's wrenched her back, but she's wiggling her toes and she's not biting her lip to handle the pain, so I think we'll be back home after I get a spine scan as a precaution. I'll call from the hospital and let you know how it's going." Tom shifted the phone. "Jen—" He laughed. "Hold on, Jack. Give me the towel, honey. You really don't want to have your monogrammed towel chewed up. Jack…I'm glad you were near a phone. Jen was sleeping, the housekeeper went to the store, I got delayed by a page on the way back…everything went wrong."

"It was my pleasure. And Tom, when she gets a little more coherent, ask her what she bought you for Christmas. You might have a problem."

There was a deep pause. "Is it alive?"

"To tell you the truth…I'm not sure."

Tom laughed. "I'll check. Thanks for the heads-up. We're heading out now. I'll call when we get there."

The call ended. Jack shifted his phone from hand to hand before folding it closed, feeling lost as all the responsibility for the crisis shifted entirely to Tom.

Jennifer. Jack took a deep breath and let it out slowly, grateful that he was very rarely asked to be the point of first contact for a family crisis. It was one thing when it was a stranger and an entirely different matter when it was family.

Cole walked over. His friend had been listening in via the dispatcher in Houston.

"Thanks for the help."

"Trust Tom. Jennifer is going to be just fine."

"From this."

"Jack, don't give up hope. A lot of people are praying for her."

Jack knew Cole was one of those people. While he didn't understand how they thought prayer could change things, he knew how sincere they were about it. At this point he'd take just about anything that might help. "I appreciate that."

"Is it okay if I tell the guys what's going on?"

Jack was peripherally aware that several of the firefighters had stepped outside in the last half hour to see if there was anything they could do. "Please do. Rachel?"

"She hung up on me when I passed on the news Tom had arrived. My guess is she's going to be here very soon."

"Cole—"

"She's not going to cry all over you."

"So you say." Jack wished with a passion that his brother Marcus was in town. This was the stuff his older brother handled with ease. "Let me know when she arrives. I'm going to try and track down Marcus and Kate."

"I'll do that." Cole headed inside.

Jack turned the phone toward the light that had come on at the back of the building in order to pick out the numbers. He paged his sister Kate to start informing his family of what was going on. As he looked up from dialing, a splash of red caught his attention.

Cassie was sitting at the picnic table. Her head was bowed. She was praying.

And the appreciation Jack felt was incredible.

"Hey, lady." Jack slid onto the bench across from Cassie.

"You're shivering."

Cassie's quiet observation had him realizing she was right. He'd been holding his jacket the entire time, not willing to set down the phone long enough to put it on. He rectified that, pulling on the jacket. The warmth was immediate. He turned his phone so he could see the signal strength and make sure the batteries remained strong. He reached his sister Kate and she was going to track down everyone else so he could leave his phone free for Tom's callback.

Cassie had pulled on a coat and gloves, but she had to be getting chilled just sitting there. Jack would suggest they go inside but it would remove any chance to have a private conversation. It wasn't the most comfortable place to chat—beneath his hands the wood was rough, the paint beginning to curl after a year of exposure—but after this day the discomfort didn't matter as much as the chance to have a moment with her.

She picked up a thermos from the bench beside her and spun open the top. The aroma of hot coffee drew a final shiver from him as she handed him the cup. He curled his hands around it, grateful.

"You never told me your sister had cancer." There was no reproach in the words, just quiet concern.

"I'm sorry about that. I didn't mean to hide it." He circled the coffee mug around a knot in the wood. "It's all happened pretty fast. She didn't tell the family until the weekend after the Fourth of July."

"Protecting the family from bad news."

Jack gave a slight smile. "Temporarily preempting my job."

"Jack, she didn't make a mistake in calling you. Jennifer might have been confused, but she knew exactly who she wanted to intervene. How bad was the fall?"

"Four stairs. Maybe it was an accident, but I'm afraid it's going to prove to be something worse. The cancer is around her spine, touching her liver. She's had a brief remission, but this may be the first indication that has ended." Jack ran his hand through his hair. "If the remission doesn't last through Christmas…" He shook his head.

"I'm sorry."

Her words were a mere whisper. She did understand. Cassie had spent Christmas last year in the hospital. And while she'd had visitors during the day, when Jack had swung by the hospital after he got off shift on Christmas day she'd been alone.

The foot-tall ceramic Christmas tree had looked pitiful, and all the Christmas music in the world hadn't been able to change the fact it was a hospital room. She'd had skin graph surgery on her right arm ten days before. She'd had her arm elevated, resting on a pillow, and any time she tried to shift on the bed she'd paid an excruciating price.

Cole had been there earlier in the day but had been called away by a page. Jack had taken Cole's place, picked up the crossword puzzle he had been reading aloud for her, and teased her into smiling as they debated words.

His Christmas gift to her had been a copy of the *How the Grinch Stole Christmas*. She had laughed at it, as she'd laughed at everything else going on. He watched her by force of will refuse to let the pain win, refuse to let the despair take hold.

If Jennifer was in the hospital, he'd deal with it. But creating moments of lightness in such a dark day was not what he wanted for his sister. Not on what might be her last Christmas.

"She was at Johns Hopkins for weeks, then released to go back to Texas. Her wedding was two months ago. She was so happy, Cassie. They've got plans to come here for the Christmas holidays so Jennifer can see old friends from high school. If Tom calls and reports the cancer around her spine has returned and become aggressive, she's likely to be going back in the hospital for the foreseeable future."

"I'd say don't borrow trouble but it's probably best to be prepared."

The phone call had been a shock. He was definitely not prepared and he had to get there fast. "Thank you for praying."

She glanced over, surprised.

"Jennifer believes."

"I'm glad," Cassie replied.

"She needs something to hang on to—she chose the idea of heaven and the practical reality of marrying Tom."

Cassie looked at him, then down at her coffee. She dumped the small amount that remained and had grown cool onto the grass behind her, then reopened the thermos to pour more. "You think heaven is a myth."

"I mean no offense, Cassie, honestly." That was the last impression he wanted to leave with her. "It would be nice to think eternal life did exist. But why should Christianity's claims about heaven be more relevant than the claims of any number of other religions? Christianity rests on the idea a man rose from the dead. That's pretty tough to swallow."

"Not if Jesus was the Son of God. Are you familiar with what the Bible says about Him?"

"Jennifer talks about Him a lot." And frankly confused Jack, not that he'd tell Jennifer.

"You need to get to know Him. Then you'll understand why Jennifer believes. Why I do."

"How?"

"You could try reading the Bible."

It took him a couple seconds to realize the dry humor in her answer, to understand the smile she was trying to stop. He lightly kicked her foot under the table. "How did I know your answer would be to read a book?"

She reached over and tapped his knuckles with hers. "I know you, Jack. A look at the evidence and what Jesus said and you'd get your answers. Jesus is not a myth."

"If you say so."

"It would be easier to handle Christmas with Jennifer if you would look at it again with an open mind. Did you ask Cole to call in a replacement for you? The odds are good we're going to be rolling out again tonight and you're going to be busy for the next few hours. Ben can come in and cover your shift so you can focus on your family."

The arsonist. The reminder was a wrench back to another painful reality. "If I'm not working he probably won't start a fire."

"Jack—"

"Don't tell me that isn't the current theory. I may be slow to put together the pieces, but I get there."

She slowly nodded. "It's a possibility."

He rubbed the back of his neck, surprised she had been willing to put it into words. He didn't know what to do about it. Pull himself off active duty? He'd wanted to be a firefighter since the day as a child he'd seen his first fire. He couldn't imagine being anything else. He had an obligation as well as responsibility to his men, but if that was what it took…. "I'm a firefighter. This is what I do, who I am. If someone does have a beef with me—" He shook his head. "I'll cross that bridge when it's more than a possibility." Tom would be calling back in the next couple hours. "Any more coffee in that thermos? It's going to be a long night."

"I'll go get us a refill." She slid from the bench. "Jack—you're interesting to watch in an emergency. You're the first guy I've seen who likes to pace and kick rocks while you cajole the world around you to get what you want. You did a good job."

"Flattery, Cassie?"

She squeezed his shoulder as she walked behind him. "Truth."

His cellular phone rang.

Twenty-five

The district offices were dark but for the lights on in Cole's office. The clerical staff, other arson investigators, and building inspectors had gone home. Rachel would either park in the visitors' lot beside the district office or along the street just past the fire station. Cole paced in the conference room where he could see both the lot and the street. Where was she?

He'd scared her with that phone call regarding Jennifer and he hated knowing that.

He interrupted something; Rachel's hello had been distracted. As soon as she heard why he was calling, she practically swallowed her words. She scrambled to get him Tom's car phone number, talking to herself in frustration as she searched for it and couldn't quickly find it.

Cole was going to graciously forget what she had said aloud to herself even while he remembered it as an issue he'd have to soon tackle. Stupid had been the kindest name Rachel had called herself as she'd taken not knowing the number from memory, a misplaced purse, a jammed clasp on her address book, the tumbling out of dozens of business cards all as somehow being her fault.

Under the stress of a family crisis he'd gotten a glimpse beneath the layer of poise Rae normally maintained and learned just how hard she was on herself. He didn't like it, not one bit.

She had to read him the phone number twice as she transposed digits the first time, and he finally had to stop her with a quiet word and remind her to get her reading glasses.

There hadn't been time to reassure her. He was forced to leave the call with her open while he worked with the dispatcher to expedite getting help to Jennifer. And in the time that he had been talking with the dispatcher and waiting for Tom and the rescue squad to get to Jennifer, Rachel had been able to hear only thirdhand what was happening.

He'd passed word to her just as soon as he knew help had arrived. Her response was to abruptly hang up on him. He was afraid she had been crying.

Cole tapped his knuckles on the edge of the table.

She should have been here by now.

The phone in his office rang. With one last long look at the dark street, Cole moved to take the call.

The coordinator for the state crime lab was on the phone. "Hold on, Kevin." Cole unlocked the secure file cabinet to retrieve his case index log. While he had a great support staff to keep track of case numbers, assigned officers, pending evidentiary tests, and court dates, it made his life easier to keep his own reference log that could go with him. "Okay. Give me the case numbers."

Kevin read a list of six. The last two numbers Cole knew by heart. The popcorn case arson numbers were burned into his memory.

Cole turned and punched in his secure number on the fax, which would enable encryption and provide the requisite date and time log to make his life easier when he inevitably had to testify at trial. "How much paper are you dumping to me tonight?"

"Forty-two pages."

"Oh, joy." Cole checked the paper supply. "Shoot them to me. And thanks for the evening response."

"Thank your administrative assistant. Your paperwork always arrives complete, with tracking numbers and labels preprinted for my convenience. I don't mind expediting requests that only need my signature to prep. She's even started sending the stamps."

Cole smiled. "Before you ask, no, you can't hire her away from me.

I'm working on a raise if I have to pay it out of my own pocket." The fax machine by the window came to life. "I see paper. Thanks, Kevin."

"Anytime."

Cole dropped the phone back into the cradle.

Forty-two pages were going to take a while to come through the fax. Cole rubbed his forehead at a rare headache and reached over to the inbox for the top inch of paperwork already waiting there to be read.

The problem with having an efficient staff was that paperwork that needed his attention rarely got delayed. If he initialed or signed something, made the mistake of writing an e-mail, action happened immediately. Inevitably that meant follow-up status reports coming back. His own success with hiring great staff often felt like the making of his own downfall. He could delegate work; he couldn't delegate responsibility.

An official-looking binder with the red stamp budget was on top of the stack. It was a problem that would not go away. Every time Cassie got a draft that would work someone else on, the committee would make more changes.

He set aside the report to take home with him. It was part of the reality of command. He and Frank were fighting the bureaucracy. Between the two of them he had no doubt they would eventually get the aggressive training program they wanted in place, but it was like rolling a boulder uphill—all the pressure was coming from the other direction.

The next item was a blue folder clasp, used for personnel matters to protect confidentiality. Cole opened the folder and slipped out the two pages. The bottom line through the official paperwork: Chad wanted to come to work for him. A message from his assistant noted Chad had called again that afternoon. Ben had caught him yesterday over lunch to mention the doctor was releasing Chad for light duty.

Telling a firefighter on disability he couldn't come back on shift work was hard, telling him there wasn't even a place for him in the administrative side of the house felt like hitting a brother when he was down.

There wasn't a seniority card he could play. He'd done that with

Cassie. She had enough seniority he could authorize paying her out of his own budget. To justify bringing Chad off disability meant having a clear permanent position available he was qualified to take.

Cole found a pen and made a note to his assistant that he would call Chad. He'd find some way to at least give the guy hope at Christmas, even if it meant calling in favors at every other fire company in the surrounding counties until he found someone with an opening. Ben was absolutely right, firefighters had to take care of their own. Cole dropped the paperwork in his out box.

The fax finally went quiet. Cole reached for the stack of pages, then sorted out the reports.

The third report was for him. Lab work was done on the evidence he had expedited from the fire department fire. He started reading.

The first popcorn arson fire had been pinned down to a match dropped with the right wind, humidity, and temperature conditions. In those fires, it had been the popcorn signature linking them.

The structure fires were different.

The fires starting in the walls had a strange burn pattern. They were very hot, with characteristics of a flash fire. That suggested a spark-triggered accelerant. But there were also odd characteristics of a slow, sustained burn.

Cole wasn't surprised when the report pointed to chemical traces of fertilizer. That would explain the heat and flash characteristics of the fire.

The gold mine was found on page 2 of the report.

Tar.

That explained the way the fire clung.

He'd read just about every arson report this district had written in the last decade to strengthen his own understanding of what type of cases he would have to deal with. Tar was an interesting choice. An unusual one.

He reached for the phone book. He was about to get a crash course in how many stores and businesses sold tar.

Car headlights moved across the window. From his office, Cole couldn't tell if the car turned in the visitor lot. There was the faint sound of a door slamming. That had to be Rachel. He locked away the reports and his log book, then grabbed his coat.

When he reached the door he caught a glimpse of Rachel already rushing along the sidewalk. Cole pushed open the door and hurried down the handicap ramp. He darted around the railing and caught her arm as she nearly got by. "Hold on, Rachel."

She stepped on his foot. He was wearing boots, but he still felt it and wasn't entirely sure it had been an accident. She'd been driving while crying. The realization made him mad. She should not have been behind the wheel. "I promised Jack you weren't going to cry all over him. Don't make a liar of me."

"Let me go."

"Not until you get your composure back." He was bigger and broader and he got in her way, refusing to let her past. A sidewalk wasn't the place to have this conversation, but she wasn't in a mind-set to slow down at the moment. "Rae—Jennifer's okay. She's got some pain in her back from the fall, but she's got good mobility; she's alert. Tom's going to call as soon as he has news."

"You don't understand. Where's Jack?"

Her voice wobbled. He wanted to wince when he heard it. Rae normally handled crises so calmly that he was having to scramble to get in sync with where she was at. He hadn't been expecting this, wasn't ready to handle it, and he blamed himself for being the one who had put it in motion. If only he'd handled the situation differently when he called her. "We'll find Jack in a minute." He turned Rae back the way he had come. "Come on. Dry your eyes. You really don't want to cry all over him, do you?"

She wiped her face with the back of her jacket sleeve.

Inside the building she turned to walk on through to the fire station, instead he turned her toward his office. Someone had been raiding his Kleenex box; he found it tucked on the bottom shelf of his bookcase atop a copy of an old edition of the fire science journal.

"You don't understand," she repeated. "I talked to Tom last night.

Some preliminary blood panels came back...." Rachel wiped at her eyes and blew her nose.

The fact she didn't care that she'd shown up in an old Northwestern sweatshirt with spaghetti sauce splatters on it, a pair of faded jeans, and running shoes told him more than she realized. "The remission is over."

"Tom—he hasn't told her about the panels until he gets the results from a more sensitive series over the next couple days."

Cole pressed another Kleenex into her hand and guided her into a chair. "That's why he went out to buy a dog today," he murmured, adding another piece to the puzzle of what had happened in Texas. He felt for Tom, having to face the fact Jennifer was taking a turn for the worse so that he needed to move the holiday presents up.

"Yes."

It was serious if Jennifer's remission was indeed showing signs it was over, but it didn't explain this. Rachel was falling apart.

Cole had watched her step into trauma situations on a moment's notice where she faced putting back together the shattered lives of children. He watched her deal with Jennifer's cancer for five months. Rachel had gone through far more difficult crises than the incident tonight without this kind of fight for emotional control.

He wished their relationship was such that he could ask what was wrong and she'd trust him enough to answer. Something was very wrong.

It was not the time to try and pry.

He reached over and squeezed Rachel's hand. "I'll go get Jack."

Twenty-six

An interesting shift."

"That's an understatement, Cole." Cassie pushed a mug of coffee across the table to him and resumed her seat. It was approaching 1 A.M. The fire station was quiet. The skeleton crew working through the night handling routine paperwork and monitoring dispatches in the various districts had retired to the communications room. "Every moment past midnight has been a relief. I've never watched a clock like this before."

"It's tough to watch and sit on edge."

"Should I take coffee down to Rachel and Jack?"

"Let them be."

She wanted to head to bed as she was so tired she was about to fall asleep in her chair, but it didn't feel right to leave Cole sitting alone at the kitchen table. He showed no sign of leaving even though she knew he had been here before 6 A.M. He had to be exhausted too. She straightened, abruptly realizing the obvious. "Your car keys are in your office."

"Yes."

"Cole."

"Let it go. Rae needs Jack's attention, not an interruption."

"I thought the phone call at eleven was good news. Jennifer's home with only bruises and the need for a heating pad for her back. I know they were going to conference call with the others in the family, but that was some time ago. Do you have any idea what they could still be talking about?"

"I've got a suspicion."

Cassie hesitated. She wasn't in the same position as Cole who had known both Rachel and Jack for years. "Is there something I should know?"

"Stay close to Jack. He's going to need a friend."

"Jennifer's cancer?" Cole didn't answer her. He didn't have to say it. His expression told her what he feared. "Christmas with his sister dying," she whispered.

"It looks that way."

An arsonist targeting him. Jennifer taking a turn for the worse. Jack had a freight train coming toward him. *Jesus, what am I supposed to do to help?*

"Cole," she hesitated. "I was hoping I'd be able to show Jack the real meaning of Christmas this year. He's been asking a few questions." She amended that. "He's been asking hard questions."

Cole smiled at her observation. "Cassie, don't get fooled. I've watched you take Jack at face value over the years and you're making a mistake by doing that."

"What do you mean?"

"His questions don't surprise me and they shouldn't surprise you. He's forthright and transparent in a way I admire. He laughs at life. But under that tapestry—you let his humor and casualness suggest that is how he also thinks. That's a mistake. Watch him around the station. He's a natural leader in his instincts. He listens, probes for details, is not afraid to make a difficult decision and act on it. When Jack talks about faith—he's got a lot of respect for the people making the claims, but he's not comfortable the claims are right. So his response is to respectfully keep listening. That's very revealing. He's trying to understand."

"I'm simplifying, but he seems to think Christianity is nothing more than a myth that grown-ups believe in."

"He's not yet convinced that a baby in a manger and the King of kings should and could logically be the same person—Jesus."

"A hard question to resolve."

"Don't feel like you have to force the questions, or worse, force his conclusions. God has been tugging at him for a long time. Jack will slowly keep working through the claims to decide what he thinks."

"I wish it were easier to start that conversation. I feel like I'm stumbling around sometimes. He hadn't mentioned Jennifer's cancer."

"Cassie—" Cole winced and rubbed his forehead.

"Need more aspirin?"

He shook his head with much more care. "A little less caffeine."

"What were you going to say?"

"How long have we been friends?"

"Long enough probably to handle what you're about to say."

"I wish you and Jack could get on the same page." Cole leaned forward and folded his arms on the table. "I see the frustration he feels at times, but I don't know that you see it."

"Over what?"

"You're honest, but not open. And it has an impact when you try to talk about something like religion and why you believe. In a rush to convince Jack of the truth, you gloss over eighteen painful months. Faith doesn't stand in a vacuum. He knows you're not telling him everything when you talk about other things, so he listens to you talk about God and wonders what it is you're not saying."

"Cole—"

"Just listen, Cassie. You hurt him when you hide the scars. Not just the cosmetic ones, but the deep ones. Jack knows it's been a rough eighteen months, yet you're wanting to tuck it away and downplay it with him on the assumption that it would be a drag on the friendship. Over Thanksgiving it would have helped had you been straightforward that you were fighting the depression of a holiday without Ash."

She winced.

"I don't mean it in a harsh way. I know where you go when you are retreating as a means to cope. I know the things you turn to and hold on to. But Jack doesn't have that history with you. So he gets worried.

And he's a man who prefers to act, not worry. He about took my head off for this insane idea of you riding along on the fire calls."

There was a balm for the searing truth of his observation in those last words. "So...Jack's giving you a hard time about me."

"You don't need to sound so amused about it," Cole replied, pushing a napkin toward her to put under the straight pretzel sticks she was stacking into a log cabin square. "Start being more open with him. God can use openness on your part to touch Jack's heart."

"Cole, I understand your point, but I don't know if I can."

"No one ever said witnessing was easy. You've got to step back and get your priorities straight. It's wrong to flirt and mess up Jack's head only to draw back later because you can't marry someone who's not a Christian. Be a true friend and convince him about Jesus."

"I can't change his mind."

"Try."

She made a face at him. "Easier said than done."

"You got through the last eighteen months because the option was to give up and you refused to do it."

"Yes."

"So just decide to do it and don't give up. Jack's got that kind of crisis coming. It would help him if you'd let him learn from what you've been through."

"I'm not wise about how to cope just because I've been forced to do it."

"Yes, you are. You sat outside in the cold because what you most wanted on your own bad days was someone to talk to, so you instinctively gave that to Jack. That's wisdom learned from experience."

Cole reached across the table. "Watch your square of pretzels." He pulled a lower one out. The pretzel wall shifted, then held because the side walls held them in place. "As the pressure builds, Jack's going to be reaching for strong things to brace himself against. And I do expect him to look toward God because that's who Jennifer is resting against."

"The O'Malleys will close ranks. They're doing it with the conference call tonight; they'll do it through the holidays."

"Yes."

"I envy them that."

Cole smiled across the table at her. "Jack would be glad to share. There are times having four sisters drives him absolutely crazy."

"If that's where Jack is at, what about Rachel? How's she handling this?"

Cole pushed aside his coffee mug.

"Cole?"

"Unlike Jack, Rae is impossible to understand."

"She's gracious, thinks about others, helps in practical ways, is there to do whatever she can in a crisis—what's so hard to understand?"

Cole didn't answer her, just looked at her, let her think through what she had said. Cassie knew she was getting tested, but she just didn't see what he did. She shook her head slightly, not understanding.

"What's she leaning against to get herself through this?" Cole asked quietly.

The truth hit like a brick through glass. Rachel was leaning against herself. "Cole—"

He shook his head. "She's my problem." There was a grimness to that statement. "I'll deal with it."

"What are you going to do?"

"I have no idea."

Twenty-seven

R achel pushed her car door closed and wiped at the tears that made her eyes burn. The tears would simply not stop. She'd cried all over Cole. Cried all over Jack. Was still crying. She was losing Jennifer, and the grief had grabbed hold and shook her so hard she could not get it subdued. She headed into the apartment building.

The phone call—one simple little trigger and the wall holding back the tears had burst. It wasn't Jennifer's fall that was the entire embarrassing reality of tonight. Jack had even lost his ability to offer a joke to help lighten the moment because she'd so flustered him with her tears. She dealt with too much grief in her life already through the tragedies of others, she simply didn't have the strength to face it on a personal level. Not grief this overwhelming.

She had denied what was happening with Jennifer since July, denied the reality of what it could lead to. She knew it, could clinically see the pattern of denial she so often counseled against in others. She knew this break in the wall holding back the tears was inevitable, and yet when it happened it caught her by surprise.

The entire family had seen her lose it. Five months of bottled-up tears were all getting shed in one night. The conference call had lasted so long because everyone in the family had been trying their best to offer reassurance that Jennifer would be okay. Jennifer was home. Even if the remission was ending, the doctors had not exhausted treatment options.

Rachel had been in Florida early in July when Marcus had sent the initial emergency page about Jennifer. She caught the next flight out in the middle of the night, learned the news about the cancer diagnosis very early that next morning, and by that afternoon been on a plane to Baltimore to join Jennifer at Johns Hopkins.

It had been so easy to simply do what she did professionally. To step into the role of helper. To be there. To do whatever needed done. To not only help Jennifer get through the chemotherapy and radiation, but on Jennifer's behalf to also undertake the complex job of implementing wedding plans in Houston so that Jennifer would have that upcoming day of joy to focus on rather than be forced to delay it. Rachel was grateful there was a way to help; it had been her gift to her sister. To pull it off she spent hours on the phone, had made several round-trip flights between Houston and Baltimore.

The wedding had been a wonderful day. And her relief that it was over had been real.

Jennifer in remission, the wedding over, Rachel had been looking forward to a chance to step away and catch her breath. Instead, she had walked into the situation with Gage and rearranged her plans.

Now this.

She simply did not have anything more to give. She was given out.

And now the tears would not stop. She walked up the stairs in the apartment building, sorting through her keys. She struggled to get the key into the lock.

"Rachel."

She leaned her head against the door. Not this. "Go away, Gage."

Behind her on the stairs going to the next floor, Gage stood. "Cole called me."

Cole had called Gage…no need to wonder what impression she had left with that man. She pushed the key into the lock. "Come on in," she whispered. She was too tired to fight anymore and he'd come in regardless.

Gage caught the door before it could close on him. "You should have called a cab."

She ignored the comment and tossed her keys into the dish on the table in the entryway. Her home was an eclectic place that Gage rarely visited, not because he wasn't welcome but there was barely room to turn around and he hated the lack of space.

The rooms were stuffed with furniture. The hallway was lined with pictures. There were enough pillows tossed on chairs and the couch to outfit a small hotel. She liked it this way. Her apartment in Washington was more functional. This was her nest. Not that she would defend it that way to Gage.

He paced past her into the living room and tossed his jacket on the couch. "What's going on?"

"I'm tired."

He shot her a frustrated look. "Shall I interpret tired or do you want to get a little more expansive on the language?"

She pushed aside his jacket so she could sink into the cushions on the couch. She was very aware Gage would have already grilled Cole for the details. "You're the writer," she muttered. "Tired: as in go away so I can go to bed."

"As if you would. I know you too well, Rachel LeeAnn. You grieve by turning on the TV, curling up on the couch, eating ice cream, and staying up to see the dawn. Where do you keep the aspirin?"

"I already took some."

"I haven't."

It nudged enough sympathy she thought about the question. "Try the bathroom cabinet."

He reappeared minutes later, shirtsleeves shoved up, a glass of ice water in his hand. He tossed pillows to the floor and dropped into the chair across from her. "Tabitha used to say crying her eyes out was incredibly therapeutic."

Rachel opened her burning eyes. "She was lying."

Gage chuckled, albeit forced.

He was studying her with a frown on his face, and she could almost hear him thinking there was so much coiled energy apparent just in how he sat. She was a problem to be solved and he was figuring out where and how to begin. He had a habit of probing everything in a way that would strip a subject bare, although he rarely did it to her. Under the abrupt exterior there was still a softer Gage loath to hurt her feelings.

"You held Jennifer's hand through weeks in the hospital, stepped in and planned her wedding, provided a shoulder to your family for the last five months. Now you've got to find the strength to get through Christmas with Jennifer's health failing. Forgive me for being astonished by your habit of assuming you are strong enough to deal with everything."

She was startled at the amount of raw emotion in his words. "I've got no choice but to deal with it."

"You could have called me; you could have talked to me."

"And say what?"

"How about something honest like, 'Gage, I'm scared'?"

She wiped at tears and didn't answer him.

He let the silence stretch out for minutes. "Did you think I wouldn't understand?" There was so much tenderness in those quiet words.

"I feel like a fool."

"Been there, done that. You live through that one."

She smiled at his prompt reply, knowing he was speaking from experience. There had been days around the anniversary of Tabitha's birthday when she wondered not if he would make it, but if she would, after the all-night sessions on the phone when she refused to hang up because Gage was prowling like a caged lion. Months later he had sent her roses in memory of those evenings. He'd survived. It just didn't always happen without a few scars.

She leaned her head forward into her hands, heavy of heart, weary, and honestly not sure what she should do in the next few minutes, let alone the next day. Just the idea of facing tomorrow was beyond her at the moment.

"Where are the sleeping pills?"

"You know I dumped them," she muttered. It would be so simple to reach for sleeping pills to push away this stress, to smother it. Gage had turned to alcohol to numb his grief; she couldn't afford to go back to using sleeping pills.

They had been a blessing at first, recommended by her doctor. But they had begun to cover the stress of her job and make her think she was dealing with it when in fact she was relying on the pills. And the day had inevitably come last year when she'd scared Gage, scared herself. He'd called in the wee hours of the morning and she answered the phone for all practical purposes incoherent.

Severe jet lag from a delayed flight home from Los Angeles followed by a sleeping pill had been a mistake. She'd spent three weeks dealing with the fallout of a suicide pact among four high school football players and she just wanted to get some sleep. She'd gotten it. She managed to answer the phone, mumble an answer, and drop the phone without hanging it up. She'd gone immediately back to sleep only to be aroused shortly thereafter by Gage pounding on the door.

She'd dumped the pills.

"Go to bed and put in one of your favorite tapes: the ocean waves one that makes you seasick or the one of those crazy loons on a pond."

His description of the relaxation tapes she had once made the mistake of loaning him drew a smile as she knew he had intended. "I'll compromise with the radio station."

"If I leave, you promise to go to bed?"

"Yes."

"You'll call if you can't sleep?" There was no question there was an edge of skepticism in the pointed query.

She pushed herself to her feet. "I will."

He pulled on his jacket. "I want a call when you wake up."

"Gage—"

He hugged her, taking her totally by surprise. She not only was swallowed up with her face pressed into his jacket, her ribs got squeezed until her breath was lost. "Don't scare me again," he whispered. "If you want to cry, do it on my shoulder. Don't ever again do it alone."

Years of friendship boiled down and focused to one point in time.

She'd always wondered if he understood her core concern for him. He had; he was mirroring it back to her. "Thank you," she finally whispered.

"Crying alone is a waste of good emotion."

She rubbed her cheek against his jacket and hugged him back. "Go home."

"I'll go home."

She was smiling as she locked the door behind him, the relief of his visit real.

She turned out lights, confident she'd be able to sleep.

The bedroom was chilly as the wind had picked up, and she had not yet put up weather stripping to better seal the window frame. Last week she had added extra blankets and changed to flannel sheets. She slid under the weight of the blankets and wrapped her arms around a pillow.

She owed the relief she felt to more than just Gage. A brief battle over that fact ended when she reached for the phone. She punched in a number.

"Yes?"

"Cole...thanks."

"Rae." She'd surprised him but clearly not woken him up.

"Calling Gage was a nice thing to do."

He floundered for a moment. "Better than doing nothing."

She curled her hand under her cheek. She'd embarrassed him. "He handles tears better than you do."

"Oh, really?"

She chuckled. "You want to solve them."

She expected a quick reply and instead he was quiet for so long she was afraid she offended him.

"No. I want to remove the reason for them."

The breathtaking scope of what he reached for—how could she have so misread the man not to have seen that coming? He was not offering it as a casual statement. Their conversations over the years had often revolved around the subject of religion and tragedy as he asked about what crisis she was dealing with at work and how she was approaching it. But the few times he tried to make it personal, she avoided the conversation.

She had a choice to make. Did she want to have such a conversation? One word would step her back, the other... She took as big a risk as he had when she answered. She so desperately wanted the peace Cole had. "There is no remedy for tears when the reason for them is inevitable. Jennifer is dying."

"The despair can be remedied." He spoke to the heart of the matter.

"Only by denying the pain of the loss."

"If death is permanent, despair is the right conclusion. If death is a brief separation, it's merely a reason to be sad," he replied gently.

"Heaven." She'd seen people cling so hard to that conclusion in the face of tragedy. She had known he would base his position there; it was where those who believed anchored themselves.

"The reason for this Christmas season—*Unto you this day a Savior is born.* There's hope, Rae."

They were nice comfortable words that were said so often at this time of season. But she'd heard the words so many times said by others in the face of tragedy that it had become something of a panacea. Cole believed those words; she didn't doubt his sincerity. And because it was him, for the first time she was willing to press the contradiction she saw.

"There's hope, but only if I accept the premise that God loves man so much it rationalizes the fact He would allow His own Son to be killed."

"You think God acted arbitrarily." She'd stunned him.

"Is it rational to do wrong in order to do right? He let His Son be crucified supposedly to save mankind. Where was the love for His Son?"

"Rae—"

"I don't buy loving someone at the expense of someone else."

"Love can't be inclusive? A parent's love for a spouse and a child? Equal and yet unique."

"The Bible says because God loved us He sent His Son. Jesus would later cry from the cross, 'Why have You forsaken Me?' The Bible contradicts itself on God's character."

"Rae—you've got it wrong. Giving His life was Jesus' own choice. He came to save us and the way to do it was to die in our place."

"Maybe."

She was met with silence. An absolute silence. "I can hear the hurt," Cole finally replied. "You've obviously thought about it. Would you be willing to talk about it another time?"

It didn't sound like she'd offended him, but it did sound like she disappointed him. She buried her head in her pillow. "Of course." She'd listen, even if the emotions behind her conclusions ran deep. "Buy me breakfast some morning." She had no idea she was going to make the suggestion until it was made.

"I'd like that a great deal."

She'd offered it, she couldn't easily back out. "Good."

"Sleep well, Rae."

She looked at the clock, which showed most of the night gone. "I'm going to try."

"If you're awake in half an hour, I expect a call and we'll talk about it tonight."

The two guys in her life expecting the same thing...she smiled, hoping she didn't find herself awake and forced to choose between the two of them. "Good night, Cole."

Twenty-eight

Jack, I don't want to move to this apartment complex. It's too new and pristine and…well, yuppy. I want a place where rust on the car in the parking lot isn't considered an eyesore to be scorned."

Jack leaned against the side of his car, smiling at Cassie's definition of the apartment complex. It had been built two years ago. There was a swimming pool, two tennis courts, a weight room, and a large community center. The one-and two-bedroom apartments were spacious with high ceilings and large closets. It was the opposite of what she had now. "You haven't even see an apartment here and you don't like it."

"I just know I won't."

She was so sheepish about it that Jack had to bite back a grin. This was the fourth complex they had looked at on Tuesday their day off, and with every stop her excuses got more and more nebulous. They had plenty of time and the full attention of an apartment complex staff eager to rent an open apartment, but Cassie wasn't biting. "Admit it, Cassie. You don't want to move."

"Yes, I do. There is a mouse now living with me who I didn't invite to be my guest."

"You could put out a trap; you could let me find him."

"I'm not going to put out a trap that I'm the one most likely to step on."

He'd expected that to be her answer, although he suspected it was for a far more fundamental underlying reason. He moved away from the car and opened the passenger door. "Come on. Let's go get lunch."

"No. It's okay, we can look at the apartment while we're here. I promise I'll keep an open mind."

"There's no need. I know what you want."

"What's that?"

He chuckled. "To look like you moved without actually moving. That can be done too." He waited for her to get in the car. He closed the door for her and circled around to get behind the wheel. "Paint. Wallpaper. New curtains." He added one more just to tease her. "A cat."

"The building manager would never agree."

"Sure he will. I'll do the asking." If it came down to it he was sure he could find someone who knew someone who knew the owner of the complex to get the approval.

"I don't like wallpaper."

"You need a flowery border for the kitchen. Trust me on this."

"Then I don't need a cat. I don't want a dead mouse. I kind of like my mouse."

"What's his name?"

"Her."

He barely heard her. "What?"

She sighed and spoke up. "It's a her. T. J."

"A cousin of J. J.?" Jack glanced over at Cassie, amused by the choice of name. "I'm jealous. At least your mouse is alive." Despite her protests, he'd suspected she was attached to the unexpected guest. "I promise I'll find and rescue your mouse. We'll build you bookshelves; you can do your spring cleaning early and get everything in your drawers and closets nice and neat and organized. It will be just like you've moved."

"Maybe I had just better move. This sounds like work."

"I'll recruit help."

Twenty-nine

Cassie bit the tip of her tongue as she carefully cut the Christmas wrapping paper to give an inch overlap. She set aside the scissors and smoothed the paper, folding the corners of the paper and neatly creasing them. Jack leaned across what she was doing. "Hey—"

"You're hogging all the bows." He selected a huge red one from the plastic storage bin sitting beside the Charlie Brown-size Christmas tree he'd insisted she get for her apartment.

"Well, you're hogging the tape."

"I need it. There are only five days to Christmas and I've got close to a zillion packages to wrap."

He added the bow with a flourish to what had once been an envelope box and was now a colorful if rather interestingly wrapped package. He added the box to a growing mound that was threatening to topple over.

"What was that?"

"A new toothbrush for me."

"Jack—" She laughed.

"Cole said to buy what I want and give him the bill."

"A toothbrush."

"A Wile E. Coyote that will not be mistaken by any other guy at the station in the early hours of the morning."

"I take it back. That's a good gift," Cassie agreed.

"I thought so. What did Cole get you?"

"He's actually buying my gift himself and I have no idea what he's getting. Last year at least he asked for a list of what I wanted. This year—he just gets this grin on his face."

"It's got to be something noisy," Jack speculated.

"Please. Cole has not bought into the idea that color and sound somehow make the gift better. I think, I hope, it's a book."

"You have a truly boring Christmas list. Books, gloves, a new coffee-pot."

Cassie smiled. "I asked for what I want."

"You asked for what you need. Books to you are like food. Is there a second tape dispenser around here somewhere?"

"Try the box you labeled this afternoon: everything-that-has-nowhere-else-to-go."

"That's what you told me the stuff was," Jack protested.

"I meant it in frustration, not to be taken literally."

Jack got up from the floor to head to the hallway and search for the box. If someone had suggested to her at Thanksgiving that Jack would be so intertwined in her life that a day off when she didn't see him would feel like a loss, she would have laughed at the suggestion. Jack had transformed the holidays for her.

Lord, he's wrestling with a simple question. Who You are. If You're a myth or real. I need an opportunity to talk with him. Please show me an opening. Now that I've got my nerve up to try, it's hard to wait for that right moment.

"Cassie, what's this small box marked hot stuff?"

She smiled, having wondered how long it would take him to ask. "Salsa for the department Christmas party. Remind me to take it over to the station tomorrow."

"I see you finished packing the front closet."

"I got it done last night."

At Jack's suggestion she had brought in packing boxes and was doing what he defined as spring cleaning. His method was extreme. It was to empty the drawers so that furniture could be moved away from walls while they painted and so that stuff, as Jack described it, could be put back where it should go instead of where it had been.

It was effective. It felt like she was moving. The good thing was she didn't have to carry boxes outside in mid-December. The bad thing was her apartment hallway had become a floor-to-ceiling stack of boxes.

Jack came back with tape. "Where did you put those books of wallpaper samples?"

"A couple of them are on the kitchen counter, the others in the bedroom."

"Have you thought about wallpaper for the bathroom?"

"Paint."

"Then do something other than white." Jack leaned over to tap the end paint sample strip spread out on the carpet. "What about this blue for the trim?"

"Too dark."

"It would look sharp. You need bold colors."

She shifted the paint strips. "Maybe a soft rose."

"That would look good too."

"As long as it's color."

"Exactly. White is boring." He tore open the plastic wrap on a new package of Christmas wrapping paper. "Have we decided what to get Cole?"

"We?"

"Come on, Cassie, help me out. He's my friend but he's also a boss. It's not easy."

"He wants a copy of the movie *Apollo 13*."

"Easy enough."

"And a copy of the movie script."

"Where am I supposed to find that?"

She looked at him and smiled.

He sighed. "How much is it going to cost me?"

"I'll be kind."

"Sure you will." He spread out paper, sized a box to wrap, and liberally cut the paper. "You didn't ask what Christmas gift I wanted from you."

"Jack—"

"Ask."

She'd already bought him a game player after meeting with his sister Rachel to find out what he really wanted. "What do you want me to get you for Christmas?"

"See, that wasn't very hard. I want you to come to the O'Malley family gathering with me."

She set aside the scissors rather than cut the paper and make a mistake. "Your family Christmas gathering?" She was enjoying spending time with him, had known she'd see him sometime over the Christmas weekend around the shift on Sunday, but his family gathering— "You're sure?"

"Yes."

"I don't want to crash your family gathering." Maybe he didn't know what that implied, maybe he did. She wanted his friendship because it was going to be hard to spend Christmas without Ash, and she certainly didn't want to spend it alone. But going to Jack's family gathering—

"I want you to come," Jack insisted. "You already told me you don't have other plans."

"Maybe not, but spending Saturday night with your family would be presumptuous."

He leaned over to crowd her space to pick up the scissors. "Jennifer wants to meet you. You have to come or I'm going to be in the doghouse with her. You wouldn't want that, would you?"

"Come because your family wants me to?"

He caught her off guard by sliding his hand along her cheek. His laughter turned serious. "*I* want you to come. Please."

Her gaze held his. The last thing she wanted to do was hurt him. But if she said yes, it would just complicate a friendship. She leaned against his hand, appreciating this man's strength, and tried to calculate the cost of a yes.

The radio on the counter sounded dispatch tones. The conversation stopped as a fire dispatch came across. The address was given.

Cassie paled. "Cole—"

Jack surged to his feet, pushing back wrapping paper and packages. He caught her hand to pull her to her feet. "Get your jacket. A call will find out if he was working late at the office."

The dispatch address was Cole's home.

Thirty

Smoke was curling up behind his house, and Cole didn't have to see the source to have a good idea of what was burning. As soon as he opened his car door he got confirmation. It smelled like what it was: the stench of burning garbage. Someone had set his trash cans on fire.

He had a big backyard with his garage set to the back of the lot, the trash cans along the side of the garage next to the alley. It wasn't the first time someone had set fire to his trash and it probably wouldn't be the last. At least this time it hadn't dropped sparks and spread to the grass.

Engine Crew 21 had been able to pull into the alley to within fifteen feet of the fire. Under the distant streetlight there was some light to work with, but most light at the scene came from the engine's own halogen spotlights. "There's a garden hose and water hookup on the east corner of the garage," Cole called over to the lieutenant as he reached in the back of his car for his fire coat. Two men had just about suppressed the fire with fire extinguishers, but the area would have to be wet down to handle any smoldering remains.

A car pulled in behind him, headlights briefly lighting the scene. Cole turned and recognized Jack's car. Cassie was with him. Cole wasn't surprised that his address in the dispatch would have caught attention. He was surprised to see them together.

"Cole?" Cassie called, worried.

"Everything is fine. It's a nonevent." He'd have to replace some boards and repaint his garage in the morning, then do some digging at the local school after the Christmas break to find out who had thought tossing a match would be a fun thing to do, but it wasn't a crisis. It was the typical complication that showed up when he least needed another problem on his plate.

Cole slipped his hands into his back pockets and watched the fire-fighters do their jobs. He was tired enough he was willing to stand back and let others take care of it.

"Who called it in?" Jack asked.

The breeze changed and Cole gave a rueful smile. "I suspect any-one downwind." His pager went off. Cole glanced down and saw the return number for the office. "Come on up to the house if you like. I need to call the office."

Cole walked around the curving stone walkway through the trees up to the house. "Watch your step. There's wandering ivy across the stones."

He dug out his keys.

"Cole." Jack caught his elbow, stopping him. The alarm in Jack's voice would have halted him without the hand reaching to stop him. "Back of the house."

Cole looked up. Jack swept his flashlight over the area.

The back door was hanging at an angle from its hinges, wood from the door frame torn open.

"Cassie—" Cole waited until she looked his direction and held up his keys. He tossed them toward her. "The phone in my car. Get me the arson squad coordinator and the police liaison." It would keep her out of the way, which was nearly as important as the task he gave her. She nodded and turned back toward the cars. "Jack, come with me."

The floor was littered with popcorn.

"Wait for the police," Jack cautioned.

Cole took a careful step around the shattered door. Someone had taken an ax with at least a five-inch blade to it. The door frame had been shattered at the lock and at the top security bolt.

Murderer.

Cowards.

Cole wondered cynically what he was going to get tagged with. *Trash man?* The guy had torched his garbage cans. But why the vandalism? Had there really been a change in MO? The popcorn said it was the same guy. "Jack, get back to Cassie and clamp a hand on her. He may still be in the area. When the cops get here, you two can look around."

He expected Jack to do it. Instead, his hand came down hard on Cole's shoulder. "Outside."

"This may be set to burn. I need to know where and how." He was not letting tar and some spark mechanism send his home up in flames when they were early enough to prevent it.

Jack muscled his way in front of him and got in his face. "Outside. Now. Or so help me, Cole, I will take you out."

Jack was furious.

And it drew Cole up short.

"It's your home...but it's not worth people's lives. Get out, and tell the firefighters coming up the walk to stay out."

And in that moment the man facing him moved from being a friend to being a lieutenant correctly reading the scene and flexing his right to take charge and assume authority. "We'll wait for the cops."

Thirty-one

Cole shone his bright torchlight around the living room walls. Jack swept his light across the floor behind him.

"Somebody doesn't like you," Jack said tersely.

"Now whatever gave you that idea?"

The word *liar* was sprayed repeatedly across the walls. They had waited forty minutes after the cops arrived to make sure the house wasn't going to explode on a timer before entering to begin the arson sweep. The room where he relaxed to watch a football game, read a book, make his regular Sunday afternoon phone call to his aunt in California now looked like a whirlwind had blown through. Bookcases had been dumped, tables overturned.

"He didn't bother to torch your place; he just trashed it."

"He knew if it burned down, I'd get compensated."

"Annoying little man."

Cole silently agreed. *"Liar.* It's an interesting word choice." The man had hit out at him. It could have been worse. He could have lashed out at someone else.

"You're an honest man."

Cole chuckled at the fact Jack felt the need to say it. "Nice to know you think so." He studied the words and the way they were spray painted literally from floor to ceiling. The letters were huge. It wasn't necessary, and thus it probably meant something, but he had no idea what. "Who's going to be next? And what does he want?" Cole murmured, thinking aloud.

"You need to ask Rachel to profile this."

"No." He rejected that suggestion immediately.

"Cole, if you reject what she does, you implicitly reject her."

"She's got enough on her plate."

"Give her a chance to get back on her feet. It will help her to have work to look at over the holidays."

Cole didn't want to add another burden on her. He already felt guilty about seeking Rae's opinion over the word *murderer* and telling her of his suspicion regarding Jack being a target. Had he understood what else was going on in her life, he would have never added that pressure. "I'll think about it," he replied noncommittally. "Did you notice that this time Gold Shift was off duty?"

"We're losing the ability to predict his behavior."

"A wonderful thought."

"Cole?" The faint call came from outside.

"Cassie, stay outside. I'll be right there." Cole looked at Jack. "Who's with her?"

"One of the cops. He knows we'll be having words if she gets out of his direct reach."

Cole nodded. Jack and Cassie had spent an hour looking around the area, and Cole was relieved their search had come up blank. If he did continue to allow her to rollout to fires to look for the man, and he hadn't yet decided if he would, there would have to be someone assigned to stay with her. This had moved from just an arsonist they needed to spot, to someone who took an ax to a door. There was too much violence here.

Cole stepped around the men working to get plastic sheeting in place to cover the broken windows and exited the house through the destroyed back door.

Cassie was waiting at the turn in the walkway.

The police officer standing literally a foot behind her cast a nervous glance at Jack. Cole bit back a smile. There had clearly been a rather frank warning given. Cole couldn't blame Jack. Whoever had trashed his place, set a fire, and scrawled the word *liar* was not someone either one of them wanted Cassie ever again coming face to face with.

"Gage is here," Cassie told him.

The press. It was the last thing Cole wanted to hear.

"Do you want me to talk with him?" Jack offered.

Jack and Gage were oil and water. Cole didn't need that tension brought into the situation. He needed the press limiting how much they said. Gage knew how to dig for facts, and the details of this fire and the fire station would be in his sights. "I'll talk to him."

Cole glanced from Jack to Cassie and decided it would be best not to have her seeing what had been done inside the house. She was worried enough about Jack as it was. "Jack, do me a favor. Would you go over to the station and start clearing my calendar for tomorrow? There's a couple court hearings that will need to be postponed. And Cassie, if you can print out another copy of that draft budget for Frank he can cover the finance meeting. It will be several hours here before I'll be able to do anything more constructive beyond watching the investigating officer do his job."

"I'll take care of it," Jack agreed.

Cassie looked troubled at the thought of leaving. "You're sure?"

"Cassie—this is bad, but it's stuff. I'll deal with it. I'm more concerned with who is next."

"How many popcorn arson fires does this make?"

"Eight." Cole followed the investigating officer as the vandalism was cataloged. They had worked cases together many times; Joe was an old friend. It was five in the morning, and at this point Cole wasn't sure he was drawing reasoned conclusions after being up most of the night. To keep some perspective, he was using his friend as a sounding board. "It's strange that he goes from creating a huge fire at the station to now settling for burning trash."

"Any odds this was a copycat?"

"Slim to none. Neither the popcorn nor the words are known signatures to the public." And unless Gage was snowing him, the reporter didn't have either of those facts yet.

"Then it's not the fire that he's impassioned about. It's the message."

A very interesting conclusion. "The words have got to be the key. Murderer. Cowards. Liar—they intersect somehow to make clear who this is." Cole picked up an autographed baseball which now had its seams slit. For the first time he felt sick. It had been a gift from his dad. He rubbed his thumb over the gash in the ball that scored through the autograph. The ball could not be restored. "Do the words suggest someone to you?" he asked Joe.

"Not really. But it does sound like there was an event that occurred."

"I've searched the cases we've worked for the last two years and I'm still drawing a blank."

An officer appeared at the doorway. "Sir, there's someone out here to see you."

"I'll be right there," Cole replied. He looked to his friend. "If there is anything here that would suggest a possible suspect, I could really use something to put my hands around."

"You'll get anything I can find as fast as I can," Joe promised.

"I appreciate it. I'll be on my pager if you need me."

There was nothing he could do here beyond watch. His possessions had been trashed. His home turned into a crime scene. And he was tired enough that it was hard to even get angry. Exhaustion overrode the emotions. Cole left his friend to the task of finding evidence and went to see who needed him. It was setting up to be a very long day.

He ducked under the plastic sheeting put up to stop the snow flurries swirling in through where his back door had once been. His steps slowed when he realized who it was. "Rachel."

She was waiting just inside the police tape.

He wasn't surprised to see her here. For Rachel not to respond when something like this happened to someone she knew would be contrary to her nature.

That said, she'd had a rough few days, and he was distressed to see her here. At this time in the morning she should be asleep, not standing outside his home on a cold late December morning. She wore a long black dress coat and black leather gloves, a deep red scarf setting a bold splash of color. She was dressed up and he wondered briefly if she hadn't also been hit with the unexpected and a call that was going to take her away over the holidays.

She gestured to his house. "How bad is it?"

He pushed his hands into his back pockets as he walked down the path to join her. "It's trashed but he didn't get as far as the kitchen dishes or my closets."

"This is personal."

"Very."

She looked down, shifting her booted feet on the walkway stones. "Can you leave for twenty minutes?"

He could see Rachel was clearly hesitant to ask. "What do you need?"

She glanced up at him. "Breakfast."

Rachel saying she needed something… She was saying he needed something but was suggesting it in such a way that it was her need. He smiled as he dug out his keys. "Let's go to breakfast."

Thirty-two

Would you relax?" Rachel was still very ill at ease with him and Cole didn't like it. He handed her the sack with breakfast burritos. He wasn't into bacon and eggs for breakfast when he could have something more substantial.

"I don't like eating breakfast in the car."

"Sorry, but I'm not dressed for the public. I'm not planning to share you with a crowd, and at least the car is warm." He was too tired to be anything but frank with his answer. He handed her the carrier with two coffee cups, then turned to get his change from the drive-through clerk.

"I hear echoes of my mother over the propriety of eating in the car."

Cole smiled at the comment. "I grant a waiver. I stop here for breakfast most mornings, and while you can quibble the nutritious value, I can vouch for the fact the food at least tastes excellent."

"I don't mean to criticize the food. This is fine."

"No offense taken. And like I said, please relax. It's not yet 6 A.M. If there was ever a time for going with the flow it's now."

He took them to the community park where he could park and they could watch the dawn come up without the morning rush-hour traffic flowing around them. He occasionally came to the place to have morning devotions, for it was a peaceful place to walk.

Rachel handed him the first breakfast burrito he had ordered. Cole unwrapped it and picked up a napkin. He closed his eyes and took thirty seconds out of a day that had not ended for him. *Lord, I'm exhausted. Rae needs something or she wouldn't have sought me out. I'm hardly equipped to give it at the moment. Later today I have a case to work and a home to try and repair. I could really use some energy.* The emotions of the night flowed out in the quiet words. Cole opened his eyes. He reached for the coffee and considered the odds if adding sugar to the caffeine would keep him awake when he finally found somewhere he could sleep. It wouldn't be his own bed for the foreseeable future. He opened the coffee and drank it black.

Rachel nibbled at her breakfast burrito; he ate his.

Cassie had been right when she said Rachel was gracious. She allowed him to eat in peace, passed him the hash browns when he finished the burrito, and when he was done with them handed him the second burrito.

The food helped. He leaned his head back against the headrest as he wadded up the napkin.

"What do you pray for when you bow your head?"

He was surprised with her opening question. "In one word? Comfort."

"Someone to listen and care."

"Yes."

"I need to ask you something."

He turned his head toward her. "I'll do my best to answer."

"Jennifer is coming to town Saturday. Tell me how I can find the strength to smile and not cry when I see her."

It was very hard to get handed such a question, to know the door was open to the basis of her doubts about Jesus, and yet know he was at his lowest ebb for constructing a coherent answer.

"If Jennifer needed a bone-marrow transplant to heal her cancer and you matched—you'd jump to do it."

Rachel nodded.

"You'd do whatever was in your power to help her because you love her."

"Yes."

"Jesus loves her too."

He waited for that loop to circle, hoping she'd draw the obvious conclusion and make it simpler for her to hear him.

"Rae, unlike us, Jesus can do something about it. He had the power to come and lay down His life for her. He chose to do so. He opened the door and gave Jennifer the opportunity for eternal life. As the Bible says it, He took away the sting of death."

Cole tried to sort out some way to answer the contradiction Rachel had presented him a few days ago what she thought was present about God's love.

"I don't see a contradiction in God's actions. People die physically from things like cancer, but we're dying in a more fundamental way from sin and the evil that pervades the world. Jesus knew that. He chose to lay down His life to save us. And God the Father let Jesus make that choice, not because He didn't love His Son, but because He had decided in turn to express His own love for His Son and raise Jesus from the dead. God honored the sacrifice His Son made."

"But Jesus didn't just die," Rachel whispered. "He was crucified and abandoned by His Father."

"Rae—Jesus made a huge sacrifice. But I think God the Father actually made a larger one. He let the one He called His beloved Son be humiliated and murdered. Can you imagine how hard it was to sit on His hands and allow that to happen? He wasn't being contradictory. God was in agony, but He loved us enough to allow it to happen."

"The Bible says that?"

"Look at the anger God feels against anyone who rejects what His Son did. *Hell* is a mild word for the reality. Based on what Revelation says, when God the Father acts at the end of time it is going to be unlike anything mankind has ever seen. Men will beg to be spared that wrath. God loves His Son, and He's going to call the world to account. Every knee in heaven and earth will bow to the fact Jesus is Lord, and if they don't do it by choice, they will do it in judgment."

Cole tried to focus on the emotion he knew Rachel was struggling to cope with as she faced the fact Jennifer might be dying. "Please understand. I'm not saying don't cry. I'm not saying don't be sad. I can't and don't minimize what it is like to face losing someone you love. For the rest of your life that void will be there. I'm saying cling to hope. Grab hold of it and brace yourself against it. It is the only way you are going to get through what is eventually going to come, whether it is months or years away. Jennifer has that hope in Christ. Claim it, Rachel. I don't know how better to package it for you. It's waiting there for you. Christmas is all about hope."

She was crying.

He pressed a napkin into her hand and didn't say anything else as the sun came up.

"He's changing behavior, which suggests new triggers are arising," Rachel offered.

Cole nodded. "The suggestion was made that it's not the fire that he's impassioned about as much as the message in the words he is leaving."

The sun was rising on the horizon and shining through the side windows of the car with a gold cast. Rachel had retreated to talking about the arson cases and Cole had accepted it. She needed time to think about what she had asked him, and he knew the value of time to let questions settle and to let God work on her heart. He was relieved the tears had ended.

He knew she had a headache, but she was doing her best now to turn her focus to what he was dealing with. Rae's sense of fairness wouldn't let her talk about her situation without talking about his.

"Why did he go after you?" Rachel asked.

"If I had some idea of a suspect maybe I could figure it out. *Murderer. Cowards. Liar.* Possibly *chicken* although that's suspect. He's being extremely blunt."

"He's going after authorities."

"Fair conclusion."

"Any idea on why he changed to vandalism?"

"An arson fire in an arson investigator's home—there is not enough sting to it, I imagine." He finished his coffee. "Give me your opinion. He goes after the man responsible for public safety and calls him a murderer. He goes after the men responsible for facing down fires and calls them cowards. Finally, he goes after the man, me, whose essential job is to discover the truth and he calls me a liar."

"Questioning integrity," Rachel concluded.

Cole nodded his agreement.

"You also know he's setting fires at the edge of the district," Rachel added. "He doesn't want you to be able to respond in a timely fashion to what he is doing. You know he's watching the scene. So he feels some responsibility for the results of his actions. You've got a contradiction in front of you. Cassie said she saw a thoughtful man. Trashing your place—that's the action of a man in a rage and out of control. For those to be two sides of the same coin…it's a man who has snapped and is fluctuating like a pendulum between two extremes."

"How do I stop him?"

She didn't give him an immediate answer. He looked over at her.

"Cole, you've got one slim hope. He's escalating. That's being caused by something. Everything revolves around this district so the trigger is probably here as well. If that can be removed you've got a chance to change his behavior, slow down his escalation in time and type of fires. That might give you the time you need for the investigation to give you enough information to identify him."

"How are the holidays going to affect him? Christmas, New Year's?"

"The season is a stressor even for people who otherwise have happy lives—the pace, the financial pressure, the people pressure. And I doubt this is a man with a stable family with whom he spends the holidays. He's probably alone. If you haven't found him by Christmas—" She shook her head. "He'll hurt someone, Cole. There will come a point where he doesn't care."

Thirty-three

Jack paced the terminal waiting for Jennifer and Tom's flight to arrive. The O'Malley family was assembling from all corners of the country and he was the designated chauffeur. For the fifth time he glanced at his watch. This was going to be tight. He had an errand to run after he took Jennifer and Tom to the hotel, and then he had to get back here to meet his brother Marcus and his fiancée Shari.

Since the family gathering had grown from seven to fifteen with the addition of spouses, fiancées, and dates, they had decided to make it easier on Jennifer and arrange the whole event to be at the hotel where she and Tom would be staying. They had been able to reserve a block of hotel rooms and had hired the hotel to cater the gathering.

Jack knew it was the best compromise. They'd hopefully be able to keep Jennifer from overextending her energy and get her to agree to call it an early night if she knew everyone would still be at the hotel and around for breakfast.

The relief that she was able to come was intense. That decision hadn't been made until early yesterday morning, the twenty-second. Jennifer hadn't wanted to leave her puppy behind, but other than that, when he talked to her yesterday she'd been eager to get here.

The family had taken her fall as a warning of what was coming. They were eager to have this weekend as a full family celebration of not only Christmas but also New Year's. All of them realized that the next time the family gathered as a group it might be around a hospital visit. Jennifer was going back on chemotherapy in January. She'd pleaded for the extra week before it began. She had been so wiped out last time that her doctors had agreed a few more days of recovery before she was hit again with toxic drugs would mean she'd have a better chance of success.

Jack checked the wall clock to confirm his wristwatch time was correct. If this flight was late, he would have to track down Stephen and see if he could handle meeting Marcus and Shari. Jack did not want to be late picking up Cassie. She was nervous enough about the idea of coming with him to the family gathering that he didn't want to give her any excuse to back out.

Jack knew Cassie had to be tired. They had spent most of yesterday and part of this Saturday morning at Cole's helping him deal with the mess the vandalism had created. They had rebuilt the back door yesterday, then replaced the last windowpanes this morning. Cole had hired a professional painter to come in because it would take a blackout paint to cover the glowing spray paint and not have it show through the next coat of white paint. Jack knew he'd have to make it an early night for both of them. He didn't want Cassie walking away from tonight with anything but fond memories.

The flight finally arrived. Ten minutes later people began to flow from the gateway. Jennifer and her husband Tom appeared at the end of the first group.

Jack had been braced to see her looking ill, to have lost weight, to look tired, as she had during the hospital stay. Instead she looked wonderful—her color was good and she'd gained a little weight since being released from the hospital. She dropped her bag at Tom's feet and raced toward him. Jack caught her.

"Jennifer." He took care with his hug knowing how injured her back was. "Hi."

She hugged him back. "Oh, it's good to see you." She'd turned into a bubbly blonde with the choice of the wig to deal with the loss of her hair. She caught his tie and tugged it as she laughed. "You dressed up for me?"

"Cassie actually, but you get the benefit of it." A suit jacket and dress slacks were not what he would normally wear to an O'Malley gathering but he knew Cassie. She was going to be dressed up, and he wanted something that at least felt like a comfortable middle ground.

"Did she pick out the tie?"

"An early Christmas gift."

"I thought so."

"I like this tie."

"You hate ties."

"I hate ties, plural. I love this specific tie."

She giggled. "In that case, I'm buying you a tie for Christmas."

"Jen, while I'm not opposed to wearing two ties to this O'Malley family gathering and recreating my clown costume, on basic principle it will look kind of bad if I don't wear just Cassie's tie this time."

"Very good save. So shall I buy you cuff links instead?"

"I really don't want to dress up that much."

"Unless Cassie gives them to you."

He conceded that point with a sheepish nod.

"I can't wait to meet her."

"She's coming. Would you look after her tonight for me? She's not used to large, boisterous families."

"I'd love to." She slid her hand through his arm. "Where are we heading first?"

"How much luggage do we have to deal with?"

Jennifer smiled.

"That bad?"

"I'd hate to ruin my reputation."

He glanced over at her husband Tom. "Let's go to baggage claim. If needed I can bring the car to the lower level. Then I'll take you over to the hotel. The party gets under way at seven."

Jack glanced at his watch and sprinted up the steps. He was late and Cassie was a stickler for punctuality. This was not the impression he wanted to leave with her.

She had buzzed him into the building so he wasn't surprised when she immediately answered his knock on her door. Her coat was over her arm and her keys in her hand.

"Sorry I'm late." And then what she wore registered. "Wow."

Her smile was immediate.

She was wearing a pink cardigan and a black pleated skirt with an explosion of color along the bottom four inches. She looked absolutely gorgeous. He spun his finger.

She swirled to show it off.

"Beautiful."

"Thank you."

She was blushing and her voice wasn't quite steady. He tilted his head, surprised at that. He hadn't expected the nervousness before they got to the party. "Jennifer can't wait to meet you," he offered. He took her coat and held it for her as she slipped it on.

"It's mutual."

He squeezed her shoulders. "You'll have a great time. I promise."

She smiled as she pulled on her gloves. "Nice tie."

He glanced down and ran his finger across it. "It's quite grown-up."

She slipped her hand under his arm and companionably walked the stairs with him. "I also bought you a much less grown-up one." She leaned over against him to admit.

"Did you?"

Jack opened the apartment building door and the snow swirled in. She was wearing flats that looked like they had smooth soles. "The walkway is slick," he cautioned. She clenched his arm as she took the first couple steps, slipped, then got her footing.

"The tie was a joke, you know. Cole dared me to give you one."

"I know. But never let it be said I can't take a gift in the spirit it was intended." He wrapped his arm around her shoulders. "What's this?" A small, gold chain glinted in the cold evening air and tumbled from his hand to dangle by a finger. He lowered it into her palm.

"I do wish you would quit doing that," she said, and then she looked at what he had pressed into her hand. It was a gold heart with the flowing word *Cassie* across it. Jack saw unexpected tears get blinked away. He'd had it made for her thinking it would look good with whatever outfit she chose for tonight.

He tugged her toward him and pressed a kiss against her hair. "Merry Christmas."

Rachel had brought Gage. Jack drew up short when he saw the man across the room talking with his brother Marcus. Rachel stood beside him.

The hotel meeting room was set up with casual, adjoining groups of sofas, a faux fireplace providing a focal point on one wall, and floor to ceiling windows on another wall, giving a spectacular view of the city skyline. From the thirty-fourth floor the skyline was a sparkling set of lights spread out like a blanket. A buffet table was on the east wall.

It looked like he and Cassie were the last to arrive.

Jack was surprised Gage had agreed to come. But knowing how difficult the last few weeks had been on Rachel, Jack suspected the man would have found it next to impossible to tell her no when she made the invitation.

"Call a truce."

Jack glanced at Cassie. "I wasn't the one who started it." He was more than willing to bury the hatchet, but he wasn't the one keeping it alive. Gage had reason to hold on to his anger. Christmas for him without his wife Tabitha had to be unbearable.

"Jack." Cassie pulled on his arm. "We're going over to say Merry Christmas and to shake hands."

"Later, Cassie." Jack didn't want to intensify that grief by interjecting himself into the man's Christmas. But Cassie was heading that way, and it didn't matter that he wanted to wait. There was nothing he could say that would eliminate the unease that the entire group would feel. Beyond Merry Christmas there was little safe territory and Rachel would land all over him later should he say the wrong thing. Cassie had no idea what she was asking of him.

Gage spotted them coming and leaned over to say something to

Rachel. Moments later he came across the room to meet them, surprising Jack. "Cassie, Merry Christmas." He leaned down to hug her.

"It's good to see you, Gage."

He looked over at Jack and his smile faded. Jack flinched at the coolness. "Can I talk to you a minute in private?"

Jack glanced at Cassie, loath to leave her before she'd been introduced around. Abandoning her in the midst of his large family was not the way to ease her into meeting them. The O'Malleys as a full group could feel overwhelming; Jack was under no illusions about that. His family was great, but you had a cop, a U.S. Marshal, a paramedic, and a doctor, to name just a few of their jobs, and the conversations were not going to be about the latest television comedy. Shari was here and there was a good chance Marcus's fiancée had the title congresswoman in her future.

Rachel was coming toward them. At Cassie's slight nod toward Gage, Jack reluctantly accepted he had no choice and agreed to Gage's request. "Of course."

"Cassie, I'm so glad you could come." Rachel greeted her with a smile, grasping her hands. "The guys had us outnumbered. Come with me. Let me get you a glass of punch and I'll introduce you around to all of these O'Malleys."

"I've worked with Stephen many times in the past," Cassie offered.

Rachel seized on it as Jack knew she would. Rachel was a natural hostess. She would do what she could to ensure Cassie was comfortable. "Since he was the only one who dared show up alone, we'll start by pestering him about why that happened," Rachel said.

"I told him he should invite someone," Jack protested when Rachel looked pointedly at him. He offered Stephen more than one suggestion about whom to bring. Jack looked to Cassie to back him up.

Cassie glanced up at him once again to offer him a distinctly amused smile. "He tried."

Since Cassie didn't have a big family, Jack had been forced to deal with her laughter at the idea he was working to play matchmaker for his brother. Jack figured it wouldn't take long for her to figure out just how involved the topic was in his family. The questions directed to Cassie regarding him would be subtle but they would come. Before the night was over Cassie would catch the drift.

The ladies headed toward the punch bowl. Gage gestured toward the hallway. With some reluctance, Jack nodded and headed that direction. Gage closed the door behind him, and they walked in silence to where there was an open area near the stairway.

Gage had requested this conversation, so he was the first one to speak. "Popcorn."

Jack waited for the rest of it.

"It's appeared at all of the arson fires."

Since Gage was not a man to allege facts, Jack confirmed it just to find out where this was going. "Yes."

"That signature has leaked. It will hit the papers tomorrow or the next day."

"Who has it?"

"The *Daily Times* and the ABC news affiliate. Do you want to go on record?"

"No."

"Jack, I suggest either you or Cole do so because you've got a problem. I've been sitting on the words used in the fire station arson and at Cole's home, but it's only a matter of time before someone else gets those. Once that happens I'll have no choice but to lay out the connection with all the fires."

"No one else has the words?"

"Not that I've been able to ferret out."

"Gage, we don't need public panic, not over the holidays."

"Reporter's discretion only goes so far. You can duck the news becoming public and react once it does, or you can intervene to shape it before it comes out."

Jack understood the man's position, respected the way in which he worked to get the details confirmed even if Jack didn't often like the specifics of what Gage wrote. "Talk to Cole. And if you can, sit on it a while longer."

"Do you even have an unofficial suspect?"

Jack didn't reply.

"That's what I thought." Gage nodded back down the hall toward the room. "I'm glad you brought Cassie. She needs a good Christmas."

It was a generous statement from a man who understood just what it meant for Cassie to be here. "I'm glad you came with Rachel," Jack replied, meaning it. He looked down and studied the pattern in the carpet. He wanted to say he was sorry for what had happened in the past but didn't know how. Straightforward was still the best approach. He looked up and locked his attention on Gage. "I'm sorry about Tabitha. We tried, Gage. We couldn't get to her."

"My son would be celebrating his first Christmas this year," Gage said softly.

Jack knew how deep that grief went. He'd watched Rachel be the one to reach out to Gage and listen to that pain. Had the situation been reversed, Jack wasn't sure he would have handled it as well. For Gage to face this Christmas without his wife and son had to be a shattering thing to handle. "I know."

"You were late."

"We were late. It wasn't in our control, but it happened." Jack held Gage's gaze. "You want to take another swing at me?" he asked, hopeful. If a black eye would help, he'd give Gage a free shot.

"Yes, but then Rae would take one at me."

The two men looked at each other.

"It's history."

Jack's relief was intense, for he hadn't expected Gage to give at all. "Good. Are you going to date my sister?"

The question rocked Gage back on his heels. "You don't waste any time in shifting to brother mode."

Jack simply held up four fingers.

"I hear you. Marcus already gave me the elder brother look." Gage laughed. "No wonder Rachel wasn't worried about how her family would react to my coming along. She already knew."

"She's an O'Malley."

Gage conceded the point with a nod. "We're friends. And as her brother, you've got a right to know if that changes." He gave a glimmer of a smile. "That said, I might tell Marcus first." Gage gestured down the hall to where the gathering was under way. "Anything else you want to say before we go back in?"

"Not at the moment. But when I do, I know where to find you."

They headed together to the party. And Jack felt like he had managed to put to rest a burden from the past. He knew Rachel would be relieved.

"Cassie, it is a delight to get to meet you. I'm Jennifer."

Cassie was feeling overwhelmed with O'Malleys by the time she was finally introduced to the youngest of the seven. The hug she got from Jennifer was long. The petite lady leaned back, smiling at her, and Cassie smiled back somewhat tentatively.

"I know, you don't know me," Jennifer said, "but the way Jack talks about you I feel like I know you. How's your mouse? Jack said you named her T. J.? And how did you ever get my brother to dress up and wear a tie? He looks great. By the way, I was ordered to make sure you didn't get overwhelmed, but it appears you already are. So would you like to come find a seat with me or get a piece of cake? I'll tell you anything you want to know about Jack."

Cassie grinned, charmed with Jack's sister. "If I could get a refill on the punch and find a seat, I would love to chat with you."

She followed Jennifer, keeping a lookout for Jack's return.

"I hear you are a good firefighter."

Cassie leaned over to hear what Jennifer said, missing a few of the words but getting the heart of the question. "I used to be," she replied. "I got hurt a couple years ago so I'm pretty much on the bench doing paperwork now while I watch Jack do his job. He's pretty good."

"What happened? Jack's only given me the highlights. The doctor in me is intensely curious if you don't mind talking about it."

⎯⎯∞∞⎯⎯

Cassie was politely smiling. It startled Jack. She wasn't enjoying herself?

It mattered that Cassie enjoy tonight and he felt a sense of panic at the idea she wasn't. The ladies in the gathering had split off and were sitting on the two couches by the fireplace, Cassie sitting in the chair beside Jennifer. Cassie was politely smiling at his sister Lisa, glancing over at Jennifer as she spoke, her head turning back and forth as she followed the conversation.

He'd been able to stay close to her during the first hour of the gathering before the dynamics of the family had split them into groups. For the last hour he had been trying to work his way back to Cassie's side.

No one in his family would want to exclude Cassie, but if the conversation had drifted into issues of only family interest, they might have unintentionally done so. It had been hard to get Cassie to agree to come, and if it turned out to be a mistake…and then he realized the truth.

He'd seen that polite expression on her face before. The background Christmas music, the half dozen conversations going on in the open room…sound was bouncing. Cassie couldn't understand what was being said.

"I'll catch up with you later, Stephen." He broke off his conversation with his brother midsentence and headed over to intervene.

He was mad at himself for letting this happen. He hadn't warned Jennifer that Cassie would struggle with the noise level; therefore, Jen wouldn't know what to watch for. Cassie was so good at assuming adapting to a problematic situation was her issue and not that of her host. She was wrong. He was her host, and he'd just blown it.

He had wanted one thing more than any other—to give her a good Christmas. Instead he had just reinforced what was the most difficult part of her transition to accepting the limitations imposed by the accident—the feeling that she no longer easily fit in.

Jack maneuvered around the room, his grim look causing a couple conversations to stop as he strode past. He forced himself to shake off that intensity before he joined her. It wasn't Cassie's fault; it was his. Stopping behind her, he smiled over at Rachel and rested his hands lightly on Cassie's shoulders.

She started at his touch.

She looked up at him and he leaned down close to her left ear. "You can't understand a word of what's being said, can you?"

She couldn't hide the chagrin.

He searched her face, rubbing his thumb in small circles along her shoulder blades. She hadn't wanted to rock the boat. He wasn't sure what to do. He wanted to hug her but settled for reaching down and catching Cassie's hand in his. She rarely offered him her hand, as if the scarred skin made it less than perfect to hold. When he wanted to hold her hand he had to reach for it.

There were times someone needed to protect Cassie from herself, and this was one of them. Jack shot Jennifer a smile. "I'm tired of sharing." His remark drew a laugh from the group. He gently tugged Cassie to her feet. "We're heading out. Okay if I join you for breakfast?" he asked Jennifer.

His sister noted their entwined hands and smiled. "Please do."

Jack settled Cassie's coat around her shoulders. "You should have said something."

"It wasn't so bad at first; it just got confusing as the evening wore on."

She pushed her hands in her coat pockets as they walked down the hotel hallway. Jack didn't like the subdued, frankly exhausted impression he got from her. He tried to figure out how to say he was sorry for putting her in this position without making her feel worse. He didn't know the right words.

"You've got a wonderful family."

"I think so."

"Jennifer is a very special lady. You would never know she was ill from casually meeting her."

"She's normally a brunette."

Cassie gave him a small smile. "So she told me."

He pushed the button for the elevator to take them down.

She rubbed her eyes as she leaned against the wall, her slight frown marking her headache. "Did you see Jennifer's pictures of her puppy? The husky is adorable."

"She's in love with him," Jack agreed.

When they reached the lobby, he reached again for her hand. Her hand tensed in his and then relaxed, curling around his. The lobby was crowded with people flowing from the restaurant and a Christmas party going on in the lounge. He was relieved when they stepped outside and out of the noise.

Garland and Christmas lights were wrapped around the streetlight. The night was cold and clear. Cassie shivered with the impact and stamped her feet. She slid her hand into the crook of his arm to keep her balance on the slick pavement.

The silence during the drive told Jack a lot. Cassie's exhaustion was nearly as bad as what he had observed at Thanksgiving.

"I'm sorry you had to leave the family gathering. I didn't expect to have it affect me this way."

"This is not your fault."

She hesitated, started to say something, then stopped herself.

"What?"

"It's not your fault either." She sighed. "I couldn't hear Jennifer very well. Her voice was too soft...and I so wanted to."

He reached out his hand and waited for her to take it. When she finally did, he squeezed it gently and held on to it. "Give me time, Cassie. I didn't intend to put you in such a difficult position tonight. I just didn't think everything through."

"I did enjoy the party."

"My family loved you."

She gave a slight smile. "I envy you them."

He let the rest of the drive pass in silence. The apartment complex where she lived had been dressed up with Christmas lights on the entryway trees. It was at least a small reflection of the season. He parked near her building and came around the car to offer a hand.

He had one hope to redeem this day.

When she unlocked her apartment there was a gift-wrapped basket with a large bow set in the middle of the hall. Jack had arranged for her neighbor to bring the gift over after they left for the party.

Cassie bent down to pick up the basket. She looked at the contents and cast him a puzzled look. "Jack? This is from you?"

"Yes." And he was suddenly very nervous about this being the right gift.

"What do I need cat food for?"

He smiled at the wary tone in her voice and reached past her to turn on the other lights. "Go on through to the living room. Your neighbor helped me out."

There was a large box very carefully gift-wrapped waiting for her. He'd spent a week making the arrangements. "It's the last gift of the season. I promise."

Cassie pulled over the ottoman and lifted off the box lid.

The kitten was incredibly small, heather gray in color, asleep on a bed of monogrammed towels.

"She's not much bigger than your mouse so I don't think she'll be any threat to your other guest. Her name is Benji, B. J. for short."

Cassie reached in the box and the kitten woke to stretch. Cassie carefully picked her up.

"I brought everything you would need for her. Cassie—" he waited for her to look up at him—"don't feel like this is a gift you have to accept. You can borrow her for a couple weeks and then B. J. can move to my place." He smiled. "I don't even know if you're allergic to cats."

She nestled the kitten against her sweater. "I think I'll keep her for a while if you don't mind."

Her voice had gone so soft. Jack breathed a sigh of relief because he really gambled with choosing such a gift. Jennifer had been so overjoyed with her puppy. Cassie's apartment complex only allowed cats.

Cassie glanced up at him. "B. J.'s a good name."

"I thought so." He pointed to the box. "There are extra mono-grammed towels with her name on them and the equivalent of a cat bed and several play toys in the second box. The basket should have everything she'll need to eat for a few weeks. There's also more milk in the refrigerator."

"You thought of the details."

"I hope so."

He stepped close and ran a finger along the kitten's back.

He wanted to kiss Cassie good night. He pushed his hands into his pockets instead. "I'd better go so you can get some sleep."

She carefully got to her feet so as not to disturb the kitten.

"I will catch your other guest when I come over to help clean out the closet so we can start painting."

"I'll appreciate both." She looked up at him. "I love the kitten, Jack."

"I'm glad." Relieved was the better word. "Shift starts at 8 A.M. tomorrow. Do you want me to pick you up?"

"If you wouldn't mind. Christmas weekend and snow flurries—there will be a lot of calls."

"But hopefully no fires."

She looked down at the kitten and stroked a small ear. "I'll have to leave B. J."

"I have a feeling she'll sleep most of the time you are gone," he promised.

"Would you do me a favor and call me when you get home? The roads are slick."

It meant a great deal that she would ask. "I will."

"Oh…she's purring. I wish I had bought you a better gift."

He laughed. "Cassie—" He waited until she looked up. "You already gave me the Christmas gift I wanted." He ran a finger along her jawline, leaned down, and swiftly kissed her. "Good night, beautiful."

Someone needed to remind her she was supposed to sleep before she went on shift. Cassie curled her hand up under her cheek as she watched the kitten sleep on the second pillow.

Jack had her tied in knots. No one had kissed her since the accident, and that simple act still had her head spinning. Jack had caught her off guard.

She was in wonder over the fact he would like her that much. That he would consider the fire and its aftermath to be something he could look beyond.

Jesus, I'm in over my head. I don't want to hurt Jack's feelings. This feels awful. He doesn't know You. I've been hesitant at witnessing, but now I need to reach out and find a way to do so.

She reached over and ran her finger over the soft fur of the kitten.

She had faced a fire and been hurt. If she was going to get involved with a firefighter, she would only be able to handle it with someone she didn't have to worry about should the worst happen. *Lord, give me the strength to resist my feelings for him.*

If only Jack believed…

He'd overstepped. He knew it.

Jack tightened his grip on the steering wheel as he headed home. That kiss had been spur of the moment, and as soon as he had done it he knew he'd made a mistake.

The problem with rushing fences was he all too often knocked them over. Hadn't he learned the basics? She'd blinked at him, not exactly frowning but definitely not smiling, and he wisely left before she could react more than that.

The kiss was wonderful. It had just been badly timed.

Two strikes for the night. The noise, the kiss…he certainly hoped the kitten turned out to be considered as nice a gift in the morning as it was tonight or it was going to be three strikes all in one night.

This was not the Christmas weekend he had planned and hoped for.

Thirty-four

Cole balanced the paintbrush on the edge of the can and stepped down from the ladder to answer the doorbell. He was not going to get the living room done today if the interruptions continued, let alone his hope of also finishing the hallway. The phone had been ringing ever since he got home from church; now he had visitors.

The blackout paint had covered the spray paint but it had dried a chalky white. The quicker he got at least the first new coat of white on it, the better. Right now there wasn't a room on the first floor that wasn't in some state of chaos with furniture moved out of the way or recovered items packed in boxes waiting to go back on shelves.

Cole wanted his house back.

He picked up a towel and wiped at the paint splatters on his hands as he maneuvered around two sawhorses balancing long pieces of trim for the stairway to replace the damaged pieces. He unlocked his new back door.

"Rachel." He was stunned to see her. "Please, come in." He pushed open the door. She'd been over Friday with Jack and Cassie helping him sort out the mess. He hadn't expected her back today.

"I tried to call. Your phone was busy."

"It's been ringing ever since I got home from church."

"You're painting."

He tossed the towel on a box and gave a rueful look at his hands. "Yes."

It didn't look like she'd come over to help. She was dressed to the nines in a blue silk dress. She was absolutely lovely and if she was feeling tired or stressed it was not apparent in her looks. There wasn't a good place to have a conversation where she wouldn't get paint on her dress or snag it on something. So he leaned his shoulder against the wall, deciding where they stood in the hallway was probably the safest place. He was delighted to see her even if he wasn't sure why she had come over.

"I had breakfast with Jennifer and Jack."

"How is Jennifer?"

"Recovered from her fall. She's going back on a new round of chemotherapy after the first of the year."

"How is she handling it?"

"She says she's going to worry about it next year."

"Are you going to wait to worry about it too?"

Rachel gave him a small smile and didn't answer. Instead she looked around. "You're making good progress."

"You want to come shopping with me sometime this next week? The insurance guy took one look around and said it would be cheaper to replace versus repair. He handed me an early Christmas check."

"Can I replace the blue monstrosity you call a recliner?"

He enjoyed that glimmer of a smile she gave him. "Just because you got stuck in the chair and had to have help getting out…"

"It's not a very lady friendly chair."

"You're welcome to help me find another one." He waited a beat until it was clear he knew she was hesitating on saying more. "What's up, Rae?"

She reached into her large bag and drew out a square-wrapped package. "Merry Christmas, Cole."

He accepted it slowly, caught off guard. "Can I open it now?"

She bobbed her head.

Intrigued, he split the tape. "Your gift will be at your place in the morning by the way."

"Really?"

"You'll like it."

Rachel laughed at his confidence.

He had bought her new luggage. An expensive gift, but it had taken only a brief consideration of her job and schedule to known what she needed was something practical and pretty. He checked with her family to make sure he wouldn't be stepping on her independent streak. He'd been assured the gift would be well received. He'd know tomorrow if that were true.

Cole lifted the lid on the box. "Rachel."

"Cassie told me," she said quietly.

He slowly moved aside the tissue paper. "It has been a very long time since someone so surprised me." He lifted out an autographed baseball to replace the one that had been cut open. "Where did you—" He was at a loss of words to know how she had found the same autographed baseball.

"My dad would have liked yours. He followed the same team."

It was one of her few mementos from her own past. And as a gift it was incredibly generous. It was a family heirloom. "Are you sure?"

She smiled. "It's a baseball, Cole. It's important enough for me to hold on to for a lot of years, but I had it in a drawer. You obviously had yours out on a shelf to be enjoyed."

"I'm grateful."

"You're welcome."

"Listen—" he pointed to the kitchen—"would you like to join me? I'll make sure I find a safe place you can sit down."

"Another time. I'm heading over to go shopping with Jennifer."

He tried to bury the disappointment, understanding that higher priority. "Would you please wish her a Merry Christmas for me?"

"I will. I'll let you get back to painting."

"Rae—" he tossed the ball and caught it on the way down— "thanks."

—∽∾∽—

"We should have brought Jack to carry the packages," Rachel said rue-fully as she unloaded the department store sacks from the car trunk and prepared to carry them to her apartment. Snow swirled from the trunk lid inside. The wind cut through her wool coat and even with earmuffs, hat, and gloves she found the weather unbearable.

"I've never seen a man more delighted to be able to say he was working than Jack over breakfast when he heard our plans for the day," Jennifer agreed, picking up the shoe boxes and the sweater box.

Rachel wasn't so sure Jack was having a good day, not with holiday traffic, snowy roads, and this cold. She would be surprised if he got time to thaw out between dispatches.

Jennifer nudged the trunk closed. "This has been so much fun. I always love to shop with you."

"I notice it's primarily my wardrobe getting extended again."

"Cole will like the peach sweater."

"Jenny."

"Don't look at me like that. You were the one who had me up until 2 A.M. on the phone while you debated the implications of giving him that baseball."

"I still don't know if it was smart. He acted like I'd given away a priceless heirloom or something." Rachel shivered as she stepped inside the building and the warmth hit her. She held the door for Jennifer and then led the way upstairs.

"After having his place trashed, I suspect having the one item that would be the hardest to replace taken care of first meant a lot." Jennifer retrieved Rachel's keys and unlocked the apartment. "The door wreath is beautiful."

"Thanks. Gage gave it to me." It was a spectacular Christmas wreath with dried white rosebuds woven into the evergreen and a satin red ribbon wrapping it. "Toss the keys in the bowl," she suggested to Jennifer. Rachel maneuvered with her packages through the apartment as best she could without knocking items off the tables.

She had been in a rush this morning. She was able to make the bed, had pushed the dark green comforter up, but her numerous pillows were scattered, some on the bed and others on the floor. Two plastic storage tubs were pushed against the wall near the closet. She'd been exchanging her fall lightweight sweaters for the heavier sweaters for the winter.

Rachel lowered the packages onto the bed.

"How's Gage really doing? Last night he was being his charming self, but it was hard to tell how deep that calm extended."

"Gage is...well, let's put it this way. He's decided to pretend Christmas Day tomorrow doesn't exist on the calendar. It's a decent way to get through the day, I suppose."

Jennifer set her packages down on the floor beside the bed. "Worried about him?"

Ice crystals had formed on the inside of the windowpane. Rachel frowned when she saw it and knew she'd have to check the weather stripping again.

"I'll always be worried about him. But no, I think Gage turned the corner this last month. His grief has less anger in it." She tugged open the closet door and pushed clothes around, sorting through her closet to find empty hangers. "Did you hear Jack bought Cassie a kitten?"

Jennifer piled pillows against the headboard and sat down on the bed, leaning against them. "He told me he was going to. I think Jack likes her."

"Whatever gave you that idea?" Rachel shot her sister a grin as she opened the first box and folded back the tissue paper to retrieve the new amber blouse with pearl buttons. "The fact it's the first time he's ever brought someone to a Christmas family gathering?"

"He cheated and told her to come so I could meet her. I thought that was interesting. I liked her."

"So do I."

Jennifer picked up the book on the nightstand. "Rae, I thought you were going to do light reading for the holidays. *Causes of School Violence?*"

"I'm trying to get ready for the commission next year."

"I wish you had passed on that assignment."

"It's what I do for a living, Jennifer. Someone has to figure out a way to get around the problem. And you know quite well that I was chosen because I'm an unknown and can manage the volume of material so others can be the face of the committee."

"It's a lot of stress."

"Had I known last spring what my new year would be like I would have graciously declined, but I said yes. I gave my word. I have to do it." Rachel knew the concern for her was real, knew Cole would probably think the same thing as Jennifer if he learned what she had volunteered for. It was a prestigious assignment. She hoped she had the reserves to deal with the stress.

"If there is anything I can do to help, you'll ask?"

"Of course."

Jennifer looked over at Rachel. "Without being intrusive, how bad were the burns on Cassie's arms?"

"Severe. I don't think Jack cares," Rachel replied.

"She does."

"You noticed that too?"

Jennifer nodded. "It's more than vanity. She knows the subject often makes people uncomfortable." Jennifer tugged her wig. "She's got great empathy for my no-hair status."

"Jack gets protective around her."

"I thought it was cute."

Rachel started folding up the empty sacks. She'd cut tags off the new purchases later. "I thought I'd fix salad and soup for lunch."

"Sounds wonderful. Want help?"

"Without wanting to say no, at the moment the kitchen only has room for one. I'll call when it's ready."

"Fair enough." Jennifer tossed the pillow to the floor and stretched out. "How long of a nap did you promise Tom I would take?"

"Twenty minutes."

Jennifer looked at the clock on the bedside table. "Then wake me in twenty-one because I am not sleeping away my Christmas vacation."

"Deal. You still want to meet Kate and Lisa for Christmas Eve services?" Rachel was leery about going to church, but she knew it was a big deal for Jennifer and would go along for that reason.

"Absolutely. And Rae?"

"Hmm?"

"I'm going to beat this cancer. Believe it."

Rachel was stunned by the unexpected comment, and by the fact Jennifer had obviously clicked into the subject that had been just off center stage all day as they shopped. Rachel was chagrined at the realization that her agreement with Tom to keep an unintrusive eye on Jennifer had not been so subtle after all. "If optimism can affect it, you will."

"Prayer will," Jennifer said easily. "Wake me in twenty-one minutes."

"I'll do that," Rachel said quietly. She closed the bedroom door and leaned her head against it.

She wished she felt comfortable calling Cole. Jennifer had an assurance inside that she would be okay. Cole was pointing toward that same assurance, encouraging Rachel to reach out and grasp it too. She needed to have someone to talk with who would listen to what she was thinking and just be a sounding board.

She wanted so desperately to believe. She wiped at the tears. She had to talk to someone. Jack. He was a good sounding board, and he'd keep the conversation private. And better yet, he wouldn't try to convince her God's love existed. If anything he'd try to convince her she was wrong.

The reality she feared was Jennifer heading back into the hospital, and Rachel was going to need to find the strength to go along and help her. Not to do so...it wasn't an option.

A decision had to be made. She couldn't carry on like this much longer; the weight of what was going on was too heavy. How many people had she seen break under the weight of impending grief? Too many. She couldn't do that to her family. She had to be strong enough to get through this.

But her sister was dying...and Rachel was dying along with her.

Jack stretched out in Cole's spare office chair, trying to relax while he could because this shift had the markings of a hard one. They'd been out on four calls already. He tried to find a clear spot to set his soda, couldn't, and ended up setting it on the floor under his chair. The piles of file folders, books, and printouts had grown into mountains.

The map on the wall tracking the location of the arson fires was new. Jack studied it. There was no clear clockwise or counter-clockwise to the pattern. "He's going to do something over Christmas."

Cole used both hands to wrestle a file cabinet drawer back on track. "Very likely."

"Who's setting these fires?"

"Not you." Cole shoved the file cabinet drawer one last time, gave up, and propped his foot on it. "I don't know, Jack. It's the same answer as the last five times you landed in that chair to ask me."

"It wasn't Christmas weekend last time. I don't want my men hurt."

"Join the crowd."

"You've got to at least have some suspicions."

"Several."

"Names? Someone I know?"

"None you need to know about, and not when you're going on shift. I don't need you distracted, Jack."

"I'm trying to help here, Cole, and you're not making it easy."

"Live with it."

"I don't want Cassie rolling out with us today."

"Any particular reason?"

"I don't need her getting hurt on Christmas Eve," Jack replied, ready to argue the point.

Cole just held up his hand. "She'll ride with me today. I don't particularly want her in the middle of this either. Did you read that nursing home report I gave you?"

"Yes. I wish you would tell me what you're looking for."

"The words murderer, coward, liar. He's angry. And he's leaving popcorn with a flourish. The nursing home was the fire where popcorn became a calling card. There were other signatures he could have copied: the gas can and red bandanna for a fuse, padlocks on the doors. Why not the fireworks signature that made such a splash in the press last year? He chose popcorn for a reason."

"We've already looked at the people who died in the nursing home fire, their relatives."

"It's time to rethink it. Something is there."

"Ash disappeared," Jack said quietly.

Cole just nodded. "Has Cassie said anything about that fire?"

"No."

"She's a key to this, Jack. Just like you are."

Jack scowled. "I don't know why he's focused on me, this shift. I've racked my brains for names. Does Ben have any ideas?" Tones sounded. Jack pushed himself to his feet.

"Be careful."

"Always, boss."

There was new caulk around the sink in the fire station women's locker room. Cassie added her toothbrush to the blue spin rack, opened the cabinet, and found on the shelf below the towels an empty basket with her name on it nestled between others overflowing with shampoo bottles, makeup, cotton balls, and hair dryers. She tossed her toothpaste and hairbrush into her basket.

She had been on enough shifts she had finally decided to bring enough items to the station to effectively move in. She hadn't wanted to appear presumptuous about her position for she knew it was day to day based on how long it took for them to find the arsonist.

Living at a fire station wasn't all that different from her days living in a college dorm with the exception of a few unique realities—behind her, hung on a shower curtain rod, one of Margaret's uniform shirts dripped dry. It had been soaked to remove blood stains acquired while working at the car accident earlier that morning.

Cassie walked back into the women's dorm room. Bunks were made with precision; rugs covered the concrete floor. The room had been turned into more than just a place to sleep. There wasn't much privacy to be found at a fire station, but an effort had been made here to make it a place to relax. Two comfortable chairs had been moved in along with a small television. Bookshelves had been built along one wall. A desk had been squeezed in.

Cassie picked up the folded yellow T-shirt that had been waiting for her on her bunk. Jack had snuck in a gift. The shirt was one from last year's chili contest, boldly proclaiming Company 81's standing as the hottest company. The Post-it note simply said Jack. He'd begun the effort to shift her loyalty to Company 81.

It was trivial, but she thought it was his way to add something light to counter what had felt like an awkward parting. She had seen him only briefly today, and only long enough to casually pass a few general remarks. He was out on another dispatch.

It was another day where she was stuck at the station while Gold Shift rolled out numerous times to car accidents caused by the snowy day. She hated being stuck in the station.

Lord, is there anything different I could do to help find this man?

She could feel the tension that grew with every shift and the awareness that a fire would come. With the two holidays what was normally a festive time of the year was markedly different this year, almost grim. She was worried about Jack. But there were many other families equally being affected by the threat this arsonist presented.

They needed a different game plan. They had to be able to find him.

Cassie went to find Cole to see what she could do for the rest of the shift. If it was paperwork… She sighed at the idea. She was coming to be proficient at it, and she knew Cole was relying on her and giving her more and more to do. It was a love-hate relationship. When Jack was here at the station, being here to work on paperwork was a nice reason to be in his world. When Jack was out on a dispatch, she found herself watching the clock and paying close attention to anything over the dispatch radio.

Maybe if Cole didn't have anything really urgent for her to do, she could retreat to the kitchen and do some baking. The guys always relished having big, fresh cookies available. They had all the ingredients for Italian beef sandwiches that could be left in the Crock-Pot and kept hot for when the guys returned. It would be great to also get a soup started. The guys coming in and out of the station through the night would be cold and very likely hungry. A bite to eat and some desperately needed shut-eye would be high on their list of priorities.

"Got an extra one of those?"

Cassie looked up from the sandwiches she was cutting to see Ben had paused to lean around the kitchen door. "Sure, Lieutenant. Roast beef, mustard, and hot peppers? Heated?"

"Perfect. Cole around?"

"His office I think."

"Thanks. I'll be back in a few minutes."

Cassie fixed Ben a thick sandwich and turned to take out of the oven the pan of brownies she had left there to keep warm. She wasn't surprised to see Ben, even though it was only eight hours since he'd gone off duty. He'd been home, gotten some sleep, and come back to where he was needed most.

Ben rejoined her as she was peeling apples for a pie.

"Cole's a miracle worker. He may have found Chad a job."

Cassie slid Ben the sandwich. "Not the arson investigator slot he hoped for, but a community safety officer is a pretty good option." She'd helped Cole find a way to get it created. "Think Chad will accept?"

"He should. It's a good job, but will he?" Ben looked uncertain, and in the tightness around his mouth a touch of anger. "If he's ready to accept he won't be able to fight fires any more."

Cassie studied the older man, knowing how hard he'd been trying to help his nephew, understanding also how hard it would be for Chad to adjust to the disability. "He's depressed?"

The man's discomfort increased. "It's the holidays."

"Anything I can do?"

Ben shook his head as he wadded up his napkin. "You adjusted; he's got to do the same. It's time he faced reality and got back to work. Would you do me a favor and make two pies? Black Shift loves your baking."

"Glad to."

The phone rang. Ben motioned for her to stay put and got up to answer it. Cassie wondered if she should point out Chad had been making those steps back—the application to Cole, stopping by to see Cole. Chad was trying, but she knew the job offer that would have him talking about fires instead of fighting them would hurt. It would really hurt.

"Jack!"

He struggled to turn in the ditch where the blue sedan had flipped. He squinted against the blowing snow, holding up his hand to block the wind as best he could. Daylight was dwindling, vehicle headlights were becoming brighter in the fading light. Traffic was rushing by and throwing up dirty snow and ice creating a background of constant noise.

"No joy on the tow," Bruce shouted to be heard over the traffic. "Mark the car to be pulled out later."

Jack waved his hand acknowledging that he heard the message. He struggled to get the top pocket of his winter gear open. He took out a bright red fluorescent seal and unfolded it.

Christmas Eve was proving to be the day that would not end. Jack marked the wreck by putting the red seal on the shattered back window so patrolling cops would know the vehicle had been checked out. This car was trashed, but the driver had walked away once they had been able to get the door pulled open. He was on his way to the area hospital to be checked out as a precaution.

Jack struggled to work his way back up the slick incline. Snow had begun to fall midafternoon and already his boot tops were disappearing as he walked. It wasn't expected to let up for hours. Snow-packed treads, slick roads where salt melted the snow into mush, drivers hurrying to get home—as the temperature fell, the wind picked up, and as the snow got heavier the number of accidents grew exponentially. The spinouts and fender benders were coming faster than dispatch could take the calls.

He was cold and miserable, and the odds were good he was going to be cold and miserable for the next several hours. Jack slipped and jarred his wrist as he stopped the fall. He brushed snow off and tried to get it out of his glove.

Cole had arrived, his SUV parked behind Engine 81, red and blue lights flashing to warn traffic. His friend had come back to work shortly after 4 P.M. to help out Frank with command and control. Prioritizing scenes was crucial when bad weather hit.

He wished traffic would slow down to a moderate speed so they didn't have someone else end up in a ditch before they got done packing up from this one.

Cassie was standing near Cole's vehicle, bundled into winter gear. Jack wasn't thrilled with the idea of her being out in this to help Cole, but he was grateful to see her. The wind felt like blowing ice as he walked over to join her.

She wiped the snow off his face. "The shift is half over."

He leaned against her hand. "I volunteered to work part of tomorrow."

"I know. You'll survive."

He gave a weary smile. "Promise?"

"I brought you a hot roast beef sandwich and the biggest thermos of coffee the station had. They're in the engine cab."

"Bless you. I've forgotten what food was."

"Cole is sending me home at 10 P.M. He doesn't want me rolling out if we have a fire tonight."

Jack heard the unasked question of his role in that decision. "It's Christmas Eve. You need a chance to enjoy it."

"Protecting me, Jack?"

He hoped she would understand. "Trying to."

She squeezed his arm. "Be careful tonight."

"Guaranteed. Want to share my coffee?" The radio broadcast tones for another car accident. He scowled at it as he listened to the mile markers. It was about a mile north.

"Find a few seconds to eat the sandwich before dawn," Cassie sympathized.

"Did you put on hot peppers?" Jack asked, walking backward as he headed toward the engine to join the guys.

"Absolutely."

"Did you save me any of that cake you were baking?"

"I already set a big piece aside with your name on it."

"Enjoy Christmas Eve, Cassie."

"I will."

Cassie drove home very slowly when she left the station; the last thing she wanted to do was add another accident to what the guys already had to deal with. The radio was playing Christmas music with no commercials.

Her windshield wipers struggled to keep up with the falling snow obscuring the window. The car heater still blew cold air. She was glad to get home.

Jack had added bags of sand to her trunk in case she hit ice and spun out. The added weight helped. Plows had come through the apartment complex parking lot, piling the snow into large mountains. The parking lot had been cleared but the sidewalks had not yet been shoveled.

Lord, this is a strange night. I didn't expect to spend it alone.

She envied Jack the fact he was working tonight. He was making a lasting difference in people's lives. People died in car accidents, people were injured every day of the year. But when it happened on a major holiday—the memory of that holiday was destroyed for years to come. For everyone Jack was able to help tonight, someone escaped a painful memory for the future. *Jesus, please keep him safe tonight as he tries to keep others safe.* She hoped the new year brought some clarity to her own future. She desperately needed to find it.

Thirty-five

Jack considered thumping the snowblower with a wrench on the assumption that action would have as much success at fixing the thing as the last two hours of effort.

He was spending Christmas Day trying to fix it because he didn't want to shovel snow by hand. If he had started shoveling the snow by hand when he got home from the fire station, he would have been done by now. Instead he had yet to begin.

He'd finally gotten off work at 1 P.M. Jack wanted to get the snow cleared so he could go over to Cassie's and talk her into building a snowman or having a friendly snowball fight. He shifted on the carpet remnant he was using to block the cold from the concrete.

The door between the house and garage opened and Rachel came out to join him. She was bundled up in a ski suit that would make a professional skier jealous. Jack was willing to bet Jennifer had been behind that gift. Rachel often ended up working at natural disasters where cold and wet were part of her long days.

"Here. Warm up."

He accepted the hot chocolate. "Thanks. This garage is like ice." His hands were painfully cold even with the palm and half-finger gloves.

"Jack, Jennifer believes in Jesus. I think I finally understand why." Rachel perched herself on the bag of salt he planned to spread on the walk once it was cleared of snow.

"Hold it, Rachel. You walked in, said hi, and now we're talking about religion. Give me two seconds to shift gears."

"It's Christmas."

"And frankly I'm going to be very relieved when this holiday is over." He'd had his fill of snow, car accidents, and drunk drivers. Jack drained the hot chocolate. "Do we really have to talk about this now?"

"I went to church with Jennifer last night."

They *were* going to be talking about it now. "Okay…" He hadn't expected that but wasn't totally surprised by it, not if Jennifer had asked Rachel to go along.

"What if Jennifer is right?"

It sounded like instead of talking about Jennifer's puppy and plans for New Year's Eve, it was going to be the subject of religion. Jack rubbed his eyes, annoyed at the grime on his hands, and tried to give Rachel his full attention, knowing he was about to be left behind in the dust with this conversation. She didn't mean to talk over his head, but Rachel was comfortable talking in-depth about subjects like psychology and law. If she was now adding religion— He figured he could get in one statement that sounded intelligent before he got confused. "You think Jennifer might be right to believe Jesus is alive."

"Yes."

He picked up the wrench and considered stripping apart the carburetor. He had spent hours on this snowblower over Thanksgiving to avoid just this situation. He needed this thing to start. "Why? You've been the one saying for months that it didn't make sense."

"She's happy."

He was expecting a profound answer and instead she surprised him with a very simple one. "I could have told you that." He grimaced as the wrench slipped and he scraped his knuckles against the concrete.

"She's got cancer, her remission is officially over, and she's going to be fighting for every day of her future. In the face of that she's able to be happy. Even being married can't explain that joy."

"You're using an emotional argument to justify why she is right."

"Yes."

He shook his head, confused. Rachel was logical as well as empathetic with people, able to sort out what seemed like contradictory human behavior and shape it back into some order, but there were times he simply could not follow her reasoning. He looked at her and was surprised by the almost pleading expression.

"When you're dying, you can't easily lie to yourself. Jennifer's gut tells her Jesus loves her and has given her eternal life. The fact that the closer she gets to death, the stronger she believes tells me she's right."

Jack didn't feel it wise to point out the contradiction in her statement. She had just said Jennifer was in denial of the fact she was dying. Rachel wanted him to agree with her, and he couldn't do it, but neither could he discourage her. He'd missed that sound of hope in her voice. "What are you going to do?"

"Am I blowing smoke with that conclusion?"

"Sounds reasonable to me."

"Good. Because you need to read the Bible. Jennifer wants to talk to you."

"Rae—" he instinctively protested. He did not want to get into a discussion of religion with Jennifer. The last thing he wanted to do was disappoint her, and he would if they talked about that subject. She wanted him to believe too and he couldn't yet say that he did.

"Tough. You need to wrestle it to the ground. If I do choose to believe, that leaves only you and Stephen on the wrong side of the decision."

He glanced at her, hearing the line being drawn with a smile. "If you're right, everyone has to agree with you."

"About this, yes. I want company on this scary step."

Being told by his sister to read the Bible after being told by Cassie the same thing, he was willing to concede at least the fact he couldn't ignore making a decision any longer. "Is there a large print edition that I don't have to squint at, written in something better than Old King's English?" When she nodded, he sighed. "Get me a Bible for a Christmas gift, then I'll see what I think."

She beamed at him. "I already did. It's the package on your kitchen counter."

"Am I that predictable?"

"You hate to tell family no."

"I'll start working at it."

She laughed. He smiled at her, then looked back at the hunk of metal that was the bane of his existence. "Do you know how to fix a snowblower?"

"I'll kick it for you."

"Doesn't work." He finally grabbed hold of it, tipped it, and shook hard. A screw tumbled to the concrete floor. "Now I wonder where that was supposed to be?" He went back to searching.

He finally leaned over and pulled the cord. The snowblower started.

"It works." She said, surprised, smiling at him.

"Good, because you get to use it on the drive while I use the shovel on the steps."

It was snowing. Cassie hated winter as a rule, but on Christmas Day she made an exception. The snow was building up on the kitchen windowsill. The sun was out, and the reflection off the snow was so bright she had to narrow her eyes as she looked around. Long icicles hung in neat rows along the building gutters. The world outside looked new.

She had given herself the luxury of sleeping in until ten and fixing flavored coffee. The apartment was toasty as the building heat had shifted into its too hot mode. She was wearing sweats, but she could easily be in short sleeves and be comfortable.

"Come on, Benji." She picked up the kitten from the couch. B. J. had curled up on the new leather jacket Cole had given her for Christmas. It was gorgeous. She owed her friend a hug although he'd get embarrassed if she did it.

This was the day she had targeted as her turning point and she had woken in a good mood, was absolutely loving the day. There was no stress, no bookstore to worry about, or shift to go to. It was a day off and totally free. She hummed along with the Christmas music on the radio as she finished unpacking the gifts she brought home from the department party and set on the couch last night.

After all the painting and wallpapering was finished, she'd basically have a new apartment by the end of the week. The bookstore business through the month of December had been wonderful. She planned to catch up on paperwork tomorrow and do the final budget planning for next year. The owner of the bike shop was talking again about moving to a larger store, and that put the option of expanding the bookstore back on the table. She was excited about that possibility.

Jack should be home from his shift by now. She would call him and wish him Merry Christmas, but she was afraid she might wake him up from a much-needed couple hours of sleep. The wind had tapered off around midnight and the brunt of the storm had skirted north. She hoped Jack had an easier end to his shift.

She put Benji down on a pillow she pulled to the center of the bed. The kitten loved to play and equally loved to sleep. As a gift Jack couldn't have found a better one.

Cassie looked around her bedroom. Everything short of the walk-in closet had now been Jack's definition of spring cleaned. She had toyed with the idea of starting the painting on her own, but then decided for simplicity's sake to wait for Jack.

She stepped over the vacuum cleaner and went back to work on the windows. She'd been finishing up the cleaning. When this was done, she was going to look at baking some cookies. Jack hadn't said whom he had recruited as help, but knowing the odds, she figured planning to feed them would be a good idea. She reached to clean the top of the windowpane.

A snowball splattered against the window. Startled, she took two steps backward and then warily returned to the window to see the source. Jack stood on the curb looking up at her window, his hands on his hips. She cracked open the window and shivered at the cold.

"Can Cassie come out and play?"

"You're crazy, you know that?"

"Gloves, woman, and get yourself down here."

"Hold on." With a laugh she closed the window.

She opened her closet, got out her long blue coat, hat, and black gloves, then went to join Jack.

Jack had a girlfriend. He drank hot coffee as he watched the two of them struggle to roll a growing snowball across the hilly ground. They were having a good Christmas. At least someone was. He'd listened to a near suicide threat; the holidays doing what time had not, nearly causing another casualty in his family. Popcorn fell on the car floorboard. He shook the box to spread out the butter better. He was getting tired of it all.

The snowman grew. Acquired eyes and a nose.

Cassie tumbled back in a snowdrift and made a snow angel as Jack stood watching and laughing.

The pressure had to increase and this was the most vulnerable point. He sighed. No one had found his last message, his most elegant message. It was frustrating as he had worked hard at it. But this situation…it had possibilities.

They went in and the lights soon came on in her apartment.

He stepped out of the car to check out the snowman.

Jack stretched out on his back on the living room floor, exhausted but happy. Benji, sitting on his chest, made a tentative swipe with her front paw at the pretzel stick Jack twirled in front of her. The kitten pounced and butted his chin. Jack laughed softly because the fur tickled, and the kitten tumbled, an earthquake rumbling beneath her. Jack nudged Benji back to the center of his chest to prevent her tumbling off.

Jack rubbed his cheek with the back of his hand. Just before they came in Cassie had hit him square in the face with a snowball. He had frozen feet, cold hands, and a wet shirt. And he was happy.

"Cassie, did you get lost?"

"I'm drying out."

"Bring me another towel when you come. I'm melting all over your carpet here."

She reappeared in the doorway, and the towel lobbed his direction caught him upside the head.

"Thanks." She sat on the floor beside him and dropped a monogrammed towel for Benji beside the kitten. "B. J. still has a milk mustache."

"She's getting better at it. At least she didn't tip the bowl this time."

Cassie was towel drying her own hair. She'd made a snow angel and come up looking frosted afterward.

She changed into a gray short sleeve shirt. She'd never done that before with him. Jack noticed it immediately. The burns that scarred her forearms curled back around her forearms to behind her elbows. Her upper right arm muscles looked deformed by the results of the fire, contracted and withered.

A glance at her face told him she knew he had noticed. He didn't say anything, but he did relax. She'd trusted him. That meant a lot. She was also wearing his pendant. And that meant even more.

He carefully started drying off Benji's milk mustache.

"Thank you for her." She reached over to stroke the kitten.

Jack caught her hand, turned it, and kissed the back of her hand where the scars marred her skin.

Startled, her hand curled. "Why did you do that?"

"To kiss it better," he said matter-of-factly. "You hide your hands. Now you don't have to."

"Jack—"

He quirked an eyebrow when she struggled with words. She finally just offered a smile to him. He smiled back and turned his attention to the kitten, now trying to eat a button on his shirt pocket.

"Who do you think is going to be his next target?"

"Our firebug?"

Cassie nodded.

"So far he's gone after the fire board, the arson group, and the fire department. It's pretty obvious he's trying to get us to react, so take your pick at what he strikes at next."

"Cole thinks it's a firefighter."

Jack nodded. It was depressing but given the situation probably accurate. "Do you think it's someone from the old Company 65?"

"No."

"It's no one in Company 81."

"It can't be someone we know," Cassie agreed. She hesitated, and then added, "I'm worried about the next fire."

He heard an undercurrent of something deeper under that general comment. "You're worried about my getting hurt."

She nodded.

"It's a possibility for any firefighter." He reached over and gently traced the scar that ran from the back of her hand across her wrist. "Would you have not gone into the nursing home had you known this would happen?"

"I would have gone in."

"Don't borrow trouble, Cassie. If something happens, we'll deal with it. Until then worry is wasted emotion."

"You're not going to take Ben up on his suggestion that you and he change shifts, Black and Gold, and find out if it's you or Gold Shift itself?"

Jack shook his head. "I would be leaving Nate and Bruce and the guys. I can't do that to them if it's Gold Shift who's the target."

The mood was becoming way too serious, the laughter of the afternoon replaced with a more somber mood. She'd had one Christmas wish, and he was unable to help fulfill it. "I'm sorry you are not able to spend Christmas with Ash."

"So am I. I think something happened to him. I can't imagine him not being here for Christmas if he could."

"Again, please don't borrow trouble."

"He isn't a man to abandon me like this."

"It took you the better part of two years to reach acceptance of what happened. Ash held on to his anger for much longer than you did. He needs the time. Let him have it."

"He felt responsible for what happened."

"That's his right," Jack cautioned her, understanding why Ash would have reacted the way he had.

"I just wish I knew where he was spending this day."

Jack needed to shake her out of this growing melancholy. "Do you want to try and find your mouse tonight?"

"Are you up to it?"

He smiled at her doubt. "I think I can find the energy if you can."

"I tried to sort through some of the boxes, but I found the closet has been used as the place to store everything I didn't want to unpack in the last move so it's a bit chaotic." Cassie stood and offered Jack a hand to pull him to his feet.

Jack set Benji in the small box that had become her bed.

Cassie turned on the lights in the bedroom, opened the closet doors, and turned on the lights in the walk-in closet. "Where do you want to start?"

"I'll hand out the boxes if you want to stack them in the hall."

"There's no room in the hall. What if we stack them between the dresser and the bookcase in here?"

Jack was doubtful that they would fit, but it would mean she had to carry them a shorter distance. "We can try it."

He moved aside the hanging clothes. If he worked clockwise around the closet... "This mouse is white."

"Yes."

"You're sure it lives in here?"

"I've seen it three times."

Had he known there were this many boxes he would have suggested it another night. Maybe if he got them at least shifted away from the walls so the mouse wouldn't have a place to hide... Jack picked up the first box, deciding to first clear out enough space so he could turn around. He made sure Cassie had both her arms under the box and that the heavier part of the box was toward her left arm before he released it.

As he started to move clothes around on the rods to reach boxes below them, he realized she had been wearing only a fraction of her wardrobe since Thanksgiving. It was past time to take her out to a nice dinner. "This box has broken tape on the bottom."

She took it gingerly. "Got it."

"Jennifer wants to talk about religion." Cassie had trusted him; he was going to return the favor. Frankly he needed some advice.

Cassie bobbled the box. "Does she?"

"Where am I supposed to start reading the Bible?"

"Jack, we jumped from a mouse to a discussion about Jesus. Did I miss something?"

He shot her a smile. "I am so glad similar shifts in conversation levels confuse you in the same way it does me. Every time Rachel does it I get lost."

She looked relieved at that. She carefully set down the box atop others. "You want me to tell you where to start reading the Bible."

"It's a thick book."

"Actually, it's sixty-six books put together into one book."

She laughed at his look.

"You've read them all," he guessed.

"Yes, although I admit some of them are easier to read than others. What exactly does Jennifer want to talk about?"

"Jesus."

"Try opening the Bible to the middle, then open the section to the right in the middle again. That will probably put you in the book of Luke or John. Those books are basically biographies of Jesus' life."

"I don't suppose there are CliffsNotes?" he asked, hopeful. He glanced over at her. She was doing her best not to laugh. "I didn't think so."

"Jack, it's not a hard book to figure out. Read it with common sense. When does she want to talk about it?"

"She's heading to Johns Hopkins on January 3 to start the next round of chemotherapy. Sometime before then, I imagine."

"Start with the book of Luke. It's practical. I like it."

"Jen's going to tangle me in word knots like Rachel does."

"Not intentionally," Cassie offered sympathetically.

"They never do it intentionally," Jack countered. He pushed aside shoe boxes, looking to see if any had corners chewed out. He was reaching the last wall of boxes and so far there had been no sign of her uninvited guest.

"What are we going to do for New Year's Eve?"

Jack liked the assumption of we. "Besides cut drunks out of car wrecks?" he asked, remembering last year.

"True. Besides that."

"I'm not big into late night parties."

"Do you want to bring over a movie? We could invite Cole, Rachel, make pizzas."

"Sure, we could do that."

"Your family wouldn't mind?"

"Nothing formal is planned. We're scattering to different parties this year." Jack picked up the next box. "Be careful with this one. I feel something sharp on the right side." He was getting down to the last of the boxes. "I don't think your mouse was home tonight."

"Or he's inside one of these boxes," Cassie offered, worried.

Jack tipped forward the next to last box labeled books. "Get him!"

Cassie scrambled toward the scurrying mouse that darted into the room and headed toward the dresser, trying to cut the mouse off. She was too late. "It's a her," she corrected, using her foot to block the path the mouse had used.

Jack sat on the carpet in the now almost empty walk-in closet and rested his arms across his upraised knees. "She just went behind the boxes we just moved."

"I'm afraid so." Cassie looked at him and she couldn't stop the giggles.

"It's not funny."

"Yes, it is."

She walked over to the closet doorway and leaned against the door frame. "You got beaten by a mouse."

He tossed a wadded up sock at her.

"I could go get Benji and let her try," Cassie offered.

"As you're the one who has to sleep in a room with a mouse, I wouldn't laugh too hard. Do you have some cheese? We can at least try to lure it out of the bedroom."

Cassie pushed her hands deeper into her pockets as she stood on the curb and watched Jack scrape the frosted windows of his car. He had declined to let her help. "Would you call me when you get home?"

"Of course."

"I don't mean to imply you're a bad driver."

Jack laughed. "Just that everyone else is."

"Exactly."

He opened the passenger door and tossed the windshield scraper onto the floorboard. "I had a good Christmas, Cassie."

"So did I."

"I see someone has added a hat to our snowman."

She looked toward the playground. A baseball cap had been pushed down on the snowy white head with a carrot nose and charcoal brick eyes. "He looks dashing." A gust of wind blew snow from the overhang. She shivered and wrapped her arms tighter around her waist. "I'm going to head in before I freeze."

Jack grinned at her. "Good idea, you're turning blue. I'll call."

"Thanks." She hurried back up the walkway.

A car door slammed to her right and she glanced over. Her feet went out from under her and she fell hard on the sidewalk. "Ash."

Thirty-six

She heard someone rushing up the walkway, then realized Jack had seen her fall. Her attention was focused solely on the man standing by an old Plymouth. There was no mistake about who he was. Ash was a ghost of the man she remembered—thinner, a suggestion of hesitancy where there had once been obvious confidence—but he was really here. "Ash."

He started walking toward her, pushing his hands into his pockets. "Hello, Cassie."

Rather than help her up, Jack stood between the two of them. Cassie grabbed the edge of his coat, using the hold to get leverage to sit up. "It's okay, Jack. The man I saw at the fire was not Ash," she murmured, understanding Jack's instinctive move. Ash had grown a beard; his clothes were flannel and denim and his leather jacket looked beat-up.

She caught Jack's hand and forced him to give her his attention. He reached down and helped her up.

"I would have been here earlier but the snowstorm slowed me down. I wanted to spend Christmas with you," Ash said quietly, stopping a few feet away. "Hello, Jack."

"Ash."

Cassie felt like she was dreaming. He was really here. The prayer she had prayed for months had been answered. She hadn't been expecting it and that made her feel ashamed for doubting. "Please, come in," Cassie urged. Months that Ash had been gone...she wanted to know all the details. And she was nervous about those answers. Her hand around Jack's tightened painfully, hoping he'd offer to stay without her needing to ask him.

Jack didn't even give her a choice about it. He took the keys from her and settled his arm around her shoulders, putting himself between Ash and Cassie. "Were you driving into this storm?"

"Skirting along its edge. I was in St. Louis yesterday coming up from the gulf."

"You do look like you've got a bit of a tan," Cassie offered, getting her first good look at her partner in the light from the front door. He'd aged. The man she admired and trusted and followed without question into a fire was different tonight than the man she remembered.

"I was out chasing a sunburn again."

He looked different, but he was starting to sound the same.

Upstairs, Jack unlocked the apartment door and returned her keys.

"You're moving?" Ash asked, on seeing the boxes.

"Cleaning house," Cassie replied, shooting Jack an amused glance.

"You're a brave man. I helped her move in originally," Ash commented to Jack.

Cassie started to slip off her coat and Jack stopped her. His hands on her shoulders tightened and he leaned down. "Go change into something with long sleeves," he whispered.

She shot him a look, saw the sympathy, and understood. "Keep Ash company?"

"I'll host."

Cassie went to the bedroom before she slipped off her coat. She changed, choosing her best sweater, a soft pink cashmere. On their first meeting Ash didn't need to encounter her most vivid scars from the accident. She was relieved Jack had caught her attention before she slipped off the coat. She ran a brush through her hair and went to rejoin them.

The two men were standing by the patio door. Their conversation was pitched too low for her to hear.

Jack turned when he heard her come back in. She smiled as she saw he was holding Benji. He walked over to join her. "I'll leave and let you two have a chance to talk," he said softly. He handed her the kitten.

"Jack." She didn't want him to leave.

He hugged her. "Listen to him, honey," he whispered. "Then call me."

He wasn't giving her a choice; he was pulling on his coat. "I'll call." She reluctantly walked him to the door and locked it behind him.

Ash hadn't moved from his place beside the patio door. "Jack gave me the kitten for Christmas," she commented as she set B. J. down on her towel, suddenly nervous as she didn't know what to say.

"I won't stay long."

"Ash—I've been hoping so long to have you back, but now that you're here, I don't know what to say." She sat on the couch and gestured to the chair. "Why didn't you tell me you were leaving? Where have you been? Why didn't you call? Oh, it's good to see you."

"Cassie." He waited for her to run down. "I got a call from an investigator looking into a fire in Tallahassee. It fit the pattern of the fire we had here, so I decided to go check it out."

"That abruptly? You couldn't tell me you were leaving?"

"I was tired of pacing, of being able to do nothing. I didn't mean to abandon you; I just felt like until I could find something out, I had nothing left to offer you. And I wanted out. I'm not proud of it, but that was where my head was at."

Cassie wished he understood how much he had been doing just by being there for her. She heard so much lingering pain in his voice. "The accident wasn't your fault. And the man who set the nursing home fire died in a car accident in New Jersey."

"I heard about his accident."

"But you still didn't come back."

"It's taken the last couple months to decide if I wanted to have a firefighter's life again."

"What changed your mind?"

He gave her a small smile. "The memory of your determination to get to this day and have your new beginning. I decided I needed one too."

"I'm glad." She leaned her head back against the couch. "I don't think you've changed, Ash. You're still stubborn, impatient. And you would have gotten answers faster had you stayed here instead of taking off on your own."

He smiled at her. "You look well, Cassie." The subject changed abruptly. "What's been going on here that I missed? Besides Jack getting his act together."

The reference to Jack made her smile; the other question really disturbed her. "There's been some fires."

"Arson fires?"

She nodded. She got up and from her desk sorted around to find the file where she had collected the newspaper accounts. She handed him the file but didn't immediately release it. She swallowed hard, feeling incredibly guilty. "I thought I saw you at the scene of the Wallis fire."

He stilled. "Did you? Why?"

Water was dripping. Jack listened hard to the quiet in his house, trying to decide if the sound was coming from inside or outside. It sounded like it was coming from the bathroom. He was going to have to replace the seal on the sink.

Jack shifted around and grabbed one of the extra pillows on the bed beside him and tossed it at the open door to push it closed and block out the sound. In the middle of the night small, unnoticed sounds from the day grew loud and annoying. Water dripping was one of the worst.

He turned the page of the Bible, wondering why they made the pages so incredibly thin. The words might be large type, but it was still a bit like reading a newspaper with its two-column format.

Come on, Cassie, call. He was struggling to stay awake.

Ash was back.

The shock of that was still settling in. Jack had a feeling his life had just gotten more complicated.

Ash felt like part of this. In the same way Cole was part of it, as Jack himself was. Ash was one of those people connected to the department that had this arsonist's attention. Someone, something had triggered the arsonist to start to act. And while it might be coincidence, the calendar said Ash had disappeared; then the fires had begun. Now Ash had reappeared—it was going to create a reaction. That was what Jack uneasily sensed in his gut. Why had the fires begun after Ash disappeared? What had that triggered? And what would happen now that he was back?

Jack was glad Cole was involved to help sort out those questions. They were agonizing ones, and not something that could be talked about with Cassie. She would try to protect her partner. Jack wanted to protect her. And he was afraid their two goals might collide.

He fingered the page of the book, considered closing it, but accepted he couldn't duck this issue as easily as he could the other. Jennifer wanted him to consider this, and Cassie… Religion certainly mattered to her.

He had to find a middle ground on this that showed he respected their position without offending them. He adjusted the bedside light and turned his attention back to what he had been reading for the last two hours. He wasn't calling it a night until he heard from Cassie. And if he didn't hear from her in the next half hour, he was going to call her.

Who was Jesus Christ? This should not be so hard to figure out. Jack ran his hand through his hair, frustrated with how difficult it was to make sense of the book of Luke.

Before reading the book Jack would have said Jesus was a man who was a good teacher who had ended up being martyred, and His followers were so impassioned about what He had taught they insisted He rose from the dead so they could claim they followed someone living rather than dead. It was a rather brutal opinion but common sense said claims of a resurrection had to be a myth.

Luke presented something so much more complex. Jack got hit in the first pages of the book with talk of the angel Gabriel, of how the virgin birth came about. Long sections of Luke dealt with Jesus healing the sick. There were references to Jesus knowing men's thoughts. His teaching was blunt and searing to the heart of the matter. He was called a King, the Son of God. He claimed to be able to forgive sins. It was already an incredible statement of the man before Jack ever reached the chapter that described the Resurrection.

To swallow any part of this, he just about had to swallow the whole. But to reject it because the Resurrection was implausible would do a serious disservice to the whole thing presented. There was so much here. It was a massive package.

Jack was annoyed Jennifer and Rachel had simplified things in the past when they talked about it. It was easier to see a big, deep picture and possibly accept the Resurrection as part of it than to support it as a single stand-alone event. Was this why Jennifer and the other O'Malleys believed? Because of the whole?

The phone rang. Jack glanced at the clock and reached for the phone. "Cassie, I was getting worried about you. It's almost 1 A.M." He shifted the phone to his other side and bunched the comforter as a pillow, closing the Bible he had been reading. "How did it go?"

She didn't say anything. "Cassie?"

"I wish you were here so I could get a hug."

"Honey, go get some Kleenex."

She went away and eventually came back. "Sorry. It was just so good to see him. I'm happy. I cry when I'm happy."

Jack gamely accepted that because he had no choice. "Okay. That's good to know."

She laughed around the tears. "Ash is going to come by the station this week and nag Cole into letting him come back to work."

"I'll enjoy having a chance to talk with him. Cole was relieved when I called to let him know Ash had returned; he'll be eager to talk with him too." Jack was relieved to hear her quieting down. He wanted desperately to change the subject. "I was reading the book of Luke tonight," he offered, hoping to divert her.

"Really?"

There was hope in that one word and he was glad he raised it. "Cassie, is Jesus alive?"

"Yes."

"How do you know for sure?"

She hesitated.

"Tell me."

"In the dark days after the fire, Jack, Jesus understood all of it. The nightmares of being trapped in the fire, the pain, the despair. I could talk to Him and read His Word, and it was talking to someone who was there. He was always there. He answered me in so many profound ways, through events, through people, through His Word. He heard me."

Jack closed his eyes as she spoke. The man she called Jesus had been there to comfort when no one else could. No wonder Jennifer believed if that was what she had also found in the midst of the cancer.

"Do you want to come to church with me next Sunday?" Cassie offered. "Pastor Luke explains things so much better than I do."

"Maybe." He heard a beep on the line. His frustration was immediate. "Hold on, Cassie, I've got a call coming in." He accepted the call. "This is Jack."

"It's Ash. What's Cole's number? I've got a problem at my place."

"Something happen?"

"Does popcorn mean anything to you?"

"I'm on my way."

"No. I've got cobwebs growing on the message. Cole can handle it. If you come, Cassie will hear and have to come. It's not the way I want her ending her Christmas."

"Then I'll call Cole for you."

"I'd appreciate it."

Ash hung up. Jack warned Cassie he would be a minute coming back; then he called Cole, wondering what the message was that Ash had received.

—∞∞—

"This is quite a welcome home, Ash." Cole shone his light on the living room wall revealing a huge mural of a fire. No wonder the arsonist liked big, sweeping letters. He liked to paint murals. It had been here a while for there were cobwebs in the corners of the room.

This had taken several hours if not days to create. Cole walked back into the hallway near the front door where the painting began. He crouched down to study it. There was amateur skill in it and a good understanding for how fire began. The painting began low, just above the floor, as black smoldering impressions. As he walked down the hall it slowly rose on the wall. There was a flash as flames briefly flared for the first time and then it fell back to a steady burn and slowly grew.

Cole traced his light up as the fire moved from the floor to the ceiling. The ceiling fire then dropped burning embers to the floor. There was an incredible burst of fire as the room was shown to reach the flash point. "Any spray paint cans?"

"Not that I've found. Who paints murals?"

"A young man who likes elegant graffiti." Cole replied. It had to be a young man who knew all about fire. This was too accurate for how a fire moved and breathed to be chance. Cole stood back, looking overall at the problem. Ash's home had not been trashed, and that was interesting. "How did he get in?"

"Someone scratched the back door lock."

"That was Cassie breaking in. She lost her key."

"Then no, I don't have any idea."

Cole frowned. After he painted the arsonist had taken the time to move the furniture back to their original spots, had taken the time to rehang pictures. And Cole found it interesting that he didn't see any picture out of order. Why the arsonist had hit him, it made sense. He was part of the district leadership. But Ash—this had been painted when there was no idea when or if Ash might return.

"Did you stay in touch with anyone here? Did you call someone? E-mail anybody?"

"I was planning to leave it all behind and permanently end any idea of being involved with a fire department. I didn't call or write anyone. I came back simply to see Cassie for Christmas."

"I'm tempted to give you a headache for giving Cassie cause to worry about you."

"Let's not and say you did. I didn't hurt her intentionally."

Cole looked at his friend, having understood more than Ash probably realized. "There is a reason they call those nightmares you were having flashbacks."

"They stopped about four weeks ago."

"Admit it, you've been bored without the firefighter job."

"If you think I was safety picky before, you haven't seen anything yet."

Cole nodded and made an offer he'd been hoping he would one day have the opportunity to make. "Frank and I have the budget in shape to increase the training funds. If the board gives us the final approval at their next meeting, we're going to need someone to run it."

"Cole—"

"I want you back on rotation, and I want you teaching at the academy. It's time to get back in the game and help me out."

"I suppose I owe you one."

It was a grudging admission, but Cole would take it. "In a month you'll tell me you love it."

"Rookies? Please. I've done too much training through the years. I know the reality. It's like corralling a bunch of show-offs." Ash stopped by the entryway to his office. "At least he left this room alone."

"He called you chicken in the e-mail message he sent you."

"I wish he'd had the courage to call me that to my face." Ash walked around the room to see if anything else had been touched. "Cassie said you think this is a firefighter."

Cole leaned against the doorjamb, watching Ash prowl around the room. "He's setting fires within the walls using small flowerpots."

Ash stopped, then turned on his heel. "My signature?"

Cole nodded. He knew it would get a rise and he watched, interested in knowing exactly what that reaction would be.

Ash looked grim. "One of my students."

Cole understood the emotion clouding Ash's voice. The idea this was a firefighter bit hard, and the realization it was someone they might have worked with was hard to swallow. "I don't know if borrowing the signature is another way to turn the knife, like he's doing using the popcorn and setting fires at the edge of the district, or because he knows it's the best way to start fires in the wall."

"More than one rookie has washed out because they failed the training."

Cole nodded.

"Getting my address would be easy to do."

Cole let Ash think, hoping he would be able to put a name to the details.

"What's the base he's using?"

"Tar," Cole replied.

From the front of the house came the sound of car doors slamming. Cole walked back to the foyer and turned on the outside light. His friend Joe, the police investigator who had worked the vandalism and garbage fire at his place, was coming up the drive.

Cole held open the door for the man. "Sorry for interrupting your Christmas."

Joe stopped long enough to stamp snow off his feet before coming into the house. "Don't worry about it."

Cole gestured to the living room. The investigator stopped at the door to the room and whistled.

"Tell me about it," Cole agreed.

"No fire at all with this one?"

"None." Cole was worried about that. It was a change in MO and any change was a sign of possible coming trouble.

"I'll pull the same team that worked your place as they'll have a better sense of what to search for. This is going to take a while. Give me a couple days."

"It would help if there was a way to figure out the brand of paint. He's gone through a lot of it recently."

"I'll see what I can do."

"I appreciate it. Come on, Ash, you can spend the night at my place," Cole offered. "I just got the spare bedroom put back together. You and I need to talk."

"I'll take you up on that."

Thirty-seven

I t can't be Charlie. He's older than the man I saw." Cassie tossed the blue folder into the eight-inch-high cardboard box collecting files of people they had ruled out. She tried to shift around in her chair and nearly kicked over her drink sitting on the floor by the box.

"How many people did you train over the years, Ash?" Beside her on the table was a sliding stack of files to go through, and every hour more of them came from the records archive. Since she had seen the man they thought had started the fire, she was given the job of going through the files first. If she could absolutely rule out the person, it meant one less file for Ash to deal with.

Ash lowered his feet from the corner of Cole's desk so Cole could get back to his chair. "About three hundred, give or take how many you count from the year I was an assistant at the training academy."

Cassie knew he had done a lot of training. Like most firefighters he had a specialty within the district, and his happened to be structure fires. She had not known the extent to which he had trained over the years.

Ash was paging through a roster for a class six years ago. Learning who Cole suspected, Ash had dug out the class material and old rosters from a box in his attic. "Cole, do you remember a Larry Burcell?"

"He's working with the forest service in Montana."

"That's a guy I could see setting a fire."

"Ash, you've gotten cynical in your travels," Cassie protested.

Cole laughed. "You're just now learning your partner was a closet cynic? Where have you been all these years?"

Ash laughed. "It's called loyalty, Cole. I inspire more of it than you. Cassie still thinks I walk on water."

"The muck is getting deep in here." Cole picked up one of the files Ash had quietly passed him to review. The two men were bantering back and forth as they worked, while underneath it was very serious business.

Cassie was feeling a little out of her depth. She and Ash had been partners; they had worked for Cole. And while Cole had been her friend as well as her boss, she had not realized the extent of the friendship between him and Ash. She was hearing for the first time about a shared history.

"Cassie, where's that list you put together of businesses that sell tar?"

She shot Cole an annoyed look at the idea of having to find it. What she knew for sure was that it was buried. Cole just laughed at her look.

Trying to avoid the whole stack of files spilling across the floor, she moved the stack of files from her lap to the floor. The last time she had seen that list it had been somewhere on the round table with notes scrawled by Cole and three Post-its marking corrections. "You could print another copy."

"That's work."

She started searching. "Here's the phone list of attorneys you lost last week." She checked the portfolio and found the page of the minutes from the budget meeting. She scanned a list of restaurant take-out order phone numbers. Cole had to eat better than this. She finally found the printout he requested and passed it over to Cole. "I was able to eliminate a few of them as being irrelevant to what you were looking for."

"Do you remember any of these being art, supply-type companies?"

"Spray paint can be bought at a hardware store as easily as an art supply store."

"The guy has to have a job somewhere. We know he likes art."

"He's an amateur," Ash pointed out. "I would suggest you try frame shops or the like."

Cassie sorted through the files, trying to figure out if there was some way to get them in roughly chronological order for the age of the individual. Jack had been doing that for her, but he disappeared about twenty minutes ago to return a phone call. "I think Jack has gotten lost." She appreciated the help even if Jack had been driving her crazy this morning with his teasing.

"I asked him to see if the conference room schedule could be moved around so we could take all this stuff down there," Cole replied.

"It is a little much for your office," Cassie agreed.

Ash handed Cole another file of a possible suspect. "I still think the words should tell us something," Ash commented, going back to a conversation they had had several times over the course of the day. "Doesn't calling you a liar imply you made a promise to someone?"

"Calling you a chicken probably implies someone ran into your cautious safety streak."

"I want to know how he got my e-mail address."

Cassie reached down to the red milk crate beside her holding temporary file dividers. She found last year's training course catalog that was mailed to all departments in the surrounding counties. She flipped through it, spotted what she remembered on the back of the catalog, and tossed it in Ash's lap. "That's how."

"My picture too? Man, I look like some fugitive from the seventies."

"You still do."

"Ooh...cruel, Cassie. You wound me."

"If you're coming back on shift you have to get a haircut," she pointed out. She reached to the floor into the bag of chips she had carried back from lunch. Startled, she jerked her hand back up, then looked down. "Jack!"

Cole and Ash broke up laughing.

She very gingerly picked up J. J., the traveling mouse.

Thirty-eight

J ack, where are the new curtain rods for the window in Cassie's bathroom?" Rachel asked, coming into the kitchen where Jack was working. He glanced back at her. It was Thursday, and he had recruited most of his family to help with the painting and wallpapering so it could be done in one long day.

"I set them inside the hallway closet so they wouldn't get tripped over." He shifted his paintbrush to his left hand and reached for a rag to wipe paint off the countertop where a break in the masking tape had let paint touch the caulking. "Leave them for me. I don't trust you to get the braces tight enough."

"Didn't I hang all the curtains in my apartment?"

"Didn't I fix all of them?" he countered, smiling.

"Fine." Rachel looked around. "Stephen, I need curtain rods hung. The wallpaper is finished."

"Hey—" Jack protested, looking over at Rachel. "I said I'd do them."

She nudged him aside to reach for a cold soda. "You're busy."

"So am I," Stephen replied, lifting the globe light fixture into place, "but I'm almost done. Jack, what do you think?"

Jack leaned back to see around his oldest brother Marcus. As usual Marcus was ignoring the debate going on between the rest of them. "Looks good to me."

Stephen used the power screwdriver and secured the fixture.

"I'm going to start on the wallpaper in the hall then," Rachel offered.

Jack pointed to the sack on the countertop. "The double rolls are there."

"Stephen, after the curtain rods, I need someone helping me with the wallpaper."

"I nominate Jack."

Jack smiled at Stephen. "You're taller. And I would hate to rob you of the fun."

"You just want to paint the ceiling in the living room."

"It is more fun," Jack agreed.

Laughter from the bedroom interrupted the football game commentary on the radio. Jennifer, Cassie, and Marcus's fiancée, Shari, had taken over painting in the bedroom and were having a great time. He had known Jennifer and Cassie would become friends. He hadn't expected them to shove the guys out of the room so they could have girl talk.

Benji wandered into the kitchen.

Jack nudged the ball of yarn, which had rolled up against the dishwasher, toward the kitten. B. J. pounced on it and tumbled over. In the space of a week the sleepy kitten had disappeared and been replaced with a kitten full of energy.

"Jack, I want a hug."

He barely got the paintbrush out of the way before Cassie invaded his space and wrapped her arms around him.

Bewildered, he looked over her head at Marcus. His brother just rescued the dripping paintbrush, offering no help on this situation at all.

Jack indulged Cassie and wrapped his arms around her, enjoying the chance to hold her.

She leaned against him, didn't say anything, and he got more confused as the moments passed. She rubbed her cheek against his shirt, tightened her arms, then stepped back. "Thanks." She disappeared toward the back bedroom before he could get a good look at her expression.

He turned to Marcus. "Do you understand women?"

"No."

Afraid he'd missed something, Jack was grateful for the clarification. "Okay, then." Since his brain had short circuited, he left it at that. He picked up the brush and slapped paint on the wall.

"You've got a mushy smile on your face."

"She likes me."

Marcus laughed as he punched his shoulder. "Good job, Jack."

Jack used a rubber mallet to tap the paint can lid down. "What was all of that about earlier?" The last of his family had headed home. In one long day Cassie's apartment had been transformed. The place smelled of drying paint and it was enough to give a person a headache. They opened the patio door for a while this afternoon despite the cold in order to air out some of it.

Cassie was rolling up paint-splattered newspapers. Her jeans were speckled by paint and her sweatshirt was marred by wallpaper paste. He was intrigued at the reality she was blushing. Jack reached over and tipped up her chin, amused. "Cassie?"

"Did you really tell Jennifer I was gorgeous?"

It was his turn to get a bit embarrassed. "Maybe." He remembered telling Jennifer Cassie was adorable; gorgeous had probably showed up in the description along the way.

"That was cute."

He grinned. "Worth a hug at least."

Cassie reached for the black garbage bag and shoved the newspapers inside. The plastic sheeting used to protect the furniture had been rolled and folded into the black trash bag.

Jack scanned the room, seeing a few pieces of furniture that were close but not exactly back in place. Once the paint had dried he'd directed Stephen and Marcus as they moved furniture back against the walls. "Do you want to unpack any of the boxes tonight? We could do your desk, or start on the new bookshelves."

"Another day. You might have energy to move but I'm a puddle of mush."

Jack laughed at the image. He gently rubbed her shoulder. "It was a very long day."

"I think it would have been easier to just move." She nodded to the bookshelf. "That was a really nice addition."

"You're welcome. Stephen likes to build stuff."

"The bookshelf should be full in a few weeks."

Jack got up to sort out the wallpaper remnants, deciding what should be kept for repairs and what small pieces should be thrown away. "Would it be okay with you if I just threw away the paintbrushes rather than try to clean them?"

"Sure."

Jack closed the garbage bag. "Your mouse didn't reappear."

"I think my mouse and Benji have been flirting with each other. Lisa looked everywhere to try and find her."

"My sister likes odd pets."

Cassie gathered up catalogs. There had been discussions with Rachel and Jennifer on what kind of new furniture she should consider buying. "Jennifer said you were joining her tomorrow?"

"Planning to." He sighed. "I'm going to get grilled." For the past six months the subject of religion had been a quiet undertone to his conversation with Jennifer. With the end of the cancer remission, conversations she had been willing to pace with time were now being brought forward.

"She just wants to talk. Why are you absorbing so much pressure about this?"

"I don't want to argue with her, Cassie. If the worst happens, Jennifer doesn't have much time. Having a division now—" He shook his head, finding the idea intolerable.

Short of agreeing with Jennifer on the issue of religion, he didn't know how to find the right words. Respectful disagreement was not how he wanted the conversation to end. That would hurt Jennifer. He would do anything he could to protect her. "Can Jesus stop Jennifer's cancer?"

"Yes."

"Will He?"

When she didn't answer, he looked over and found she had stopped what she was doing. "Jesus is not Santa Claus. He's God. There's a huge difference. He does whatever He wants."

"I find it fascinating that you believe in Him so absolutely." How was that possible?

"I know Jesus loves me."

"Even though He let you get burned?" he risked asking her. He had thought about it many times, thought he would offend her with the question, so he hadn't asked it before.

"Do you know what I decided back when I was lying in that hospital bed enduring the slow passage of time until the next shot of painkiller?"

Startled by an answer that again opened a door into what she had been thinking during those days, he stopped what he was doing and gave her his full attention.

Cassie raised her hand, flexed it, and the scars near her thumb tightened, whitened. "God made the ability to feel pain. He didn't have to, you know. He made the ability to feel pain and He also made it possible to feel joy. Should I hate Him for allowing one and praise Him for allowing the other? God knew what He was doing. I may not always agree, but that is part of what respecting His authority means."

She rubbed her thumb across her palm, glanced up at him, and smiled. "Jack, I personally know Jesus. I have no doubts about the fact He loves me. He helped me get through those long hours, sometimes minute by minute. I found out life is tough, but God is tougher."

"No matter how good she looks and tries to act, Jennifer is very sick."

"I know," she whispered.

"I'm supposed to believe Jesus is okay with this?"

"He's got a plan in mind that will maximize her joy. Jack, I know that—" She flung out her hand. "No, Benji!" She caught the kitten but she had already walked through paint. "Oh, Benji. White and blue paint in the same day…" Cassie got to her feet, talking to the kitten as she headed for the kitchen.

The phone rang as Cassie was coming back into the room. She gave Jack a frustrated look and turned to answer it. It was Linda; it quickly became apparent the conversation would go on for a while. The opportunity to talk lost, Jack got his coat, carried the trash downstairs to the dumpster, then carried the paint cans down to the car. *"Maximize her joy."* Cassie's perspective didn't mean Jennifer would necessarily get well. Jack sucked in a deep breath of cold night air. Jennifer had to get well. He couldn't handle losing a sister.

It felt good to be back at the bookstore. Cassie shoved the last box of Christmas decorations across the threshold into the storage room. The shelves Jack had helped her build were now filled with shipping boxes, packing tape, preprinted lists of current inventory specials, and rolls of bubble wrap. Jack had helped her custom build a worktable that could fit in the corner of the room so she didn't have to haul the shipping material into the other room when she filled orders.

Soon, this would once again be her full-time job. The arsonist wasn't going to linger out there for more than a few more weeks before Cole had enough information to locate him.

Cassie turned her attention to the next box of books to be priced. Linda had already entered them into the inventory database.

Jack was meeting with Jennifer today.

Lord, please let that conversation go well. Cassie was worrying about it, about how Jack was dealing with the subject of faith. He was obviously feeling pressured, and that was the wrong way to get anyone to consider such a fundamental question of who Jesus was. She hadn't helped matters.

She glanced at her watch. She was meeting Jack after he saw

Jennifer, and she needed to get home in time to change.

Cassie looked around the bookstore.

It no longer felt like an albatross to see herself as a bookstore owner as the place where she put her passion. She enjoyed the department work, but she had missed this place. Her days here in the last few weeks had been more focused on filling orders and keeping up with the paperwork than stepping back and dreaming about where she wanted to take the business.

She found she missed that time to dream and it was a good thing to learn about herself. She no longer felt the attachment to the past and clinging to what had been as necessary to be content. There was a future here in the bookstore business.

And Jack would worry less about her.

She knew he was nervous about the job she was doing for Cole, rolling out to look for the arsonist. He didn't like her doing something that had that element of risk. And since she was nervous about him simply fighting fires, she well understood his concern.

"Hello, Jack." Tom let him into the hotel suite on the fourteenth floor.

Jack pushed his hands into his pants' pockets. "How is she?" he asked softly, worried, having received the call changing plans as he was getting ready to leave his apartment. Their lunch plans had been scrapped.

"Jack, I'm fine. Quit whispering to my husband," Jennifer said. She was stretched out on the couch by the large screen TV that had the news on. She set aside the book she was reading. She had received a number of books for Christmas, had been especially thrilled with Cassie's gift of an autographed copy of a T. Emmond mystery.

"She's fine," Tom reassured. "She's just ordered to the couch for the next few hours."

Jack crossed the suite to join Jennifer and leaned down to hug her. "Faking it, are you?"

"I pulled my back. Tom doesn't want me walking because he hates my shoes or some such nonsense."

"I'm going to ignore the fact you're questioning my medical advice," Tom called back to his wife as he picked up his pager.

"You're sure that is all?" Jack whispered to her. No disrespect to Tom, but Jennifer's medical opinion had been the one that always carried the most weight.

There was no hesitation or shades of gray in her reassurance. "Yes."

"Jen, I'm heading over to meet Marcus for lunch. Anything you need before I take off?" Tom asked.

"Tell my brother I want to see him and Shari for dinner before we fly east."

"Will do, honey. See you later, Jack."

"Tom."

Jack sank into the plush chair across from Jennifer, relaxing. She turned down the volume on the television then set aside the remote.

Appearances were deceiving. Her health was precarious. She was in that edge of reality with the remission ending and the next round of chemotherapy beginning. The last round had taken all her energy and left her voice so soft it had been a struggle to hear her. Jack had spent enough time staying with Jennifer during the last hospital stay that he knew the best hotels near the hospital. He wasn't looking forward to that return trip.

"It's going to take me a while to get used to this," Jennifer said.

"What?"

"Your suit and tie."

Jack ran his hand along the tie. It was burgundy and blue to match the dark jacket and wool slacks. "I'm taking Cassie out later." And he was trying his best to make a good impression.

"I like her."

Jack looked at Jennifer, hearing a lot more in those three words than were on the surface. Jennifer's opinion in this family carried a lot of weight. "What's the family grapevine opinion?"

"Very positive. She's upbeat in her outlook despite everything that happened. She surprised me a bit with that dry sense of humor. Lisa really enjoyed talking with her."

"Cassie was equally complimentary. She enjoyed herself." Jack stretched out in the chair, studying his sister. "I've got the rest of the afternoon free, so what would you like to talk about first?"

"Oh, I think I've got a few more dozen questions about Cassie to start with..."

He laughed. "You're so predictable."

"You're not. You surprised us with that invitation to bring Cassie to the party. I want to hear how you met her."

"You look a bit shell-shocked." Cassie leaned against Jack's arm to get his attention, worried about him. She wasn't used to Jack not joking and laughing, smiling at life. Dinner out had been enjoyable, but she'd felt like he was struggling to keep up with even the general conversation he offered. He had been subdued ever since he picked her up.

"What?"

She handed him the bowl of ice cream. She added chocolate and two cherries to the vanilla ice cream; the smiley face she had drawn was rather lopsided. They had come back to watch a movie after dinner but she didn't think his heart was in it. She curled up on the couch beside him, tucking her feet underneath her and tugging down the afghan. "What did you and Jennifer talk about?"

Jack smiled. "You." Then his smile disappeared. "Family history, her cancer. God. A lot about God."

Lord, what's wrong? This is a man who looks like he's been hit by a two-by-four. She rubbed his arm. "You've missed what I've said a few times. Do you want to just pass on tonight? You've got a lot on your mind."

"I'm sorry. I don't mean to be so scattered."

"Don't worry about it. I've been there many times."

He set aside the ice cream and pushed his hands through his hair. "Yes, it's probably best I head home."

"Call me later?"

"Sure."

She put her hand on his arm and squeezed it. "If you don't call me, I'm calling you."

"I'll call."

She pushed aside the afghan, then got up to fetch his coat from the hall closet. She waited by the door as he pulled it on. "Don't forget your gloves."

He tugged them out and slid them on, smiling at her as he did so.

"Want a hug?" she asked softly.

She'd taken a risk asking the question, but his expression of relief was deep and it confirmed she'd made the right decision. He opened his arms and she stepped into them, his arms wrapped tight around her. He sighed and she could feel the exhaustion in him. "It will be okay, Jack. All of it."

"Pray for me," he whispered.

Her throat closed. She hugged him tighter, fighting the tears. "Sure," she choked out.

When he finally stepped back, she searched his face, looking for anything that would help her know how to help. "She's dying, Cassie."

He was reeling from it. It was coming home to him emotionally, and he was walking the tightrope of figuring out how to accept it. For all the benefits of knowing Jennifer was sick, the extra time just made each step along the journey a roller coaster for her family.

"Love her, Jack. That's what she needs from you most," she whispered.

Jack gave a sad smile. "I'm sorry to ruin tonight."

"You didn't ruin anything. Go home, get some sleep, then call me."

He nodded. "Good night."

"G'night, Jack." She locked the door behind him. And she leaned her head against the door. *Lord, Jack needs hope.*

She rubbed the back of her neck, no longer afraid of the hard conversation, no longer afraid of how vulnerable it might make her. She wanted to help Jack more than she wanted to make it easier on herself. She hoped he called. She needed him to call.

Thirty-nine

The phone call woke Cole up. He pushed aside pillows and saw on the bedside television that Jay Leno was talking with an actor. Cole waited for Ash to get the phone; his houseguest was the one receiving most calls tonight as plans for the department New Year's Eve celebration were being put together.

At the third ring Cole forced himself to reach toward the phone. Only then did he see the clock and realize that rather than ten o'clock it was 1 A.M. and it was a replay of the *Tonight Show* on TV. He braced for news of another fire, a big one this time. "This is Cole."

"It's Rachel."

"Rae—" He sat up and turned on the bedside light. "What's wrong?" Had something happened to Jennifer? She rarely called him, and she'd never called before at this time of night.

"Your arsonist."

Cole blinked, surprised at the topic. "Did something happen?" he asked sharply, fear leaping inside at the very idea that she had also been touched by the events going on.

"No, nothing like that. I couldn't sleep, I was thinking about the cases."

She couldn't sleep...his voice softened. "You should have called me rather than lie there awake."

"What do you think I'm doing now?"

"Don't get annoyed. Tell me what you've been thinking about."

"It's just an idea."

Cole reached for the pad of paper on the nightstand, knowing with Rachel she didn't have what-if ideas, she had well-formulated suggestions. And her voice told him she thought this idea was significant.

"It's hyperbole, Cole. The mural, it's more than just a paint form he likes to use. It's a grandiose painting with things made larger than life. The words he chooses—he's doing the same thing. He's overblowing facts in the same way."

Cole started to click into what she had realized. She was on to something. He knew it as soon as she said it. And the implications were startling. He clicked on his pen and pushed the notebook to a blank page. The paper curled on him and he fought the spiral binding. Overblowing facts Cole started offering specifics to Rachel, interested to get her reaction. "The word *murderer.*"

"Think smaller," she offered. "Someone might have come close to dying. He may have transformed what came close to happening into the conclusion of what it would mean had that death occurred."

A near fatal accident... Cole winced as he mentally thought through the size of a report listing injuries that had happened in the district over the last year. He'd have to have help to even get that report categorized. "Cowards."

"It's an extremely personal remark, again, a conclusion he reached. He probably knows the men who worked at that fire station or at least knows of something they did. They probably exercised normal caution and he saw it as timidity."

He was taking notes as fast as he could. "Liar."

"The most personal of all. Look for something you tried to accomplish that didn't happen. It would have affected him or someone he cared deeply about."

"Any suggestion for that one? Are we talking about an arson investigation that didn't get closure? A personal decision? A financial one?"

"I'm not sure, Cole. It does imply that you are a known figure to him, not just a name. I find it interesting that he set your trash on fire.

That suggests he knew it had been done to your house before."

"Popcorn."

"Contrary to your assumption, I don't think it's a reflection of the nursing home fire in the sense of being a jab at what happened. The man who set that nursing home fire was a professional arsonist. Instead, I think the popcorn reflects an admiration of the man who set the fire and the reaction he got. Think about the popcorn as a way for him to suggest he's got the capability to be like that other arsonist."

"That man did arson jobs for profit motives."

"I think it's a good assumption that this man does have financial problems. You don't lash out without it being a reflection of intolerable stress."

Cole thought about that image she was drawing. The profile they had of this man was becoming more and more specific. Cassie had given him the rough age and appearance; the location and type of fires being started were good indications of his background; Rachel's suggestion was a very good look at how the man thought. He needed to find this man before someone got hurt. "Anything else strike you? This is good, Rachel."

Silence met his question. He twirled his pen, giving her time to think. He was surprised that she had spent her time unable to sleep thinking about this, but it was obvious her thoughts were more than casual. "Anything," he urged. "I'm not looking for professional conclusions here."

"The mural with no word."

Cole flipped some more notebook pages.

Rachel clearly hesitated over her choice of words. "That one is very serious, Cole. He went mute."

"He assumes he will no longer be heard," Cole concluded, understanding what she feared. And if he was done talking, it meant there would be an explosion coming.

"What's it mean that that message was left at Ash's home?"

"It means he knew Ash was gone and not likely to return for a while. A mural has to be painted in layers and allowed to dry between each one so the paint won't mix. Even spray paint takes a few hours to set. And it takes planning. I think he had visited Ash's home before because that trail of fire motif implies he thought long and hard about actually torching the house, then decided instead to leave just his signature."

His house had been trashed, Ash's just painted...the arsonist didn't want to burn a fireman's home? Cole wondered, and wrote himself a note to think about that some more. "What is the probability he also knows Ash?"

"Very high."

"The e-mail word *chicken?*"

"One of those cruel taunts, like a school yard pushing match."

Cole hesitated but had to ask. "And Jack?"

"It has always revolved around Jack and Gold Shift."

"Will he be targeted?"

"When is his next shift?"

"Today."

"Can you take him off the shift?"

"Rae—"

"Please."

"I can't."

"You have to."

"Rae—I can't." He had accepted the reality weeks before. He could protect Jack, but not at the price of robbing Jack of his job. "I'll talk with him," he struggled to reassure her. "I'll do everything I can short of taking away his job."

"Don't do this, Cole. Take him off duty before he gets hurt."

She would never forgive him if something happened. "I'm sorry."

She hung up on him.

Cassie struggled to follow Ash through the smoke-filled corridors of the nursing home. She'd helped eight nursing home residents get out, and there were more waiting to be rescued. There was no way to hurry now as the heat and smoke built. Over the radio came the terse messages of rescue crews as rooms were cleared throughout the building.

She swung her light along the room numbers: 1613, 1614, 1615. All rooms they had helped clear. The fire was above them, in corridors to the east. As soon as the last rooms were checked she would be glad to get out of here.

Ash's torchlight shot upward, and his hand shoved her hard. She hit the wall, an instant before something struck a glancing blow on her shoulder and she went down, training tucking her toward the wall with hands to protect her neck.

Something struck her air tanks, and then the world exploded with flames and weight, burying her, pinning her.

She was burning. She screamed as she realized she couldn't move. The debris was crushing her. The burns touched nerves and she coiled into her mind against the agonizing pain.

She was dying. She fought the panic and the pain. She wanted to live. Oh, she wanted so badly to live. She strained to try and move.

"Cassie!"

The yell was the most blessed sound she had ever heard. "Ash…" She couldn't think against the pain. "Get me out."

"Hold on. I'm coming, Cassie." Debris began to move from near her face. Ash strained against the beam pinning her.

Agonizing time passed. He couldn't move it. She desperately struck her free hand against anything she could reach. She couldn't wiggle out of the debris and he couldn't move it.

"I've got a fulcrum."

There was a moment in time when she felt the weight move and then it settled back. She was going to die here. She gasped against her air. Her partner was going to die here too because he wouldn't leave her, because she didn't have the strength to get free.

Her air tank began to chime. She was running out of air.

Ash started kicking the beam pinning her.

A good life, and she hadn't enjoyed it nearly as much as she should have. She'd been too busy trying to get ahead.

Her air ran out. Her ability to move her hand dropped, consciousness was fading.

Her mask was pulled off, the smoke and heat hit her face, and Ash desperately pushed his mask against her face. "Breathe, Cassie. Breathe," he ordered, choking to say the words as he got as low to the floor as he could.

She breathed, revived. Ash removed the mask and grabbed a breath. Then his mask was tight against her face again.

They were both going to die here. His air canisters had only a few more minutes of air than hers. She wanted so desperately to at least be able to tell him good-bye. The tears were choking her so hard she couldn't get the words out. Jesus, don't let me die....

Her partner grabbed her free hand. She used what strength she had to squeeze it.

The shrill ringing phone woke her up. Cassie leaned her head over the side of the bed and heaved at the remembered tears, struggling to breathe. *Lord, the fire...* She fought to get away from the remembered panic. The memory was alive, in her memory, in her emotions, the panic so real she could taste the bitterness of the smoke.

She groped for the phone. "Hello," she choked out.

Silence, and then, "Cassie, what's wrong?"

"Jack, don't go to hell. Please don't go to hell. It's awful." She struggled to hold the phone, shivering, closing her eyes against the remembered flames.

"The fire."

She gasped a desperate half laugh. "The fire."

"Oh, honey."

"Promise me you won't go to hell."

"Cassie—"

"Come over and take me for a walk. We've got to talk."

His hesitation was brief. "I'm on my way."

Cassie had on her coat and gloves, her keys in her pocket, and was waiting in the downstairs landing when she saw Jack's car come into the lot. She went out to greet him and leaned into the hug he offered, wrapping her arms around him and resting against the solid comfort of the man.

His jacket was cold against her cheek and his arms strong around her. "Shh, it's okay." He rubbed her back as he whispered the words.

"I wanted to be a hero that day. I nearly became a victim."

"Fire doesn't respect a person, good or evil; it will grab and kill whomever it can reach."

"Satan is just like that, Jack."

He went still and she tipped back her head to look at him. "Jesus is alive. And unless you trust Him, someday you are going to be caught in a fire like hell that never ends."

He tightened his arm around her shoulders and pointed her to the walkway. "Come on. Let's walk."

There was no finesse to her approach tonight, only a heartfelt passion. If she offended him, she'd accept that. The hesitation to force the conversation had disappeared under the weight of her fear. If something happened to Jack during this arson investigation, she'd never be able to live with herself.

"When we found you and Ash in the nursing home, you were barely conscious. Do you remember what you were saying?"

She shook her head, puzzled. She'd avoided talking about that day, not wanting to relive the details any more than she had to.

"I was cushioning your head while we moved you to a backboard. You were whispering from a psalm the phrase 'The Lord is my shepherd' over and over again."

"I reached for Him that night and He was there."

"Jennifer said essentially the same thing, when she described the night she met Jesus."

She tightened her hand around his. "Don't wait for tragedy to strike like I did, Jack."

"Did you ever hate God over what happened, when you saw the burns?"

"A man I knew kissed them better," she whispered.

He dashed a glove across his eyes. "I've got so much on my mind it's hard to sort it out, Cassie. Heaven and hell, the Resurrection—it's a huge step to accept it all."

"Trust Jesus. Trust what you do understand. The rest will come. I'm scared for you, Jack."

He rubbed his gloved thumb across the back of her hand. "I appreciate that, Cassie. And I promise, I am thinking about it."

She searched his face, longing to find he meant it. She saw a reassurance there. She squeezed his hand. "Thank you."

"I'm so sorry you dream about the nursing home fire. I dream about the fires too, and it's hard to wake to those memories."

"The fear. And the sound of the fire…"

"The awareness that it's going to happen and there is no way to stop it," he finished for her.

"Yeah."

"They'll go away with time."

"Oh, I hope so."

He slowed her as they walked up the sidewalk. The apartment building lobby door had been propped open.

She tightened her hand on his. "Jack."

"Stay here."

She didn't listen but followed him instead.

Popcorn littered the hall.

"He was watching us, watching her," Jack said to Cole, feeling the fury and the helplessness. This was becoming so personal it was like living a real nightmare. He didn't know what to do with the fear. If he hadn't come back tonight, would it be a fire here matching the popcorn? He watched Cassie sitting in his car to keep warm, and he was terrified for her.

Police officers were sweeping the grounds, but they had found nothing so far.

"Go in for shift early, take her with you, sleep at the firehouse, and let me sort this place out."

"Cole…" Jack did not want to say the words but he had to. "If I go in to work, he'll strike. The man is escalating. Maybe it's better if I don't report in, if we change our plans."

His friend squeezed his shoulder. "I don't think it's going to matter to him anymore whether you're there or not."

"I can't live with someone getting hurt."

"The best thing to do is accept it's a foregone conclusion and be ready to respond when he next strikes. In case you didn't notice, he just acted close to the firehouse rather than at the edge of the fire district. Odds are good we're not going to have a long time to wait before he acts again. Get Cassie to the station. I'll join you once the canvass is done here."

Forty

Gage, couldn't you have at least tempered the article a bit?" Rachel scowled at her friend as her headache throbbed. She tossed the folded paper down on the table. "You waved a red flag in front of the guy." Gage had reported the mural, the words, the popcorn, and the sequence of eight fires in his Weekend Focus article. There was more information in the article than she had known.

She'd joined him for breakfast in order to talk about plans for New Year's Eve. She'd borrowed his newspaper. Now she wished she hadn't.

"Rachel, you can't have it both ways. You asked me to help you out. He's a serial arsonist, and that mural painting is a signature someone who knows him will recognize. This article is a public service. Someone knows the man and this will generate the leads Cole needs."

"Couldn't you have at least warned Cole?"

"I asked him for a quote. He knows. Quit scowling at me. I'm doing my job."

"You should have told me."

"Rae—"

She shoved back her chair "I'm going home."

"You just got here."

"And now I'm leaving."

"Sit down."

His quiet order caught her off guard. She looked back at him. "Sit down."

She sat.

"Jack knew this was running. Cole. Ash."

She sank back as what he said registered. "Jack is planning to use his presence on the shift to draw the arsonist out," she whispered.

Gage just looked at her.

She underestimated Jack so many times in the past; she'd done it again. "If he isn't on shift, the arsonist just goes underground to strike out another way."

"Jack's not going to take unnecessary chances. Cole won't let him. But they've got to do something."

She didn't want a noble brother; she wanted one who was selfish and thought of himself first. She rubbed at the headache. It was going to be a very long day and night until he came off shift.

"Finish breakfast. Stay for the day. I'd like the company."

"You just don't want to come to my place in order to hold my hand."

Gage smiled at her and nudged her orange juice toward her. "You can help me dust."

"Can I now tell you I told you so? You shouldn't have fired the housekeeper."

There was ice in the rain. Cassie leaned against the engine bay door watching the pellets bounce when they hit the pavement. She was scared. And the longer the day went, the more scared she got. The arsonist had been at the apartment building last night. Why? Following her, or worse, following Jack? Jack had just given her a hug this morning when she tried to raise the concerns and she understood why. He couldn't offer anything more definite but that silent reassurance. He'd protect her. That was what worried her the most. *Lord, protect Jack.* With night would come the odds of another fire. On top of that, there was this incoming weather disaster.

The weather station was on in the lounge. They had spent the day watching the ice storm come their direction. The front edge had arrived. The day before New Year's Eve, one of the busiest travel days of the year, and they had an ice storm coming through. Somehow Cassie didn't think people were going to be wise enough to stay off the roads. Mandatory callbacks of all shifts had begun forty minutes ago.

"Cassie, you're riding tonight on Engine 81. Check your gear."

She turned to look at Cole as he strode by, stunned. "Who, me?"

"You're drafted. And if I can get the blasted fax machine to work so I can get a waiver issued for Ash, he's drafted too. As soon as he gets here find him gear."

"Yes, sir."

"Has Ben reported in yet?"

"I haven't seen him."

"Holler when you do."

She nodded.

She was on active duty on Engine 81. It took her a moment for that to sink in. There was no question they would be rolling out nearly continuously during the next hours. If Cole was drafting her and Ash, he considered this to be an emergency shift requiring all manpower available. She hurried to her locker and started checking out her gear. She knew it was ready, but it wouldn't hurt to check it again.

"Cassie."

"Jack, don't protest to me. Cole said I was rolling out with you. Take it up with him."

His hand came down on her shoulder and she paused long enough to look around. "A face mask. You're going to need it to avoid frostbite," he said, handing her the blue cap. "And I asked for you."

"Oh, thanks."

"Thank me after you spend a few hours trying to walk on a skating rink. Ash was going through some gear a couple days ago. Do you know where he stored it?"

"The unassigned locker next to Frank's. Ash had checked out

everything but the boots. I think some came from the warehouse earlier today."

"Your partner is riding with us in Engine 81 as well. Stay beside Ash throughout the night, understood?"

"Not a problem." She was willing to accept any conditions he set just so she wouldn't have to sit here at the station while they went out.

"Medical runs; I want you on the cardiac kit. If we hit a wreck and have to do an extraction, you're my mouse. Be prepared with the blankets to go under or into the wreck if necessary. Any signs you've acquired a taste of being claustrophobic?"

"Not a bit."

"Good. Where's Cole? We need a plow assigned full time to work with us tonight."

"Heading back to his office. He was working that problem earlier," she offered.

"Toss extra gloves and socks into the Engine 81 cabinet. You'll need them."

"Yes, lieutenant," she said, and meant it with absolute respect.

He grinned at her and tossed her a bright orange packet. "For your coat pocket." It was an instant hot pack; break the seal and it heated to 105 degrees. Jack glanced around the bay. "Bruce, find us at least one extra thermos of coffee. Ash takes it sweet like Cassie."

Forty-one

"C" an you get in there?" Jack leaned in near Cassie to be heard above traffic.

She shone her light on the crumpled metal of the van tailgate. She had to squint as stinging pieces of ice were striking her face. "I can get in there." The van had been broadsided by a sedan and then hit from behind by a taxi. It was the third accident of the night she had worked.

"In the passenger side door of Engine 81, there's a canvas bag with a Velcro tab on top. You'll find a handheld tape player, a pair of child sized earphones, and a bunch of *Sesame Street* tapes. Get them and a thermal blanket. Try to hold the boy still. He's going to react when we take the Jaws of Life to the roof, and I don't want him moving that leg. I'm certain it's fractured."

Cassie nodded.

She struggled the ten feet back to the engine, the scene lit by its flashing lights and halogen strobe. Walking on ice was impossible and more than one firefighter had fallen. As tough as the job was, she loved being back on the job. It was good to be useful again. She was getting proficient at how Jack liked to work.

Even with gloves her fingers were frozen. She struggled to get the door open. *Sesame Street* tapes: It shouldn't have surprised her knowing what she did about Jack and his habit of being prepared, but it did.

She was grateful he had them available.

With the blanket and the cassette tapes, Cassie worked her way to the boy, her world closing down to the size of the air pocket inside the crumpled vehicle. She was able to use Ash's help to get leverage.

"Hi, Peter." The boy was screaming and for once she was glad she was partially deaf. "I'm Cassie." She shoved aside the coloring books that had tumbled out of a child's backpack and winced when her knee landed on a metal Matchbox car.

The boy was buckled into a car seat, but when the impact had happened the entire bench seat had been thrown off its tracks and had crunched into the driver's seat. The boy's left foot had been caught. The paramedic had been able to work an air splint around his lower leg and inflate it. Now they just had to get a way to move the boy out. If they tried to bring him out the way she had wrestled her way in, his leg would have to turn. Cassie strained to get the blanket across him.

She clicked on the cassette player and the sound of the familiar music startled the boy into stopping midcry to look around at her. "This is for you," she reassured, adjusting the volume and then slipping the headphones on him. She used the blanket to wipe his wet face and running nose. The screams had become broken sobs. She put her arm across him and silently gestured to Jack for him to get started.

Exhausted, feeling a crick in her neck that refused to ease, Cassie stood back as the ambulance pulled away. The boy had been whimpering rather than crying, clearly relieved to be out of the van, clutching the bear the paramedic had offered him. His mom had already been transported to the hospital. Both were stable. It was the way the accidents were supposed to end.

"Good job."

She looked over at Jack and offered a weary smile. "Thanks."

The sleet had temporarily ended but the wind had picked up. She adjusted the face mask, knowing exactly how Jack had felt on Christmas working in the snow.

"Climb up in the engine and thaw out while we finish the cleanup. Ash and I need another ten minutes," Jack recommended. Behind him the whine of a tow truck winch started.

Cassie nodded, more than willing to accept the offer. "Deal."

She was grateful for Bruce's help up into the engine cab. She gave a relieved sigh as she stripped away the frozen face mask and the cold gloves.

"Coffee, drinkable hot."

"Thanks, Bruce." She warmed her hands around the cup as she drank the coffee.

Cole's vehicle was parked immediately in front of Engine 81, its lights flashing. She watched Cole walk cautiously from the wreckage back to his vehicle.

Jack and Cole made a good team.

Tones sounded. It was for Company 81 but served as a heads up for Cole. She saw him duck into his vehicle and knew he was talking to dispatch. He got out of the vehicle and called something over at Jack. Moments later tones for the engine and truck crews sounded.

She opened the door and braved the wind to hear Cole.

"We've got a report of smoke at an apartment complex. We're pulling out from here to check it out. Rescue 81 will finish up with the taxi driver and join us."

Cassie could feel the fear and dread building. It was a fire call. She was glad she was not responsible for driving the rig. A million dollar rig on icy roads was not a job for the faint of heart. She leaned forward from the back bench to hear Jack as she worked the buttons on her fire coat and turned up her collar. "Make sure you keep an eye on where the hose teams are to try and keep out of the water mist."

She nodded. She'd worked many fires during the winter and the advice was something she knew well. Bathed in water and moving into the wind was a prescription for frostbite.

"Do you think it's him?" she asked, worried.

"Maybe. If conditions are such you are able to look around the scene, you have to stay with Cole or Ash. No exceptions."

Wandering around on her own was the last thing she wanted to consider. She had no desire to meet him alone. "Will do." She was grateful Ash was with her. Her partner was checking his gear beside her as if nothing unusual was going on. He was a good man to have around in a crisis.

Cassie leaned forward and peered into the night. She recognized the red and white light display on a white house with pillars. She had been in this area recently, and they were heading to an apartment complex— "Jack, this street. There's only one apartment complex out this way."

He nodded, his expression turning grim as he picked up the radio to call Cole.

The smoke wasn't heavy, there was no sign of flames, but it was definitely not a false alarm. The smoke curled into the night sky lazily, not sure of its movements, with the exception of the east end of the building where the rise of smoke was stronger, indicating more heat was present.

It was either good luck or bad that they had approached the one building she and Jack had visited when viewing one of the apartments to rent. Had she wanted to move, this complex had the best layout of those she had looked at. Engine 81 pulled to the front of the building, as close as they could get given the cars in the handicapped spots.

Cassie hurried to join Cole as they did a fast planning powwow. "Jack and I were in this building less than two weeks ago to look at an apartment."

"Where exactly?"

"East wing, one of the end apartments."

"Jack—you, Ash, and Cassie check the east wing. Bruce and Nate, handle the west. This is defensive only, so take no undue risks. I'll start generating a head count out here. Feed me temperature and smoke data, and I'll have the next arriving units laying hose. But dispatch just warned it's going to be a few minutes. They've got a pileup on the tollway slowing them down."

Cassie looked to Jack for directions. "We go in carrying air. Be ready to don it at a moment's notice."

She walked carefully across the slick pavement. Ash was already bringing out the self-contained breathing apparatus canisters. Cassie accepted one. The weight helped, making it easier to walk on the slick sidewalks. Cassie held on to that truth as she tightened the harness and clipped the face mask to the harness within immediate reach. She refused to consider the fact that this time she was wearing SCBA with a good likelihood she would need to use it. "Relax, Ash."

"Stay between Jack and me." He was worried about her and not bothering to hide it.

She smiled and clamped her hand on his forearm, dislodging a thin film of ice from his coat as she did so. "Fine with me. You carry the ax, I'll handle the extra torchlight."

The number of people coming from the building had slowed. Cassie winced at the realization two of the ladies had taken enough time to retrieve not only purses and coats, but one was carrying a photo album and the other wall pictures.

Bruce jammed a wedge-shaped piece of wood under the front door as a doorstop. He followed Nate into the building.

Building fire alarms were piercing.

Cassie followed Jack inside. She got hit with a wave of warm air. The lights were on in the building, the hallways wide and empty of people. It smelled smoky but no smoke was visible. It was a smell not much different than a grill in a neighbor's backyard, a lingering whiff of something close to lighter fluid.

"We've got dormant water," Jack indicated, using his torchlight to point out the sprinkler head on the ceiling. "Watch for heat spots that may suddenly trigger it."

Ash used the fire department master key to unlock the steel box where building master keys were kept. He handed keys to Bruce and

Nate. Cassie closed her glove around hers. It was an odd key, *T* shaped for grip, master fit to open every door in the building. She nodded and pushed the strap around her glove.

Jack led down the east hallway.

"I bet it's a Christmas tree fire. I'm smelling whiffs of pine," Ash said.

"There's something sharper underneath it." Jack paused. "What's that?"

Ash used the handle of the ax to turn over the package. "Someone dropped a Christmas present as they rushed out."

Cassie nudged the box to the side with her foot so it wouldn't be trampled as she left.

From behind them came the sound of voices as Bruce encouraged someone to go outside, insisting it was necessary even if no smoke was visible and it was bad weather out there.

They reached the turn in the hallway into the east wing proper. Smoke lingered in the hallway, hovering around the ceiling and surrounding the hall lights, creating an impression of a fog coming down.

The hall was warm and edging toward hot, but still no flames were visible. Cassie watched the walls and the ceiling for any clue of the source.

Jack pointed her to the first apartment door to the left, Ash to the first one on the right. The three of them moved down the hallway checking doorways. They opened one apartment after the next, checking to confirm everyone was out.

The fourth apartment on the right had small wisps of smoke coming from under the door. The smoke burned her eyes.

Jack tentatively closed his glove around the doorknob and tried to turn it. The door was locked.

"Go to air. Cassie, stay within arm's reach of me."

She nodded, slipped off her helmet, and donned the mask. Her breath hissed inside the mask and her hands grew clammy at the thought of what she was doing.

Jack reached over and rested his hand heavily on her shoulder, setting the maximum distance. "Ash, open it. We search clockwise."

Ash nodded and popped the lock open.

There was a quiet whoosh and an inward flowing breeze as the room drew in air. It was an eerie feeling. The apartment was dark.

Cassie felt her fear level leap. The movement of air was a good indication the fire had found itself a flume for the heat.

Cassie shone her torchlight inside and saw only thicker smoke. It was hard to tell if it was coming from a ceiling or a floor fire; the smoke simply hovered.

She looked toward Jack, letting him make the critical decision. He nodded and gestured for Ash to watch the ceiling. Jack led them inside single file. Cassie was grateful to be between Jack and Ash.

A cat darted out between their feet, startling Cassie and causing Ash to trip a step back. It was an occupied apartment. And most residents rushing outside would probably have stopped to grab their pets. Odds had just increased to fifty-fifty that someone was still in here.

It was the same layout as the apartment she had looked at briefly during her short consideration of moving. Jack led the way through the smoke toward the bedrooms.

She could hear the fire.

Forty-two

The apartment was laid out with the bedrooms to the left and the kitchen and living room to the right. Jack made the turn toward the bedrooms, hating the way the hallway narrowed down. Two bedrooms on the left, bathroom straight ahead, Jack moved forward from memory.

He stopped at the doorway to the master bedroom, feeling incredible heat. He put his hand back to pause Cassie, not sure what they were facing. His light disappeared in the smoke, touching what might be the edge of a bed but unable to pierce the smoke. His light crisscrossed the floor, then stopped. Someone had tried to reach the door and gone down about three feet inside the room.

"Cassie, with me. Ash, see if you can break out a window."

He moved toward the victim. An adult male. Cassie's light joined his and together they turned him over. "Chad." Jack was horrified to see someone he knew. He had been expecting smoke inhalation, ready to grab and carry to get him out, but it took a moment for the realization to set in that there was blood staining the man's chest. What had been a dark blue shirt had a huge stain.

"No."

Jack tightened his hand on Cassie's arm to steady her. The man's stiffness was rigor mortis setting in. His light picked up the gun the man had been lying on. Self-inflicted? Murder? He couldn't tell.

Glass shattered. Ash took out both windowpanes and the room exhaled, smoke and heat rushing toward the new vent as a warm wind. All the panes had been in the window, the front door had been locked, the apartment hadn't shown an obvious source of entry. Jack mentally cataloged it as he tried to decide if they could stop the fire so as not to disturb the scene. That suggested suicide. The fire, something much more sinister. Ash moved back toward them, his torchlight now able to pierce through the clearing smoke.

Jack saw something that frightened him, and he grabbed his torch and swept it up. He lifted his light to the wall behind the large headboard.

There was a mural on the bedroom wall. A mural of flames. Big, bold, red flames. It shocked him.

Cassie got to her feet, locked her hand onto his shoulder, and aligned her light with his.

The word atop the mural of fire was huge. *Burn.*

Fear rippled through Jack's muscles from his toes up to his back.

The huge word flickered.

The paint peeled back.

He shoved Cassie toward the open windows. "Get out!"

The wall exploded toward them.

"I've got five trapped. Go to three alarms," Cole ordered the dispatcher coolly, not having time for emotions. Around him people were screaming and trying to run backward, falling on the slick pavement. Rescue crews were not going to get here in time. He needed help. Unfortunately he only had himself.

The dispatcher was swift to put out tones.

Natural gas, that was his first hunch. The explosion had ripped through the back of the east wing of the building. He couldn't see the wall that had collapsed at the back of the building, but he saw the effects the instant it blew out. The crown of the roof snapped and the second floor shifted backward.

Lord, have mercy. Cole was depending on the truth of that mercy.

He dropped air on his back. Five people. He didn't have the wisdom of Solomon, but he now needed it. He had two in the west wing hopefully only trapped; he had three in the east wing who were likely injured. And he could only go one direction.

The police officer working to keep residents back got a terse message from Cole. "When firefighters arrive, tell them three are down in the left wing and two in the right. Do whatever you must to keep other people out. Untrained help won't be a help, no matter how good the intentions." He looked at the man hard to make sure that message was received. "This building is going to collapse at any time." Unsaid was the simple reality that five firefighters might give their lives if that happened, but he'd allow no one else to join them.

The cop grimly nodded.

Cole headed into the building to try to reach Bruce and Nate. It would take more than one to have a chance to reach the others.

Forty-three

Nate, pass him across." Cole braced his feet to take Bruce's weight. It made more sense to go out a window than try and work back through the hallway. The shock wave of the explosion had taken out almost all the windows.

Considering what might have happened, Cole was relieved Bruce only had broken ribs to deal with. He lowered the injured man as carefully as he could to the ground. Nate dropped to the ground beside them.

"Leave me here. You two go get the others out," Bruce bit out, his hand fighting the straps to remove the air pack.

"You can walk if you have to?" Cole asked.

"Yes...go."

Additional help still had not arrived. Cole looked at Nate. "Let's try to get in through the back of the building."

Cassie was looking up at Ben. He hovered over her, blocking the worst of the stinging sleet. She was outside, the shattered wall lying around her dotting the snow. She'd been blown through it. She struggled to think as adrenaline surged, as the agonizing impression formed that he was the man she'd seen watching the Wallis house fire. "Ash. Jack—"

"They're in there?"

She struggled to nod, her ears ringing with a white noise that surrounded and swallowed her. She fought the nausea to turn her head.

It had exploded. The outside wall of the apartment had blown out. Part of the second floor had collapsed into the void. It was a blackened shell with a glowing red flame flickering in the heart of the destruction. The fire was beginning to spread.

She was left lying in the snow as Ben headed into the building.

Cassie rolled onto her stomach, gagging. She fought the waves of pain as she struggled to try and get to her feet.

She had to get inside.

She had to find a way inside.

Lord… She fell again, hard.

"Cassie!"

Cole caught her. She wanted to cry at not having seen it. No fires on Black Shift— "Ben. It's him. He's the arsonist."

Gloved hands caught her face and helped lift it. "You're sure?"

She nodded, and she felt betrayal so deep it hurt to breathe. Not Ben. Not someone she admired.

"Nate, get her farther back," Cole ordered. He headed into the building.

Jack fought to keep focused. The pain in his shoulder was not yet a broken bone, but it was agonizing to be alert and trapped. He was face-down, the only thing visible the flickering light of flames and the edges of something wooden. Where was Cassie? Jack fought against the panic and the fact he couldn't move. He was going to die here, and it wasn't nearly as ugly a thought as knowing Cassie was somewhere in this exploded rubble.

He listened to the hiss of his air exhalation valve. The heat was building. His air was running down. He hoped they went after Cassie first.

Jesus.

The awareness of someone coming back from the dead now rippled as something more than a myth. The desire to live was incredible. If

Jesus truly was the author of life and had overcome death...

He was crying inside the mask. He remembered the words the thief said to Jesus as he hung on the cross beside Him: *"Remember me when you come into your kingdom."* Jack desperately wanted Jesus to remember him too. *Jesus, I'm a sinner. Save me. I don't want to die.*

He struggled to get air into his lungs. He was at the mercy of someone he couldn't see, could only believe in. A calm replaced the fear. Lie still, conserve energy. When his air tank ran dry, push off the mask and hold on....

Cole yanked Ash from under burning carpet. Cole's elbow struck a walnut dresser lying on its side and his hand momentarily went numb. The owner of the apartment above had loved walnut furniture, and all of it was in the way now that the floor above had collapsed. "Hold on, Ash."

The man had broken his leg but the time for finesse was later. Where was Jack? Where was Ben? He had to prove Cassie wrong. It couldn't be Ben. Not a friend, not a man who had spent his life fighting fires.

"Cassie forgot to say getting buried in rubble was like being landed on by an elephant," Ash bit out, able to help some by protecting his leg as Cole finally pulled him clear. "Did you get her out?"

Cole paused long enough to grab a breath and get a firmer grip. "She's got a concussion." He was guessing on that but it fit her total disorientation and uncoordinated movements trying to get up.

"Jack?"

"Not yet. Let me get you to Nate, then I'll find him," Cole gasped out. This was a job that needed several people; instead he had Nate and himself.

"Chad's dead."

Cole felt like he'd been kicked in the gut. "Chad?"

"We found him just before the inferno ripped through. Gunshot to the chest, maybe self-inflicted. He was lying on the gun."

Cole tightened his grip on the back of Ash's coat and hefted him into a fireman's hold. Ice hit Cole and a sharp wind bit as he got out of the protection of the building.

"Cassie, knock it off!" Cole ordered. She was fighting Nate, trying to get up. The sight scared him to death, for her movements were uncoordinated and would increase injuries she was too adrenaline blocked to feel.

"Dump me beside her," Ash ordered. "I'll deal with her."

Cole lowered him down as carefully as he could, grateful it looked like Ash had a simple fracture. Cassie looked horrible. Her face wasn't white as much as it had a grayish cast. The only thing keeping her moving had to be adrenaline. And it was obvious by her actions that she was not thinking clearly.

Ash stripped off his gloves and started unbuckling Cassie's fire coat. "Both of you go get Jack," Ash ordered. Ash turned Cassie toward him and gingerly cupped her face. "What did you do to yourself, partner?"

Confident Ash would be able to help her, Cole headed back inside the building with Nate.

Cole worked his way back into the destroyed apartment, knowing where Ash had been found. He made a guess that if Jack had been with him, he would be buried somewhere nearby.

There was a gas line feeding the flames, and the fire was growing in intensity. As more and more material and carpet ignited, the smoke became denser.

The only thing working in their favor was the way the structure had settled. There was a wind tunnel effect coming through, pushing the smoke back into the structure and keeping the air near the floor clear, if freezing cold. It created an odd explosion of sparks upward as the dampness in the air snapped and popped as it was blown into superheated air.

Nate grabbed his arm and pointed.

Cole added his torchlight to Nate's. In the wavering light Cole spotted Jack by the smiley face on the back of his fire coat.

Seeing his position was almost a dagger in itself.

The fire was close. Getting from here to there...even if they could get to him, digging him out was going to be nearly impossible before the fire swept the area.

"Nate, we need new sixty-minute cylinders, an extra one for Jack, and a cutting torch to deal with that ductwork. On the second trip be thinking about how to suppress that gas line fire."

Nate nodded and immediately headed out for the gear.

Cole shoved aside furniture and ducked down to get under the door tilted on its side now holding up part of the ceiling.

He tested if an overturned bookshelf would take his weight. He didn't have room to move it aside. He climbed over it and winced when the back panel gave way and his booted foot crashed through. The heat started to make him feel like he was getting a sunburn.

"Jack." He slapped the man's leg when he got near, looking for a way to get him free.

"About time."

"Get on air," Cole growled.

"Get this thing off my shoulder and I can move. It's hot."

"That thing is a personal safe and it's wedged under what looks like the central ductwork for the furnace."

Cole heard his response but decided to ignore it. He had no choice but to wait for Nate. He started moving away anything he could that would burn. The mural would have been interesting to see as a whole. Cole tossed chunks of plaster out of the way, the red flames in the paint mirroring the reality of what was around him.

"It was a good painting. My gift to Chad when he used to dream about being a fireman as a child. It's been a long time since I painted, but the skill returns." The voice rasped from the wrong side of the room.

Cole froze.

He looked across Jack and into the dark building where the only light came from reflected flames.

The man clicked on a torch.

He stood in the apex of the wind tunnel, the hot air and sparks blowing toward and swirling around him. Ben. Cole took a deep breath and suppressed the emotion that surged as the horrible reality was confirmed. He had suspected it might be Chad, but never Ben. Cole ignored the danger obvious in Ben standing there and kept moving debris.

"The painting haunted Chad after the accident. He wanted to paint over it, but I wouldn't let him. I kept promising him he'd come back to work. But I couldn't give him back the job he wanted, being a firefighter. He shot himself, Cole."

Cole wanted to reply and couldn't afford to get drawn into the pain the man was feeling. He heard a shrill hiss and knew the gas line was building toward another explosion. He was not going to let Jack be caught in it.

"The department destroyed us. My marriage. My nephew. And they'll destroy the community if they don't reopen the fire stations they closed."

"Why Jack? What did he ever do to you?"

Jack had stopped moving, hearing the conversation.

"I sleep during Red Shift. Jack was the one on duty when I was awake. Awful, isn't it, the randomness of who gets to be a victim?"

Cole squeezed Jack's leg to apologize for what he was about to do. He put his strength into shifting the safe, knowing that because of how it was resting, moving it would actually cause the corner to dig harder into Jack's shoulder. If he could get two inches, Jack had a chance of sliding back....

The best Cole could do was raise it a fraction of that distance. He was forced to let it settle.

"Use this. I went into the fire to get it." There was irony under the words. Ben tossed him a crowbar.

Cole picked it up.

Ben grabbed the ductwork from his side and put his weight on it, shifting it back. "All they had to do was restore the stations they closed, Cole. Rehire the men they let go. That's all they had to do."

"Shut up," Cole said coldly. The safe slid up ever so slightly. "Move," Cole ordered Jack, as he fought to keep the safe from slipping back.

Jack's hand grabbed hold of Cole's boot to use it as a leverage. Jack pulled himself back. The rubble shifted and Cole got his feet knocked out from under him. He landed hard atop Jack and rolled.

The dragon lashed out.

Cole felt agonizing heat brush his face.

Jack grabbed the back of Cole's coat and yanked him back. "Move!"

Cole struggled to his feet. He pushed Jack ahead of him. As soon as Cole saw Jack was able to get out under his own power, he turned back toward Ben. They were divided by the ductwork that had come down. He reached out his hand. "Come on."

"Not this time."

Cole heard his tank begin to chime.

"Ben—"

The man turned back into the burning apartment.

Cole wanted to dive after the man. Ben was making his decision, and it was agonizing to realize Cole didn't have the time to change it. He prayed for words but none came. He closed his eyes, turned, and struggled to get across the rubble. Twenty seconds later he was breathing icy night air.

A second explosion ripped through the building.

Forty-four

You look horrible."

Cole struggled to open his eyes. The emergency room was not the place to try and overcome a headache. He ached. He licked lips that were cracked. "Rae."

"You got a fire sunburn."

He gave a painful smile. Her hand touching his was so tentative it felt like a feather. "Some," he whispered. Most of the flash burns from the second explosion were at worst first degree; they'd heal. "How's Jack?"

"Pacing until he can see Cassie. Jennifer is keeping him company."

The relief was incredible.

"Thanks for getting him out."

There was a lot he could say. About duty, about friendship, about feeling responsible for what Ben had done. He passed it all by to say what he wanted to most. "You're welcome," he whispered.

Cole struggled with his memories of the man he had known and the man he had changed into. It was senseless. Ben had been pushing him on the budget, for more personnel, to get at least one of the closed stations reopened, but Cole had missed the desperation Ben felt.

Ben felt he had to force change to happen—setting the fires, focusing on Jack and on department officers to get across the point they were stretched too thin to fight the arson fires. Using popcorn and vicious words to make his actions something the public would react to with alarm. Making it personal, raising the stakes by threatening a former victim— Cassie being in trouble had gotten Cole a call from the fire chief and a push to find a solution. Eventually what Ben had been after would have happened. Only Chad had cut it short by taking his own life. Had Chad read the paper that morning and realized the arsonist was Ben? The young man had been smart; the mural information Gage presented would have been enough to convince Chad it was Ben.

Cole had failed them both. Rae's hand slid under his. "Can I stay a while?" She spent her career trying to heal trauma from events like this.

She was doing that for him, being here right now, trying to heal his trauma. His hand closed around hers. "I'd like that." He took a shallow breath feeling the pain in his ribs. "No jokes."

Her smile was worth the attempt at humor. "No jokes," she promised.

"Jack, sit down."

Jack paced the ER waiting room and ignored Jennifer. "I should have seen the warnings when I went toward the master bedroom. I let Ash and Cassie stand there as the wall blew up."

Jennifer grabbed his hand, caught him by surprise, and pulled him down to the chair beside her. "Great, blame yourself for what Ben caused. Just because he's dead and you can't be mad at him does not mean the answer is to be mad at yourself."

He rubbed his sore shoulder that had been so bruised he could not lift his arm without agony. "Ash busted his leg, Cassie's got a concussion—" Jack shook his head.

"Would you quit changing the diagnosis? She does not have a concussion. The doctor said a bad headache and a disoriented inner ear impact with her balance."

"What's the difference?"

"She'll want to go home in the morning is the difference."

Jack pushed his hand through his hair. "How long before they are going to let me see her?" he muttered.

"You asked me that three minutes ago. Soon."

He got up to pace again. Cassie had been his responsibility. Instead of protecting her, he'd come close to killing her.

"I know what Cassie must have felt when she got hurt. Trapped, desperately worried about friends, hoping for help to arrive, dependent on others. It was awful."

Jennifer didn't say anything. He looked over at her.

"Cassie needs someone who understands her. God gave you a chance to taste what she went through. I'd consider it a gift."

He smiled. "One I would have been glad to pass on. But it did get me off the fence to make a decision."

"You chose to believe," she whispered.

He simply nodded.

"I'm glad."

He leaned over and hugged her. "Between you, Rachel, Cassie…the three of you are pretty persuasive. Hell is a scary place if tonight was any glimpse of what it will be like."

"It will be much worse."

"Will Jesus heal you, Jen?"

"He's the I Am. He doesn't explain Himself. But I trust Him. If He heals me, it will be a gift I'll treasure. If He doesn't…there's something gracious still in His plans for me, something that will bring Him glory. He loves me, Jack. I trust Him."

The doctor came into the waiting room, interrupting them.

"Cassie, can I see her?" Jack demanded.

"She's being admitted for the night for observation. You can go with her as she's transferred to a room if you like."

"Definitely."

"Do you want the lights off, not just dimmed?"

"They're okay," Cassie reassured Jack. She was relieved to finally be done with the moving around and the doctors prodding her.

Her headache had become a throbbing reality. The world still had the nasty habit of spinning when she moved her head. The explosion had set her left inner ear ringing, and as a result, messed up her sense of balance.

Jack had pulled over a chair but it was obvious he was having to force himself to stay sitting. She could see the tension in him, or rather inferred it from her impression of him. Even with her glasses, which she'd begged him to find for her since she hated a fuzzy world, at the moment nothing was very clear given this headache.

Jesus, thank You for keeping him safe. Jack could so easily have been killed.

"Tell me what happened," she whispered. "I remember your hand coming back and propelling me toward Ash. Then the next thing I know I'm looking up at the night sky with Ben standing there."

"He had been setting the fire to cover up Chad's suicide. He wanted a fire that would crawl through the walls and floors. I got a glimpse of the holes between joists in the drywall at the base of the walls just before the paint began to peel back. The way the wall came back at us, something explosive ignited."

"He disabled the building sprinklers?"

"Either that or they never worked."

"Please don't blame yourself," she whispered.

He touched the back of her hand. "Is this going to bring back all the memories of the nursing home?"

It was a worried question and it brought a lot of comfort that he would ask. "If it does, it will fade. How's Cole?"

"He got caught by the second explosion and has some flash burns. He'll recover."

Jack walked back to the window.

Cassie watched him and sensed there was a lot more here than what he had said so far. "Are you going to tell me?" she asked softly.

He was prowling around the hospital room struggling to push down emotions. She'd seen it before.

He sank back down in the chair beside her bed and buried his

head in his hands, raking his fingers through his hair. "Jennifer's here.
It's so hard, Cassie. I don't want to accept she is dying. I have no choice
but to accept it."

Her heart hurt at that broken admission from him. She knew how
tight Jack held to his family, how close he was to Jennifer. He would do
anything to protect her. "If you don't accept it, you're just going to hurt
yourself," she whispered.

"Jesus loves her as much as I do?"

Tears filled Cassie's eyes. She felt the depth of those quiet words.
"More."

"I know Jesus is alive; I got past that hurdle tonight while I lay there
helpless. It's finally more plausible that He is who He claimed to be
than not. I just resent not being the one in charge when it's Jennifer
we're talking about."

Tears welled up in her eyes, of relief that he had finally wrestled
through the question of who Jesus was, of sadness that he was so
deeply hurting. Cassie shifted her hand to his shoulder. "Being a fol-
lower isn't so bad. Jack—" she waited until he looked at her—"when
it's time for Jennifer to go to heaven, let her go with grace. That's the gift
you most need to give her."

He looked at her and in the silence Cassie finally saw if not peace,
then at least acceptance.

"Jesus loves her," Cassie whispered. "Really loves her."

His hand brushed back her hair. She closed her eyes and relaxed
into the touch. She was so thankful he believed. Where this was going
now… He leaned over and kissed her forehead. "Get some sleep."

The one good thing about a hospital on a holiday weekend was that
dawn came and lightened the room before a nurse appeared to interrupt the peaceful stillness. Cole could see the edge of pink in the dawn
and could tell the coldness outside by the occasional brush of wind
against the windowpanes. Cole heard footsteps in the hall and turned
to look as the door was slowly pushed open.

"Cole?"

He raised his hand to warn Jack.

Rachel was asleep. He'd been watching her for the last hour. She was asleep in one of the hospital chairs, curled sideways, her legs drawn up, her head resting against the curve in the high back of the chair. It had to be the most awkward place to sleep. It was a tribute to her fatigue that she slept without any sign of movement.

Cole saw Jack's expression soften and shared that reaction. Rachel had come up last night when they transferred him from the ER to a room, had helped in so many small ways to make the transition easier to accept. Just having her available to make calls for him had been invaluable. The burns weren't too serious, but the smoke inhalation was enough to make him glad he was flat on his back. He thought they talked about her getting a lift home with Frank, but now that he thought about it, she'd just nodded as he gave her options.

"I'm going to take Cassie home," Jack whispered. "She's getting stir-crazy at the idea of staying."

"Good. Thanks. You'll keep her company tonight for New Year's Eve? I don't want her even thinking about going to the department party."

"I will."

Cole nodded toward Jack's arm. "How's the shoulder?" Cole still hated the memory of what he'd been forced to do to get Jack out.

Jack stopped at the side of the bed. "It aches but I'll live."

Cole raised his hand to his chin and looked at Jack enquiringly. "How bad's my sunburn?"

"Enough Rachel will want to sympathize but not enough Jennifer will do more than suggest you swallow aspirin."

"That's what I thought." He glanced at Rachel. "She stayed the night."

"She likes you."

"Yeah. I think so. It feels nice."

"Do you want a lift home later today? I can plan to come back in."

"I'll call if I do. Before I make plans I want to hang around and see when Ash is going to get released." He didn't want to ask but he needed to. "Is Gage here?"

"Working on his follow-up piece," Jack confirmed.

"If you see him, please ask him to come up." Cole knew he needed to talk to the man professionally but also for much more personal reasons.

"I'll ask him to come up." Jack nodded to Rachel. "Take care of her."

"I plan to," Cole reassured, feeling it as a promise.

Forty-five

"Are you falling asleep before midnight?" Cassie leaned over the edge of the couch to look down at Jack. He was stretched out on the floor, his head resting against a pillow near the center of the couch, his eyes closed. She was now wide awake and headache free. He wasn't in so good a shape. "The new year is eighteen minutes away."

"Come kiss me awake in seventeen minutes."

She blinked at that lazy suggestion, gave a quick grin, and dropped Benji on his chest.

He opened one eye to look up at her as he settled his hand lightly on the kitten. "That's a no?"

She smiled. She was looking forward to dating him, but she was smart enough to know he'd value more what he had to work at.

He sighed. "That was a no. How much longer am I going to be on the fence with you?"

"Is that a rhetorical question or do you want an answer?" If this was the right relationship God had for her future, time taken now would improve it, not hurt it. She was ready to admit she was tired of being alone.

He scratched Benji under the chin and the kitten curled up on his chest and batted a paw at his hand. "Rhetorical. I'd hate to get my hopes up."

She leaned her chin against her hand, looking down at him. "I like you, Jack."

"You just figured that out?"

"I'll like you more when you catch my mouse."

"The only way we are going to catch T. J. is to turn this place into a cheese factory and help her get so fat and slow she can no longer run and hide."

"Or you could move your left hand about three inches to the right and catch her."

Jack opened one eye and glanced toward his left. The white mouse was sitting motionless beside the plate he had set down earlier. Jack closed his eye again. "Let her have the cheeseburger. You put mustard on it."

"You're horrible."

He smiled. "I'm serious."

"So am I."

Jack leaned over, caught Cassie's foot, and tumbled her to the floor. "Oops."

"That wasn't fair. You scared my mouse."

Jack set the kitten down on the floor. "Benji, go get her mouse."

The kitten took off after it.

"You're teaching her to be a mouser."

"Working on it. Come here. You owe me a kiss for the new year."

"Do I?" She reached over to the bowl of chocolates on the table and unwrapped a kiss. She popped the chocolate kiss in his mouth. "I called your bluff."

He smiled and rubbed his hand across her forearm braced against his chest. "That will last me until next year."

She glanced at the muted television. "That's two minutes away."

"Two minutes to put this year behind us." He slid one arm behind his head, adjusting the pillow.

She patted his chest with her hand. "That shouldn't take long." She felt him laugh. "It ended up being a very good year," she offered.

"Next year will be even better."

"Really? Promise?"

"Absolutely." He reached behind her ear and a gold coin reappeared. "What do you think? Heads you say yes when I ask you out, tails you say no?"

She grinned at the idea. "Are you cheating again?" She took the coin. "This one isn't edible," she realized, disappointed. And then she turned it over. "A real two-headed coin?"

"A rare find." He smiled. "Like you."

"That sounds like a bit of honey."

"I'm good at being mushy."

"Oh, really?"

He glanced over her shoulder. "Turn up the TV. There's the countdown."

She grabbed for the remote and hit the wrong button. The television came on full volume just as the fireworks went off. Benji went racing past them spooked by the noise to dive under the collar of the jacket Jack had tossed on the floor. The white mouse scurried to run into the jacket sleeve.

"Tell me I didn't see what I think I just did."

"I won't tell you," Jack agreed, amused. He watched the jacket move and raised an eyebrow. "Am I supposed to rescue the kitten or the mouse?"

Dear Reader,

Thanks for reading this book. I deeply appreciate it.

Fire has always fascinated me, even more the men and women who fight them and why. It's a special person who stands guard to protect the public. I've had the honor of knowing such men and they are guys you can count on when trouble comes. In Jack and Cassie's story, I hope I captured a slice of their lives and was able to convey the deep friendship that ties them together.

Jack's story also offered an opportunity to ask a profound question: Who is Jesus? Cassie Ellis has found the real meaning of Christmas and Jack is still searching to understand. To Jack, Jesus seemed to be the serious myth that people believed in at Christmas, Santa Claus the childish one. Watching Jack with Cassie, with Jennifer and Rachel, as he searched for an answer, was a chance to see a man honestly asking why and not shying away from making a life-changing decision.

By the way, about Rachel...Cole and Rachel were an added bonus. I had no idea this man existed until I wrote the opening chapter of this book. I'm looking forward to telling Rachel and Cole's story in *The Healer*.

As always, I love to hear from my readers. Feel free to write me at:

Dee Henderson
c/o Multnomah Fiction
P.O. Box 1720
Sisters, Oregon 97759
E-mail: dee@deehenderson.com
or on-line: http://www.deehenderson.com

First chapters of all my books are on-line; please stop by and check them out. Thanks again for letting me share Jack and Cassie's story.

Sincerely,

Dee Henderson

The publisher and author would love to hear your comments about this book. *Please contact us at:*
www.multnomah.net/deehenderson

> "Dee Henderson is an extraordinary author whose writing connects with your heart and soul. The O'Malley series is a classic meant for your 'keeper' shelf."
>
> —The Belles and Beaux of Romance

the Negotiator
1-57673-819-1

THE GUARDIAN
1-57673-642-3

THE TRUTH SEEKER
1-57673-753-5

The O'Malley Family Series

The Negotiator—*Book One:* FBI agent Dave Richman from *Danger in the Shadows* is back. He's about to meet Kate O'Malley and his life will never be the same. She's a hostage negotiator. He protects people. Dave's about to find out that falling in love with a hostage negotiator is one thing, but keeping her safe is another!

The Guardian—*Book Two:* A federal judge has been murdered. There is only one witness. And an assassin wants her dead. U.S. Marshal Marcus O'Malley thought he knew the risks of the assignment.... He was wrong.

The Truth Seeker—*Book Three:* Women are turning up dead. Lisa O'Malley is a forensic pathologist and mysteries are her domain. When she's investigating a crime it means trouble is soon to follow. U.S. Marshal Quinn Diamond has found loving her is easier than keeping her safe. Lisa's found the killer, and now she's missing too....

"I highly recommend this book to anyone who likes suspense."
—Terri Blackstock, bestselling author of *Trial by Fire*

Don't miss the prequel to the O'Malley series!

Sara's terrified. She's doing the one thing she cannot afford to do: fall in love with former pro football player Adam Black, a man everyone knows. Sara's been hidden away in the witness protection program, her safety dependent on being invisible— and loving Adam could get her killed.

ISBN 1-57673-577-X

Uncommon Heroes…They do more than make promises—they keep them.

Palisades Pure Romance

TRUE DEVOTION

DEE HENDERSON

Uncommon Heroes Series #1

Kelly Jacobs has already paid the ultimate price of loving a warrior; she has the folded flag and the grateful thanks of a nation to prove it. Navy SEAL Joe "Bear" Baker can't ask her to accept that risk again—even though he loves her. But the man responsible for her husband's death is back, closer than either of them realizes. Kelly's in danger, and Joe may not get there in time.…

ISBN 1-57673-620-2

"Dee Henderson has done a splendid job mixing romance with the fast-paced action of a Navy SEAL platoon."

—Steve Watkins, former Navy SEAL and author of *Meeting God behind Enemy Lines*

The Truth Seeker

Women are missing. It's been happening for years.
Lisa O'Malley's found the killer, and now she's missing too.
U.S. Marshal Quinn Diamond is not about to lose the woman he loves
to the man he hates....
The drama continues with book three in the O'Malley series.

Lisa O'Malley was sitting on the side step of the fire engine, silent, one tennis shoe off as she'd stepped on a hot ember and burned the sole, her stockinged foot moving slowly back and forth in the soot-blackened water rushing down the street toward the nearest storm drain. Her gaze never left the dying fire. Her brother Stephen had wrapped a fire coat around her, and she had it gripped with both hands, pulled tight.

Quinn Diamond kept a close watch on her as he stood leaning against the driver's door of a squad car, waiting for a callback from the dispatcher. She was alone in her grief, her emotions hidden, her eyes dry. She'd lost what she'd valued, and Quinn hated to realize how much it had to resonate with her past.

Kate sat down beside her.

Quinn watched as the two sisters sat in silence, and he prayed for Kate, that she would have the right words to say.

Instead, she remained silent.

And Lisa leaned her head against Kate's shoulder and continued to watch the fire burn, the silence unbroken.

Friends. Deep, lifelong friends.

Quinn had to turn away from the sight. He had so much emotion inside it was going to rupture into tears or fury.

He found himself facing a grim Marcus O'Malley.

"Quinn, get her out of here."

"Stephen has already tried; she won't budge."

"No. I mean out of here. Out of town," Marcus replied. "The killer goes from notes and phone calls to fire. He's not going to stop there."

Marcus was right. Lisa had to come first. "The ranch. She's going to need the space."

"Thank you."

"I'll keep her safe, now that it's too late."

"Quinn—we'll find him."

That wasn't even in question. He was going to hunt the guy down and rip out his heart.

The Guardian

You've fallen in love with Marcus O'Malley,
now watch him fall in love....
Don't miss book two in the O'Malley series.

It was a good night for a sniper, Marcus realized as he checked with the men securing the perimeter of the church property. They were running behind schedule and Marcus could feel the danger of that. Twilight was descending. In the dusk settling in the open areas around the church across the clusters of towering oak trees, the shadows themselves spoke of hidden dangers.

It was time to move.

Marcus raised Luke on the security net. "I'm changing the travel plans. We're going to take the family out the back entrance. Cue us up to leave in five minutes."

"Roger."

He reentered the church.

Marcus had been too occupied during the last hour to really look at Shari, an unfortunate reality that went with the job. It was everyone else who was the threat. He looked now and what he saw concerned him. She was folding; he could see it in the glazed expression, the lack of color in her face, the betraying fact her brother had noticed and now had his hand under her arm.

Definitely time to leave.

Marcus moved to join them and relieve Craig.

Shari saw him coming and broke off her conversation to join him. "Marcus, could—"

The window behind her exploded.

Shari heard someone gasp in pain and the next second Marcus swept out his left arm, caught her across the front of her chest at her collarbone, and took her feet right out from under her.

She felt herself falling backward and it was a petrifying sensation. She couldn't get her hands back in time to break her fall and she hit hard, slamming against the floor, her back and neck taking the brunt of the impact. His arm had her pinned to the ground, his hand gripping her shoulder. He wasn't letting her move even if she could.

"Shari—"

She couldn't respond, her head was ringing so badly.

That had been a bullet.

She wheezed at that realization, her lungs feeling like they would explode. Around her people were screaming.

Another window shattered.

Marcus forcibly pulled her across the floor with him out of the way. "South. Shooter to the south!"

She could hear him hollering on the security net, and it was like listening down a tunnel. Who was bleeding? Someone was bleeding, she could see it on his hand.

It was coming home to her now, very much home. Someone was trying to kill her...again.

The Negotiator
Don't miss book one in this captivating new series!

Dave waited until Kate's brother Stephen disappeared up the stairs. "Why didn't you tell me yesterday? Trust me?"

"Tell you what? That I might have someone in my past who may be a murderer?" Kate swung away from him into the living room. "I've never even met this guy. Until twenty-four hours ago, I didn't even have a suspicion that he existed."

"Kate, he's targeting you."

"Then let him find me."

"You don't mean that."

"There is no reason for him to have blown up a plane just to get at me, to get at some banker. We're never going to know the truth unless someone can grab him. And if he gets cornered by a bunch of cops, he'll either kill himself or be killed in a shootout. It would be easier all around if he did come after me."

"Stop thinking with your emotions and use your head." Dave shot back. "What we need to do is to solve this case. That's how we'll find out the answers and ultimately find him."

"Then you go tear through the piles of data. I don't want to have anything to do with it. Don't you understand that? I don't want to be the one who puts the pieces together. Yesterday was like getting stuck in the gut with a hot poker."

He understood it, could feel the pain flowing from her. "Fine. Stay here for a day, get your feet back under you. Then get back in the game and stop acting like you're the only one this is hurting. Or have you forgotten all the people who died?" He saw the sharp pain flash in her eyes before they went cold and regretted his words.

"That was a low blow and you know it."

"Kate—"

"I can't offer anything to the investigation, don't you understand that? I don't *know* anything. I don't know him."

"Well he knows you. And if you walk away from this now, you're going to feel like a coward. Just what are you so afraid of?"

He could see it in her, a fear so deep it shimmered in her eyes and pooled them black, and he remembered his coworker's comment that he probably didn't want to read the court record. His eyes narrowed and his voice softened. "Are you sure you don't remember this guy?"

She broke eye contact, and it felt like a blow because he knew that at this moment he was the one hurting her. "If you need to get away for twenty-four hours, do it. Just don't run because you're afraid. You'll never forgive yourself."

"Marcus wouldn't let me go check out the data because he was afraid I would kill the guy if I found him."

Her words rocked him back on his heels. "What?" He closed the distance between them, and for the first time since this morning began, actually felt something like relief. He rested his hands calmly on her shoulders. "No, you wouldn't. You're too good a cop."

She blinked.

"I almost died with you, remember?" He smiled. "I've seen you under pressure." His thumb rubbed along her jaw. "Come on, Kate. Come back with me to the house, and let's get back to work. The media wouldn't get near you, I promise."

Marcus and Stephen came back down the stairs, but Kate didn't look around; she just kept studying Dave. She finally turned and looked at her brother. "Marcus, I'm going back to Dave's."

Dave gave in to a small surge of relief. It was a start. Tenuous. And risky. But a start, all the same.

Danger in the Shadows

RITA Award winner—the highest national award given
for excellence in romantic fiction
National Reader's Choice Award Winner
Bookseller's Best Award Winner
Read the prequel to the bestselling O'Malley series.

The summer storm lit up the night sky in a jagged display of energy, lightning bouncing, streaking, fragmenting between towering thunderheads. Sara Walsh ignored the storm as best she could, determined not to let it interrupt her train of thought. The desk lamp as well as the overhead light were on in her office as she tried to prevent any shadows from forming. What she was writing was disturbing enough.

The six-year-old boy had been found. Dead.

Writing longhand on a yellow legal pad of paper, she shaped the twenty-ninth chapter of her mystery novel. Despite the dark specificity of the scene, the flow of words never faltered.

The child had died within hours of his abduction. His family, the Oklahoma law enforcement community, even his kidnapper, did not realize it. Sara did not pull back from writing the scene even though she knew it would leave a bitter taste of defeat in the mind of the reader. The impact was necessary for the rest of the book.

She frowned, crossed out the last sentence, added a new detail, then went on with her description of the farmer who had found the boy.

Thunder cracked directly overhead. Sara flinched. Her office suite on the thirty-fourth floor put her close enough to the storm she could hear the air sizzle in the split second before the boom. She would like to be in the basement parking garage right now instead of her office.

She had been writing since eight that morning. A glance at the clock on her desk showed it was almost eight in the evening. The push to finish a story always took over as she reached the final chapters. This tenth book was no exception.

Twelve hours. No wonder her back muscles were stiff. She had taken a brief break for lunch while she reviewed the mail her secretary had prioritized for her. The rest of her day had been spent working on the book. She arched her back and rubbed at the knot.

This was the most difficult chapter in the book to write. It was better to get it done in one long, sustained effort. Death always squeezed her heart.

Had Dave been in town, he would have insisted she wrap it up and come home. Her life was restricted enough as it was. Her brother refused to let her spend all her time at the office. He would come lean against the doorjamb and give her that *look* along with his predictable lecture telling her all she should be doing: puttering around the house, cooking, messing with the roses, something other than sit behind that desk.

Sara smiled. She did so enjoy taking advantage of Dave's occasional absences.

His flight back to Chicago from the FBI academy at Quantico had been delayed due to the storm front. When he had called her from the airport, he had cautioned her he might not be home until eleven.

It wasn't a problem, she had assured him, everything was fine. Code words. Spoken every day. So much a part of their language now that she spoke them instinctively. "Everything is fine"—all clear; "I'm fine"—I've got company; "I'm doing fine"—I'm in danger. She had lived the dance a long time. The tight security around her life was necessary. It was overpowering, obnoxious, annoying…and comforting.

Sara turned in the black leather chair and looked at the display of lightning. The rain ran down the panes of thick glass. The skyline of downtown Chicago glimmered back at her through the rain.

With every book, another fact, another detail, another intense emotion, broke through from her own past. She could literally feel the dry dirt under her hand, feel the oppressive darkness. Reliving what had happened to her twenty-five years ago was terrifying. Necessary, but terrifying.

She sat lost in thought for several minutes, idly walking her pen through her fingers. Her adversary was out there somewhere, still alive, still hunting her. Had he made the association to Chicago yet? After all these years, she was still constantly moving, still working to stay one step ahead of the threat. Her family knew only too well his threat was real.

The man would kill her. Had long ago killed her sister. The threat didn't get more basic than that. She had to trust others and ultimately God for her security. There were days her faith wavered under the intense weight of simply enduring that stress. She was learning, slowly, by necessity, how to roll with events, to trust God's ultimate sovereignty.

The notepad beside her was filled with doodled sketches of faces. One of these days her mind was finally going to stop blocking the one image she longed to sketch. She knew she had seen the man. Whatever the cost, whatever the consequences of trying to remember, they were worth paying in order to try to bring justice for her and her sister.

Sara let out a frustrated sigh. She couldn't force the image to appear no matter how much she longed to do so. She was the only one who still believed it was possible for her to remember it. The police, the FBI, the doctors had given up hope years ago.

She fingered a worn photo of her sister Kim that sat by a white rose on her desk. She didn't care what the others thought. Until the killer was caught, she would never give up hope.

God was just. She held on to that knowledge and the hope that the day of justice would eventually arrive. Until it did, she carried a guilt inside that remained wrapped around her heart. In losing her twin she had literally lost part of herself.

Turning her attention back to her desk, she debated for a moment if she wanted to do any more work that night. She didn't.

As she put her folder away, the framed picture on the corner of her desk caught her attention; it evoked a smile. Her best friend was getting married. Sara was happy for her, but also envious. The need to break free of the security blanket rose and fell with time. She could feel the sense of rebellion rising again. Ellen had freedom and a life. She was getting married to a wonderful man. Sara longed to one day have that same choice. Without freedom, it wasn't possible, and that reality hurt. A dream was being sacrificed with every passing day.

As she stepped into the outer office, the room lights automatically turned on. Sara reached back and turned off the interior office lights.

Her suite was in the east tower of the business complex. Rising forty-five stories, the two recently built towers added to the already impressive downtown skyline. She struggled with the elevator ride to the thirty-fourth floor each day, for she did not like closed-in spaces, but she considered the view worth the price.

The elevator that responded tonight came from two floors below. There were two connecting walkways between the east and west towers, one on the sixth floor and another in the lobby. She chose the sixth floor concourse tonight, walking through it to the west tower with a confident but fast pace.

She was alone in the wide corridor. Travis sometimes accompanied her, but she had waved off his company tonight and told him to go get dinner. If she needed him, she would page him.

The click of her heels echoed off the marble floor. There was parking under each tower, but if she parked under the tower where she worked, she would be forced to pull out onto a one-way street no matter which exit she took. It was a pattern someone could observe and predict. Changing her route and time of day across one of the two corridors was a better compromise. She could hopefully see the danger coming.

Sara decided to take the elevator down to the west tower parking garage rather than walk the six flights. She would have preferred the stairs, but she could grit her teeth for a few flights to save time. She pushed the button to go down and watched the four elevators to see which would respond first. The one to her left, coming down from the tenth floor.

When it stopped, she reached inside, pushed the garage-floor parking button, but did not step inside. Tonight she would take the second elevator.

Sara shifted her raincoat over her arm and moved her briefcase to her other hand. The elevator stopped and the doors slid open.

A man was in the elevator.

She froze.

He was leaning against the back of the elevator, looking like he had put in a long day at work, a briefcase in one hand and a sports magazine in the other, his blue eyes gazing back at her. She saw a brief look of admiration in his eyes.

Get in and take a risk, step back and take a risk.

She knew him. Adam Black. His face was as familiar as any sports figure in the country, even if he'd been out of the game of football for three years. His commercial endorsements and charity work had continued without pause.

Adam Black worked in this building? This was a nightmare come true. She saw photographs of him constantly in magazines, local newspapers, and occasionally on television. The last thing she needed was to be near someone who attracted media attention.

She hesitated, then stepped in, her hand tightening her hold on the briefcase handle. A glance at the board of lights showed he had already selected the parking garage.

"Working late tonight?" His voice was low, a trace of a northeastern accent still present, his smile a pleasant one.

Her answer was a noncommittal nod.

The elevator began to silently descend.

She had spent too much time in European finishing schools to slouch. Her posture was straight, her spine relaxed, even if she was nervous. She hated elevators. She should have taken the stairs.

"Quite a storm out there tonight."

The heels of her patent leather shoes sank into the jade carpet as she shifted her weight from one foot to the other. "Yes."

Three more floors to go.

There was a slight flicker to the lights and then the elevator jolted to a halt.

"What?" Sara felt adrenaline flicker in her system like the lights.

He pushed away from the back wall. "A lightning hit must have blown a circuit."

The next second, the elevator went black.

True Devotion
UNCOMMON HEROES...
They do more than make promises—they keep them.
Don't miss book one in this exciting new series!

Kelly slipped her hand into Joe's as they strolled down to the water's edge then turned north to follow the beach toward the Hotel del Coronado where their evening had begun. Music from the Ocean Terrace restaurant at the hotel drifted toward them, the colorful lanterns lit around the Terrace reflecting on the water. It was a festive mood.

"One of the last memories I had in the water before you rescued me was from the last time we walked this beach."

"Really?"

She nodded. "Friday night after dinner. You indulged me with a walk down to the Terrace to buy a frozen fruit smoothy. Remember?"

"I remember the smoothy—it gave me an ice cream headache."

"I had forgotten that."

"I haven't."

"What I remember is holding your hand while we walked, deciding how nice it was not to be walking alone."

He squeezed her hand gently. "Thank you. You're welcome to hold my hand anytime you like."

Kelly returned the pressure, communicating without words her pleasure, and they walked in silence along the shore. This was the best memory maker of the evening. The restaurant, the movie, roses, and the bear—of all the images of the evening, this was the one she treasured most. She had walked this beach with Joe before, but this time it was different. This time in a new way she belonged beside him and it felt that way: special.

The evening was going to end eventually, and she didn't want that to happen. Would he kiss her good night? There were already stars in her eyes; that would certainly cap this evening with the best ending possible.

The moonlight flickered as clouds skimmed over the sky.

Joe stopped.

She looked at him, puzzled, and saw his eyes narrow as he gazed ahead.

There was only the dark shadow of the surf and the resulting white breakers. The sound clued her in, an odd interruption in the withdrawing surf as it pulled back to sea.

They both began to run.

A limp body was rolling in the surf, being thrown by the sea to the shore.